ANNABELL'S SEARCH FOR THE HOLISM

A Fantasy Novel

Written by
Alan Davies

MAPLE
PUBLISHERS

Annabell's Search For The Holism – A Fantasy Novel

Author: Alan Davies

Copyright © 2024 Alan Davies

The right of Alan Davies to be identified as author of this work has been asserted by the author in accordance with section 77 and 78 of the Copyright, Designs and Patents Act 1988.

First Published in 2024

ISBN 978-1-83538-365-0 (Paperback)
       978-1-8-3538132-8 (Hardback)
       978-1-83538-366-7 (E-Book)

Book Cover designed by Alan Davies and Book layout by:
       White Magic Studios
       www.whitemagicstudios.co.uk

Published by:
       Maple Publishers
       Fairbourne Drive, Atterbury,
       Milton Keynes,
       MK10 9RG, UK
       www.maplepublishers.com

Contents

Chapter 1 – Annabell's Search for The Holism 5

Chapter 2 – YEAR: AD 2222 7

Chapter 3 – The Parchment Is Analysed 16

Chapter 4 – The Shark World 26

Chapter 5 – Annabell Meets The Queen 41

Chapter 6 – Annabell Meets The Parliament 55

Chapter 7 – The Delvi 65

Chapter 8 – Annabell Confronts The Delvi 82

Chapter 9 – Annabell Returns To Shark World 99

Chapter 10 – In Search Of Chloe 115

Chapter 11 – In Search Of The Fox 131

Chapter 12 – Annnabell Finds The Narwhal 152

Chapter 13 – Stamp 162

Chapter 14 – Looking For The Polar Bears 193

Chapter 15 – The Half Blind Eel 210

Chapter 16 – Another Piece Of Parchment 217

Chapter 17 – Annabell Meets Don Baker 231

Chapter 18 – The Smartalex 243

Chapter 19 – Levid 257

Chapter 20 – Saving The Passengers 267

Chapter 21 – The News Conference 292

Chapter 22 – The Search For Kevin 314

Chapter 23 – Meeting Kevin 337

Chapter 24 – The Outback 355

Chapter 25 – Gone Fishing 381

Chapter 26 – Elvid 407

Chapter 27 – The Monster In The Lake 433

Chapter 28 – Kevin Is Resurrected 443

Chapter 29 – Kevin Gains Powers 455

Chapter 30 – Annabell Goes Home 470

Chapter 31 – The Last Piece Of Parchment 480

Chapter 32 – Annabell Goes To India 494

Chapter 33 – Annabell Meets The King 502

Chapter 34 – The Red Bottle 519

Chapter 35 – Annabell Tries To Save The King 530

Chapter 36 – The King Tells His Story 540

Chapter 37 – The King Rights His Wrongs 547

Chapter 38 – Anja 570

Chapter 39 – The Search For The Dragon 587

Chapter 40 – Finding The Dragon 614

Chapter 41 – Annabell Gets Married 630

Chapter 42 – The Mysterious Figure 650

Chapter 43 – The New Earth 675

Introduction

Annabell's Search for The Holism

Annabell *"the special one"*. Annabell has now grown-up. She's twenty- one years old and she's considered to be the most beautiful woman in the world despite her being born different from anybody else that has ever lived on the earth. She has powers which she has already demonstrated to earth people.

Annabell has been born on the earth for a reason - she's the only person who can save the earth from total destruction.

Earth's evolution is complete. Four seeds created all life on earth. The creator wants the seeds back. Annabell has got one already. The land seed, which gave her powers. She has to find the other three.

Her task will not be easy, because the devil has its own seeds. Anti - life seeds. These were put on the earth at the same time as the good seeds to destroy life as we know it.

The devil seeds have been dormant. But now they've activated!!!

There are five of them, anyone of them has the capability of destroying life on the earth.

Annabell has to find the good seeds while encountering the devil seeds.

She will be given clues as to where to find the good seeds, which are scattered around the globe. She will also be given cryptic clues of how to defeat the devils. The clues are not easy to follow - she will need help.

Will Annabell be able to defeat the devils? Will she be able to find the seeds of life?

The battle: Armageddon has begun!

⊷◈⊶

Chapter One
YEAR: AD 2222

Armageddon was predicted the final battle between good and evil - the outcome of the battle would decide the fate of the Earth, it was expected that good would prevail over evil but this cannot be considered to be a pre-determined outcome.

Year AD 2222 had arrived - this was the year that the Devil had decided that the final battle (Armageddon) would happen.

2222 meant something to the Devil - what it meant, human kind will never know. But God knew what it meant, and he had been preparing for this year. Annabell had been born to the Earth in preparation for the final battle but she would have to stand alone. The Devil though would unleash everything in its power, and there would be mighty forces of evil that Annabell would have to face. Annabell wasn't aware of her purpose in life but shortly she would find out.

She was now a grown-up woman of twenty-one years old, and she was extremely beautiful. She was even regarded by a lot of people as the most beautiful woman in the world though she did look rather strange.

She wrote numerous books about her adventures and was hardly ever out of the news. She had become a very famous and wealthy woman, but she donated much of her wealth to the welfare of animals and children.

Annabell had become a very important person in the world. The magical powers that she had gained, she used to help the Earth whenever she was able to. She kept her promise to her mother and had always used her powers for the good.

People said that she had been gifted by God. But obviously nobody really knew that, but she was certainly a very unusual person and a great asset to the Earth.

One day she was back at Cherry Tree farm talking to her horse Charlie, who didn't look a day older than he did thirteen years ago, and neither did Annabell's mother and father. It seemed like nobody associated with Annabell was ageing.

Something came fluttering down from the sky and hit Annabell on her shoulder. She looked up to see where it had come from but there was nothing there, it seemed like it had just floated down from the heavens. "Must have blown in the wind," thought Annabell. She assumed that it was a leaf that had blown from a tree but soon dismissed this when she looked down to the ground to see what had actually hit her.

She picked it up. It was a piece of very old, crude type of paper more like parchment but she wasn't sure what it was. She scrutinised it. It had a sort of symbol on it with strange writing. The symbol was a circle cut into four quarters. In the centre was what looked like a red stone. Annabell was fascinated by the symbol because the quarters looked exactly like magic object on her necklace.

She matched it up with the drawing on the parchment. It was a perfect match! The piece of parchment that she had looked like it had been torn from something else. Annabell assumed that there must be other parts to the parchment.

Annabell read the words. They wouldn't make any sense to other people because it was written in a strange language that only Annabell was able to read.

It read to Annabell in English as follows:

I bring life to this world by way of the four quarters, they are the seeds of all life.

Plants - Insects - Water life - Land life The stone in the centre is the catalyst. When North...South...East...West join back a new world is born. The one born red is the chosen one. Earth is complete. You, my daughter, the red one, must find the seeds and bring them to me. Only you will be able to do this, you have the powers. You have the seed of land life already, you must find the rest. The seeds must be joined back. It's time. The whole is greater than the parts.

But beware, your search will not be easy - there are dangers in the form of five other seeds. The seeds of all evil, anti-life, Devil seeds. But you have the powers to defeat these evils.

Follow the signs.

The Creator.

Annabell was very puzzled as to what it all meant. "Who is the creator?" she muttered to herself. "It says, I'm his daughter. But...I'm my Ma and Pa's daughter. It says that I must find the seeds. The *'red one'*- that has to be me! But I don't understand this."

The next day Annabell went into the city to see a Professor Nicolls. He was regarded as the leading expert on old parchment according to what she had been told.

She went to the University of Ancient History, where the professor worked. She knocked on his door. "Hello who's that?" Came a very gruff sounding voice.

"It's Annabell Jacobs, is that you, Professor Nicolls?"

"Yes…Yes, please come in, Annabell. I've been expecting you."

Annabell entered the room and was met by a frail old man well into his seventies. He had very little hair but what was left was a dirty grey colour and his teeth had seen better days. He was wearing a grubby white shirt with a frayed collar as usual for professors and scientists! He was wearing spectacles that were worn half way down his rather long nose.

He'd spent most of his life working on parchments. What this man didn't know on this subject, so Annabell was told, wasn't worth knowing. Annabell was confident that he would know what it was.

"It's a pleasure to meet you, Annabell, in fact it's an honour," said the professor shaking her hand affectionately. "You've made an old man very happy - very happy. I've followed your adventures in your books and they're fascinating - fascinating. What an experience you've had and who could ever forget you riding that Brachiosaurus; what a sight...what a sight... Wonderful! - wonderful!" The professor was repeating himself continuously.

"What can I do for you, Annabell?"

"It's this, Professor." Annabell produced the piece of parchment from her handbag.

"I want to know what it is? And what it all means? I've been told that you will know." Annabell handed the parchment to the Professor.

"Well...Well...Well, this is interesting, wherever did you get it from, Annabell?"

Annabell told him that it just fluttered down from the sky.

"What is it, Professor?" She was very impatient to know.

"Give me a chance, Annabell. Rome wasn't built in a day you know!- you know!"

The professor looked at it, felt it, put it under his magnifying glass. Looked in all his books. He held it up to the light. He made numerous phone calls.

Over an hour passed. The professor was now sitting at his desk, beads of sweat could be seen on his balding head and were trickling down the side of his face, he was constantly wiping his brow. Annabell just sat there twiddling her red fingers.

The professor looked up at Annabell. "Well," he said, with an air of authority. "You've got me with this one, Annabell. I'm sorry, but I've got absolutely no idea … and I mean, no idea whatsoever what this parchment is. In all my considerable years that I've worked in this field, and it's quite a lot of years I can tell you, I've never come across anything like this Annabell… and the writing on it - my goodness me, is of no known language. And…" The professor paused to wipe his brow again. "I've got no idea what the symbol represents. I'm baffled! I can tell you, baffled! I'm so sorry Annabell, but I can't help you. If I can't read what it says, I don't stand a chance of being able to understand what it all means." The poor Professor obviously felt very embarrassed.

"I know what the writing says," said Annabell out of the blue.

"Do you? How would you know that Annabell?" The professor was shocked.

"I don't know Professor, but I know that I can read it." Annabell handed the Professor a piece of paper. She had already written down what the words on the parchment read.

The Professor studied the words and he was shaking his head in disbelief. He was muttering to himself. "No...no...can't be! This is impossible. This is..."

"What is it Professor? What's wrong? Please tell me."

"Ummm...This is some sort of religious thing, Annabell, it's like a *Holism.*"

"What's a '*Holism*' Professor?"

"Holism ...ummm... mainly applies to religious scriptures, it means...umm.. The whole is greater than the parts."

"What does that mean?" Annabell was really baffled now.

"It means that umm; when all the parts are put together, the whole thing is stronger than just bits of it. But it usually applies to scriptures, biblical writing, it doesn't mean objects. But according to what you've written down Annabell, it says that the symbol is the holism and whoever wrote it, says that the bits are the seeds of life and that you must find them and bring them to the creator. It's beyond me, Annabell. I understand the message, but it's too incredible to be true. You need to get the parchment scientifically analysed because it's something that I have no understanding of."

"Who is the creator, Professor?" Annabell asked.

"*GOD!!* Annabell, you should know that. It appears that you have a message from the Almighty. This is all so incredible, I can't believe this."

Annabell looked shocked. She kind of knew that it had something to do with religion.

Chapter Two
The Parchment Is Analysed

The professor wrote down name of a person that he knew. It was another professor by the name of Pamela Smithson. She was the Head of the University of Scientific Research.

"Here, Annabell, take your parchment to her. She'll be able to analyse it for you, we'll have to try to get to the bottom of this. Please let me know the results. I'll be very interested to know what this parchment is made of, and what sort of year the material was made in. This is absolutely fascinating stuff...fascinating," repeated the professor.

Annabell thanked him for his time and left, somewhat confused.

The next day she made an appointment to see Pamela Smithson. She arrived at the university and went to the main reception.

"Can I help you?" asked a young lady at the reception desk not looking to see who it was that was standing there

"I've got an appointment to see Professor Pamela Smithson." said Annabell politely.

"Name, please?"

"Annabell Jacobs." The young lady looked up she knew this name.

"Annabell...? WOW!" she screamed. "Look everybody, it's Annabell."

But everybody had already noticed Annabell walking into the building.

People clapped and cheered. She was a heroine in America and throughout the world. People in the building were scrambling to take pictures of her. Annabell didn't mind, she was used to being famous now.

When all the fuss had died down Annabell was escorted to the office of Pamela Smithson by a very pretty girl in her early twenties. She asked very shyly if she could have her autograph. Annabell laughed, she couldn't understand why people were so in awe of her. She asked the girl what her name was. "Carol," replied the girl.

Annabell signed her autograph for her. "Thank you, Thank you," said Carol. "I shall treasure this forever."

"Why?" asked Annabell. "It's only a name."

"Yeah, I know," said Carol "But it's your name and you're so famous, Annabell."

Annabell felt a bit embarrassed by the whole thing.

They walked down a long corridor which had lots of doors with people's names on them. Eventually they came to a door that had a sign:

'Professor Pamela Smithson' written on it.

"We're here," said Carol. "This is Pamela's room. I should call her Professor really but we're not that formal here, Annabell." Annabell liked this attitude, she herself didn't like formality although she accepted that sometimes she had to be formal especially when meeting important people. Annabell knocked on her door.

"Please come in," said a soft voice.

Annabell entered the room and was met by a middle-aged lady. She was very smartly dressed and well-spoken and wearing as is usual for professors, spectacles!

"Hello Annabell, I've been expecting you." Annabell shook her hand.

"Um... Professor Nicolls tells me that you have something very interesting to show me, he's got himself in rather a fluster over your piece of parchment, let's see if we can sort this out. There's always an explanation. We have some very advanced machines here at the University that will be able to analyse what it's made of, and how old it is. I was surprised that the professor didn't know what it was. He's usually very good at knowing what these things are The professor thinks that it's religious. He's been telling me that he thinks that God wrote it!! My goodness me, the silly old fool is going senile. God, indeed!" Pamela smiled at the ridiculousness of such a suggestion.

Annabell handed the parchment to Pamela. "My... my, this is interesting...ummm, very interesting. The professor tells me that he doesn't believe the writing to be any known language. Well, we'll soon find out." Pamela asked Annabell to follow her.

She was taken into a big room with lots of computers and there were several people that Annabell thought were scientists at work on different projects. Pamela shouted out.

"**Can I have your attention please**? We have a celebrity with us today who needs our help."

Everybody shook the hand of Annabell and told her that it was a pleasure to meet her.

Pamela took Annabell into another room. Inside was a huge computer. It took up most of the room. Lots of lights were flashing on it. It looked really impressive.

"Annabell this is *NOALL*! Pamela was pointing to the computer. Annabell laughed at the name.

"He's the most advanced computer the world has ever known. He's been running non-stop for years, and years, gathering all the knowledge of Earth, and some of beyond. He never stops learning. We call him *NOALL,* because well, he does know it all." Annabell sniggered. She was amused by this name.

"He'll sort it out for you, it won't take a minute."

Pamela put the parchment into a slot that was on the front of *NOALL.* This slot analyses sample material. Pamela then typed out the questions that Annabell wanted to know.

She asked *NOALL* Three questions: What is the parchment made of? - And when was it made?- And what is the language written on it?

She then pressed a green button. *NOALL* lit up like a Christmas tree and there was a loud sort of ticking sound. The ticking got faster and faster until in the end - it was going so fast that all you could hear was a whistling noise.

Annabell and Pamela waited patiently for the results. Ten minutes went by but nothing happened.

"That's unusual." remarked Pamela -"It usually only takes a few seconds."

They waited and waited. But *NOALL* didn't seem to know the answers!

Over forty-five minutes passed and still *NOALL* hadn't produced an answer.

Pamela called all the scientists into the room. "What's happening here?" she asked them despairingly but nobody knew.

Over an hour passed. Suddenly smoke could be seen coming from *NOALL* electrical circuits and there was a puff of smoke from the slot that the parchment was put into. The parchment suddenly shot out onto the floor smouldering. Annabell picked it up.

"Oh, no, it's ruined!" She yelled, but it wasn't damaged at all, there wasn't a mark on it, despite it seemingly catching fire!

Sheets of paper came cascading out of the computer, it was like *NOALL* was being *sick!* There was a hissing noise coming from the machine. Alarm bells were ringing. Lights were flashing on and off at a phenomenal speed.

"He's overloading!" Somebody shouted out. Smoke and flames was coming out of *NOALL!!* Pamela told everybody to *run*!

Suddenly there was a loud bang as the final piece of computer paper shot out of *NOALL* and hit the wall. Pamela instinctively picked it up, and told everybody to run for their lives!

They all ran to the door as fast as they could. *NOALL* was well on fire now! And the smoke was getting dense.

They all just managed to get outside the building by this time all the fire alarms in the building were ringing. The sprinkler system had come on but wasn't able to put out the fire. Suddenly there was an almighty explosion. *NOALL* had blown himself up!

All the windows in the building shattered! Fragments of glass were cascading onto the street below - people were running for their lives, trying to get away from the burning building.

The fire service were quickly on the scene and were trying hard to put the fire out but it was now raging out of control.

The brave firemen's efforts to put out the fire was all to no avail. The building, and *NOALL* were totally destroyed.

Pamela was still clutching the result sheet, she was shaking with fright. "My God! what on earth has caused this?"

Annabell turned to Pamela and said, "I don't wish to be insensitive, Pamela but I would really like to know what *NOALL's* analysis of the parchment was."

Pamela was still shaking and was looking very pale, she was saying over and over again. "My God! My God! What am I going to do? All the scientific research of the last, God knows how many years has been destroyed. Oh this is a disaster! It's a disaster."

She turned to Annabell. "Sorry, I know that the results mean a lot to you but this is a disaster for us. I can't believe what's happened."

Pamela looked at the result sheet, her hands were shaking uncontrollably, she turned even paler with the shock at what she had read.

"What's wrong Pamela?" asked Annabell, she was very concerned about Pamela, she could see that she wasn't very well. Suddenly and not really unexpectedly Pamela fainted and fell to the floor. Annabell comforted her while they waited for the paramedics to arrive. They arrived very quickly and revived her with smelling salts.

She was put into an ambulance and rushed straight away to the hospital.

Annabell noticed that the result sheet was still lying on the ground where Pamela had dropped it. She picked it up and read it - only four words were written on it. It read:

NOT OF THIS WORLD!!!!!!!!!!!!!!!

Annabell was shocked. Poor Pamela! The piece of parchment that Annabell had asked her to analyse had probably ruined her life. It proved too much of a challenge for *NOALL*. It was an impossible question to answer.

Annabell walked away feeling very sad and responsible for the damage that the parchment had caused. But she wasn't to know, nobody could really blame her but she would put right the damage that the parchment had caused, and hoped that Pamela would be able to resume her job along with all the other people who used the university.

Annabell walked around the city for several hours not knowing what to do.

She came upon a park and just walked around it thinking and wondering. The words of *NOALL's* last thought kept coming into her mind. *Not of this world.* She came to a bench and sat down and closed her eyes. She was deep in meditation, when suddenly she was pecked on the shoulder by a magpie.

Chapter Three
The Shark World

"I've been sent to give you this." The magpie had in its beak another piece of the parchment. Annabell pulled it from its beak and asked the bird who had given it to him

The magpie told her that. The creator asked him to find the red person and that he was to give her the parchment. "Who's the creator?" asked Annabell. The bird didn't answer.

Annabell shouted at the bird, "Please tell me, is the creator God?" But the bird just flew away without so much as a goodbye.

Annabell looked at the parchment - it had the same Holism symbol as the first one, but with a different part of the seed missing and there was another message written on it : it read as follows:

The land seed you have - Its powers you have gained.

The water seed is next - 66- degrees - 32 minutes North is where it lies.

Go to the sea and seek a fish - But beware! You'll waken the Delvi when you enter the water: The Delvi is evil beyond belief but it has a weakness that you'll least expect.

Remove the "e" from least to last - This word will make the creature past.

Follow the signs.

The Creator

Annabell didn't understand the clues, she was talking and thinking to herself. "*Go to the sea.* What sea? *Follow the signs.* What signs? *Beware of the Delvi.* What's a Delvi?" She already knew that the parchments were not of this Earth. But where had they come from? She had no idea.

Annabell was sitting on the park bench talking to herself! People were walking past her and saying, "Hello." but she was so deep in thought that she was oblivious to them.

She studied the first piece of the parchment again and re - read it, she thought that maybe she could get some clues as to what it all means.

I bring life to this world by way of the four quarters - They are the seeds of all life.

Plant - Insects - Water life and Land life. The stone in the centre is the catalyst - When North - South - East and West join together a new world is born.

The one born red is the chosen one. Earth is now complete. You, my daughter, must find the seeds and bring them to me - Only you can do this. You have the powers

The seeds must be joined back together.

It's time.

The whole is greater than the parts.

But beware, your search will not be easy - there are dangers in the form of five other seeds.

The seeds of all evil, anti-life, but you have powers to defeat this evil.

follow the signs.

The Creator

Annabell was beginning to understand now that she had to find the rest of the pieces, it appeared that it was her destiny, she had always been special, she knew that, to be born red made her different from all other people.

Nobody could ever find the reason why this happened to her. It couldn't be explained by any scientific or medical knowledge. She had always felt in her inner feelings that she herself was not of this world, although she was born to normal human beings. She was so different to normal people and she had gained incredible powers by wearing the piece of the Holism which Professor Nicolls believed was from God.

Annabell knew that she had to follow the directions on the parchment. She suddenly felt an inner strength, like she'd been *enlightened*. She knew what she had to do now, but it was all so incredible and hard to believe that this could be happening to her.

The next day she made her way down to the sea. The parchment didn't mention any particular sea. She just went to the nearest point.

Annabell thought this to be a billion to one chance.

Annabell stood at the sea's edge just watching the waves coming in.

Twenty minutes passed, absolutely nothing had happened.

Annabell had no idea as to what she was supposed to do next. She took off her shoes and went in for a paddle. But she had forgotten something.

The parchment warned her that she would wake the D*elvi,* when she entered the water but she didn't have any choice, she had to go into the water.

Thirty minutes passed, nothing had happened. Annabell was just about to give up when something nibbled her toe. She looked down into the crystal clear water and saw that it was a very small fish.

"Pick me up," said the fish, Annabell bent down and cupped her hands and scooped up the little fish. It swam in a circle around her hands.

"Who are you?" asked Annabell in a gentle voice. "You're a lovely little thing and just look at you? You're the same colour as me!"

"My name is Polp," replied the tiny red fish.

"Hello Polp, it's a pleasure to meet you. I don't suppose you know anything about the holism, by any chance, do you?"

"No I don't. I've been sent to find you though, you have to come with me."

"Come with you, where?" asked Annabell.

"Into the water, you've got to come into the water. I've got to take you somewhere. Come on, hurry up!"

"But...but...I can't swim Polp!" said Annabell anxiously. "I can't possibly come into the water, I'll drown!"

"No you won't." said Polp confidently. "You'll be surprised at what you can do. You have powers you know. Use them! Come on, hurry up, we haven't got all day there's work to be done."

Annabell wasn't sure about this. She couldn't remember ever learning to swim! In fact she hated water!

"Come on, put me back into the water, and follow me," said Polp impatiently.

Annabell gently lowered Polp back into the water, and he slowly swam off.

Annabell slowly, very slowly! waded out. First up to her knees.

"Further." shouted Polp. "You must go all the way. Do not be afraid."

Annabell was now up to her waist. She wasn't reassured by Polp's confidence. She was now up to her neck. "I don't like this Polp," she screamed, "I don't like water."

Then suddenly a big wave came in and went right over her head! Annabell was under the water now.

"Follow me, and try to keep up," said Polp swishing his fins.

"Alright! Alright!...Don't get your fins in a twist!" Annabell laughed at her own joke.

Suddenly she realised that not only could she talk and hear under the water, but she could breathe as well. Polp was right. Annabell had powers that she didn't know about.

Polp swam out into the open sea. He was quite speedy for a small fish.

"Where are we going?" enquired Annabell. Impatiently.

"You'll see. You've got to keep up. Come on, I haven't got all day!"

"Why haven't you got all day? Why do you keep saying that?"

"I don't know," replied Polp.

"Who told you to meet me, Polp?"

"I don't know - I just know that I had to meet you and take you somewhere. It's some sort of instinct thing, I think? Something is guiding me."

Annabell held out her arms in front of her and kicked her legs. She was amazed at herself, she was able to swim really fast, even though she had never learnt how to.

She swam like a *mermaid!!*

They swam together for over an hour until they reached a group of rocks.

"We're here," said Polp.

"We're here, where?" asked Annabell. "Where are we, Polp?"

"This is where I've been told to bring you."

"But who told you to bring me here?" Polp didn't answer the question. He just swam away and said, "Bye. I'm off." He sped away so fast that it was just like a flash of light as his red body disappeared in the distance.

Annabell was now all alone not knowing why she had been brought to this place.

She thought she was alone, but out of the corner of her eye she caught sight of a huge Great White shark, and it was big! At least twenty feet long! And it must weigh at least two thousand pounds!

He came right at her and opened his huge mouth showing off his big white razor sharp teeth.

Annabell screamed. The shark came at her again like he was going to eat her! But turned at the last minute and swished his tail causing Annabell to become unbalanced by the swirl of the water. She turned over and over, like clothes in a washing machine until finally all was calm again.

The shark started to circle her. He seemed to have a smirk on his evil looking face. He circled around her for several seconds.

Annabell shouted at it. "Get away from me." She realised now why Polp had sped off so fast. He must have known that this shark was around "You're not going to eat me! I won't let you," shrieked Annabell. "Get away from me, I'm not frightened of you. I've seen bigger things than you. You can't hurt me anyway, I've got special powers you know, if you try to eat me you'll be sorry."

"I'm not going to 'eat you'," said the shark with a smirk on his vicious looking face.

"Then what do you want?" Annabell shrugged her shoulders, and screwed up her face.

She knew that this creature was the most ferocious and feared thing swimming in the sea. She knew that this species of shark was a killing machine and would attack anything that moved so she wondered why it didn't want to eat her.

"If you're not going to eat me, then why are you circling around me?" said Annabell, inquisitively.

The shark opened its huge jaws and spoke. "Because I was fascinated by the colour of you, that's why. I've never seen a red human before and I've seen and eaten lots of them! You're quite tasty you know, but don't worry I'm not going to eat you. You're very special. I've heard a lot about you. You're famous here in the sea, everybody knows you. News travels fast you know, just because we're here in the seas doesn't mean we don't know what's going on - on the land. We've all heard about what you did for the Dinosaurs, that was fantastic. Now then...um, the main reason why I've been sent here is to take you to see someone. I know that you're looking for some special object, well, so I've been told."

"Yes. That's right, I'm looking for the part of the holism that created life in the seas. Do you know where it is, shark? It's very important. The creator has sent me to find it, but I don't know who the creator is. Do you know where the holism is, shark?"

"No, I don't know where it is, and by the way my name is not 'shark'! It's the Right Honourable Albert Stein and I'm at your service, madam."

"What are you on about?" Annabell laughed - "The Right Honourable Albert Stein? That's a human name, *Honourable*? How can you be *Honourable*? You have to be awarded a peerage or membership in a chivalric order by the British Monarch to hold such a title."

"Not in the seas, you don't," replied Albert in a stern voice. "We have our own Monarchy down here! We don't live in the dark ages, you know. You human's think that you own the planet! Well you don't! I was awarded the title by Her Royal Highness, Bolvina, the third, Queen of Sharks, for my service to the crown. So there you are."

Annabell shrugged her shoulders and muttered underneath her breath "*Fish Queens!* whatever next?"

"What's that you say, madam?"

"Nothing!...nothing!... I was just talking to myself. Where are you going to take me? And who told you to take me there? I want to know. I demand you tell me, Mr Stein."

"I'm not at liberty to tell you, madam, but it was somebody in higher authority than me. Please follow me."

The shark, Albert Stein, swam off at a tremendous rate. Annabell found it difficult to keep up with him. "*SHARK!*" she yelled. "Slow down, how do you expect me to keep up with you? I'm not a fish you know!"

The shark turned back and grabbed Annabell with its big sharp teeth. He was careful that he didn't bite her. He closed his jaws just enough to hold her. Annabell was now dangling from the mouth of this ferocious creature but she didn't fear him. He swam for quite a while until he reached a sort of underwater mountain range. Albert opened his jaws and released Annabell.

"What's this place?" asked Annabell.

"This is Queen Bolvina the Third's residence, madam. It's also the sharks' secret world. Only sharks are allowed here normally, but I was told to bring you here, so I'm following my orders. You're very privileged to be allowed to come here. Sharks have lived in this place for hundreds of millions of years. It's the most important place in the whole oceans for sharks. The sharks' *Mecca*, you might say. Queen Bolvina the Third is expecting you, so we'll better not keep her waiting," said Albert in a pompous voice.

Just as the shark finished his sentence, six huge shapes appeared from a hole inside the mountain and enclosed Annabell in a tight circle. She now had seven Great White sharks surrounding her.

The Right Honourable Albert Stein went up to the front and the six other sharks spread out, three on each side of Annabell so that she was in the middle. This was obviously an escort. They swam inside the underwater mountain by way of an entrance that was guarded by several sharks mainly Great Whites.

The entrance led into a huge cavern, that was the size of a small town. There was lots of smaller caverns situated around the sides of the main cavern. All species of sharks were here and it appeared that each species had its own cavern.

The sharks had somehow managed to decorate the walls and ceilings of the entire place with gold and silver coins, which created a mosaic effect - Annabell was puzzled as to how the sharks had managed to accomplish this. She felt that it must have taken hundreds of years scavenging the seas for sunken ships' cargoes to be able to have accumulated enough to cover the entire cavern with the coins, and she had no idea how the sharks had managed to get the coins to stick onto the rock.

Inside the caverns mysterious orbs gave out light. The light reflected onto the coins which made them sparkle. To her it felt like she was in a fairyland. Annabell was in awe of this incredible place.

Almost in the centre was another substantial cavern that the sharks had led Annabell into. Like everywhere in this magical world the walls and ceilings sparkled in this cavern but it was different here, there were gold and silver objects of all descriptions everywhere. There were piles of jewellery and vast amounts of ceramics from all centuries and cultures. There were even clothes here, which surprised Annabell.

To humans this place would be like finding *King Solomon's Mines?* But this was sharks' treasure! And not just any shark. It was the Great Whites' treasure. It is unlikely that if any human was to find this place they would live to tell the tale.

To a normal human being this would be a frightening place to be but she wasn't frightened at all. She loved it here and marvelled at the beauty of it.

Annabell was taken through a corridor which led into another smaller cavern. This was laid out like a banqueting room just like you would expect to find in a palace.

In the centre of the room hanging from the ceiling was a massive chandelier that was made out of solid gold and it had diamonds hanging from it. The chandelier was lit up by orbs. The light from the orbs lit up the chandelier and made it sparkle like stars.

Annabell had no idea what was powering the orbs. She felt that it couldn't be any known power that land people would know about. She thought that maybe it was some sea creature that were the orbs but what creature, she didn't know.

In the front of the room was a big throne also made of solid gold and inlaid with precious gems. Annabell was provided with a chair to sit on. Albert Stein remained at her side, the six other sharks positioned themselves around the room.

Ten minutes passed, Annabell asked Albert what they were waiting for. "You'll see."

Chapter Four
Annabell Meets The Queen

Twenty minutes later a fanfare of trumpets was played. Albert told Annabell to get up from her chair and to bow her head, which she did. The fanfare lasted several minutes and then stopped abruptly. A normal person would not have been able to hear the trumpets.

Two sharks entered the room. Annabell laughed. The two sharks were wearing evening gowns!! Albert prodded her and told her to *"SHUSH!"* But Annabell couldn't stop laughing this was the funniest sight she had ever seen!

"What on earth are they?" laughed Annabell "Why are they wearing clothes? Fish don't wear clothes!" Annabell was in hysterics.

"Don't laugh! What's so funny anyway?" Albert was not amused. "These are very important sharks, they're ladies in waiting to her royal highness.

"Oh, Sorry! Sorry!" Annabell was very apologetic. "Sorry! Sorry!" she said again but she carried on laughing. "I'm really sorry, Albert, but they look so funny. This is silly!"

Albert looked at her sternly. She eventually stopped laughing and composed herself.

Another fanfare of trumpets started playing. Albert once again prodded Annabell with his snout and told her to show respect. "You mustn't laugh, Annabell.

The Queen will be here any minute." It was obvious that Albert was a bit annoyed by her behaviour. "Now keep your head bowed. You, naughty girl!" Albert told her.

Annabell was very important, but obviously to Albert his Queen was far more important.

The Queen of all sharks entered the room. Albert made an announcement.

"Her Royal Highness Queen Bolvina, the Third. May I present to you, your majesty, the one that you had asked me to find, Annabell, the land red person."

Annabell didn't look up, she was now following Albert's orders to the letter.

The Queen was dressed in the most magnificent gold and maroon evening gown and was adorned with beautiful jewellery including a diamond tiara that sparkled in the crystal clear water. The Queen swam towards Annabell, her magnificent gown was flowing like wings - she was like an angel, flying in the sky.

The Queen swam around and around Annabell, eventually she spoke in a very graceful and posh voice.

"My - my - my. You're so beautiful. Lift your head up young lady, let me see you properly. My, you're the most beautiful land person that I've ever seen. Just look at the colour of you! You have such beautiful eyes and hair. My you're a treasure. All the stories that we've been told about you are true. How are you able to breathe and talk under water, Annabell? No land person can do that."

"I don't know ma'am," Annabell answered. "I just can - but it could be because I have a magic object." Annabell showed the Queen her necklace which held the object.

"I need to talk with you Annabell," said the Queen. "Word has got to me that you need our help. The message has come from the dolphins, they say that it's of the utmost importance that we help you."

"But how did the dolphins know that I needed help? Who told them?" asked Annabell.

"I don't know," said the Queen. "That was all that we were told - that we must help the red human. Which of course is you." Annabell wasn't too sure what was going on.

"ALBERT STEIN!" The Queen shouted.

"Yes, yes, your majesty."

"Go and assemble parliament at once and please inform them that we have a very important person with us who urgently needs our help. Please make haste sir."

Albert bowed his head to the Queen and replied that he would see to her request immediately. With a swish of his huge tail he left the room.

The room was very exquisitely designed with luxurious furniture everything seemed to be big. There were sofas and tables and chairs but they were huge. The tables were made from high quality marble and were very long.

The Queen asked Annabell if she was hungry.

"I'm starving ma'am. I could eat a *horse!*" she replied.

"I'm sorry, Annabell, but we don't have horses in the sea. So I'm afraid you can't have horse for your dinner. You'll have to pick something else."

"Ma'am, I was only joking about eating a horse. It's just a saying that we have on land, it means that I'm really hungry, I would never eat a horse."

"Oh!" replied the Queen. "That's a strange thing to say. What would you like to eat then? You can have anything you want as long as it's not a horse." The Queen laughed. "I've been told that land people consider caviar a bit of a delicacy, would you like that?"

"Ugh!...no thanks ma'am, they're too salty for me. I really can't eat fish eggs! Ugh! - no thanks. Can I have some lobster please? I like that."

"Certainly you can." The Queen banged a golden gong that was by her side and into the room came a small shark dressed up as a chef.

"Please serve Annabell our finest lobster, and I'll have the tuna today with oysters to start. Mmmm... would you like a starter, Annabell?"

"No thank you, Ma'am, the lobster will be fine."

"Right chef." The Queen spoke with authority. "Right, we're ready to eat now, will you please bring us our meals." The chef rushed off at some speed to fetch their meals.

"I'm really looking forward to eating the lobster, ma'am," said Annabell licking her lips. "I love lobsters they're so tasty and I haven't had one for a long time."

"Well, you won't be disappointed Annabell," said the Queen. "All our food is served fresh."

A few minutes later two sharks dressed as waiters came into the room. They weren't Great White sharks, but another species called Hammer Heads. They were really strange looking fish, they had heads that resembled *dinner trays*!! Ideal fish to be waiters.

One of the Hammer Heads swam over to Annabell. On top of its head was a silver bowl with a lid on it. It slid the bowl gently off its head onto the table in front of Annabell.

"Thank you," said Annabell to the waiter politely. Annabell licked her lips again in anticipation of the forthcoming meal.

"I know that I'm going to enjoy this." she said excitedly. She took the lid off the bowl and out *crawled* a big fat lobster!!! Annabell screamed! "Whatever is the matter?" The Queen was concerned. "Have you hurt yourself, Annabell?"

"No ma'am… It's… just, Ugh! - It's crawled out of the bowl ma'am ! It's alive!! Ugh! I can't eat that!"

"Why?" asked the Queen somewhat surprised. "It's as fresh as you can get, Annabell, and you said that you liked lobster and just look how plump he is."

"But ma'am. We land people like our lobsters, **cooked**!"

"Cooked?" The Queen was puzzled by the word. She called over the head waiter and told him to ask the head food chef why he hadn't *cooked* the lobster.

Two minutes later, the waiter returned and whispered something to the Queen.

"Oh, it appears, Annabell, that our top food chef doesn't know what *cooked* means, can you please explain to him what it is?"

"It means ma'am, that you've got to boil it … or roast it in an oven…or fry it in a frying pan with hot oil. But lobsters are usually put in boiling water, and I'm embarrassed to say this, ma'am, but they're put in the boiling water when they're alive!"

"What is boiling water, Annabell?"

"It's very, very hot water, your highness."

"That's a strange thing to do," replied the Queen. "Seems a rather cruel thing to do to me but I suppose you land people have different eating habits to us. Everything here in the sea is eaten fresh. I'm sorry Annabell but it's not possible to boil the lobster. *Crom,* is his name, he's been specially bred for the table! You've had a good life, Crom? We've looked after you, haven't we?"

"Yes, your highness," said Crom waving its pincers from side to side. "It's been a privilege, and an honour to be bred for your table, ma'am. I knew that this day would come, it's part of life, you receive and then you give. You've given me a good life. I've wanted for nothing - if it wasn't for you breeding me then I wouldn't have had any life at all."

"That's right, Crom, well said, I'm proud of you." said the Queen. "That's the sort of gratitude that I like to hear. Have you any children, Crom?"

"Yes, your highness, I've got 364 girls and 354 boys, or it might be 355? I'm not sure. My eldest boy is coming to the age where he will be transferred to the dinner waiting list and he's really looking forward to it, in fact he can hardly wait. He knows that he'll get the finest food to eat and he'll be allowed to get married and have babies of his own. He'll live like a king, if you pardon the expression, ma'am - until the day arrives when like me, it'll be his turn to be your dinner."

"Well said, Crom." The Queen clapped her fins together. "I'm so proud of you. I can see that all our work has paid off, you're a fine outstanding specimen of a lobster, you're going to make a lovely meal for Annabell."

"It will be a honour, your highness. I'm ready now, enjoy me. I hope that I'm tasty."

"Crom is ready now, Annabell, so enjoy your meal," said the Queen.

Annabell grimaced. "Sorry ma'am but I cannot eat Crom," Annabell spoke in a stressed voice.

"No! - no! you mustn't say that," Crom moaned. "It's my destiny, you've got to eat me, if you don't, I'll be the laughing stock in the lobster world. I'll be an outcast, my family's reputation will be at stake, we'll be known as the lobster family that was rejected for the Queen's table and none of my family will ever be allowed to go to the dinner waiting list ever again. My family will be kicked out of the palace."

"Come - come, Annabell, pull yourself together, young lady," said the Queen. "It's part of the sea law. We're all food down here you know. Even me! - One day those horrible crabs or even Crom's kind will eat me when I die! These creatures are the scavengers of the seas, they'll eat anything, even you, Annabell. Isn't that right, Crom?"

"Yes ma'am. But I'm the lucky one, I've been looked after, I've had all the food that I've ever wanted, I've wanted for nothing - look how fat I am?" Crom rubbed his belly with his pincers. "It's true, I have eaten bits of land people!! That you've kindly given me, I know that it was just the leftovers that you sharks didn't want. They're really tasty, land people are. I would love to eat one now."

Is it possible your majesty for me to take a bite of your guest? I'll only take a little bite just for old times' sake. Just to have something to chew on! One last request you might say before I go to the promised world. Would that be alright, your majesty? Who is she anyway? If it's not too rude of me to ask, I would like to know who's going to eat me."

"No!... no! You can't take a bite out of our guest, Crom," said the Queen angrily.

"You're not to eat her! She's to eat you. She requested to eat you. Isn't that right?" The Queen turned round to Annabell and waited for her acknowledgement.

"Well...yes ma'am... I did say that, but I didn't expect it to be alive!!"

"Surely you must know who this land person is Crom? - She's probably the most famous person known to us sea creatures - Look at her! You haven't seen a land person like her before have you? Look at the colour of her skin! You've seen white skin people. Brown skin people. Black skin people. But you've never seen a red one, have you? This is Annabell. The special one from the land. You must know of the stories. Annabell saved the Dinosaurs, Crom."

"Oh yeah. I remember, how stupid of me not to know her. WOW!! I'm going to be so famous, to be eaten by the special one from the land. What an honour! How can I ever thank you, your majesty? You've made my day! Just wait till my family and friends hear about this. Oh, I'm going to be the most famous lobster the sea has ever known. Everybody will remember Crom. Of course, your highness, it would have been an honour to have been your dinner, you're very special too, but Annabell is known throughout the whole world. Cor!

I can hardly wait now. I'm so excited. Right then, I'm ready. Come on, Annabell, open your mouth and eat me. Come on, hurry up. Open wide – Let's see those lovely teeth."

Annabell shook her head in disgust. **"NO! NO! NO! NO!NO!"** She screamed…"How many more times do I have to tell you? I'm most certainly not going to eat you, not now, not ever - in fact, I'm never going to ever, ever, ever eat a lobster again, and I mean that."

"But!…but!" Crom pleaded with Annabell.

"There's no but's. Don't even go there. I'm sorry your majesty, I appreciate your hospitality but I just cannot eat Crom. No!- no! I can't do that."

Crom was very disappointed and he lowered his head in shame.

"Oh, very well Annabell. I'm sorry you feel like that but I respect your wish. Come over here, Crom."

Crom slowly crawled across the table towards the Queen and quick as a flash the Queen gobbled him up!! - She give out a little burp! "Mmm.. delicious." And then she spat out the remains of Crom's shell into a cloud of thousands of small particles. Just like an exploding firework! "You don't know what you've missed Annabell." remarked the Queen.

"Crom was delicious. It's aright Annabell, Crom's gone. Annabell, you can open your eyes now."

Annabell had put her hands over her eyes - she got a bit of a shock, she wasn't expecting the Queen to eat Crom. She gave out a sigh and wiped away what looked like a tear from the side of her left eye.

"What's the matter Annabell?" asked the Queen.

"Poor Crom! I liked him."

"Don't you eat food, Annabell?" asked the Queen sarcastically.

"Yes ma'am, of course I do but I wasn't expecting you to just gobble him up like that."

"Well what were you expecting Annabell? We don't cook food here in the sea - how could we? That's what Crom was for, Annabell. He was bred for the table. Don't you land people do the same thing? You breed animals to eat. Don't you?"

Annabell had to nod her head in agreement, because what the Queen was saying was true.

"Crom had a wonderful life. We've looked after him ever since he was born. He was getting to the end of his life anyway. He was really old you know. He didn't have much longer to live, only about another two weeks. He was at the end of his life that's why he was chosen. It's far better that he was my dinner rather than those horrible, nasty crabs getting him. Crom wouldn't have wanted to be eaten by them."

"I understand that you're, majesty, it was just a bit of a shock for me." Annabell had seen reason now, and had calmed down.

Albert Stein returned into the room where the Queen and Annabell were dining, but Annabell hadn't actually eaten any food.

Albert Stein informed the Queen that her parliament was assembled and waiting for her as she had requested. "Let them wait, the silly old fools," said the Queen, quite sternly, and then she turned to Annabell and smiled.

"I'm having a conversation with somebody far more important than those decrepit and conceited group of twits!!" she informed Albert.

Chapter Five

Annabell Meets The Parliament

"Very well your highness, I will inform the members of your parliament that you will be slightly delayed." With that Albert Stein bowed his head and left the room.

The Queen and Annabell had a long discussion about the sea world in general. The Queen told Annabell that the sharks had been living on the Earth long before the humans arrived.

"Your kind have caused great harm to the sea's life," said the Queen. "They had no regard for other species or for the future survival of the sea world. They've hunted Whales to near extinction and have decimated fish stocks, which, of course, is our food. This is our home, we don't, and can't anyway come onto the land and cause you the damage that you've done to us. It's not fair, Annabell." The Queen appeared to be angry.

Annabell at that moment felt ashamed to be part of the human race.

"But ma'am. They have finally learnt what they were doing was wrong. Whales are beautiful creatures. They are now protected and have been for a long time. The fish stocks have been replenished. Earlier humans, didn't realise what they were doing to the seas but now they have respect for all sea life. Please don't attack humans anymore, ma'am, we wish you sharks no harm, surely we can all live in harmony together now - that's what I want."

The Queen was very touched by Annabell's words and promised that she would relay what she had told her, throughout the shark world - I promise we'll never harm humans again. That's only if they don't harm us, of course, otherwise they'll get these!" The Queen opened up her mouth to show her sharp teeth as a kind of threat.

Annabell thanked the Queen and felt really pleased that she had contributed to the harmony of the sea and land worlds.

After nearly one hour of discussion the Queen moved away from the dining table. "Come with me- let's go and face those miserable motley members of my parliament." They came to a place that strongly resembled the British House of Parliament!

Annabell was very surprised at what she was seeing. "Ma'am, um, if you don't mind me asking, but why have you copied the human way of society? This is almost an exact copy of the British House of Parliament."

"Yes I know," replied the Queen. "It was meant to be like that."

"But why ma'am? This is really strange, I didn't expect to see anything like this." Annabell shook her head to show her disbelief.

"It's all explainable Annabell. The British, as you call them, almost ruled most of the land world. They were very strong and innovative humans and stood out from all others. This didn't go unnoticed by the sharks. The humans were organised and at that time the sharks were living in a haphazard world with no moral standards.

My ancestors realised that the British humans were right with their Royalty and organised parliament. We learnt all this from the information that we salvaged from the shipwrecks. So we created an identical world. Law and order is very important in all societies. It may surprise you but we too have our own police force. Hospitals, to care for the sick and injured are here in the seas, and we've even got prisons to punish bad sharks. Everything here in the shark world is run the same as the human world."

Annabell was fascinated by what the Queen was telling her but she couldn't imagine sharks having hospitals and a police force. To Annabell this seemed absurd.

"We had no idea ma'am, that you were so far advanced. We always knew how intelligent the Dolphins were. In fact some humans believe that they are the superior species on earth but I'm not sure if that's true.

When I get back home I will try to explain to human people what I have been told and seen for myself about your world, but I don't think that they're going to believe me, ma'am."

"Never mind, Annabell, whatever will be, will be. You'll know that it's true."

All the members of the Queen's parliament were assembled in their seats.

The Queen and Annabell were escorted to the front bench alongside the Prime Minister, Albert Stein. Albert stood up on his tail and started the debate, he now knew why Annabell had been sent to the shark world.

"Your Highness, Annabell and my right Honourable Ladies and Gentlemen. We have been sent here today a very special land human, who I'm sure, needs no introduction. May I have the pleasure to present to this House, Annabell, better known to us as, *The Red One*. You have all now been briefed as to why the red one has been sent to us. She needs our help. The creator of all of us has sent her on a mission to find the missing pieces of all life here on Earth."

Albert turned to Annabell and asked her if she would be so kind as to show the House what it was that she was searching for.

Annabell stood up and held the piece of the Holism. It was glowing in the crystal clear waters with all the colours of the rainbow.

Annabell addressed the parliament:

"Your highness, my right Honourable Ladies and Gentlemen. It's an honour and privilege to meet you all. As you all know, I've been sent on a mission by the creator of all life to recover four pieces of an object - I have one piece, which I'm holding in my hand. This is the seed that created all life on land. I'm now in search of the seed that created all life here in the oceans. I don't know why I've been chosen to find the pieces, nor do I know the reason why the Creator has sent me to find them. All I know is: it's of the utmost importance that I find them. The only clues that I have to whereabouts of the seed is that it's somewhere at 66 degrees - 32 minutes North, and I've been told that I must follow the 'signs'. What the signs are, I do not know?. With those words Annabell sat down.

The Right Honourable Francis Flip member of parliament for the species of Thresher sharks put up his right fin, trying to draw the attention of whip of the house.

(The Whip is an elected representative member of parliament who has special responsibility for ensuring discipline).

She was the right honourable Mavis Davis. Elected member of parliament representing Hammerhead sharks. Mavis Davis was an elderly lady shark, and had been a member of parliament for over 26 years. She was very well respected by all the elected members of the parliament and always maintained order.

The Right Honourable Mavis Davis gave permission for Francis Flip to speak.

Francis Flip had been born with a speech impediment and had never spoken in the house in all the twenty years that he had been a member of parliament. He stood up on his tail and started to speak: "Six... six...sixty six...thir...thir...thirty...two min...min...minutes...nor...nor...north. Yo...yo....you... s...s...say? W...w...well....I...I...I've... al...al ...always... un...un...under...st...st...stood...tha....tha...that...t...t... b...b..be...th...th...the...n...n...north...p...p...pole."

"**HERE!**"... "**HERE!**" shouted out all the members of the parliament and they stood up and clapped and cheered the right honourable member Francis Flip for his maiden speech. The cheering and clapping lasted for several minutes.

All the members of the House knew what an effort this had been for him.

"Well...well...well... spoken sir," shouted out, one of the members representing the Great White sharks. This was the right Honourable Charles Chip. A rather arrogant fish who wasn't really giving Francis Flip any praise for his enormous effort but was making fun of his speech impediment.

The House erupted in fury with loud booing, because Charles Chip laughed at his own joke. He thought that it was so funny that Francis Flip had such difficulty in getting out his words.

"ORDER!...ORDER!...ORDER!." shouted out the Whip, Mavis Davis.

"Would the right Honourable gentleman, Charles Chip, show more respect to the right Honourable gentleman Francis Flip, and the House ...and please remember we have her Royal Highness with us today and our special guest Annabell. Whatever must they think of you all? You should be ashamed of yourselves for this kind of behaviour. I will not tolerate it, do you understand? All of you please be quiet and show respect."

The Queen turned to Annabell and said, "What did I tell you? I told you they were a load of *twits*. I apologise for the behaviour of these dim wits, Annabell."

"That's alright, ma'am. We have the same sort of behaviour from some members of our political parties on land."

All the members of the parliament apologised for their outburst, except for one!! Charles Chip. The Whip Mavis Davis ordered him to apologise immediately to Francis Flip. But he refused. This left the Whip with no choice but to have him suspended from parliamentary duties until further notice. Charles Chip was escorted from the house in disgrace.

"We will not tolerate this kind of behaviour here in this House," Mavis Davis informed the members of parliament. "I hope that you all understand this - Any further outbursts and I will suspend the lot of you." The House went quiet.

Albert Stein stood up and thanked the right Honourable Francis Flip for his contribution to the discussion. "This seems to be a very intelligent suggestion made by our right Honourable friend, Francis Flip. I thank you sir. "The North Pole?" Albert paused for a moment. "Yes! umm, Yes! I agree. This is what the clue must mean. The North Pole after all is the farthest north that you can go. I propose that we should take a vote whether the members of this house believe that the clue given to Annabell does actually mean to look at the North Pole for the seed that created us all here in the oceans. All those in favour would you please raise your fins now...?"

Every single member stood up and raised their fins in approval.

"Vote carried," said Albert

Francis Flip positioned himself back into his seat with a look of self- importance blazed across his face. This was the happiest moment of his whole life. He had finally achieved his ambition to make his maiden speech in the House of Shark Parliament.

Albert Stein turned to Annabell and asked her if she agreed with the decision that the piece of the holism could be at the North Pole?

Annabell nodded in agreement. "Right then, that's settled, the search will commence immediately. I propose that we send out one thousand of our finest soldiers to scout the seas and ask all our sea friends if they have any knowledge of the whereabouts of the said object."

All the members of the House agreed and the meeting was ended.

The Queen invited Annabell to stay at the Shark World while the search for information commenced.

Chapter Six
The Delvi

Several days passed, and then a week but no news was forthcoming regarding the piece of the holism. Annabell was having the time of her life at the Shark World. She was given a comfortable cave room to live in, and she and the Queen became very good friends. The Queen loved Annabell, she was so unusual although she had human features she didn't behave like a human!! She swam around the Shark World like she was a fish!

Two further weeks passed. At last, there was a breakthrough. News was filtering through to the Queen that one of the soldier scouts had some interesting news. He was summoned along with Albert Stein to come to the Queen's residence immediately.

The Queen and Annabell waited in one of the cavern lounges for the scout soldier to arrive. Both the Queen and Annabell were getting very excited in anticipation as to what this news might be.

Suddenly there was a bang on the gong that was outside the lounge cavern. "Please enter," said the Queen. Albert Stein entered the cavern lounge accompanied by a very nervous soldier shark who was wearing a soldier uniform that comprised of just a cap that was a sea shell, probably a clam that was stuck on top of his head somehow.

"What news?" asked the Queen. "Come...come, hurry up soldier."

The soldier shark was stricken with nerves. Standing there in front of the Queen and the Prime Minister was too much for him, he was bolt rigid unable to move or speak.

"Oh, please," said the Queen. "Relax sir. What is your name, soldier?"

"257893 Private Mortimore at you service, **sir.** Oh, I mean your Highness...umm... ma'am. Majesty," Mortimore was getting tongue tied.

"Oh, for goodness' sake, sit down Mortimore, and try to calm down," said the Queen getting a bit agitated with the soldier.

A large chair was pulled forward so that Mortimore could be close to the Queen and Annabell who were both sitting on a large sofa.

Mortimore tried to position himself onto the chair but managed to fall over the back of it knocking over a priceless *Ming* vase which was smashed into pieces!! He landed flat on his back with his fins in the air. His face turned from a grey white to a vivid pink colour!!

Annabell and the Queen couldn't help but laugh at Mortimore's antics.

"Mortimore!"

"Yes sir? Oh, I mean your highness ma'am - sorry!"

"What's the matter with you? Are you accident prone?" asked the Queen. Annabell laughed.

"I'm sorry! - I'm sorry! your highness , sir - ma'am. Oh,... I'm getting all mixed up, it's just that... I'm so nervous." And then Mortimore shuddered.

"How long have you been a soldier Mortimore?" asked the Queen sarcastically.

"Umm... six years... five days, your highness... and loving every minute of it, sir."

"Oh, dear! We haven't taught you very much, have we, Mortimore? And why do you keep calling me 'sir'?" The Queen was now teasing poor Mortimore.

"It's because....umm .... I'm used to only talking to my commanding officers....and umm. I have to call them, sir - sir. It's a habit now. Sorry your highness I don't mean any disrespect to you. I am a good soldier, honest I am, it's just that I get nervous in front of others that I don't know."

"But you know me Mortimore. I'm your Queen."

"Yeah, yeah, I know that your highness but I never ever thought that a humble soul like me would one day be standing face to face with you. It's such a honour for me, I can't believe it."

"Mortimore, I believe you have news for us? Now in your own time, and there's no need to be nervous. Myself and Annabell would love to know what the news is - it could be very important."

Motimore tried to compose himself before he spoke.

"Your highness."

"Well that's a good start," said the Queen. "Now carry on."

"I came across a Humpback whale that was heading to the North Pole, her name is Chloe. She told me that she'd heard a story told many years ago that an artic fox, had told a Narwhal, who had told a story about a Polar bear who had seen such an object that we are searching for and indeed it was at the North Pole."

"But how could Chloe be so sure it was the piece of the holism?" asked Annabell, slightly dubious about the story.

"Because ma'am, the fox said that the polar bear felt some sort of magic when he held it in his paw."

"What sort of magic?" asked Annabell. "Only I have the power that the holism gives."

Mortimer explained to Annabell that the fox was told that when the Polar bear held the object his fur turned red!!

Annabell was shocked by what she had heard -"No!-No! you're kidding with me, this cannot be true. You're making it up."

The Queen was not amused by Mortimore's story.

"Mortimore!" she shrieked. "If you're telling lies, I'll have you thrown out of the army with a dishonourable discharge."

"NO!...NO!....your highness, I'm not making fun, I would never do that.

I'm an honest shark. I don't know if the story is true. But honestly, this is what Chloe the Humpback was told."

The Queen turned to Annabell. "What do you think, Annabell? I don't think Mortimore made it up. Could it be possible for other living things to be able to generate power from this object?"

Annabell thought for a while and then remembered the story of the dinosaur who gained magic from the holism. She realised that maybe some animals may be able to gain the object's powers if it was absolutely necessary.

The story that Pete told her was that when the dinosaur laid her eggs on the piece of the holism that she now had, the eggs hatched out. She must have also gained powers from the holism. So it was possible.

Then Annabell remembered the words on the parchment. 'Follow the signs'. The polar bear turned red!! Maybe this was the sign?

"MA'AM!" Annabell screamed out excitedly. "I think this is it!! It's the *sign*. The red polar bear is the sign. It must be - we must find Chloe, the whale. I've got to go to the Pole ma'am. Francis Flip was right. It's there… must be. Oh, I could kiss you, Mortimore," and she did!!

Mortimore went a bright pink colour again!

"Where about was this whale Mortimore?" asked Annabell very excitedly.

"She's about five or six hundred miles from here and she's already heading North."

"Oh! How will I ever be able to catch her up? How many other whales are with her, Mortimore?"

"There… were… well, umm, like, hundreds of them ma'am."

Oh my God! Mortimore, it's a hopeless task," said Annabell, very disappointed.

"No ma'am, it's not hopeless." said Mortimore unexpectedly

"What do you mean?" asked Annabell. "If there are hundreds of whales how would you know which one is Chloe?"

"I would know which one of the whales is Chloe," said Mortimore proudly.

"How would you know this, Mortimore? You said there were hundreds of them. They all more or less look the same, don't they?"

"Well, yeah they do, you're right, but I've put a tag on her fin, she's got a red-coloured shell tied to her back fin, and believe me ma'am, it wasn't easy putting it there. I was risking my life messing about with a creature as big as her - but I've got it around her pretty well. It won't come off, I don't think,"

"Brilliant work, Mortimore," said the Queen, "I'm proud of you. You're a soldier of the highest quality, it's a pity about your nervous disposition though, you'll have to try and sort that out. Remind me when it's medal time to award you one for your gallantry."

Mortimore felt so proud and held his head up. "Thank you, sir...oh, sorry!... I mean of course your highness, ma'am."

"You may leave the room now, Mortimore." said the Queen, pointing her fin to the lounge cavern exit.

Mortimore bowed his head and left the cavern.

"Now then, how shall we work this, Annabell?" asked the Queen. "We've got to somehow get you to Chloe the Humpback whale as quick as we can."

Annabell didn't answer, she was trying to think of what to do.

"Have you any ideas Albert?" asked the Queen.

Albert thought for a moment. "Yes, your highness, I have an idea. Why don't we get Birling Ross? To take

Annabell. He's fast and strong and we'll get Tames Blunt to go along as well."

"That sounds a good idea, Albert," said the Queen. "Please go and inform Birling, and Tames that I would like to have a word with them."

"Yes your highness, I will go immediately. Not too sure where they are at the moment though. It may take some time tracking them down."

Several hours later Albert came back to see the Queen and Annabell.

He'd located Birling Ross, and Tames Blunt, and had informed them both that the Queen wished to speak with them.

A short while later they both arrived, and the Queen told them both that they were to take Annabell to find the Humpback whale named Chloe.

They left the lounge cavern and went away to prepare for their journey.

The Queen chattered to Annabell for several hours until the time came for her to leave the Shark World. Albert Stein informed the Queen that everything was now ready for Annabell to start her journey to find Chloe the Humpback whale.

Suddenly there were loud bangs on the gong, followed by yelling and shouting.

"YOUR HIGHNESS!-YOUR HIGHNESS! I must speak with you....It's...It's... very, very urgent."

"Come in, come in," said the Queen.

The Right Honourable Charles Chip rushed into the lounge cavern, nearly knocking Albert Stein and the Queen over! He was in somewhat of a hurry and very flustered.

"What is so urgent Charles? That you nearly knocked me and Albert over," asked the Queen.

"Sorry! Sorry! Your highness, and you, Albert. I don't wish to be rude, but we have a very serious problem here in the ocean. There's something really horrible swimming in our waters. The dolphins have brought us news that they've picked up from the humans.

"The news is being relayed all around the world. They're talking about something that is very evil, and it's here! It's coming toward us. Your highness, we're all in great danger for our lives!"

The Queen was now very concerned at what Charles was saying.

"What is it Charles? What evil thing swims in our sea? Why are we in danger for our lives? Surely we can sort this out...whatever it is?"

Charles Chip lowered his head and was very reluctant to tell her of this evil thing.

"Your highness the dolphins say that there's a creature in our waters that is consuming all the *salt* from the water and it's killing all sea life. It then turns the water to *fresh water*! The dolphins say that were all going to die if we stay here."

"Oh, no!" Annabell put her red hands over her eyes. She repeated again "Oh...no!- no!- no! this can't be happening."

"What is it Annabell?" asked the Queen. "Do you know something about this?"

Annabell thought for a while. She was too ashamed to say that she did. Finally she spoke.

"I'm really sorry to say that I do, ma'am. Oh, this is very, very serious. I think that it's the *Delvi,* ma'am. It's come alive. The creator said that when I entered the water I would *waken the Delvi.* It's all my fault."

"Delvi? What is that?" asked the Queen. "What is a Delvi, Annabell? You must tell me what you know about this."

The Queen was nervously swimming up and down the lounge cavern. Albert and Charles were side by side almost motionless in the water clearly in a state of shock and they were eagerly waiting for Annabell's reply.

"Oh, I'm so… sorry ma'am - I should have told you but I forgot. The creator warned me that this would happen. The Delvi is one of the evil seeds. The creator said that this was evil beyond belief, but I didn't know what it was."

"I know what it is," said Charles Chip. "The dolphins said that it's some sort of a *Blob!* of matter - it travels ten feet under the surface of the water and all the time it's spreading - it's now hundreds of miles long and hundreds of miles wide, and it's growing rapidly. The dolphins say that the blob is jet black !! And it's got thousands of holes on its body that suck in the sea's water. It then takes all the salt out of the water and stores it. All the time it's getting bigger, and bigger - it blows the fresh water out through holes on its back. The sea where this creature is - is now a mass of bubbles, and jets of fresh water."

The Queen was still swimming up and down listening to Charles' terrible story of this creature and was now looking extremely worried. "So how can we stop this blob creature, Charles? Have the dolphins any ideas?"

"No, your highness, they haven't. They say that it can't be stopped. The humans have tried. I don't know what this all means, ma'am, but the dolphins said that the humans have dropped what they call bombs on it. They've tried to burn it. They've tried acid on it, and chemical weapons, but nothing will stop it. The dolphins said that as a last resort they even injected every known deadly virus into it, but it was hopeless. It resists everything, and all the time it's growing at a phenomenal rate. The dolphins say that it grows by fifty miles per hour in an ever-increasing circle."

The queen turned to Annabell, "Do you know what this all means, Annabell?"

"Yes I do, ma'am, and it's very serious - it means that the humans can't stop it."

The Queen was circling around the room swimming very fast, she was now extremely concerned for the Shark World. "How far is it from us now, Charles?"

"Your highness, I'm sorry to be the one to tell you, but it's only about two thousand miles away!!

It will be here in less than one a half days! - we've got to leave here before it's too late."

"Oh,...I agree, Charles," said the Queen anxiously. "Albert, get things organised, quickly. Inform my parliament that we have to leave our home immediately. Get our soldiers organised for a mass evacuation. The females and young ones must leave immediately, we've all got to leave here and fast, we have very little time."

Albert bowed his head in acknowledgement. "Yes, yes your highness. I will see to it at once, but where will we go? This creature travels so fast, we couldn't possibly get away from it." Albert was relating to the Queen what she already knew. He knew that their plight was hopeless.

The Queen turned to Annabell, who was still sitting on the sofa with her hands still over her eyes. She was trying desperately hard to think of what to do.

"Oh, Annabell, this is a disaster for all of us sea life, if we do not stop this thing, we will surely all perish. Albert's right. We cannot out run this thing; it travels too fast."

Annabell got off the sofa - she was angry, very, very angry. "**NO!!**" she screamed, "You will not 'perish'! I will not allow this to happen."

Annabell turned to Charles who was looking down at the sea bottom like a lost soul, not knowing what to do next.

"**Charles!**" shrieked Annabell when did this creature first appear in the sea?"

"It was like you say, it was about the same time that you entered the water with the little red fish. The dolphins said that it first showed itself about two weeks ago. Masses of bubbles started coming to the surface. Humans went out to investigate to see what the bubbles were, but they never came back. The dolphins said that they were told that the humans were killed by this creature - it kills everything in its path. Several of the humans' ships have been sunk, and a lot of humans have lost their lives. We're all doomed!!"

Annabell shook her head. "No Charles, you're not *doomed!*"

Annabell turned and faced the Queen. "Ma'am, it definitely sounds like it is the Delvi. The creator told me a story that I must tell you now. When the seeds of all life were released on the earth four thousand million years ago, five other seeds were released at the same time, these five seeds were the seeds of **anti life**! (Devil seeds).

I've been sent on a mission not only to find the seeds of all life, but also to destroy the anti life seeds. The creator said that I have the powers to be able to defeat them. This sounds like the seed, Delvi. This seed, so I was told, is evil beyond belief. But I've been given clues of how to defeat it. The creator said that it has a weakness. The clue said that: if I take out the *'e'* from *least* - to make it *last* - this will make the Delvi *past.* But I have no idea what it means, ma'am. But I know that this evil creature cannot harm me. I must go and confront it before it destroys all life here in the oceans. I must go at once. Please don't leave your home, it will be hopeless anyway you can't outrun this creature, if I don't defeat it, all life on earth will surely die."

"But how will you stop it, Annabell?" The Queen was frantic with worry. "You heard what Charles said - nothing can stop it. It resists everything. We're all going to die, Annabell, we can't live in fresh water. We only have just a day to live!! What am I going to do?" The Queen was very worried and sad.

Annabell put her arms around the Queen's head in a sort of embrace. She was trying to console the Queen - she looked straight into her eyes and said: "I will beat this thing, ma'am, - I promise- I promise- I promise." She kissed the Queen, and left the cavern.

Chapter Seven
Annabell Confronts The Delvi

Annabell was eager to confront the Delvi. She believed it was her fault that this creature had appeared at this moment in time but this was always going to happen. The Devil was confident that Annabell wouldn't be able to stop this horrific creature. It wanted to test her to see if she really was a threat to its ultimate aim. The Delvi would have come to life in the not too distant future anyway.

Annabell had been born to the Earth for her to take on these encounters with the Devil seeds - if she wasn't able to stop them it would result in the end of life on Earth. Annabell had the power and she had the clues. All she had to do was to work them out.

Annabell left the Shark World and headed out in the ocean towards the Delvi. She could already feel the strong current as the Delvi was drawing water towards itself. Annabell had no need to swim fast as the current was all the time pulling her but she used her power to swim to it as fast as she could. Her eyes were sparkling which was always the sign that she was using her powers. Annabell knew that she had no time to lose - she could already see sea creatures being drawn towards the Delvi, which would result in certain death for them.

As Annabell neared this creature the current was becoming ferocious and unpredictable. The sea was erratic with forward and backward motions. One minute she was being pulled forward and then she would go back a short distance. There was no need for her to swim, now ahead of her she could see huge masses of bubbles, jets of water were being sprayed high into the air.

The Delvi now stretched for hundreds of miles. Annabell could hear a loud hissing noise like a kettle boiling. Annabell was sucked into the creature through one of the holes on its body She was squeezed into its internal organs along with hundreds of unfortunate sea creatures. The creature was extracting every bit of salt from their bodies but Annabell couldn't be harmed, she was ejected from the blob through a hole in its back. She found herself being tossed around by the bubbles and jet spray. All the time the Delvi was growing at a phenomenal rate.

Annabell looked upwards, she could see helicopters that were observing this horrible creature but there was nothing that they could do.

Annabell had a plan of how to stop it. She thought that the part of the holism that she had would have the power to kill it. She used all her strength to reach the Delvi which was ten foot under the water. She touched the creature with the holism but to her **dismay** nothing happened. She was pushed back to the surface by the force of the bubbles and jet spray. Annabell was getting frustrated, she knew that she didn't have much time to save the Shark World, and everything else that lived in the sea.

The creator had told her that she had the power to stop this creature but she didn't know how. It had resisted bombs, chemicals, fire, viruses. This was virtually everything that man knew. She wondered what weapon was left. The creature seemed like it was totally indestructible. Annabell thought about the words on the parchment:

"Take the 'e' out of least to make last, this would make the creature past"

The parchment said that it would be the **'least'** thing you would expect.

Annabell was very confused by the clues, and she found it hard to think under the pressure that she was under. But she knew that the most important word was **last -** the parchment said that this would make the Delvi **past.**

Annabell was trying to think of the meaning of the word past. She knew that it could mean having been *once here*. She thought if you were *once here*, then you're no longer here now.

Annabell thought about the word *least* - the parchment said that it would be what you would **least** expect. And to think about the word *last.*

Suddenly the clues clicked in her mind. She knew what it all meant now. She realised that if you rearrange the word *last* it would make some other word.

There was one substance that could harm this creature, all the clues on the parchment pointed to it, but it seemed ridiculous, it certainly would be the last thing you would expect to work though.

Annabell decided that's what it all must mean. She was sure that she had worked out what the creator was trying to tell her but she had very little time left and she had a big problem. She had to get back to the land to get the substance that she needed despite her being a very fast swimmer, she realised that the rate the Delvi was growing it would be impossible for her to out swim this creature as the currents were so strong.

The sea all around the Delvi was raging, the sea water was now being sucked in faster and faster as the creature was growing. Jets of water were being sprayed high into the air! The water was coming back down as torrential rain!!

The creature was now only hours away from reaching the Sharks' World and she was about an hour away from the nearest land. Annabell realised that she was in an impossible situation. She knew that she needed help - the helicopters were still hovering around monitoring the Delvi. This was her chance.

She waved frantically at them trying to get one of the pilots' attention. One of the pilots saw Annabell waving and flew his helicopter down towards her to see what she wanted. Annabell gestured to him that she wanted to be winched up to the helicopter.

This was going to be a very dangerous operation. The ferocity of the jet spray coming from the creatures back would make this task extremely difficult.

Annabell was all the time being tossed about by the water spray.

Captain John Smith, a United States navy pilot for over twenty years. Forty-two years old and a very brave man indeed knew what Annabell wanted him to do. He flew the helicopter right into the water spray, visibility was very low, but the colour of Annabell's red skin was helping the captain to see her.

A crew member was lowered down by winch - he was trying desperately to grab hold of her, but was being swung violently from right to left, and then swung around in circles. The captain was all the time fighting the controls of the helicopter trying to keep it steady.

Annabell couldn't hold her position for any length of time for the crew man to be able to get hold of her. Ten agonising minutes passed. The helicopter was being pushed and knocked about all over the place by the force of the water spray.

Annabell was now forty feet away from the man on the winch line. The captain in one last desperate attempt decided to go down even lower but he knew that he wouldn't be able to maintain this position for very long. The rotor blades on the helicopter were struggling to keep their motion, if the captain didn't get out of there soon the helicopter would be in danger of crashing!!

The man on the winch line swung himself right at Annabell and managed to grab hold of her arm, but he was having trouble holding on to her. Annabell grabbed hold of the man's left leg and held on tight and she screamed. "**GO! - GO! -GO!**"

The captain flew the helicopter upwards as fast as he could to get away from the spray. Annabell and the man were dangling in mid air! When they were clear of the jet water Annabell was winched up with the man, both were pulled inside the helicopter.

"**QUICK!**" She shouted. "I must get to the land as quickly as possible, there's not a minute to lose. How fast can this flying machine go, sir?"

"300 mph," replied captain Smith.

"Oh, thank goodness for that," said Annabell. "Put your foot flat down captain, sorry, I don't know your name."

"It's Captain John Smith. I know who you are. What's going on, Annabell? Have you got any ideas of how to get rid of this nasty creature? - What is it? Do you know?"

"Yes I do know Captain. It's the Delvi. This is something very evil. I've been sent to destroy it - and yes, I have got an idea of how to get rid of it, but I can't tell you yet, it would seem too silly for you to understand but I think that there's a way to stop this thing but we must hurry. How long will it take to reach the land captain?"

"About ten minutes, Annabell. San Cristo is our nearest landing point.

"Oh thank goodness for that, there's still time, can you go any faster?"

"No, Annabell, I'm flat out now," replied the captain. Water was dripping off his cap and running down his neck! All of them were soaking wet! It was going to be a miserable and uncomfortable journey for them.

Annabell was really eager to get back to the Delvi as fast as was humanly possible.

The helicopter finally reached the coast line of San Cristo and landed.

Thousands of people had gathered on the coast line, including the United States Army and Navy. War ships were just off the coast, they were being tossed around in the erratic sea.

The Delvi was less than a hour from reaching the land.

The ships wouldn't be able to stay off this coast for very much longer as the currents were already getting stronger.

The Delvi was drawing the sea salt water inwards, and pumping fresh water outwards. The sea was now getting very turbulent and the current was getting faster as the Delvi came closer and closer.

If the war ships didn't leave soon, they would be drawn towards it and without any doubt be sunk!

Blockades had been placed around the whole coastline. The latest advanced weaponry was put in place. When the Delvi was in range they will open fire on it - in one last attempt to kill it.

People were warned not to go into the sea. They would face certain death if they did. Several hundreds of people had lost their lives already.

Preparations had been put in place by the United States President to protect the people. But the President was at his wit's end. Nobody could come up with any solutions of how to stop this evil creature. If Annabell's plan didn't work it will surely be the end of all life on Earth.

Annabell got out of the helicopter and ran screaming and shouting at everybody to get out of her way.

The army made a path for her. She ran down the road shouting out, **"Does anybody know where a food store is?"** A little boy aged about eight years old, shouted back, telling her that there was a food supermarket just around the next corner.

Annabell ran around the corner and spotted the supermarket. She ran inside it. Everybody was shocked and couldn't understand what she could possibly want in a food store at this tragic time. Everybody knew Annabell. The media had been filming her ever since she encountered the Delvi. Her every move was being monitored and transmitted around the world.

This was the worst crisis the world had ever known, and here was Annabell getting something to eat!! If this creature wasn't stopped the world would end!!!

People were screaming and crying. **"Help us! please help us! - Annabell."**

Hundreds of people could be seen praying on the streets of San Cristo

"Please everybody get out of my way," shrieked Annabell. **"I don't wish to be rude, but this is a matter of life and death."**

She ran down the aisles of the store looking for a special item, then she suddenly stopped and picked up a small glass bottle. **"That's it!!"** She yelled. She ran past the checkout girl. **"Sorry! Sorry!** I'm not stealing it, but I haven't got time to pay you." There were long queues in the food store where people were panic buying food and water.

The manager of the supermarket shouted to Annabell, **"It's alright, take anything that you want."**

"This is all that that I want, thank you," replied Annabell as she ran out of the store.

The television crews and newspaper reporters were rushing around falling over each other trying to get her to give an interview of what she was doing going into a food store, and they were trying to see what it was that she had in her hand - all the cameras were flashing at her and they were jostling her.

"Will you please all go away, and get out of my way," yelled Annabell.

"I haven't got time to explain to you. None of you will understand anyway. You'll all find out later. Now please go away and leave me alone."

The media people did what they were told and stopped harassing Annabell and let her go on her way.

Annabell ran back down the road clutching her small bottle for dear life. The sea was now becoming a lot more turbulent as the Delvi approached the shore line.

Before she got back into the helicopter Annabell requested to talk to the President of The Unites States Of America. She told him that all the people must be evacuated from the coastline immediately because she feared that a *tsunami* might occur if she was successful in defeating the Delvi. She informed the President that if this happened the first waves would hit near Rakes Bay.

The President said that he would send out a red alert immediately and would instruct his men to evacuate the people at once and move them to higher ground. The President thanked Annabell and wished her all the luck in the world. "We're all very proud of you. The destiny of us all is in your hands, Annabell. May God be with you."

Annabell put the phone down and got back in the helicopter.

She told Captain Smith to go as quickly as was possible to get back to the Delvi.

Her plan was to jump out of the helicopter onto the top of the Delvi's back.

Captain Smith headed back out to sea. There was absolutely no time to lose.

The helicopter reached the Delvi in just a few minutes. The Delvi had grown much bigger.

Annabell didn't know if her plan was going to work. It would be the one and only chance that she would get. She knew that.

The sea all around was erupting with the violent fury from this evil creature.

Captain Smith flew the helicopter over the top of the Delvi and wished Annabell good luck. **"I'm going to need it!"** she yelled back, and then she jumped from the helicopter straight onto the blob's back! She plunged under the water, but was quickly pushed back to the surface by the force of the jet spray that was coming from the creature's back.

She slowly unscrewed the lid from the small glass bottle and yelled at the top of her voice, **"Oh, I hope this works! Please! God,"** she pleaded. **"Make it work! Please!...Please! make it work."**

Annabell tossed the bottle onto the back of the Delvi like she was throwing a hand grenade! She shouted again, **"Here, see if you like this, you evil, horrible good for nothing blob!!"**

Some of the contents of the bottle emptied out and were dispersed amongst the bubbles, but they were being held in suspension by the force of the jet water pressure.

Annabell waited and waited, but nothing happened.

"Oh no, I've failed!" she yelled, **"It doesn't work."** And she banged her fist on the surface of the water in anger. The force of her anger created a power surge go through her body, which resulted in downward current to the Delvi - a single particle of the bottle fell onto the back of the Delvi. Instantly there was a reaction from the creature - it didn't like what had just come to rest on its back. The blob stopped pumping in the sea water, it was like it had gone into a shock of some kind like it had been stung!

The bubbles and water ceased coming from its back and the creature rapidly rose to the surface creating a huge wave that was thirty feet high!!

Annabell was right there was going to be a *tsunami*. The Delvi caused it when it rose so fast to the surface.

She hoped that the people had prepared themselves for what was going to happen when the wave hit the land..

Annabell's bottle was now lying flat on the back of the Delvi.

The remaining contents from the bottle slowly emptied out in a sort of sludge onto the creature's back. At last the sea became calm. The creature wasn't moving anymore.

Holes started appearing on the back of the Delvi where the sludge from the bottle had spilled. It was like a machine gun had been fired at it, but obviously no bullets had been fired!!! Thousands of holes started appearing and the holes got bigger and bigger until they formed into one gigantic hole.

The hole then became a *whirlpool* and the big fat blob started to disperse inside itself at a rapid rate like it was *melting away*!! The creature was clearly dying!

The whirlpool got bigger and bigger! Until it stretched for hundreds of miles. Annabell was sucked into the huge hole and was tossed around. The salt that the creature had taken from the sea was now being dispersed back.

Two hours passed and finally the whirlpool stopped. The sea became very calm again.

The Delvi *was no - more.* It had been defeated by Annabell.

The creator had been correct. She did have the powers and knowledge of how to defeat it. But she also needed the help of the very brave crew of the helicopter, especially Captain John Smith and the men on the winch line.

Annabell popped up to the surface, she had been under the water for quite sometime.

She yelled out loud, **"YES! YES! YES! ... I've done it.!.. I've done it! "** She thumped both her hands on the surface of the water sending up a large spray like a fountain.

Her body surged with increased power that she had gained from the destruction of the Delvi.

Annabell swam around in circles, she was so happy. She waved to the crew of the helicopter and gave them a thumbs up sign. Two of the crew members jumped from the helicopter into the water and swam towards Annabell.

When they reached her they gave her a big hug!! They knew like everybody else would soon know that she had just saved the Earth from a catastrophe.

Dolphins swam towards her. These are extremely intelligent creatures They knew that Annabell had just saved them all. They crowded around her and they joined in the celebrations, they were leaping out of the water and making their normal squeaking noises. Annabell understood their language. The dolphins were thanking her over and over again.

Annabell had fulfilled her mission of killing one of the anti- life seeds, but there were still four more that she would have to encounter somewhere on the earth.

⬥

Chapter Eight
Annabell Returns To Shark World

Annabell was escorted all the way back to the Shark World by the dolphins. She was having some fun with them hitching a ride by grabbing their tails! But they didn't mind.

When she reached the Shark World, she was greeted by Albert. Who had already heard the news that Annabell had defeated the Delvi.

Albert was in a state of ecstasy and was grinning with the widest grin that was possible for him. "I can't believe what you have done. Whatever did you do, Annabell? How on earth did you manage to kill this evil creature? I'm all ears! Well, I would be if I had any," laughed Albert. "Please tell me, you did kill it, didn't you?"

"Yes my dear Albert, I did," said Annabell as cool as a cucumber!! "It's gone Albert and it will never come back, and now there's no need for any of my friends to leave their home. I'm really sorry that I've caused so much trouble here in the oceans, I didn't mean to."

"No, no, no, you mustn't blame yourself," said Albert, quite sternly. "It's not your fault, you wasn't to know what was going to happen - nobody knew that this creature was here amongst us, here in the seas. If it wasn't for you, Annabell, we would have all perished sometime in the future, it would surely have been the end of us all today if you hadn't defeated it."

"How did you know that I had defeated the Delvi, Albert? News couldn't have travelled that fast?" Annabell looked surprised.

"It was when the sea went calm. We knew that you must have done something, the sea was so rough and all of a sudden it went calm, and then came that enormous wave and again all went calm again. We was all finding it hard to breathe and then all of a sudden the water became salty again. We all breathed a sigh of relief I can tell you, and that's not supposed to be a joke," said Albert.

"When I saw you coming back with the dolphins, you all looked so happy. I just knew that you must have destroyed this evil creature. Annabell, my beautiful land friend, what a fantastic human you are." And then Albert gave her a kiss on her red cheek.

"Alright - Albert, that's enough of that, you're embarrassing me now.

Don't forget I was sent here to you by the creator to fulfil a mission, it was my destiny Albert, the reason why I was born, I think,"

"Come on Annabell," said Albert still grinning! "Let's go and see her Highness the Queen, I'm sure that she can't wait to see you."

The Queen was waiting outside the Shark World along with hundreds of other sharks. Albert led her towards them along with about eighty dolphins that had joined Annabell.

When they caught sight of Annabell a huge roar went up, followed by all the sharks clapping her with their fins.

The Queen swam towards Annabell and grabbed her with her fins in a sort of cuddle.

"Oh Annabell. Thank you, thank you. How will we ever be able to thank you enough? You are the saviour of the oceans, from this day forth you will be known as the sea's most virtuous entity that has ever appeared in these oceans. You shall be known as a *Saint Annabel.*"

Annabell was extremely embarrassed. "But ma'am, I'm not a saint! I don't deserve such an accolade. I was only doing what I was told to do by the creator. Ma'am really, you mustn't make me a saint," pleaded Annabell.

"No, I won't take any notice of you Annabell," said the Queen. "You're a saint to us here in the sea, you can't change it – it's done. How can we ever forget this day?"

The Queen turned to all the sharks and dolphins that were present and told them that from this day forth this beautiful and brave land person will be known as *Saint Annabell,* patron saint of everything that lives in all the oceans of the world."

A huge roar went up, every shark and dolphin present agreed with the Queen.

"We're all going to have the biggest party today," said the Queen jollily. "Today will be known as *Saint Annabell* day, and every year thereafter forever. "

The Queen turned to Albert. "Albert, what day is it today?"

"I've got absolutely no idea your highness," said Albert scratching his head with his fin!

"Maybe the dolphins know? They're usually pretty good at knowing what humans dates are."

The Queen pointed to one of the dolphins that she knew very well.

Victor Rictor was his name. He was a rather clever and brave dolphin. It was he, that got peace between the sharks and the dolphins. They were for everlasting fighting with each other, usually the dolphins won. There had been many fatalities over the years between them. Victor Rictor had more sense and saw that it was futile for the sharks and dolphins to keep fighting with each other.

One day he bravely swam into the sharks' world and said that he wanted to see the Queen to sort out the problems between them. Thankfully they did and they have been close friends ever since.

"**Victor! Victor**…!" the Queen shouted. "Come over here, please I want to ask you something."

Victor swam over to the Queen. "Hello Bolvi," said Victor to the Queen. (it was a nickname that he gave her). It would normally be disrespectful to call the Queen by this nickname but Victor was allowed to.

"What can I do for you Bolvi? Isn't this a wonderful day. She's such a beautiful human, isn't she? I just love the colour of her, she's not like normal humans - some of them are extremely ugly - I believe your kind have eaten quite a few of those ugly ones, haven't you? Us dolphins don't bother with them, we don't like the taste of them and they're too bony."

"Victor, will you shut up please," said the Queen. "Listen! I need to know what day the humans call this day."

"It's not called anything," replied Victor. "They do have some names for days - like Christmas day, and Birthday but as far as I know, today means nothing unless it's your birthday, of course!!"

"No, Victor I don't mean that." said the Queen thoughtfully. "What is the human date today?"

"Oh sorry, Bolvi, I misunderstood you. Let me think! Um….I think that its August 16th."

"Well, Victor, I want everybody to know, here in the seas, and on the land that August the 16th will always be known as *Saint Annabell Day.*"

"Hear! Hear!" replied Victor. "I agree with that…yes, I like the sound of that. *Saint Annabell Day*… I'll make it known throughout the oceans of the world and I'm sure the humans will soon find out. What a wonderful idea, well done Bolvi…brilliant!"

There were big celebrations all that day in the oceans, Annabell had a whale of a time!

It was also decided that a monument would be built as a reminder of what she did for the sea world.

The Queen declared that on the anniversary of this special day all sharks would fast as an act of religious observance in the name of *Saint Annabell,* so that other sea creatures could celebrate this day without fear of being eaten by the sharks! But she made it very clear that it was for this one special day only!

The next day Annabell was keen to start her journey to the North Pole in search of Chloe the Humpback whale.

The Queen and Albert were waiting at the entrance of the Shark World to see her off. The Queen thanked Annabell once again for what she had done.

"There's something that I need to ask you, Annabell, before you leave us," said the Queen.

"What's that ma'am?"

"How did you defeat such a mighty creature? What on earth did you use to kill it? I've heard news that you took only one small bottle of something from a human food store but nobody knows what it was. All the world is wondering what was in the bottle."

Annabell laughed and laughed, she couldn't get the words out of her mouth. After several minutes she finally was able to compose herself and blurted out the word.

"*SALT*!!!" and the she laughed out loud again. "It was salt ma'am, that's all."

Albert looked at the Queen, and then they both looked at Annabell and at the same time they said, "*Very funny!*"

"What was really in the bottle?" asked Albert.

"Salt! Albert. It was really salt. I'm not kidding you."

Albert was motionless in the water with his mouth wide open showing his razor sharp teeth - he was giving Annabell such a look. (Like humans do when they can't believe what they've just heard.)

"*SALT?*" said Albert. "What do you mean salt? That's what it eats!! Well it did! How could salt kill the creature with something that it ate? That doesn't make sense."

"Ah," said Annabell still grinning. "Ah…yes…you're right, it did eat salt, but salt was also the creature's weakness, Albert. It had no resistance to salt! Its back was the weakness! The Delvi was consuming everything which created debris, the debris created gas bubbles. The extracted salt water was turned to fresh water - everything was expelled from the creature's back as bubbles and jets of fresh water. It drew in the salt water from the holes in the side of its body and released fresh water from the holes in its back. The creature's back Albert was always in fresh water. It had no resistance itself to the salt.

"When I threw the bottle at the creature, one grain of salt from the bottle managed to land on its back, this made the creature to go into shock. It shot up to the surface, which created the huge wave, then the bottle fell onto its back and the rest of the salt emptied out, Albert. It melted away!!!

The creature was like a giant earth garden slug! Some land people, mainly gardeners, put salt on slugs to kill them. I've never really liked doing that, but I did the same thing really - it was the same as putting salt on a slug in the garden but I had no choice, I had to do it."

"But how did you know what to do, Annabell?" asked Albert. "It seems a ridiculous thing to do. Salt would have been the last thing that I would have thought of."

"Exactly, Albert, the last thing you would expect to use was salt - if you arrange the word last, the word makes salt!! - *last...salt*, same letters.

That's what the parchment was trying to tell me with the clues 'The word last will make the Delvi past'."

"But why didn't the parchment just tell you to use salt?" asked the Queen. "It would have saved a lot of trouble."

"Good question, ma'am. I was thinking that myself. But I've got absolutely no idea why, there must be a reason but I don't know what it is."

"So what was the reason for the Delvi, Annabell," asked Albert.

"The Delvi, Albert, was the seed to destroy all life on earth. The sea couldn't survive without the salt and when the creature had consumed all the salt in the seas of the world, it would have exploded itself!! Sending up a massive salt cloud in the skies, that would have covered all the land on the earth. The salt would have then fallen back to the Earth, killing every single living thing.

"This was the start of *Armageddon,* Albert. The final battle between good and evil at the end of the world.

As the parchment said, *this was evil beyond belief.* And it certainly was.

"We were all very lucky. I know that I'm going to have to encounter four more of these devil seeds!! But I don't believe, well I sincerely hope that they will not be anything like the Delvi."

Annabell turned back to the Queen. "Ma'am, I've got to go, it's thousands and thousands of miles to the North Pole, I need to find Chloe and only Mortimore knows how to find her...so if you don't mind, I'd like to take him with me."

The Queen turned to Albert and told him to find Mortimore.

Albert went off and was gone for about fifteen minutes - he returned with Mortimore.

"Mortimore!" shrieked the Queen.

"Yes ma'am," answered Mortimore adjusting his cap.

"Oh, that's a surprise, you've got my gender right this time."

"Yes sir," replied Mortimore, "I've been practising!"

"Oh well, I knew that it wouldn't last, never mind. I've got a job for you to do, but you'll have to be really brave."

"I'm your man, sir!!" replied Mortimore confidently.

"I want you to go with Annabell and help her to find Chloe the Humpback whale, do you understand?"

"Yes sir, at your service sir, umm - sorry!...sorry!... oh my goodness me, I'm doing it again, I mean your highness. Of course it will be an honour to escort this fine and very brave land person."

"Are you ready to go now Mortimore?" asked the Queen with a smile on her face. She couldn't help but laugh at Mortimore.

"Yes, your highness. I'm ready and willing."

"No! No! Don't bother to call me 'your highness' Mortimore. ... 'Sir' will do fine! There's no point in changing a habit of a lifetime, is there? But only you may call me *sir*, don't tell anybody else otherwise I'll have to put you in the guard house!! Is that clear?"

"Yes, sir." Mortimore stood to attention and saluted the Queen.

"Right then off you go, guide *Saint Annabell* to Chloe."

"Oh ma'am please don't call me a saint! Really, really I don't deserve this accolade."

"Oh, yes you do," said the Queen. "Please come back and see us, I feel like we're really good friends now. I'm really going to miss you Annabell, come here give me a cuddle before you go." Annabell gave the Queen a cuddle.

"I'm going to miss you, too," said Albert. "You be careful, you here."

The Queen turned to Albert and asked him where Birling and Tames were.

"Annabell is in a hurry to get started. Albert, can't you rush them along a bit," said the Queen motioning her right fin in a circle.

"They won't be long your highness, they're just getting themselves kitted out with special saddles so they can carry Annabell and Mortimore. Here they are now."

The two sharks approached Birling, who was wearing a saddle - it resembled one that would be worn by a land horse, probably centuries ago! It's what the sharks had salvaged from the ship wrecks. She also had some sort of steering twine that was attached to Birling's mouth so that she could hold on to him and steer him.

Mortimore had a rope or some twine of some sort attached around his girth. Attached to the girth rope was a rusty metal ring. The plan was for Mortimore to use his teeth to bite on it, so that he would be able to hold on to Tames.

Birling Ross swam around to Annabell. He was a huge shark with muscles on top of muscles! He obviously was a very athletic shark that was plain to see.

Annabell could see why he'd been the fastest shark in the sea for the last five years. Tames looked exactly the same though - these were very fit fish. They would need to be because Chloe was thousands of miles away by now.

"Hello, *Saint Annabell,*" said a friendly voice. "My name is Birling Ross, but please call me Birling."

"Oh, for goodness sake!! Please don't call me '*Saint*' ever again!" said Annabell moodily.

Annabell was not comfortable with her new title. "My name is Annabell ...just Annabell."

"Ok...ok.. Annabell" said Birling "But...we will always know you here in the sea as our *saviour,* you deserve your title, but I promise that I will not call you our saint if you don't want me to but that's what you will always be from now on whether you like it or not. Come on, get onto my back. I have to get you to your whale before the water gets too cold!! The North Pole is really cold, you know? It's too cold really for us sharks. We've got no time to lose."

Annabell climbed onto Birling's back and held onto the steering twine. Mortimore got onto Tames' back. He bit onto the ring tightly.

Annabell waved to the Queen and Albert, and then she kicked the side of Birling and shouted, "**Come on, boy. Let's go!**"

Birling Ross reared up onto his tail. **"Don't do that!"** he yelled. "That hurts!"

"Sorry! - Sorry!" said Annabell very apologetically. "Sorry!...I thought that I was riding a horse?"

"Well, you ain't," said Birling rather grumpily. "And if you do that again I'll throw you off - and don't call me boy!!"

"Sorry!" said Annabell I won't do it again, I promise."

Annabell waved to the Queen and Albert one last time and shouted, "I hope to see you soon, bye." And off she and Mortimore went in search of Chloe the Humpback whale.

Chapter Nine
In Search Of Chloe

The two Great White sharks shot off at an incredible speed. These two sharks were very competitive and were already racing each other.

"Come on Tames, you old slow coach!" shouted Birling.

"I'll beat you one day, you mark my words!" said Thames trying to keep up.

"Well it won't be today," Birling yelled back. Both the sharks were really enjoying themselves.

Mortimore didn't realise that he would be travelling at such a speed. **"WOW!"** He yelled. "This is fantastic!!" But he forgot that he was holding on to the ring with his teeth. When he opened his mouth he shot off Tames' back, and was tossed around and around head over tail. When he finally steadied himself, Birling and Tames were nowhere to be seen.

Mortimore was swaying from side to side like he was drunk! And his eyes weren't focusing properly. He shook his head from side to side trying to clear it.

Annabell was enjoying herself so much that she hadn't noticed that Mortimore had fallen off!

She was pretending that she was riding in a horse race but she didn't dare kick Birling!! She'd got the message, she knew that she'd be thrown off, if she did.

Annabell happened to look around and saw that that Mortimore was missing. **"STOP!...STOP!"** she shouted. "We've lost Mortimore."

"Where's that stupid little squirt gone now?" said Tames. "I just knew that he'd be trouble! He's accident prone, you know. He's a bag of nerves, and so erratic, how he ever got to be accepted in the army, I'll never know. They must have been desperate!"

They turned back and finally found Mortimore resting on the bottom of the sea bed still looking a bit stunned.

"Mortimore, how did you manage to fall off my back?" asked Tames angrily.

"I forgot that I was holding onto the ring with my teeth, when I opened my mouth I fell off!!... Sorry!"

"You, stupid fish," yelled Tames. In future will you keep your mouth shut. If you want to talk, pull the ring towards you and then I will know to stop. Is that clear? If you fall off again I'll leave you where you are,"

Mortimore didn't say anything he swam onto Tames back bit onto the ring and off they went again.

They headed Northwards on their long journey to find Chloe the whale.

They travelled all that day and all through the night. They travelled two more days - only stopping at food breaks. The three sharks would go off in search of their dinner - which was usually some poor fish of some sort. Annabell didn't eat anything. She could go for days without food but when she was hungry she would get moody and would have to eat. The sharks didn't care what species of fish they ate, any fish was just food to them. When they had filled their bellies up they would carry on until it was their next meal time. The two sharks were covering about four to five hundred miles a day.

Halfway through the fifth day. Annabell shouted that the whales were up ahead but none of the sharks could see or hear them!

"How do you know the whales are here, Annabell?" asked Birling. "None of us can see them? Can you see them?"

"No, I can't see them... but I can hear them," said Annabell cupping her hand around her ear. "They're about five miles ahead."

"Five miles? How on earth can you hear something from that distance?" asked Tames.

"I don't know, but I can," replied Annabell smugly.

"I can hear them talking, they're saying that they've reached the half way stage of their long journey to come back to the North Pole. They do this journey every year when they come back from breeding, and that they really enjoy coming home.

"Ah, that's good news," said Birling. He was so pleased that he didn't have to get too close to the North pole. This was far enough for the sharks. The water temperature was already getting colder.

This spurred both the sharks on. Birling and Tames really started racing each other trying to be the first one to reach the whales, but Birling was always just a little bit faster than Tames.

They eventually caught up with the whales but there were hundreds of them! Mortimore was right. Annabell was a bit despondent.

She yelled at Mortimore. "**MORTIMORE!** how on earth are you going to pick out Chloe? There's hundreds of them here and they all look the same!"

Mortimore pulled on the rope for Tames to stop, which he did.

"Don't worry I'll find her, there's no need to panic, she's tagged," said Mortimore confidently.

But they searched for over an hour. Annabell was asking each whale that she came in contact with if she was the whale called Chloe. But she hadn't had any luck.

The whales were very spooked by the presence of the sharks. It had been known for sharks to attack whales, especially if the whale showed any kind of sickness! But this has always been the rule of the seas and land that the strongest survive. It's part of nature.

"**Mortimore!**" shrieked Annabell. "Where is she then? You said you would be able to find her. So where is she? None of the whales that I've asked have seen a whale with a tag on it."

"I will find her - I will - I will, just be patient," said Mortimore. "Rome wasn't built in a day, you know?"

"Ah? What on earth are you talking about? What a stupid thing to say," said Annabell screwing up her little red nose. "Somebody else said that to me, I think that it was professor Nicolls. That's a land person saying, Mortimore. You know you're so annoying, you remind me of Bambalata, he was annoying like you."

"Who's Bambalata?"

"He's a great big bird thing that I knew but he wasn't a bird, he turned out to be a reptile. Believe me, you wouldn't like to meet him, he would eat you anyway!! Well maybe not! He liked creepy crawly things. Come on, Mortimore, where is she?" Annabell was getting impatient to find Chloe.

"Oh, I don't know maybe she's not amongst this group. There must be other shoals of whales heading to the North Pole."

"Mortimore they're not called 'shoals'," Annabell informed him. "Whales are not fish, they're mammals and they go about in *schools.*"

"No, you're wrong, Annabell, you can call a group of whales - shoals, or schools, it means the same. See you don't know everything."

Annabell didn't answer she just looked forlorn. She probably knew that Mortimore was right.

Tames was darting in and out of the whales, all the time being guided by Mortimore, who was pulling the ring left to turn left, and right to turn right.

Tames was getting a bit fed up with him now. "Will you hurry up," he shouted. "I'm getting dizzy going around in circles and it's cold here and I want to go home."

Mortimore pulled the ring for Tames to stop.

"She's not here," said Mortimore, looking puzzled. "I've searched every one of them, but I can't find my tag, it must have fallen off!! Hang on a minute!! There it is…. Look!… I can see it…look over there… it's attached to that one…. **Yeah…**" screamed Mortimore.

"**There it is,** I told you that I could do it - I wonder how many medals the Queen will give me now? It's got to be quite a few, hasn't it?"

"Oh shut up Mortimore," said Annabell. "Make sure it's your tag."

"Well, it's got to be, can't be anything else," said Mortimore confidently.

Tames swam over to the whale, but it wasn't Mortimore's tag that was attached to the whale - it was a piece of rubbish!! That had got tangled up in the whale's tail!"

"Oh, God, give me strength," muttered Annabell under her breath. "What have I done to deserve this? I've had enough!" she moaned.

Annabell was getting really fed up with the lack of success and decided to take matters into her own hands.

She got off Birling's back. "All of you stay here. I'm going on my own." She grimaced like she was in pain but it wasn't pain - it was annoyance.

She swam to the front of the school of whales and asked the leading one if it had seen a whale with a tag attached to it.

"Yes I have," said the leading whale. "My name is John by the way. Some nasty little shark tied it around the tail of one of our females. In fact, it looks exactly like that one over there," pointing to Mortimore, "the one wearing that shell on its head! Yeah, that's the one but it failed because, we took it off. It was getting on her nerves."

"Oh," said Annabell, "I knew it." **"MORTIMORE!"** shrieked Annabell

"Come here, you stupid fish, *your tag,* that you said couldn't possibly *come off* - is off!!!"

"Well you can't blame me," said Mortimore looking embarrassed. "Look at the size of these things? I thought that I was really brave even to go anywhere near them, I thought that I attached it very well."

"Well I suppose you tried your best," said Annabell, "and you did attach it but they got it off her. So I suppose that it wasn't your fault."

"There you see. I told you that I attached it - I didn't know that they would be able to get it off. She would obviously have needed help." Mortimore gave Annabell a smug sort of look, as if to say, don't make a fool out of me.

"No, I suppose not," answered Annabell, feeling a bit deflated.

Annabell faced the leading whale. "Sir, this is very important, I must find the whale that the tag was attached to. This stupid fish said that it was attached to a whale named Chloe, is that correct?"

"Yes it is, but excuse me a minute I have to go to the surface for some air!"

The whale slowly made its way to the surface and let out a great plume of water and then dived back down.

"Ah, that's better," he said, looking relieved! "Now then, you say that you're looking for Chloe? May I ask what for, *Special one?*"

Annabell wasn't sure what the whale meant by calling her the 'special one'.

"Umm…. sir… There's a story being told that Chloe supposedly told the stupid fish, Mortimore. You know him as the one who tried to put the tag on her. That she heard a story told by a fox that he had heard that a polar bear had found one of these." Annabell pointed to the piece of the holism. "It's very important that I find it."

"Well that's interesting," said the whale looking at the glowing holism. "What on earth is it?"

"It's part of a holism, sir, this one created all land life, I'm now seeking the one that created sea life. The creator wants it back. And it's somewhere here in the North Pole, and the fox knows something about it, according to what Chloe told Mortimore."

"I wonder where Chloe heard that?" said John. "I've never heard this story before and I'm the leader!! Please wait one moment while I send for her."

The whale gave out a signal which Annabell could understand. It was like a siren sort of noise, but the whale was telling Chloe to come to the front, and that there was somebody very special who wanted to talk to her.

The leading whale knew who Annabell was. That's why he called her the special one.

Chloe came swimming to the front. "This is Chloe," said the leader. "And by the way, my name is John."

"I know your name is John, you've already told me that," said Annabell not really knowing what was going on here.

"Chloe," asked John, "do you know who this is?"

"Yes of course I do," replied Chloe, "it's Annabell. Everyone knows who she is - she's our saint."

"Oh, no," said Annabell "How on earth do you know that? You were thousands of miles away when I was made, as you say, your saint."

"Are you not proud to be our saint Annabell?" asked John "You seem to be unhappy to be called that."

"Oh, believe me, sir, I'm very honoured indeed but it takes some getting used to, I've always tried hard to be just normal. I never wanted any fuss. I'm just doing what I've been asked to do by the creator that's all, it doesn't make me a saint."

"Oh yes it does," said John. "You should know that, Annabell. We've all heard about your powers and we know that you saved us all, and I mean, all. You should be proud of your title, you've earned it, after all you're our first saint of the sea and probably the last, only land humans use this title, we knew what it meant to them. So the Queen of sharks used the name for you, and we all agree with that. Are you not a virtuous person Annabell?"

"Yes, well I try to be," she replied.

"Are you a kind and a holy person?"

"Yes, sometimes I hope I am, I try to be. But it's not always possible to be good."

"Are you not good in dealing with difficult situations?"

"Yes I am, but I've been given powers for me to be able to do these things."

"Who gave you the powers?"

"The creator but I'm not sure who that is."

"The creator! *Exactly!!*" said John. "That's what makes you a special person. A saint, Annabell. Can you not see who you are?"

"No," replied Annabell. "Who am I? Please tell me if you know."

"Oh I do know," replied John. "We've been on this Earth far longer than humans - so we should know more than you! But it's something that you must find out for yourself Annabell, it's not for me to tell you." John turned to Chloe, who was patiently waiting to know why she had been called.

"Chloe. Did you tell that stupid shark, I believe his name is Mortimore a story about a polar bear?"

"Yes I did," replied Chloe. "Why, what's wrong?"

"There's nothing wrong, it's just that Annabell has come all this way to find you. She wants to hear your story Chloe."

Chloe told the story that she had told Mortimore about the red polar bear. Annabell listened with great interest.

"Would it be possible for you to take me to the North Pole to find that fox who's been telling this story?" asked Annabell.

"I don't see why not," said Chloe. "That will be alright, won't it, John?"

John nodded his huge head in agreement.

"Yes, you'll be most welcome to come with us, Annabell, but it's still a long way from here and it's really cold."

"I don't feel the cold, sir," said Annabell smugly

"Of course you don't, I should have known that. We only swim to just off the coast line, we don't come in contact with the polar bears or the fox, I don't know who told Chloe the story. Chloe... Who told you that story?"

"A *Narwhal* named Freddie, told me."

"When was that, Chloe? You never told anyone else," said John.

Chloe didn't answer. "Sorry I have to go to the surface for some air, won't be a minute." Chloe went up to the surface and was gone for a few minutes, and then dived back down. "Sorry about that. Now what was the question?"

"When did Freddie tell you that story?"

"About five or six years ago," replied Chloe.

"Why did you tell that stupid shark Mortimore the story? What's it got to do with him?"

"He came by a few weeks ago and was asking all of us, if we knew anything about a strange object or anything that had happened in the past that was unusual. I just happened to remember that story. A white polar bear *turning red* is pretty unusual, isn't it? But I don't know if it's true."

Annabell was extremely interested in this story.

"Chloe, do you happen to know the whereabouts of that artic fox? I must find him. It's very...very important." Annabell was getting excited, she believed this story.

"Yes, I know where he is. That's if he's still alive, of course. He's always at a certain place when we're at the Pole - it's nesting time for the birds. The fox hangs around the birds trying to steal their eggs. The birds say that he's a nuisance."

"This sounds like the place, I have to find that fox. So it will be alright if I come with you then, John?" asked Annabell.

"Yeah, there's no problem - it's a long way, Annabell, why don't you get into my mouth? It'll be more comfortable for you in there and you can rest yourself."

"But I don't get tired John!" said Annabell.

"No of course you don't, but you'll still be better in there out of the way."

Annabell thanked Birling and Tames for bringing her to the whales.

"Mortimore, I thank you too, if it wasn't for you we wouldn't have known about Chloe's story. Come over here."

Mortimore swam over to Annabell and she gave him a great big kiss on his cheek. "Thank you." She said very sincerely.

"Thank you?" said Mortimore. "*Kissed by a saint!!* What more could a fish ask for? Good luck, Annabell."

"Bye Birling...Bye Tames...Bye Mortimore," said Annabell waving them off.

Chapter Ten
In Search Of The Fox

Annabell swam around to face John, she wasn't too sure about going into his huge mouth but she proceeded to.

"I'm ready, John," said Annabell not really liking the idea.

John opened his mouth and Annabell swam in, surprisingly she found it quite comfortable and interesting inside. It was like being in a cave.

The huge Humpback whale travelled for over two weeks swimming non- stop, every now and again it would come to the surface for air. At feeding times John would swim with his mouth wide open gathering in thousands of small sea creatures. When he was feeding. It was like a river was flowing inside of him. Annabell soon got fed up with this. She was being tossed around in the current of the whale's mouth. She decided that at every feeding time she would get out of his mouth, and swim along with the whales. She really enjoyed this.

Then came the day that John rose to the surface. He wasn't feeding, and he wasn't taking in air.

Annabell made her way to the front of the whale's mouth and climbed out.

"Are we here, John?" she asked hopefully.

"Yes this is the North Pole, Annabell. We're home now. This is as far as we go."

Annabell could see giant icebergs ahead and there was a sound of constant cracking of ice. This was the beginning of the Arctic summer, it would stay light now for twenty-four hours a day, but only for a short period of time.

"How do I find the fox?" Annabell asked Chloe who had swum upside John.

"Look over there in the distance, can you see the birds hovering around the cliffs?"

"Yeah I can," said Annabell excitedly. "Wow! There's millions of them! Look how they dive into the sea. They're like arrows that are being fired into the water! How on earth do they manage not to hit each other?"

"I don't know," said Chloe. "I don't care really as long as they keep away from us, which they do. So I'm not too bothered really. Anyway, Annabell, you'll find the fox that you're looking for near the birds up on top of those cliffs."

Annabell thanked Chloe and John for their help and she dived into the icy water and swam to the shore. The coldness of the water would have killed a normal human being in seconds, but as we know Annabell was no normal human.

She climbed up to the top of the cliff. The birds were squawking at her but she knew what they were saying.

"Will you all shut up!" she yelled, "I can't hear myself think!! Who's in charge here?"

A big plump bird flew down, with its belly hitting the ground before its feet!!

"I am, and I know who you are. Welcome to our home *Saint Annabell,* We've heard all about what you did, I know that officially you're not a saint on the land but on behalf of all us birds it's an honour to meet you, and you're a saint to us. What a wonderful person you are…sorry about the noise, but they all got so excited when they saw you - you're so famous, without any doubt the most famous person ever known living on this earth today… But what are you doing here?"

"I've come in search…" before she could answer, two blobs of bird *poo!!* landed on her head and ran down her red cheeks!! ***Ugh!*** … thank you very much, you dirty birds. Can't you do your *poo* somewhere else?" Annabell moaned. And then several other pieces of poo started hurtling from the skies. It was like it was snowing! But it wasn't snow! Soon Annabell was covered from head to foot with the excrement.

"Oh. I'm extremely sorry, saint Annabell," said the plump bird. "How disgraceful, I'm sure that they didn't mean to do it, must have caught in the wind. But it's a natural thing for them to do, of course."

"I know that," said Annabell - in a rather grumpy voice while wiping her face with her sleeve. "But do they have to do it all over me?"

"By the way," said the plump bird. "My name is Jason but everybody who knows me, calls me *Stinker!*"

"Stinker? Why on earth would they call you that?" Just at that moment the wind changed direction and was now blowing into Annabell's face. "Ugh! What's that stink?"

"Oh, you've found out the reason for my nickname then?" said Jason (Stinker) obviously proud of his nickname.,

"What is that terrible smell? It's horrible! It smells like stinking fish!" said Annabell holding her nose.

"Yeah, that's right, that's what it is… fish." Jason (Stinker) rubbed his big plump belly. "It's all fish in there you know?" pointing to his rather large belly. "I'm filled up to the brim… I eat too many of them… my trouble is… I don't know when to stop. That's why I'm so plump and all the fish smell goes all over my feathers, it's a devil of a job to get off, you know. It's alright for the others, they've got wives who clean them, but I can't find a wife, the females won't go anywhere near me!! As soon as I get anywhere near one - she *scarpers!* I try my best, but it's hopeless. Have you any ideas of how I can get a wife, Saint Annabell?"

"Yes I have." said Annabell abruptly. "Why don't you do yourself a favour and go on a diet and have a good wash. That would be a start…That may help you? It wouldn't do any harm anyway, would it?"

"Um… I'll have to think about that. It won't be easy. Let's think…umm. Fish or wife?… Wash or wife?.. Diet or wife? Um…ok, I've decided already. I think that I'll stick to fish!! If the females won't accept me for what I am, then they're not worth having. That's what I say anyway."

Annabell thought about what Jason (stinker) had said and knew that he was probably right, you are what you are, unless you, yourself want to change, and obviously Jason (stinker) didn't want to.

"Jason, it's nice... I think? Talking to you and all that, but I need your help I need to find a fox that I've been told hangs around here. I don't know his name, but I believe you may know him as the one who eats your eggs."

"Oh yeah, I know that little devil!" said Jason flapping his wings on the ground in anger.

"He's a menace, he's always sneaking around here somewhere, We have to be on constant guard looking out for him, but he's so crafty. His name is Odi."

"Do you know where he is now? I must find him," Annabell was getting impatient, she knew that she was so close now to finding the second piece of the holism.

"I don't know where he is right now but he was here earlier, he's had his breakfast of our eggs," Jason squawked. "He'll definitely be back later for his dinner. You just have to wait here for a while."

Annabell sat there for several hours, but the time went quite quickly, she was fascinated by the birds, they would launch themselves off the high cliff and dive really deep into the water after the poor fish. The fish never stood a chance. Suddenly she caught sight of something hiding behind an ice rock, "I can see you, I know that you're a fox. Is your name Odi?" said Annabell peering, trying to get a better look at the fox.

The fox shiftily looked around the ice rock to get a better look at what it was that was talking to him.

"You might as well come out, fox, I'm not moving from here until you do," said Annabell. "I seriously need to talk to you."

The fox spoke in a grumpy voice. "Who are you? And what do you want? This is my land and you're trespassing."

"This is not your land, and I'm not trespassing," said Annabell sternly. "Is your name Odi or not?"

"What if it is? What's it got to do with you? I can't get anything to eat while you're there, and it's dinner time! Who are you anyway? I haven't seen anything like you before."

"I'm Saint Annabell," Annabell said proudly, "patron saint of all sea living creatures, surely you must have heard of me? They say that I'm the most famous person in the whole world."

"*Famous?*" laughed the fox, "well, I've never heard of you."

"Good!" said Annabell, "I don't like being famous so that suits me fine. Will you please come out into the open so that I can see you?"

"No, I won't. What do you want anyway?"

Annabell showed Odi the piece of the holism. "Have you seen one of these, I must find it. I was told that you knew something about it."

"Why are you looking for something that you've already got ?" said Odi

"No!...no!...no!...no! you don't understand, this is only one piece of it, there's three more pieces and I've been told that you may know where one piece is."

"Who told you that?" said Odi with a little growl.

"Chloe the Humpback whale."

"Well how would she know? I've never ever spoken to her, whoever she is? How could I have possible been able to talk to a whale. I never go into the water. I hate water, it makes all my fur wet."

"Oh dear," muttered Annabell "Will you please come over here, and I will explain, I won't harm you."

Odi, slowly and reluctantly crawled across the snow and ice on his belly. He was pure white! Annabell burst out laughing when she saw him. He looked like a piece of ice crawling towards her.

Slowly and stealthily Odi came to her.

"Don't know what you're laughing at me for?... Just look at the state of you!... I've never seen a red and white human before... And you stink!! I smelt you over a mile away! I thought that you was that stinking bird called Jason or should I say *Stinker*? Are you related to him in some way? You smell like him!! But you're not a bird are you? Oh, I can see what it is now. They've poo'd all over you!!" Odi laughed.

"I've had that done to me a few times, these birds are filthy creatures, that's all they ever do, poo all over the place!"

Annabell felt very embarrassed, she knew that the fox was right, she sure did stink a bit!

"You're Odi, aren't you?" Annabell was trying to change the subject of her appearance and smell as quickly as possible.

"Yes, I am known as Odi. But I haven't seen one of those things that you've just shown me. So you're wasting your time." Odi turned his nose away from Annabell. And muttered "Phew!"

"Did you tell a story to a Narwhal that you heard that a polar bear turned red when he touched some object? You must tell me Odi, it's very important."

"What if I did? What's in it for me?" Odi coughed. The smell of Annabell was wafting up his nose.

"There's nothing *in it* for you Odi." replied Annabell very annoyed.

"Do you know who the creator is?"

"Yeah, I think so," answered Odi. "Us foxes, have been taught things you know, we're not stupid. We know all about what you humans call religion. You humans think that you know it all, but you don't. We were probably here before you. So we must know more than you do. We wonder just like any other creature, of how we got here. But we have no answers to our thoughts, just like you!!"

"Well I can tell you, now," said Annabell who was getting more and more annoyed at Odi's attitude. "I can tell you now," she repeated herself, so that Odi would get the message.

"The creator : created you! ....and you see this object around my neck Odi?.... Well, this was what created all land living things. And now, I've been sent to find the piece that created all life in the sea.

The creator of everything has sent *me* to find it, so you better tell me everything you know, otherwise you'll be in big trouble."

"How do you know that the creator is a 'He'?" asked Odi.

"I don't know whether the creator is a 'He' or 'She' nobody knows. I don't even know who the creator is? But if it bothers you *She* wants it back! So where is it? I'll tell you something, Odi, if you don't tell me, I'm going to turn you red!! I don't wish to be horrible to you but I've got the powers to do it - you'll never be able to steal a bird egg ever again, because they'll be able to see you coming from a mile away! How does that grab you?"

"No, I don't want to be *red,* moaned Odi. Can you really do that?"

"Yes I can, and I will; believe me. Now where is it?"

"Alright you win."

Annabell was getting more and more stern with her speech. She was angry with Odi for mucking her about.

"Was it a Narwhal? Whatever that is? Because the story goes that Chloe was told it by a Narwhal, and she said that it was *you* who told him. But who told you that a polar bear picked up something and then turned red?"

"Look!" said Odi scraping his paw on the ice, which left a mark. "I'll tell you what I know and this is the truth.

"One day several years ago when I was out looking for something to eat a group of bears came running towards me. I thought that I was going to die! I thought that I was going to be their dinner that night! There were at least six of them, and I wouldn't have been able to out run them, but I was so relieved when they just ran past me. They saw me alright but they weren't running after me. They were running away from something!! And one of them was a *red colour*! I was shocked, I just had to find out what had gone on, this was something unbelievable, a red bear? So I followed them, they didn't know that I was about, I'm good at hiding. Then something very strange started to happen. The red bear started turning back to white again, it was then that the bears stopped running, and settled down.

"I hid close by them and heard what had happened. They said that the red bear had an object. I don't know where he got it from but when he touched it, he turned red. They were so spooked by this that they started running away from the place that had made the bear red.

"That's the story. But there is one more thing. The bear that turned red was left with a red mark which could have been the same shape as the object that you have, and it's on his right paw. I know this because I saw it."

Annabell just said, "*WOW!!!* What a story. Thank you, Odi. This has really helped me, but how do I find the bear with the red mark on its paw?"

"You have to follow the Narwhal, they'll lead you to the bears."

"What on God's Earth is a Narwhal?" asked Annabell twisting her little button nose with her finger.

Odi burst out laughing, "Oh dear, believe me madam, you can't mistake a Narwhal. They've got great big pointed tusks on top of their heads - they're very rare you know. Not many humans have ever seen one, so you'll be privileged when you do, but they're very shy creatures."

Annabell was puzzled by something in Odi's story. "How do the Narwhal get to see the polar bears, surely the Narwhal are in the sea and the polar bears are on the land?"

"Yes, you're right. It's because the Narwhal swim inland through the gaps in the broken ice. They always meet up with the bears at a certain place, I say *land,* but it's not really land - it's all ice but it breaks up at this time of year which creates kind of rivers that the Narwhal swim up. I think that they're looking for food, but I'm not sure. They come every year, and the bears will surely follow them, they always do."

"Where are the polar bears now, Odi ?"

"Last time that I saw them they were about three miles inland. But they were coming this way. They're looking for the Narwhal. So I suggest to you that if you want to find the bears then first find the Narwhal, they'll lead you to them."

"But how do I find the Narwhal?" Annabell was getting confused.

"You have to find a channel that leads inland. The Narwhal will be moving up in them now, go to where the ice is breaking. But be careful, if you find one, watch out for those spikes! I'm amazed that they don't spike each other with them, they swim so close together. Anyway…will you please buzz off now. I've told you all that I know. And I'm starving!! I need to get my dinner. Can't get anything while you're here."

"Why don't you leave those birds' eggs alone?" said Annabell with a frown on her face. She really didn't like Odi. She considered him to be a rather arrogant creature.

"Can't do that," said Odi. "I'll starve to death! Those eggs are the only decent grub that you can get around here. They won't miss one or two anyway, they've got thousands! These birds are not here all the time, you know, they only come here in the summer, they're immigrants! When it gets cold they buzz off again, and I'm left here all through the cold winter on my own."

"Oh you poor thing, I feel really sorry for you," said Annabell sarcastically. "And they're not 'Immigrants', Odi. They're migrants."

"Same thing…immigrants - migrants, they still don't belong here. I was born and bred here. This is my land."

"Well…so were the birds born here, they lay their eggs here every year – it's their birth place. So they come back and have their children here," said Annabell thoughtfully.

"Yeah, only because the fishing is good here, if there wasn't any fish they wouldn't come here!"

"If you're so lonely why don't you find yourself a lady fox, Odi? She'll keep you company."

"Because there ain't many *ladies* around here - in fact, there ain't any, it's too cold for them here, females don't like the cold. I did try one once, but ...no!... they're not for me ...I couldn't stand all their moaning and groaning! It got on my nerves! So I chucked her, and came out here to live on my own - I'm my own man now; do what I want, if I want to go fishing, I'll go fishing, I love it, fishing is my life. I'm quite a good fisherfox!

"What I do is, hide by the water's edge on my belly, and dangle my paw in the water and keep very still - you've got to be really quiet. There's a lot of skill to fishing! It's not by chance that you catch them.

"The fish see my furry paw and think that's food! And they come up and try to eat it: that's when I grab 'em! But you have to be very fast! I grab 'em with my sharp claws and flick them out of the water but sometimes they're so big that I can't flick them out, so

I have to go into the water and use my teeth and both paws to get them out. I don't like doing that because the water is so cold but if it's necessary I will go in, I don't like losing them. I like the grayling best, they're better than those trout, more tasty! and they're easy to spot, they've got a great big long dorsal fin...its like a sail. When I grab hold of them with my claws, I throw them into the ice, if the wind is blowing they really slide a long way. My best throw so far is thirty-six feet but that was wind assisted! I say wind? It was really gusting that day like a gale. But it still counts. It's great fun! You should try it."

"Sounds very cruel to me," said Annabell. "You're an evil little fox, aren't you?"

"No! I'm not 'evil'. It's called fun. Don't you have any fun?

When I was with the moaning female she wouldn't let me go fishing... she didn't like fish, so I had to catch those horrible furry things for her to eat - I hate them. And boy, was she lazy!.. I had to do all the catching, and she did all the eating!! And then she wanted to start a family!! Oh, I hate kids!! So one night when she was sleeping I sneaked out. I never saw her again, thank goodness for that. I'm doing well now, and I'm happy.

I'm getting eggs and fish, the things that I want to eat. I don't really need to catch my own fish, if you're quick, you can run up to a bird and *swipe* the fish that they've just caught, before they feed it to their little brats... Oh, I mean children or chicks as they call them. They get so angry! They attack me and try to peck holes in me! I've had many a nasty peck from them, and they poo all over me !! But it's still great fun... Sometimes I like the challenge of trying to catch my own... but I only usually fish for sport.

"You won't believe this, but sometimes I let them go. There's so many of them in the water at this time of year that it becomes too easy to catch them. Well, they're easy for me, that's because I'm a skilled fisherfox. Oh,... I haven't told you the story of when I was nearly drowned!"

Annabell frowned, she was getting really bored with Odi's stories.

"One day about a year ago, when I was fishing a great big trout grabbed my paw. I swear to you that it was a least thirty pounds, maybe bigger? Before I knew what was happening, the trout pulled me into the water, so I grabbed it with both my paws, but I couldn't get them around it - it was huge!! The biggest trout that I ever saw in my whole life... well anyway, the trout dived down to the bottom and was shaking its head trying to get me off. I couldn't hold my breath any longer and tried to let go but my claw had got caught in its dorsal fin! The trout started twisting and turning and I was pulling and shoving trying to get it off me. I started getting dizzy and I couldn't hold my breath any longer. I gave one final desperate pull and lucky for me I managed to free my paw. You know what? That horrible trout came back to me...my, was he angry? He opened his big mouth and bit my ear, he took a great big chunk out - look at that." Odi showed Annabell his half ear.

"Scarred for life I am! And do you know what that horrible trout did? He ate it!! Chewed it in front of my face! And then he swam off. Oh, how I hate those trout. The birds are welcome to them... I hope they eat them all up. If I ever see that trout again he'd better watch out."

Annabell was listening to the ramblings of Odi. And then she started laughing.

"What's so funny?" said Odi. "It's no laughing matter, you wouldn't like to lose half your ear! Would you?"

"I thought you just told me that you would 'starve to death' if you didn't get the birds eggs? And that you didn't like getting wet? And now you're telling me that you jump in the water after those poor fish and that there's too many of them for you to eat?...What a liar you are Odi....I'm beginning to wonder now if your story about the red polar bear is just a pack of lies?"

"No...no...believe me.. it's the truth! - on my ex-girlfriend's life!!...honest. It's all true."

Annabell put her hand over her eyes and shook her head. "Oh dear, after all that I've gone through, I have to meet up with you. Odi! - You do my head in, I feel sorry for you ex-girlfriend, she doesn't know how lucky she was to get rid of you....or maybe she did?"

"She didn't get rid of me! - I got rid of her!" growled Odi.

"Don't you *growl* at me," said Annabell sternly. "You're not talking to your girlfriend now! I'm going anyway - I've have had enough of your rubbish, I've got things to do, I must find those Narwhal. Bye, see you... you, miserable old fox - and if you're telling me lies, Odi - I'll be back to find you, and I'll turn you into a red fox!!"

Odi scampered off as fast as he could to get away from Annabell, he really hoped that he would never see her again, he didn't like the idea of being turned into a red colour.

Annabell started to walk across the ice, it was getting really dangerous as it was starting to break up in the warmer conditions. She walked for hours looking for the Narwhal. Suddenly there was a cracking sound and just ahead of her the ice split in two, there was a gap that was least ten feet wide, it was just like a river had sprung from nowhere.

Annabell decided that this would be a good place to wait for the Narwhal. She waited and waited for hours in the hope that the Narwhal would come through her bit of river.

⊷⊶◅◈▻⊷⊶

Chapter Eleven
Annnabell Finds The Narwhal

The ice was beginning to break up all around her, several other channels had formed.

One more hour passed. Annabell was getting really bored with just sitting there, and then something strange happened.

In the distance in one of the other channels she saw a spike pop up followed by several others. The channel where the spikes were sticking out had come to a dead end. Whatever was in it was stranded.

Annabell was so excited she ran across the ice as fast as she could to get to see what those spikes were. She was guessing and hoping that it was the mysterious creature - the Narwhal. Then she saw the creature. **"Wow!"** she shrieked."What on Earth are you?"

But she knew what they were. These were the Narwhal that she had been looking for.

Annabell was in awe of this creature, she'd never in her whole life seen anything like them

"Hello," she shouted. "Can I have a word with you?" There were several of them trapped in the channel. Not all of them had tusks. **"Hello! - Hello!- Hello!"** she shouted, but they were very shy creatures. Odi was right about that. None of them would answer her.

They had turned their backs on her trying to pretend that she wasn't there. Suddenly the ice cracked again giving the Narwhal a pathway through, and on they went up the channel completely ignoring Annabell. She ran after them and decided that the best thing to do was to get into the water with them. She swam up to them. "Please stop," she said in a gentle voice. "I mean you no harm. I need your help."

The leading whale stopped immediately, causing all the other whales to bump into each other. Luckily they raised their tusks into the air out of harm's way and just bobbed up and down in the water. "I'm very, very sorry that I've made you stop and bump into each other. But I really need your help. I'm looking for the polar bears. The fox, Odi, said that you would know where they were. I need to find them desperately. Please can you help?"

The leading whale asked Annabell how it was possible for her to survive in such cold water, it being that her body didn't have any blubber. "We've seen humans before, but nothing like you. Are you human?"

"I don't know," she replied, "nobody knows what I am." Annabell looked a little bit sad admitting that she didn't know what she was, but she had to be honest.

"I'm Annabell, you may have heard of me, I believe that I'm quite well known. I have special powers that no other land person possesses, that's how I'm able to survive in cold water - nothing can harm me. Well so I've been told, and I can understand every language, animal, and human."

There was a long pause before the whale answered, it was clear that the whale was a bit shocked at what he had just heard.

"You're Annabell? The famous land ..." Suddenly the whale for no apparent reason shouted out the word '*water*' and then continued the sentence, "...person, our saviour?"

"Yes, that's me, can't you tell?" said Annabell in a sort of joking manner, she wasn't sure why the whale had shouted out the word 'water' half way through his sentence, but she didn't say anything.

"Oh, my goodness, I'm really sorry that I ignored you, of course I've heard of ..." Suddenly the whale shouted out the word '*fish*' and then carried on the rest of the sentence "...you but I didn't know what you looked like, well that's not quite true I was told that you were a ..." And then he stopped again and shouted out the word '*water*' and then carried on again like nothing had happened "...strange colour, but I didn't believe what I was told but it was true. My, you're certainly a strange one Annabell, I don't mean to offend you, but why are you..." And then he shouted out '*fish*' and then carried on "...such a strange colour? I've seen several different coloured humans before, mainly brown ones, but I've never seen a red one!"

Annabell looked at the whale bewildered, and wondered what an earth was going on? He was saying *fish* or *water* during a sentence for no apparent reason. Before she could comment on his reason why, the whale spoke to her again.

"Hello, Annabell, my name is..." The whale paused and then shouted out the word *fish* again and then followed it with *Paul.*

The whale was twenty to twenty-two feet long, he had several scars on his body but one scar stood out amongst all the others, it was a rather nasty looking scar that he had on the back of his head and it led six feet down his back but it was well healed now; it was obviously several years ago that something had happened to him.

Annabell was a bit confused "Did you say that your name was *Fish Paul*? That's a very strange name."

The leading whale answered back in a rather gruff voice, it sounded like he had a sore throat, and he would cough now and again.

"No...no, my name is..." There was a pause and he then shouted out the name, "*Water.*"

"Water? Oh! ...alright then," said Annabell, looking surprised.

Annabell still wasn't too sure if she was hearing correctly. She wasn't sure if the whale said, 'Water' or was the whale saying 'Walter'? Annabell was getting very confused.

"Umm - whale, I'm sorry, but did you say your name was 'Water' spelt W-A-T-E-R or 'Walter' spelt W-A-L-T-E-R."

"No, no my name is Paul..." And then the whale shouted out the word, *fish.*

"So your name is Paul Fish then? Not 'Fish Paul'?" Annabell was totally confused now.

"No," said the whale. "My name is Paul."

"Paul… your name is Paul? Not 'Fish Paul' or Water Spelt W-A-T-E-R or Walter spelt W-A-L-T-E-R or Paul Fish."

"No!" shouted out the whale. "It's Just Paul. Oh, please Annabell… please call me Paul – It's Paul !- Paul! - Paul!"

The whale was clearly getting very agitated and thumped his giant tail onto the surface of the water sending up a massive splash. The water went all over Annabell.

"Sorry! Sorry!" said the whale. "I don't know what… *water* ... you must think of me?"

Annabell stared at Paul, "What is the matter with you Paul? Why do you say 'water' or 'Fish' mid-sentence?"

Paul gave out a big sigh. "Oh, oh, I… I - can't help it… Annabell. I don't mean to say those words, but I can't help it."

"Why can't you help it? Have you got something wrong with you?" asked Annabell.

She now felt like she had been a bit inconsiderate towards Paul. She didn't give it a thought that there may be something wrong with him.

Paul shook his giant head, his tusk skimmed the surface of the water like a rower's oar being taken out of the water waiting for its next stroke.

"Yes I have got something wrong with me. It's ever since I got the bang to my head!! Look at the Scar! *water*..."

"I saw the scar Paul, it's bad, what's happened to you?"

"Oh... Annabell. I was very nearly killed... I'm a very lucky.. *fish*... to be here now."

Paul shook his head again and he yelled out "Arrrrgh!" Reminiscing what had hurt him was clearly having an effect on him and he thumped his tusk on the water again and again. It wasn't in temper but anger.

Annabell could see that Paul was really hurting, and she didn't want him to go any further with his story.

"STOP!" shouted out Annabell. "Please, Paul I don't want you to carry on with how you got hurt... I know what the problem is now."

Annabell swam over to Paul and gave him a big hug and whispered into his ear, and said, "You will suffer no more my friend." She took off her necklace and held it in her hand she then placed the holism at the beginning of the scar and slowly followed the scar all the way down Paul's back like she was welding two things together. As the holism touched the scar it slowly disappeared as if by magic! After a few moments the scar was completely gone.

"There," said Annabell, and she shook her fist in the air in a show of a great victory like a sportsman or woman would do after they had passed the winning post in first place.

"It's Gone! Gone! Gone!" she yelled. "You'll be upset no more, it's as if it never happened to you."

"What have you done, Annabell?" asked Paul. He realised that he felt a bit different, but he didn't know why.

Annabell had cured Paul from his inflictions, but she didn't want any praise, it was something that she just knew that she had to do.

"How do you feel Paul!" asked Annabell. She knew the answer before he replied.

"I've never felt better in my whole life ...it feels wonderful." And then Paul started to sing. All the other whales swam up to Paul and stared at him in disbelief.

"What is it? Why are you all looking at me and smiling?" said Paul and then he suddenly realised that he hadn't said the word *fish* or *water* for the last five minutes.

He opened up his big mouth and gave out an almighty scream. Paul was in a state of *euphoria.* All the other whales clapped and cheered, they could see that their leader was now once again back to himself, it was like nothing had ever happened to him.

The horrible accident that Paul had suffered was even wiped clean from his memory, he knew that he'd been hurt, but he didn't know how or when.

Paul swam around in a circle all the time he was singing.

After a few moments Paul swam up to Annabell, "You've cured me, Annabell, haven't you? How did you do that?"

Annabell laughed, "I told you I've got powers, Paul, I can do anything... It's a wonderful gift that I've been given."

"Who gave you the powers, Annabell?" asked Paul swishing his tusk in the air like a sword.

"The creator," said Annabell, "it was the creator. But I don't know who the creator is."

Paul gave out a cry for one of the whales behind him to come to the front.

A whale that was a lot smaller than him and minus the spiral tusk swished its huge tail which created an almighty splash on the surface of the water.

The whale came up to the front to join Paul, as the whale turned to be alongside him, Annabell noticed a strange mark on the right hand side of the whale's body near its tail. Annabell didn't say anything, but she was very puzzled as to what this mark was, she thought at the time that it could be a birth mark.

Behind the whale were four smaller whales all swimming in a line, each whale was exactly half the size of the one in front. Paul rubbed himself on the body of the whale who had come to join him as a sign of affection.

❦

Chapter Twelve
Stamp

"This is my beautiful wife, her name is Jenny but I call her *Stamp!*... say hello to Annabell, Stamp. She's so famous, we all know who Annabell is, don't we?"

Stamp appeared to be a bit shy, and was clearly a bit shocked. Of course, she had heard all about Annabell, everybody had by now.

"Hello Annabell," said Stamp, she stuttered the next few words. "I don't - I don't ... umm - know what to say? I'm so humbled to meet you - I've heard so much about you, we all have here in the sea. You're a wonderful land person - I - I - can't believe I'm talking to you now out here in the North Pole, and I...umm...I... can't believe that you cured my husband and I can't believe that you can understand our language. How do you do these things, Annabell?" Stamp was in awe of her.

Annabell turned to face Stamp and was shaking her head. "Oh, please Stamp, don't praise me, it's my destiny, something that I have to do. I was destined to meet up with you, it was extremely important that I find you. I'm being guided. I don't know how I can understand your language, but I can understand every living thing. I'm really pleased to meet you. I really am."

Annabell gave Stamp a hug. Who are these four little whales that cling to you like magnets, Stamp?"

"Oh, they're my children, Annabell. Come up to the front, kids, and meet the famous land person called Annabell."

Stamp touched her nose with the nose of the biggest one.

"This is my eldest child, her name is Genique, she's ten years old, and this one here is Layla, (touching her nose)- she's eight years old, she's a very cheeky little girl, but we love her, and here's Tarlia (touching her nose), she's six years old, and here's our latest - he's so tiny, come on Samule - come to mummy."

Samule was wedged in between the three girls. He, being a boy, they spoilt him rotten. Samule managed to swim past the girls to his mother.

"Look, Annabell," Stamp said proudly. "Here he is. Isn't he beautiful? Looks just like his dad though. Say hello to Annabell, kids, this is the land person that we've heard the stories about, she's very, very special."

"Hello kids," said Annabell. "Come over here, let's give you all a hug." Annabell hugged each one in turn, but Samule was very shy and wouldn't leave his mother's side.

"Pleased to meet you Annabell," shouted out all the girls at the same time

Samule couldn't speak properly yet, he just gurgled out something in baby talk, but Annabell could kind of understand what Samule was saying. *"Pleased to meet you,"* that's what she thought he said in his baby talk Annabell wasn't certain though.

"And I'm pleased to meet you Samule," replied Annabell hoping that she had interpreted his words correctly.

Annabell turned to Stamp, "You've got a beautiful family, Stamp, you must be very proud and I must say they're all very well-behaved children."

"Thank you," said Stamp, clearly a very proud mother. "We try to bring them up properly, but it's not always easy, you have to constantly tell them right from wrong."

"Stamp!!..." Annabell paused for a moment. "I know that I'm being very nosey, and you can tell me to mind my own business if you want to. I won't be offended but I would really like to know how you got the nickname 'Stamp', it's rather unusual, is there a reason why?"

"Oh, yeah there is Annabell." And she turned and gave Paul such a look. "It's that husband of mine, he's a silly old fool!"

"I'm not old," replied Paul, "I might be silly, but I'm not old, well not that old... anyway what do you mean by old...wifey ? You're the same age as me - I don't know what you're on about. Do you think that I'm old Annabell?" Annabell didn't answer.

"Annabell doesn't know how old you are," said Stamp "How would she know? Don't be silly husband. The reason why he calls me Stamp is because... years ago, as I rose to the surface to take in some air, one of your land postage stamps that was floating on the surface of the water got stuck to my skin, we tried everything to get it off but it wouldn't budge, this stamp must have been made with some kind of special glue, anyway a few days after the stamp was stuck to me, we were having a bit of a tiff about something, it wasn't much but everybody has a little argument sometimes, it's only natural. He got the right hump with me though, because I wouldn't back down, I'm just as stubborn as he is. You know what he said to me Annabell?"

Paul was laughing to himself, because he knew what Stamp was about to say.

"He said that if I didn't behave myself, he would *post* me back to my mother... The cheek of him!"

Paul couldn't control himself any longer and really started to laugh uncontrollably.

"You think that you're so funny husband, don't you? Just because these males have those long tusks they think that they're superior to us females...don't think so!"

Stamp blew a puff or water all over Paul, not in temper! But fun.

"He's called me Stamp, Annabell. He likes giving others nicknames, so you'd better prepare yourself. He's bound to find a name for you."

"What's that you're saying, *wifey*?" Paul raised his long tusk in the air when he spoke.

"Mind your own business husband," replied Stamp. "I'm talking to Annabell, not you!"

"Oh, you mean *Ding Dong Bell,*" Paul thought that he was so funny.

Stamp turned quickly around and spouted water all over him in disgust at what he had just said.

"What did you do that for, *wifey?*"

"You know what for!! And don't call me 'wifey'. Her name is Annabell. Paul. Not *Ding Dong Bell.* Don't you ever call her that name again. It's not funny, in fact it's very insulting."

Stamp was still very angry with Paul and sprayed water all over him again. All the kids were laughing at their antics. They always seemed to be bickering but at most times, it was in fun.

"This land person is very, very special, do not insult her ever again. She has just cured you and you have insulted her with a stupid name."

Paul turned to Annabell and said, "I'm very sorry Annabell but us males are so childish."

Annabell turned and said "It's alright Paul believe me; I've been called some horrible names in the past, I'm used to it now. It doesn't bother me. You know what they say Stamp? *Sticks and stones my break your bones -but names will never hurt you."*

Stamp looked at Annabell, "I'm used to the nickname name, now everybody calls me Stamp. All that is, except my mother; she doesn't like it at all, she says that she named me Jenny ...not Stamp!" Annabell gave out a little snigger. She understood this, and then Annabell laughed. "My ma's the same. Some people called me Pinky when I was younger. My ma would never call me anything else but Annabell but my dad calls me Pinky sometimes, but just like you - I'm used to it now. Please don't apologise for Paul really, you don't have to, I don't mind having a bit of fun...I must admit I do it myself sometimes.- I'm no *angel!...* There's nothing wrong with having a good old laugh. Life can be so serious sometimes. I'm ashamed to say so Stamp, but I really teased that fox Odi, about his *half ear*...He didn't find it funny at all. He's got no sense of humour, that miserable fox."

Paul came around along side Annabell. "Sorry Annabell - Stamp is of course right, but I didn't mean to insult you - you know I would never do that. I think the world of you, everybody does. It's just the way that I am...I can't help myself."

"Oh it's alright, Paul, don't worry about it, I'm worse than that sometimes, I was just telling Stamp that I'm no angel. I like to have a laugh, but *Ding Dong Bell, Paul?* I think somebody else called me that once… um…I think that it was that good for nothing bug eater, flying reptile bat thing! Bambalata."

Paul felt a lot better now that Annabell had said that it was all right and was probably pushing his luck a bit by carrying on with the joke, but he couldn't help mentioning it again.

"It was a bit funny - wasn't it Annabell?" and he started to sing:

"*Ding Dong Bell…*" and then there was a pause, he was clearly trying to think of the next part of the rhyme. "…let me think um, how does it go?… oh yeah, I remember."

Paul started to sing again.

"*Ding dong bell, puss is in the well. Who pulled him out Little Tommy Spout*

What a naughty boy was that…

I like that song." said Paul

"It's not *Tommy Spout,* Paul - It's *Tommy Stout.,* and you've got the nursery rhyme all mixed up."

"Have I?... and is it? I always thought that it was *Spout* - like us whales do, and I don't know the whole song but I really love the land people's songs, us whales don't have anything like them - I've always been puzzled though, Annabell. What is a well? And what's a puss? *Puss in the well.* What does that mean?"

"'Puss' is an affectionate name for cats, Paul - their proper name though is felines, some humans have cats as pets. And 'wells' are holes in the ground that supply water. Cats are furry animals that live on land - quite a lot of humans keep them as pets."

Paul was baffled with the conversation that he was having with Annabell.

"Pets? What does that mean?"

"Oh,...um - um, pet, it means a tame animal or it could be a wild animal, I suppose, kept for companionship or pleasure by humans."

Paul was very confused. "You mean to say that land people keep animals for companionship? That's a strange thing to do - don't these people like their own kind for companionship?"

"Of course they do, but I've heard some people saying that they prefer their pets to people: but on the whole, pets are kept as a sort of additions to their family, and it doesn't only apply to cats: there's loads of animals that humans keep as pets - some even keep fish."

"Fish? They keep fish as companions?" Paul gave out a laugh. "Wifey, land people have a relationship with fish." Paul laughed out loud. "I've heard it all now.

The only thing fish are good for is eating - they're stupid creatures, way down the intelligence scale - all except those sharks of course - they know what's what: been here a long time, they have, but generally fish are nothing really, are they?"

Annabell shook her head in disapproval at Paul's comments.

"No you're wrong Paul - fish are quite intelligent; you're certainly right about the sharks."

Paul was waving his tusk around skimming the water when he was talking. Stamp butted in. "Why don't put your tusk up in the air out of the way before somebody gets spiked. They're a nuisance, those tusks."

"Do only males have those tusks then, Stamp?" asked Annabell thoughtfully.

"Oh, Annabell, please call me Jenny - I don't really like the name Stamp."

"Oh, I'm sorry, Jenny, of course I'll call you by your proper name."

Jenny thanked Annabell and carried on with the conversation.

"Um, it's mainly males, Annabell, but occasionally some females do grow them, they're not really *tusks* in the true sense of the word - They're um... would you believe? Teeth! We've only got two teeth and when they grow they break through our skin in our lips and carry on growing, they can grow as big as nine feet long!! Sometimes the teeth spiral around each other."

"What are they for, Jenny, are they for hunting?"

Annabell was interested in what Jenny was telling her because these were very interesting, and mysterious creatures.

"No, no - they're not for anything... They're there for no reason whatsoever, Annabell"

"Well," said Annabell, "isn't that fascinating, isn't nature wonderful?

Do you ever wonder Jenny where we all came from? Because I do. I mean... um, how did it all begin?... I mean - um..." Annabell was stumbling around trying to find the answer to what is the meaning of life!!! but little did she know that one day she would actually find out!!

She carried on talking to Jenny in a very philosophical way and then said something completely out of the blue.

"Jenny, do you think that I'm strange?"

"Ah!...what do you mean, Annabell?" Jenny was a bit taken back, kind of shocked by the question. It was obvious for all to see that Annabell was so different from other land people.

"I mean... um... look at my skin, it's red! and my bones, and look at my eyes see how they sparkle. I'm the only person born on the Earth to ever look like this. Why do you think that I was made this way, Jenny? Everybody else is either white or a brown colour. And I've been given these powers, and why is it me that has to search for the pieces of the holism? There must be other land people that could do it?"

Jenny sprayed out a puff of water, and spoke in a serious voice to Annabell - like she was about to tell her off.

"Annabell, my beautiful land person. Why are you questioning yourself? We are what we are, you of all people should know that... yes, you're unique, of course you are, and I must say you are strange looking but what a person you are! You're clearly something very *special*. Only the creator could have made you what you are, and only the creator could have given you the powers that you possess. You are a good person, Annabell, and you have used your powers for the good of the Earth."

Annabell lowered her head and mumbled something under her breath, but nobody heard what she said, but she seemed to be happy with what Jenny had said to her.

Paul had dropped back to talk to a whale at the back of the pod. This was the chance Annabell had been waiting for, she wanted to know how Paul had been hurt. So she whispered into Jenny's hearing that was located at the top part of her head.

"Um…Jenny what happened to Paul? How did he get so hurt? If you don't mind me asking."

Jenny paused for a few seconds to compose herself.

"Oh, it was terrible, Annabell…I'll never forget it - it was…um, eight years ago.

"We were heading towards here like we do every year, we come for the food, it's abundant at this time of year. We were about fifty miles from here, we'd been swimming non-stop for days, suddenly a thick mist got up, and I mean really thick! You couldn't see anything, so we decided to rest up for a while. I don't know if you know this, Annabell, but when we rest we lie on our backs! Belly up. It looks like we're *dead.* This is why you land people named us Narwhal... Narwhal means '*corpse*' as in a dead body. ...did you know that, Annabell?"

"No! I didn't, what a horrible name to give you," replied Annabell quite shocked.

"No, it wasn't a very nice name for the humans to give us but we're used to it now, and we don't really take any notice of the meaning of the name... anyway we were all resting up. Paul was as usual up in the front, suddenly, and without much warning this huge ship was coming right at us. I think it's what humans call a cruise ship. Paul quickly rushed around to get the women and children out of its path. Oh, he was so brave, Annabell, we thought everybody was clear, but at the last minute a baby swam straight into the path of the cruise ship Paul swam as fast as he could and with no fear for his own life, he just managed to push the baby aside, but Paul was hit full on. When the cruise ship had passed there was no sign of him, he was gone!! The baby was alright, thank goodness.

We gave out signals to him, but there was no response. I was at my wit's end, Annabell, I was hysterical, I thought that he was dead!!

The mist was still too thick to search for him. We had to wait hours for it to clear. When it cleared, all the men went out looking for his body, because we all thought that he had perished. Three hours later he was found. Bobbing up and down on the surface of the water. Sea birds were already pecking away at him. He had bites all over his body. He was barely alive, his head and back had been split wide open."

There was a very long pause before Jenny spoke again, she was clearly getting very distressed telling this part of the story. Annabell went over to comfort her. "Please don't carry on, Jenny, I can see that it troubles you telling this dreadful story." said Annabell thoughtfully.

"Oh, I'm all right," said Jenny. "It's just that it all came back to me, I'm ok now. When the males brought him back he was unconscious, there was blood seeping from his wounds, we had to stop it otherwise he would surely have died, several of the whales propped him up, and smaller whales lay across his head and body to stop the blood flow. This worked, after several hours Paul came to, he was very weak and didn't say anything, obviously he was in shock - it took a long time, he eventually recovered, but something must have happened to his brain, because from that day on, he had to say the words 'fish' or 'water' he couldn't help it."

Annabell listened to Jenny's story and was really sad but impressed by Paul's heroism. "He was a very brave, wasn't he?... Oh, I'm so pleased that I had the powers to cure him."

"There, what did I say to you, Annabell? See you've got your powers so that you can alter what's gone before. What a power to have!"

"Yes I can, can't I?" Annabell felt really good about herself at this moment in time.

"So the accident was nobody's fault then?" asked Annabell.

"No," said Jenny you can't put the blame on to anybody. The cruise ship couldn't possibly have seen us. All they would have felt, maybe, was a slight bump, which unfortunately was Paul!"

Paul came swimming back to the front, he was still singing he was so happy now.

"Have you shown Annabell your stamp - Stamp? I'm sure that she would like to see it. You would, wouldn't you Annabell?"

Annabell wasn't really bothered but said, "Go on then."

"It's only a postage stamp," said Jenny, "I'm sure Annabell has seen thousands of them."

She turned onto her side to show Annabell the stamp.

Annabell looked at it from a distance, it was obviously quite small on Stamp's body. It looked more like a blemish than a postage stamp. The stamp was located near her tail on the right hand side.

Annabell could see the stamp and swam closer to get a better look at it. As she got closer she was beginning to realise something, and was getting quite excited. Annabell swam right up close to it. Suddenly she screamed, which scared Jenny a bit.

"What's wrong, Annabell?"

"Wow!" shrieked Annabell, "it's the (lost) *Danny Blue.*"

"The lost what?" asked Jenny still on her side.

"It's just a postage stamp. Why has it got a name?"

"No, It's no ordinary postage stamp... It's the *lost, Danny Blue*. Wow! Wow! and another Wow! Wow! Jenny... everybody in the world has been searching for it... for years, and years. I think that it's been lost for fifty years, and you've got it - it's the rarest stamp in the whole world and it's worth a fortune in land people's money."

"Is it?" Jenny wasn't that impressed. "Well, the person who owned it must have been very rich, and very stupid to lose it, why would any human pay loads of your money for a postage stamp?" said Jenny. "I wouldn't pay anything for it! If it's so valuable, Annabell, how come they lost it? You would have thought that they would have been more careful with it."

Paul was hearing the conversation, his eyes seem to light up - like beacons! with the mention of money. He knew what money meant to humans.

"I always knew the old girl would be worth something one day," laughed Paul.

"What do you call a fortune, Annabell? And is there a reward for finding this stamp?"

Annabell laughed. "Paul, I don't know how to tell you this but this stamp is worth one hundred million pounds in English money. And the reward to the finder of this stamp was ten million pounds but I don't know what it is now. It could be considerably more because it's been lost for so long."

Paul didn't know what ten million pounds was.

"Could ten million pounds get my family enough fish for the day, without us having to hunt for it?" asked Paul innocently.

"Food for a day, Paul!!" Annabell hesitated and shook her head, and laughed.

"You could feed your family," Annabell paused. "Um, let me think…well I would say *forever!* with the value of this stamp, Paul."

Paul jumped clean out of the water in excitement and shouted "whoopee!" it was like a human winning the lottery. He came splashing down. With a mighty thump! Water splashed everywhere.

"That's fantastic! Wifey, do you hear that, we never have to go searching for fish ever again, we can stay where we want to, and live an easy life. What a bit of luck," and then he jumped clean out of the water but Annabell wasn't celebrating because she knew that Paul could never cash in this stamp.

"Annabell, why is this stamp so valuable?" asked Paul

"Because it's very special - it's a one-off. It's made from a indestructible material called *XNO – XNO* which was invented by an Englishman named Daniel Finklestein. He's now the richest man in the world. His invention changed everything, it revolutionised the world. Virtually everything now is made from this invention. Aircraft, vehicles, clothes most household goods, in fact I really cannot think of anything that isn't made from *XNO* except maybe toilet tissue, glass, and anything that you wouldn't want to use again. All my clothes are made from *XNO,* they never wear out.

"The world's people one hundred and fifty years ago realised that they couldn't keep throwing things away - land fill sites were becoming filled up. They had nowhere to put their waste, so something drastic had to be done, a new material had to be found that was indestructible. People two hundred years ago were trying to recycle but it didn't really work, there was still too much waste and Earth's resources were running low - oil which was used to make a lot of what humans were using to make things was rapidly running out so something had to be found to take its place.

Danny Finklestein discovered a replacement for oil. *XNO* is a fantastic compound it can be made into anything but once it takes a form, it remains that form until it becomes of no use, then it's recycled into a machine called *BTB*. This is the only machine in the world that is able to bring *XNO* back to its original state. It's also a fuel that now runs all of Earth's energy needs. Danny's invention has drastically changed the world. There's no more pollution on earth."

The children were beginning to get impatient and weren't that interested in Annabell's story and they were playing and making a lot of noise splashing about in the water.

"Shush kids," said Paul, "I'm trying to listen to Annabell. This is interesting."

"No, dad it's boring!" said Genique the eldest child. "We're hungry, you promised that we would find food here, come on, let's go."

"Ok, ok wait a moment, Annabell is telling a story that may affect us all. Your mummy could be worth *millions!* whatever that means? Maybe we won't have to catch our food anymore? We could all lead a life of luxury."

Of course Genique didn't know what Paul was talking about.

Annabell shook her head. "Sorry Paul but that won't be possible."

Paul was puzzled. "But why? You said that the stamp was worth a fortune...why can't we have the human's money? It's rightfully ours, we found the stamp - so it's ours, *finders keepers*, that's fair isn't it? It's not like we stole it, and you said that it was a reward for finding it - so it should be ours or should I say, Stamp's."

Annabell looked at Paul and nodded her head in agreement.

"Your right, Paul - the money would be yours but you've forgotten something."

"What?"

"The stamp is stuck to Jenny's skin, Paul. She would need an operation for the stamp to be cut off, that would mean that she would have to be taken onto the land. It's not worth the risk Paul. Jenny could die. Surely Jenny is worth more to you than human's money! Whales are not humans, Paul. No!- No! I've decided, absolutely not. Nobody must ever find out that Jenny has the stamp - some humans would come hunting for her! Some humans are like that, Paul, they're greedy, and unscrupulous. Believe me they wouldn't care if they harmed Jenny to get this stamp."

Paul suddenly realised in the cold light of day what Annabell was telling him he knew that she was right. Happiness is far more important than money. He was happy already with his wife and four beautiful children, and he did in fact like living in the North Pole and he liked catching the fish.

Suddenly Paul shouted, "I don't want the money! I want my wife and children."

"You've made the right decision, Paul," said Annabell feeling rather pleased that Paul thought more about his wife and children than money.

"I would be very interested to know, Annabell, how the stamp managed to find its way out here in the ocean," said Paul spouting a plume of water into the air.

Then he cuddled up alongside Jenny and asked her if she was alright.

"Why wouldn't I be alright?" asked Jenny, knocking herself against Paul, on purpose!

"Oh, there's no reason, I was just thinking about you, I love you, Jenny."

"That's nice - thank you, Paul, and I love you too."

The lovey - dovey talk was soon interrupted by Genique who screamed out.

"**Mummy!** We want our dinner!! Daddy promised us that we would eat soon. It's been ages since we had any food - we're all hungry!"

"The dinner is not here, kids," said Jenny. "We have to wait for the ice to break, food is just a bit farther ahead. It won't be long now. I'm sorry children but you'll have to be patient, you will eat soon, I promise; there's loads of food here, you'll all be stuffing yourselves very soon, and we'll all enjoy ourselves here. Annabell is going to tell us about this strange stamp that I have stuck to me."

Genigue moaned! "But mummy we're hungry we don't want to hear Annabell's story."

"Well, I want to, and so does your dad, so you'll have to be patient."

Annabell went to the head of the school of whales, and started telling her story.

She began: "Once upon a time, long ago - long before even I was born, my ma told me about a postage stamp, a very, very special postage stamp. In fact the very stamp that Jenny, mummy, has stuck to her now.

The stamp was made for a very special man. Daniel Finklestein was his name. The stamp was made to commemorate his wonderful invention…"

"What does commemorate mean?" asked Layla, Jenny's second eldest child.

"It means to remember something very special, Layla…anyway this special stamp was made from the material that Daniel had invented - it had his face on the stamp which was a great honour in Great Britain, because only the King or Queen of that country were allowed to have their head on money or stamps but only one stamp would be made with Daniel's head on it - so this would make this stamp extremely rare, and precious.

"The stamp was made from *XNO* and the mould that it was made in was destroyed so that no other stamp could ever be made from it ever again.

The stamp was held in the vaults of the Bank of England until the day of the ceremony. The stamp was named the *Danny Blue.* The day was chosen it was to be April the first. Some people in England call this *fools' day* because you can play jokes on people, and if you fool them - you can call them April fools. But only up to 12am, after that time if you play a joke on somebody then you're the fool.

"It was decided that this day would become a national holiday for the whole world because Daniel's invention had changed so much in the world. So it would be forever known as Daniel Finklestein *World Day.*

Unfortunately *Daniel Finklestein Day* is still known in Great Britain as *April Fools' Day,* because of the fiasco that was caused with the stamp on this day which I will come to in a minute."

Annabell had lost her train of thought. "Um...where was I?.. Oh, yeah, I remember. As I was saying, a day was chosen - very, very special humans from around the world were invited to England as guests of the British Royal Family and they were all invited to stay at Buckingham Palace which is the residence of the King. It was originally built in 1703 but was re-built in the 19th century. The King of England, King Brian the Third was to present the stamp to Daniel.

"Everything was ready. The dignitaries were all assembled in the grounds of this great palace, a special stage was erected, and the King was sitting on a throne on top of the stage with a golden platter in his hand that held the stamp which was very small, well you can see for yourself.

"A fanfare of trumpets blew, this was the signal for Daniel to make his way to the stage. Guards had been assembled all around the King and they formed a human walkway all the way to the stage.

"As Daniel walked everybody clapped and cheered him - this was to be a grand presentation, he felt so proud to be English. Film crews throughout the world were assembled to catch the moment when Daniel was to be presented with this special stamp. Daniel walked up the steps with a smile so wide that it looked like his jaw had locked.

"He was now standing in front of the King. The king made a grand speech and went to hand Daniel the stamp. He took it off the golden platter very carefully, and held it between his finger and thumb but as he went to hand it to Daniel a gust of wind, a very strong gust, blew the stamp out of the king's hand - it swirled tantalizingly in the air, never quite coming to ground.

"The king jumped up in the air with his arms aloft and just missed the stamp by the smallest margin possible. But the swishing of his hand blew the stamp away from the stage and it went high into the air. Everybody was now on their feet trying to be the one to catch it. It slowly started to flutter down like a feather, everybody held their breaths, you could have heard a pin drop! At last the stamp was in reach, it was very close to the President of the United States of America. Everybody shouted in excitement **Catch it!** but the roar of the crowd blew the stamp away from the President. He gallantly dived at the stamp in an attempt to catch it but unfortunately he missed, and knocked his head on the leg of the king!

"He always said that he did get a hand to it but this was never proved.

The stamp made its way amongst the people but it was always just out of reach, by this time these grand and important people were all looking very silly. They were knocking each other over in their attempts to catch this priceless stamp. This very special day had turned into a fiasco.

The stamp eventually came down and landed on the nose of the President of France. In an attempt to be the one to get the stamp the King of Uganda swiftly and over excitedly reached out his rather large hand to grab the stamp off the President's nose but he caught the President of France's nose full on and knocked the poor man off his feet. It was a push rather than a punch, and wasn't intentional.

"The stamp was now somewhere amongst the vast crowd of dignitaries, some of them were getting glimpses of the stamp, and were rushing around, and pushing people out of the way trying to get their hands on it.

"The King of England and Daniel Finklestein were still on the stage, and they were in hysterics at the antics of these very important people. This would be a day that nobody would ever forget, and appropriately it was April Fools' Day. The perfect Day!

"This once dignified crowd was now totally out of control, and were unaware of how ridiculous they all looked. The stamp popped up close to the Queen of Russia. She tried in vain to catch it with her hat but the hat flicked it further into the air.

"The police had to intervene to break up this disturbance, it seemed that the catching of the stamp had turned into an international competition, every dignitary wanted the prestige of being the one to catch it.

Eventually law and order was restored. The dignitaries were very embarrassed at their behaviour, and despite their valiant attempts nobody had actually managed to catch the stamp, it had disappeared.

"Rumour had it that the stamp was last seen stuck to somebody's shoe but nobody really knows if this was true, and the stamp was never seen again.

"A reward was put on the stamp of ten million pounds, which was a huge amount of money fifty years ago but nobody ever claimed the reward."

All the whales looked at Jenny. She was the finder of the stamp but she would never be able to claim her reward, if word ever got out that the stamp was stuck to a Narwhal, all Narwhals would be in danger of their lives, because some humans would kill every Narwhal in search of the stamp. So nobody must ever find out where the stamp is.

"Oh dear," said Jenny "That's not good is it Annabell?"

Annabell agreed. "We need to cover up the stamp, Jenny," she told her.

Annabell had powers but she wasn't sure of what to do. The stamp was indestructible, and she couldn't get it off Jenny's body. So they just had to leave it there and hope that nobody ever sees it. But Jenny would always have the knowledge that she would forever look a million dollars!

Chapter Thirteen
Looking For The Polar Bears

Annabell turned to Paul. She had a very serious look on her face.

"Paul, er, em… I've come here to meet you for a reason, I'm looking for a very special object." Annabell showed him the part of the holism that she had.

"I'm looking for one of these Paul, this object is what cured you, and it's very important that I find it. I don't know if you know him but the fox Odi, told me that you would know where to find the polar bears. There's a special bear here somewhere that I have to talk to. The story has it that this bear once turned red when he touched something, I believe that the bear touched one of these." Annabell pointed to the part of the holism. "Have you heard this story Paul?"

"Yes I have, Annabell - it's a well-known story around these parts, and yes I do know that fox; he's a right little rascal, and it is true the polar bears do come this way at this time of year, because there are a lot of seals here, the bears come for the seals and the seals come for the fish. We're all coming here for the food."

Annabell was pleased to hear that the story was true.

"Will you help me find the polar bears, Paul?" pleaded Annabell. "It's very important to me."

"Of course I will, Annabell - I'll do anything for you - come on, get on top of my head. I'll take you to them."

Annabell got on top of Paul's head and held onto his tusk - it was like she was riding a horse but it was more like the mystical creature the *unicorn.* Annabell thought maybe the unicorn may have been based on this wonderful creature but obviously she wouldn't know this. She was really looking forward to the ride. Annabell thought that she must be the first person ever to be riding a Narwhal.

Paul went to the front, and the school of whales started travelling further inwards, stopping now and again waiting for the ice to crack but it was breaking up pretty quickly now.

About an hour passed, and Annabell was enjoying the ride, she found it very exciting. The whales could travel at quite a speed. After about an hour and a half Paul stopped.

"We're here, Annabell! This is where the polar bears should be. I'm pretty sure they're be around here somewhere."

"How do you know that?" asked Annabell.

"Because I can smell them, can't you smell them, Annabell?"

Annabell sniffed. She wasn't quite sure what sort of smell she was supposed to be smelling. So she sniffed and turned her head in all directions and then said,

"No, I can't smell anything only you Paul! I don't mean to be rude but all I can smell is.....well, you!"

"Really!" said Paul "What do I smell of, Annabell?"

"Fish, Paul," Annabell wished she hadn't said that now.

"Fish? Oh, no please don't make me say that word again."

"Sorry," said Annabell. "I didn't mean it personally of course, I know that you had a problem with that word but you're cured now, so it's alright for you to say 'fish' now Paul."

"There are other signs," said Paul flipping his tusk up in the air like it was a giant sword.

"Look over there, Annabell," Paul pointed his tusk to something in the distance but Annabell couldn't see anything, and didn't really know what she was supposed to be looking for and had to ask him what he was pointing at.

"Look closely, Annabell - see those *holes* in the ice - the seals make them, so they can come up to breathe, and the polar bears know this, they wait by the holes for the seals to come up for air and then try and grab them for their dinner."

"Ugh! That's horrible, those poor seals," said Annabell screwing up her face.

"No, they're not poor seals," said Paul. "The seals eat the fish so the polar bears eat the seals - we're all somebody's food out here, Annabell. The humans eat the fish, and the seals and...," Paul hesitated for a moment, "...and sometimes us!"

"Really?" Annabell was shocked that humans eat the Narwhals.

"What humans eat your kind Paul?" Annabell didn't really want to ask this question but knew that it was a question that needed an answer. She couldn't imagine what humans lived out in this desolate place.

"I think the humans once called them *Eskimos* but the Dolphins told us that their name was changed a long time ago to *Inuits* which is supposed to mean the *real people.* These Inuit humans live here but I wish they didn't," said Paul a bit disconsolate.

Annabell didn't know what to say - life on Earth sometimes is very cruel but that's how earth has evolved we're all food for some creatures, even humans eat meat unless they're *vegan* of course.

Annabell got off Paul and jumped onto the ice, it was very slippery and she slid on her bottom for quite a distance. All the whales laughed especially the young ones. Annabell got to her feet and was laughing out loud herself. She was wearing ordinary boots that weren't appropriate footwear for the North Pole.

Annabell waved the Narwhals goodbye. She was sad to be saying goodbye to the whales and really hoped that she would see them again one day.

Annabell walked across the ice, it was very slippery, and she was finding it difficult to stay on her feet but she carried on as best as she could.

She was watching the holes in the ice - there were loads of them here, which indicated that there were a lot of seals here. and every now and again a seal's head would pop to the surface from one the holes. She tried to talk to the seals but every time one saw her it was gone in a flash. It was like a game at a fair, she didn't know when the next one would pop up. She was finding it quite amusing.

She waited over an hour but she hadn't seen a single polar bear. She was beginning to think that Paul had made a mistake but she caught sight or six or seven shapes in the far distance that definitely looked like polar bears. They didn't appear to be moving very much so she made her way towards them. As she was walking she was waving her hands and shouting at the top of her voice trying to get their attention. She was very excited - it had been a long journey for her in search of these beautiful creatures, and she felt that she was nearing the end of finding the second piece of the holism.

Suddenly the bears caught sight of her. "**Over here!**" Annabell shouted. "I need your help."

The bears couldn't miss seeing her now because she really stood out in the white snowy background. The bears got very excited and they all came galloping towards her at full speed thinking that she was food but when they were in striking distance of her all the bears came skidding to a full stop. They seemed to be in fear of Annabell.

"Do you know who I am?" she asked

The seven bears stood there rigid, *like snowmen*, and didn't say a word. They seemed to be mesmerized.

"Do you know who I am?" she asked again.

Annabell was getting a bit impatient, and shouted at them. This seemed to get the bears out of their shocked state, and one of them grunted something that Annabell was unable to understand.

"Right!" said Annabell quite sternly. "Now that I've got your attention, who's in charge here?"

"I am," said the biggest bear in a grumpy, and gruff voice.

"And who are you then?"

"What do you mean who am I?" said the bear.

"Well, have you got a name? - my name is Annabell - I'm quite famous you know. Don't you recognise who I am by my colour? There's no other human like me!" Annabell felt quite proud of who she was at this moment in time.

"Annabell? Um, let me think. No! I haven't heard of you," and then he turned to all the other six bears in turn and asked them if they've heard of the red human called Annabell.

They all said 'no' and then they all started laughing.

"What are you laughing at, bears?" asked Annabell with a stern looking face.

"We're only joking," said the big bear. "Of course we know who you are, who doesn't? Our eye sight is not that good, and we didn't recognise you at first."

"Really?" said Annabell sarcastically. "I was told that you have excellent eye sight."

"Well, I don't know who told you that," said the big bear grumpily.

"Oh, it doesn't matter anyway," said Annabell kicking her boot into the ice.

"What's your name big bear?"

"They call me Zappa."

"Ok, Zappa, now listen to me. The fox, Odi, told me that one of your kind found one of these." Annabell pointed to a piece of the holism on her necklace. "Is that true? Because it's very important that I find it."

All the bears came slowly forward to look at the object, and then, the last bear suddenly screamed and ran off in a mighty hurry.

"What's wrong with him?" said Annabell.

"What's wrong with her? - you mean, because she ain't a 'him', she's a 'her', and she's my wife," said Zappa

"Oh, I'm sorry," said Annabell "But all you bears look the same to me, I don't know if you're girls or boys. Anyway what's wrong with her? Why did she run off?"

"Because she's the one who you're looking for. She had a terrible experience with that object that you've got, I'm sure she doesn't want to see one of those things again, and come to that, neither do we. It turned her red you know. It was unbelievable, I don't know what that thing was but it's nasty."

Annabell was listening to what Zappa was saying with great interest.

"Zappa what is your wife's name?"

"Zavi."

"Zavi!" Annabell called. "Zavi! don't be frightened, nothing will harm you, I promise, please come here with me. I need to talk to you." Annabell was motioning her hands for Zavi to come forward.

Zavi slowly made her way back to the pack of bears but she stopped at half way. She was very frightened.

Annabell told Zappa to go and fetch his wife, which he did.

Zavi held her head down and wouldn't look at Annabell. It was probably because Annabell was red, and it reminded her of the shock that she had when she turned red herself.

"Zavi," asked Annabell, "did you find one of these?" Annabell pointed to the part of the holism but Zavi didn't look. She knew what it was already.

"Yes I did," she muttered, she sounded quite angry

"Where did you find it? - It's very important that I know," Annabell could hardly contain her excitement, she knew that she was very close to finding it now.

At last Zavi started to talk more freely, it seemed a relief to her that somebody knew something about the object that she had found accidentally.

"I was eating a part of a seal that we had caught, and I was chewing it when I felt something in my mouth that was hard. I thought that it was a bone so I carried on chewing but I couldn't chew it, because it was too hard, it would have broken my teeth, so I pulled it out of my mouth, and I held it in my paw to see what it was. You're right, it was exactly like the piece that you have. Suddenly my paw felt hot and my fur turned red!

I dropped it. I've never been so frightened in all my life - we all panicked and ran away as fast as we could. What is that thing? It's evil," said Zavi, growling.

"No! - No! Zavi it's not evil, far from it - the object that you found made all life in the sea - it has great importance to the earth. I believe that you were chosen as a guide for me. Please show me your paw, Zavi."

Zavi held out her paw Annabell shouted, "**WOW!**" There was something on her paw that she was expecting to see but she was still surprised. It was an *imprint* of the holism, it was like it had been *burnt* onto her skin.

Annabell now knew that the story was all true. "Please - please tell me where you dropped it. Do you remember? I have to find it." Annabell was so excited.

"Oh yeah," said Zavi "I know where it is but you won't be able to get it."

Annabell's face dropped. "Why?" she asked.

"Because when it fell onto the ice - the ice immediately melted, and the object dropped through it - it's somewhere in the bottom, and it's really deep, nobody would be ever able to swim to the bottom, so it's lost *forever,* thank goodness."

Annabell wasn't that anxious now she knew that no matter how deep it was she would be able to reach the bottom. It would be just a matter of locating it.

"Can you take me to the spot that you dropped it?" asked Annabell "Don't worry about the mark on your paw, as soon as I find the object the mark will disappear," Annabell didn't know how she knew this but she did.

Zappa told Annabell to climb onto his back, which she did.

He galloped off with the rest of the bears following. Zavi stayed at the back. She was obviously in no hurry to return to the spot where the holism was thought to be.

Zappa was leaping from iceberg to iceberg, and sometimes he would dive into the icy cold water head first to get back onto the solid ice. He was a very strong swimmer, all the bears were. This would have been a very scary ride for a normal person but Annabell found it really exciting.

After about twenty minutes Zappa stopped. "This is the spot," he informed Annabell.

She was puzzled - all the landscape looked exactly the same. She wondered how Zappa would know the exact spot that Zavi dropped the holism amongst all this ice in the middle of nowhere.

"How do you know that this is the spot Zappa? It all looks the same around here."

"Look closely at the ice, Annabell," he told her.

Annabell looked and looked but she couldn't see anything but ice.

"I can't see anything, what am I supposed to be looking at?"

"Look!" said Zappa pointing to the ground.

"Oh!" Suddenly Annabell realised that there was something very odd.

There was a red spot on the ice that marked the spot where Zavi dropped the holism, it was about the size of a football. Zappa informed Annabell that the red spot had been there ever since Zavi dropped the object.

"Oh!" said Annabell again, "isn't that odd!" But she remembered what the parchment had told her - *follow the signs* - and this was definitely a sign.

Annabell thanked the bears and told them to wait for her. She kicked the red spot with her right boot heel, it seemed to crack very easily for her. She made a hole about six-foot wide and then she dived in the ice cold water without any hesitation. She could hardly contain her excitement. She swam down and down. Zavi was right, it was very deep here. She swam down and down, the water was getting darker, and darker - no sunlight would ever be able to penetrate this deep. After about thirty minutes of swimming non-stop in a depth of water that would crush a normal human being to death, Annabell at last reached the bottom.

It was very, very dark but she could see everything though she couldn't see anything living here, and she couldn't see the holism. But she knew that it was here somewhere.

She swam around the bottom searching. She was waving her hands across the bottom silt hoping to expose the holism but she couldn't find it. Suddenly she caught sight of a white crab. Annabell was surprised to see anything living because it was so deep here.

She picked up the crab, it immediately locked its pincers onto her finger.

"Let go of me, crab," yelled Annabell. "I wish you no harm, what sort of crab are you anyway? How are you able to live in water this deep?"

The crab was very surprised that he could understand what this strange creature was saying to him but he wasn't frightened of her.

"I've evolved to live here, and I love it here - it's very peaceful you do know what *evolve* means, don't you?"

"Don't be stupid, of course I know what evolve means, crab," said Annabell rather sarcastically. "That's how the earth was created - everything is adapting or evolving all the time."

"What are you?" asked the crab. "What have you evolved from? You look very odd."

"Um... good question crab, to tell you the truth, I really don't know but I know that I resemble a human being."

"I don't know what a human being is," said the white crab. "So I wouldn't know if you were one or not."

"Oh, well, it doesn't really matter then, does it?" said Annabell

"Crab, I'm in search of one of these. Annabell showed the crab the piece of the holism that she had. "Have you seen one? I know that it's very close to here."

The crab told Annabell to hold the pieces of the holism closer to its eye. Annabell put it right up close.

After a few seconds the crab told her what she wanted to hear.

"Oh, yeah. I know where that is," said the white crab, confidently.

"Where?- Where? – Where, crab? You must tell me it's very important." Annabell was hyper excited. She had come a long way to find the second piece of the holism, and she knew that she was very close to finding it.

"The conger eel has got it but I don't think that he'll give it to you."

"Why?" asked Annabell.

"Because that's the thing that hurt him badly, and he's very angry."

Annabell was puzzled as to how or why the part of the holism would hurt the conger eel.

"Do you know where the eel is?" asked Annabell.

"Yes, I do, but I don't go too close to it - it's very vicious, it's always trying to eat us crabs."

"Where is it?" asked Annabell in a squeaky high pitched hyper excited voice.

The white crab that Annabell was still holding pointed its pincer in a certain direction. "It's over there hiding inside *that rock* but I wouldn't get too close to it if I were you, because it bites."

"Well everything bites," said Annabell a bit sarcastically.

Chapter Fourteen
The Half Blind Eel

Annabell swam over to where the crab said the eel was. **"Eel!- Eel!"** she yelled. "I know that you're in there because the crab told me, so there's no point in you hiding."

The eel popped his head out of the rock - it was a really big eel, about thirty pounds, and was grey/white. Annabell could now understand why the crab didn't want to come too close to it but she forgot that she was still holding the crab. Or the crab was still holding on to her?

The giant eel dashed out of the hole in a flash, and tried to grab the crab out of Annabell's hand. Annabell shouted at the eel.

"What do you think you're doing?" She quickly pulled the crab away from the eel's mouth.

"I'm looking for my dinner," said the eel calmly. "I fancied crab tonight, and you've got one, can I have it?"

"No, absolutely not," said Annabell in a stern voice. She lowered the crab to the bottom and told it to go quickly. It shot off as fast as it could go creating a cloud of particles as it went. The giant eel tried to make its way around Annabell to try and have another go at catching the crab. Annabell grabbed the eel by its head to stop it. The eel wriggled in her hand trying to get away.

The eel was none too pleased but neither was Annabell she really didn't like holding onto the eel - it was all slippery and slimy but she daren't let go. When the crab was out of striking distance Annabell let go of the eel. It quickly rushed back into its home which was a hollow rock.

"Now listen to me, eel - the crab told me that you have one of these." Annabell pointed to the part of the holism that was on her necklace.

"Have you got one? The crab said that you had."

"I don't know," said the eel, not really taking any interest. "I'm half blind so I can't see it."

"What do you mean you're half blind? If you're half blind, then you're half sighted - so use your good eye."

The eel was still trying to see if it could see the crab but Annabell made sure that he couldn't. It had gone now anyway. The eel knew that it wasn't going to get past Annabell so it reluctantly looked at the part of the holism with its good eye which was its left eye.

"Yeah!" confirmed the eel. "I've got one of them but you're not having it - one of them things blinded my eye."

"But I have to have it, eel," pleaded Annabell. "It's absolutely vital that you give it to me. I can't leave here without it. I've come a long way to find it, and I've been sent by the creator. Do you know who the creator is?" asked Annabell.

"No," said the eel. "Should I?"

"Oh, yeah, you should," replied Annabell staring at the eel in a very serious manner. "The creator is what created you, and I suppose the creator could *de-create* you. If there is such a word?"

"What does 'de-create' mean?" asked the eel rather intelligently.

Annabell laughed. "I don't know," she said "But if there was such a word, I'm sure it would mean something horrible."

Annabell quickly tried to change the subject, she knew that her threats weren't working.

"Eel, how did you get hurt by one of these objects?" pointing to the holism.

Annabell was intrigued to know the answer because she couldn't understand how a part of the holism could hurt the eel. She was concerned by this.

"I'll tell you what happened to me," said the eel grumpily. "I saw something fluttering down from above, and thought that it was a fish - so I darted out of my home and made a grab for it but I missed, and the object caught my right eye, and blinded me - it wasn't a fish at all. How unlucky was that? I've kept it ever since as a reminder to me to look before I leap."

"Oh, dear," said Annabell. "That was unlucky but you haven't learnt much have you, eel? Didn't you just leap out trying to catch the crab?"

"Yes I did, but it was a crab, so I knew that it was edible."

"Yeah, I know that it was a crab but I was holding it! Didn't you see me ? Oh, it doesn't matter now anyway," said Annabell, she just wanted to move on with getting the part of the holism.

"What would you say, eel, if I told you that I can restore your sight in your blind eye."

"Well, I would be ecstatic, of course I would, but I don't think that you would be able to do that. That's impossible!"

"I have powers, eel, I'm very famous, my name is Annabell but I don't suppose you've heard of me, you living down here, I don't suppose you get to hear about what's going on up above."

"Well, I do get to hear bits and pieces," said the eel. "But you suppose right, I've never heard of you. In fact I've never seen anything like you before, you're obviously not a fish or a crab - so I can't say what you are."

"Never mind," said Annabell. "It doesn't really matter - what matters is restoring your eye-sight. I don't like bribing you, eel, but it's very important to me. If you give me the object I promise that I will give you back your sight, believe me - I am able to do this," said Annabell sincerely.

The eel didn't really believe that she could but it knew that it had nothing really to lose. It swam into the rock backwards, and a few moments later it came back out, and spat the part of the holism out of its mouth - the part of the holism fluttered in the water. The eel was right, it did look like a fish. It looked just like what anglers would use to lure fish, when they're spinning with artificial lures.

"There you are," said the eel. "One nasty piece of work, and you're welcome to it."

The object drifted towards Annabell, and she grabbed it. Instantly it lit up and glowed with all the colours of the rainbow, and she felt a surge of energy go through her body.

"Wow!" she yelled "At last, I've got it, thank you eel."

The grey/white conger eel said, "Well, come on then give me back my sight that you promised me - I still don't believe that you can do this."

"Well you'll be wrong," replied Annabell. She told the eel to be still and she placed the new part of the holism on the eel's blinded white eye - instantly the white eye cleared, and the eel was able to see again.

"Wow!" yelled the eel. "I can see! Thank you!"

"You're welcome," said Annabell and then she said farewell to the eel and made her way back up to the surface.

When she got there she found all the bears sitting on the ice patiently waiting for her.

"I'm back," she said. "And I've found it! I would like to thank you all very much for your help, without you, and all the others who helped me, I would never have found it."

Annabell went over to Zavi and told her to hold out her paw, the one with the mark in it. She touched Zavi's paw with the new part of the holism, and the mark instantly disappeared. All was now complete everything that had been bad had been turned to good.

Annabell had a long journey back to her home in America. She turned to the bears and said, *"I wish that I could be back home in my bed."* Annabell instantly disappeared in front of the polar bears, and found herself back in her bed at home, waking up, thinking that everything had been a dream but it hadn't been a dream, because in her right hand was the second part of the holism, and it was glowing with all the colours of the rainbow.

Chapter Fifteen
Another Piece Of Parchment

Several weeks had passed since Annabell had returned from her incredible adventures in the sea world. She was enjoying her rest and was working on a book about her adventure. She was sitting by the river that was on her father's land. It was a beautiful sunny and very warm day.

Annabell was all alone. She had her feet dangling in the crystal clear water, small fish were swimming up and down the river, some of them had shoaled up around her feet and were nibbling on her red toes thinking that they were food, but Annabell didn't take much notice of them, she was so absorbed in writing her book, that she hadn't even noticed that something had drifted down the river and had attached itself to her right foot. A few minutes later though she happened to look in the water as another fish was nibbling her toe. "Oh, please leave me alone, fish, I'm trying to concentrate," she said in a friendly voice. "I'm not food!" It was then that she saw something on her foot, she thought that it was a lily pad. She splashed the water with her foot trying to kick it off but it shot out of the water and landed on top of her head!! **"Ugh! what's that?"** she yelled, water was dripping down her red face.

She flicked whatever it was off her head with her hand and it landed on the ground just in front of her right hand. She knew instantly that it wasn't a lily pad it was another piece of the parchment. She picked it up. "Where did this come from?" she muttered to herself. She read the writing on it that only she could read. It read in English as follows:

To find the seed that created plants
you have to go back out to where the bush grows
but go out first - don't put back

Find the person named Kevin Zoologong
without him you cannot fulfil your task
but to find him you have to go backwards
before you can go forward

beware of the devil seed Elvid
only it can live in its soil
Its flowers are not so sweet

look at soil - look at water

It's something that you can alter

take out S and add B

It's written down for you to see

Elvid guards the crock of gold

follow the signs

The Creator

Annabell put her socks and boots back on and started walking towards the farmhouse. As she walked she studied the parchment but couldn't make any sense of it.

"Oh!" she yelled in frustration. "What does all this mean? *You have to go back out to where the bush grows* - But what bush? There's millions and billions of bushes, and it says. *But go out first - don't put back.* This doesn't make any sense."

Annabell yelled out loud in frustration again at the message.

"What does all this nonsense mean?" She read it again, "*But go out first - don't put back.*"

She was getting more and more frustrated with the message and this was only the first part of it. She threw the parchment to the ground in temper and shrieked.

"Oh! this is so stupid, why does the parchments give me these silly clues? Why doesn't it just tell me where the seed is? It would be so much easier for me," she moaned.

She stamped her boot into the ground. "Oh, I'm not going to bother, why should I?" Suddenly the piece of parchment that she angrily threw to the ground, rose up from the ground all by itself and placed itself back in her right hand.

"Oh, no," she moaned, "I can't even throw it away - it's some kind of magic, everything that is associated with these parchments is magic."

Annabell looked up at the heavens. And spoke in a grumpy voice,

"Alright, creator. If you want me to find your seed, you're going to have to help me, because I don't know what the clues mean."

Annabell wasn't dumb but it sometimes took a while for her to understand the riddles - she felt that with her powers she didn't need to be that smart.

She walked slowly back to the farmhouse still trying to fathom out the parchment. Suddenly she yelled out again. **"BACK OUT WHERE?"**

Her father heard her yelling and came rushing out of the farmhouse to see what the matter was with his daughter.

"What's wrong with you, daughter? Are you going mad?"

"No, Pa. It's this parchment - I've found another piece of it, or should I say, it found me! I can't understand what it means, Pa. I need some help."

Mr Jacobs put his hand out for Annabell to give him the parchment.

"Let me have a look at it, daughter, I'll soon work it out for you : *us men* have bigger brains than women, did you know that?"

Annabell laughed, she knew that it wasn't true, but she didn't say anything. She just handed him the parchment - but, of course, he couldn't read it.

"Well what does it say, daughter? Now don't worry, calm yourself down, I'll soon have this solved for you," said Mr Jacobs confidently.

Annabell read out what the parchment said, to her father.

Mr Jacobs took off his cap and scratched his bald head in thought, he spent several minutes with his eyes closed thinking about it. Eventually he spoke.

"Um, daughter, can you read it again, please?"

"You haven't got a clue have you, Pa?" said Annabell, laughing.

"To be honest with you, daughter: No! I'm sorry, I haven't."

With those words of wisdom, Mr Jacobs laughed out loud.

"I have absolutely no idea whatsoever, daughter, what it's all about, it sounds all double Dutch to me."

"Oh well," said Annabell, "that proves that your brain isn't bigger than mine, Pa!"

"No it doesn't!" said Mr Jacobs. "I'm a farmer, I know a lot about that, but I'm not a code breaker, darling!!"

Annabell looked at her father with her striking, sparkling eyes.

"Oh, Pa, you're hopeless, but I love you," and then she gave him a big cuddle.

"Is there anybody that you know who could help me, Pa?" asked Annabell.

"No daughter, I don't think so," replied Mr Jacobs still laughing. "My God! I wouldn't know anybody who could work those clues out; they're very baffling, aren't they?"

Annabell agreed with her Pa and walked off. She started asking all her animal friends if they could work it out, but none of them could.

She went into the barn, she was feeling a bit mentally tired with the effort of trying to work out the clues.

There were lots of straw bales in the barn and they looked very inviting to lie on. Annabell lay on them and fell fast asleep. She slept for hours. She finally woke up to the sound of the barn owl, Charlie who was making a horrible hooting sound.

"Would you please shut-up your racket, Charlie? You woke me up," said Annabell in a bit of a foul mood. Annabell didn't really get tired as we know tiredness, her tiredness came from lack of patience, and when she was hungry it made her moody.

"What's the matter with you, Annabell? You don't seem to be in a very good mood today," said Charlie blinking his eyes.

"Oh, I'm sorry," said Annabell. "I didn't mean to be nasty to you, it's this parchment; I can't work out the clues, and it's very important. I have to know what it means."

"Well you've come to the right place or should I say - Owl. What do they call us, Annabell? *Wise old owls.* Maybe I can work it out for you; tell me what it says."

Annabell read Charlie the parchment.

"Well, that's easy to work out - the first part is anyway, but I don't know what it all means."

Annabell was a bit surprised at Charlie's revelation that he knew what some of it meant.

"Ok, if you're so clever what does it mean, clever clogs? Nobody else knows."

"Yeah, but Owls are smart, we've always been known to have a high intelligence level."

"Who said that Owls were smart?" asked Annabell sarcastically.

"I don't know," replied the Owl, "But everybody knows that it's true."

"Well I don't!" replied Annabell. "Anyway, Charlie, what do the clues mean? Please tell me."

"Well, my beautiful red lady, listen to what it's telling you; it's all logical you know, you just have to understand logic like us, Owls. It says that you have to go *back out* to where the bush grows - But go *out* first - don't put *back*. So think, you got *bush* and *back out*. What it's saying for you to do is... put the *out* before the *back* and go to the *bush*. Where is the *outback* and *bush*?"

Annabell thought for a moment and then yelled out.

"**AUSTRALIA**! It's Australia, I have to go to Australia."

"Well done," said Charlie. "I told you us Owls were smart."

Annabell was so pleased. "Yes, you really are clever, Charlie, I would never have worked that out. Thank you very much," Annabell jumped up and down in excitement.

"That's all right," said the Owl closing one of its eyes as a sign of his cleverness. "Didn't I tell you that I could work it out? Now please go away and leave me in peace, I love you and all that but I'm tired and hungry and when I'm tired and hungry I get a bit grumpy. Like you!"

"I'm not always *grumpy*," replied Annabell.

"I know you're not, you're a lovely person," replied the Owl. "I was only joking."

Annabell was so pleased with Charlie that she asked him if there was anything that she could do for him.

"A big fat mouse would be very nice," said Charlie licking his beak. "I couldn't catch anything last night and I'm starving. My eyes are not so good now, I'm getting on a bit, it's getting hard for me to catch my food, because I can't see very well. Those mice are very quick, I haven't caught one for a long time."

"Ooh, I don't like mice," said Annabell holding on to her skirt!

"Well there's a lot in here!" said the Owl.

"Why don't you get a pair of spectacles?" replied Annabell thinking that she was pretty smart to suggest such a thing.

"Yeah, that would be a good idea," said the Owl. "I didn't think of that. Can you get me a pair?"

"Yes I can," said Annabell. "Wait there! I know that there's a few pairs of spectacles that belonged to my late grandmother."

Annabell went back to the farmhouse and found some spectacles. She returned to the barn with several pairs. One pair was a perfect fit.

The Owl could see clearly now.

"Thank you very much," said the Owl. "These are great! You just wait, when I see those mice. I'll get my dinner tonight alright. Those mice have been horrible to me lately. They know that I cant see very well but they're be in for a big surprise tonight. Thank you Annabell."

"That's alright Charlie; you've earned it. Good luck with catching the mice, ugh! Bye."

Annabell ran out of the barn and went to the farmhouse that was about two hundred yards away. She ran past the ducks and the chickens, and ran straight through a puddle but she was oblivious to everything; all she wanted to do was to tell her father that the first part of the riddle had been worked out.

She ran into the house but forgot to take off her boots. Her footprints went all over the carpet. **"ANNABELL!"** shouted Mrs Jacobs. "What are you doing? Please take off your boots, look what you've done to the carpet."

"Oh, I'm sorry, Ma, I forgot, I'll clean it up, I promise. I'm just so excited, Ma, we've solved the riddle. Well, the Owl did. I can't really take any of the credit. He's so clever, that owl; he's cleverer than you, Pa."

"Really?" said Mr Jacobs who was sitting in his favourite chair, sipping on a cup of tea.

"Well, daughter, come on then, I'm all ears: tell us what it all means then?"

"Um…I don't know what it all means, Pa but the owl has worked out the first bit.

"But the owl may not be right," said Mr Jacobs spilling a drop of his tea down the front of his shirt.

"Oh, I'm certain the owl is right, Pa. The riddle was telling me to go to Australia. I have to go to the outback, the piece of holism is somewhere in the bush."

Mr Jacobs laughed, "*Bush*? Daughter the *bush* in Australia is huge… it's dense scrubland, it will be like looking for a *needle in a haystack*!"

"I know that Pa, but I have to go, I don't have any choice. The parchment says that I must find a person named Kevin Zoolagong. If I don't find this person I won't be able to find the seed. He must know where it is. And there's something else - one of those horrible devils is there. I have to find the devil seed called Elvid. This is going to be some trip, Pa. Isn't it exciting?"

Mr Jacobs wasn't happy with his beloved daughter going off to Australia, and especially going into the bush. He knew that this was an extremely dangerous place if you didn't know it, and not many people did.

"You're going to have to be very careful, Pinky," said Mr Jacobs with a concerned look on his face. "I don't want anything to happen to you, I love you very much, you're a very special person and I promised the *Ange...*" He was just about to say *The Angel* but stopped himself. Annabell knew nothing about the Angel that had appeared to Mr Jacobs before she was born.

Annabell gave her father a strange look. "What were you going to say, Pa?"

Mr Jacobs went red in his face, he didn't like lying, but in this instance he felt that he had no choice. He couldn't tell her about the angel. Not yet anyway. But the angel had told him twenty-one years before that Annabell was someone *very special* and that time would tell just how special she was. The time had come already, everybody knew that she was a very special person, but nobody knew who she really was.

"I don't want any harm to come to you, daughter. I worry about you, so does your Ma."

Mrs Jacobs was on her hands and knees scrubbing the muddy footprints off the carpet that Annabell had made and wasn't really listening to the conversation.

"Pa, I know you and Ma love me, and I love you both very much, but I have to find the seed that created plant life. I don't know why it was me who was chosen but I have to accept that I have to do it. I know that no harm will come to me and maybe when I find the last piece of the holism, I will find out who I am? I know that I'm your daughter but I feel like I'm something else!" Annabell stared at her Pa to see if there was any response but there wasn't.

Chapter Sixteen
Annabell Meets Don Baker

Mr Jacobs was well aware that the time was near when his daughter might find out who she was. He really didn't know who she was himself but he had a good idea, as had a lot of people but he always felt that it was too incredible to be true.

The next day Annabell got up early to prepare herself for her journey to Australia.

Mr Jacobs managed to book Annabell on Flight A13 MAS, Destination Hogan Airport Australia. Her flight was due to take off at 11:45am -today.

The time now was 8:00am and the nearest international Airport was at Barkstone Airport which was 200 miles away.

Annabell turned to her father, because she suddenly realised something.

"Pa, how am I going to get to the airport? We should have set off earlier!! We'll never be able to drive there in time. You'll have to cancel it, Pa." Annabell was very disappointed.

"Oh, how I wish that I could fly. I've got all these powers, surely I should be able to fly." Annabell wasn't thinking straight. She suddenly ran out of the house in a bit of a mood and dived in the air, spreading out her arms like an airplane! But she fell to the ground like a lump of lead! And to make matters worse, she had dived straight into cow poo! And it was all over her hands, face and her clothes.

"Ooh!" she moaned, "why can't I fly?"

She went back into the farmhouse with her head held down in embarrassment and the cow poo was dripping off her chin!! She walked into the house, but once again she'd forgotten to wipe her feet. And to make matters worse, when she ran out of the house she'd forgotten to put her boots on!!

Mrs Jacobs now had cow-poo footprints over her carpet!! But she didn't tell Annabell off this time, she couldn't, because she and Mr Jacobs were in hysterics at her antics.

"What are you doing, daughter?" laughed Mr Jacobs. "Are you going mad?"

"No, Pa, I'm not mad. I tried to fly but I just fell flat on my face and I've got poo all over me now. Those cows are dirty creatures, look at the state of me!"

Annabell was very despondent. Her ticket was booked but there was no way of getting the flight in time.

"Hold on, daughter, don't worry about it," said Mr Jacobs. "I've got an idea."

Mr Jacobs picked up the telephone, and talked with somebody. He talked for several minutes and then thanked whoever it was that he was talking to.

He turned to Annabell. "Well, that's sorted daughter, I told you not to worry, go and get yourself ready, darling, you're going to Barkstone Airport."

"What have you done, Pa? There's not a vehicle that's fast enough that would get me there on time," said Annabell, with a cow-poo face!

"Never mind about that. Just get yourself ready, you're going to Australia," said Mr Jacobs looking very pleased with himself.

Annabell quickly had a shower and got herself ready while Mrs Jacobs cleaned up the mess that Annabell had made.

Mr Jacobs accompanied by Mrs Jacobs and Annabell drove 18 miles to Spraggs Cross. Spraggs Cross was a small airfield that was is behind times. The airfield consisted of a single dirt track runway. Two rusting corrugated sheds that were home to two battered, very ancient, Light aircraft. The planes were made of metal and fibre glass, these materials were no longer used since the inventions of *XNO.* The planes were mainly used as crop sprayers but occasionally carried passengers on short flights. The planes were so ancient that they were still powered by old liquid fuel.

On arrival at Spraggs Cross They were met by a man named Don Baker. He was a pilot. Mr Jacobs knew Don, because he occasionally sprayed his crops. Mr Jacobs shook hands with Don and pushed something into his hand. Annabell could see that it was money.

Don Baker was a dirty, scruffy looking character. Annabell knew him, but never really liked him. Don was wearing dirty oily blue overalls that looked like they hadn't been washed for years or, if ever? He spoke in a rather unfriendly gruff voice and was a very crude man. Every other word that came out of his mouth was a swear word.

Don Baker had a craggy looking face and looked older that his forty-two years. He had beard growth that looked several days old. His teeth were rotten and some of the front ones were missing, which caused him to lisp sometimes and *spit* would fly out of his mouth when he talked.

"Hello girly," referring to Annabell, "haven't seen you for a long time. How are you?"

"I'm alright," said Annabell trying to manoeuvre her body from side to side to escape Don's spit!!

"My, you've grown since I last saw you - you still look strange though," Annabell thought, well, so do you.

"Thank you Don, I needed that," said Annabell grinding her teeth.

"Now then, I understand that you want me to take you to Barkstone Airport. That's a long way that... what do you want to go there for?"

"I'm going to Australia, Don," said Annabell trying to be amicable as she possibly could to this horrible man.

"Australia? There's only Kangaroos there, and those...what do they call them things?... those rat things? ...Wom...something? Wombat, that's it."

Annabell didn't bother to answer him. She really didn't like this man, if she'd known what her father was up to she surely would have refused to go but as she was here, she thought she might as well go.

"Jump in," said Don. "Come on girly, we haven't got all day. I have to get you to Barkstone Airport by 11am. Tall order that but I'll have a good try."

Annabell reluctantly got into the back of the plane and sat on a filthy dirty leather seat, that stank to high heavens!! She wondered if this rust bucket would be capable of taking off, let alone flying.

"Buckle-up girly," came the command from Don who was now sitting in the front of the two-seater plane. He lowered the protection cockpit cover which creaked as it lowered.

Annabell felt like she was inside a bubble and the smell from Don had now increased fourfold! Not only was it an oily smell but Don's body odour was repulsive. She wondered what on earth she was doing sitting in this rusty heap with this repulsive, crude, stinking man. She obviously blamed her father but knew that he was only trying to help her.

She waved to her parents and gave out a sigh. "Oh, dear," she muttered under her breath. And if looks could kill? - Her father would surely be dead!! Being with this man, sitting in this plane at this moment in time was probably the worst moment in her life.

Don turned round to face Annabell, "Are you alright, girly? Ready to go, are we?"

Annabell had had enough of this awful man and just had to say something before she would surely have exploded.

"Yes I am ready," she sighed. "Don, would you please! please! please! Just go."

Then Don coughed and *farted!* "Sorry about that, it's those beans that I ate this morning." And then he farted again. "Better out than in," he reasoned. But Annabell didn't agree.

Annabell sat back and covered her ears and closed her eyes in an attempt to shut herself off from this vile person. She wondered if the Devil had something to do with this man.

He then turned round to her . "Are you ready, girly?" As he spoke, his *spit* sprayed over her face!

"Ooh, God help me!" she moaned. **"DON!"** shouted Annabell. "Please just go - let's just get it over and done with." She then wiped the spit off her face with the sleeve of her coat. "Ugh!" she moaned.

She was trying to understand the mentality of this man but she couldn't.

Don pressed the ignition button on the rusty airplane, there was a big *bang!* followed by a puff of dense black smoke that came out of the engine cowling.

"Come on, you rusty bucket... start! or fart! Do something," he yelled.

He pressed the start button again. *Bang!!* it went - followed by another puff of dark smoke. "Come on you *heap of junk!*...start, will you?" Don bashed the control panel.

He pressed the start button again. It went bang!-bang! - bang! Unbelievably the engine started up, but the smoke coming out of it was incredible. Annabell could no longer see her Ma and Pa, because of the density of the smoke.

"Hold on, girly," shouted Don. "Here we go, it may be a bit rough."

The rusty old plane chugged down the dirt track sending up clouds of dust, together with the smoke, it was difficult to make out the plane - it looked for all the world that it was on fire! The plane gathered speed and somehow managed to take off, but Don hadn't judged the speed right and the plane bounced back on the dirt track with an almighty *bump!*

Don yelled. He revved up the engine until it was roaring like a lion.

The plane speeded up. **"Come on; fly!"**

The plane somehow managed to get off the ground but suddenly a strong gust of wind got up and caught hold of the plane and made it swerve violently to the left and then to the right, and then it shot up into the air and swerved to the left again. After a frightening few seconds Don managed to gain control of the plane.

He shouted out, **"That was a bit hairy, girly, wasn't it? Are you alright?** This heap will be the death of me. Mark my words. Sorry!" said Don. "Are you alright?"

"Yeah, I'm alright," said Annabell who had positioned herself in the *crash position!!*

"Just concentrate on your flying, Don, don't worry about me," she said in an aggressive tone of voice.

All through the flight Don was swearing his head off - Annabell's talk to him hadn't made the slightest difference to his attitude.

The journey took about one and a half hours, but it seemed like an eternity to Annabell. The plane landed with a jolt on the runway of Barkstone Airport at precisely 10:49 am.

Annabell got out of Don's plane as quickly as possible. She thanked him for the ride.

"Pleasure," he said proudly "When you want to come back, girly, just let me know and I'll come and pick you up."

Annabell gave him a wave and muttered underneath her breath, "*Over my dead body!* never again! - never again!" and she walked off.

As Annabell made her way to the arrivals gate - she stepped on something that attached itself to her boot. She tried to scrape it off with her other boot but it wouldn't come off. So she bent down and pulled it off, to her surprise it was another piece of the parchment.

It read in English as follows:

The Devil seed Levid you will encounter soon

this Devil is solar and electric and will consume

you will see it when others won't

you have the seeds of land and water

one seed will alter and one seed will falter

you must choose but beware of your choice

choose wrong and Levid will become strong

choose right and you will extinguish its light
and gain its flight.
follow the signs
The Creator

Annabell had absolutely no idea what this all meant - she just put the parchment into her pocket and forgot about it.

She made her way to the terminal and went inside. Suddenly people started holding their noses. "What's that horrible smell?" some of them said.

Annabell realised that *the smell* was *her*! It was on her clothes. They smelt of something *horrible.* She wasn't sure whether it was cow's poo? Chemicals or the smell of Don! But whatever it was, it stank!

She checked in, and waited in the reception area for her flight to be called. Everybody at the airport knew who she was and crowed around her. The airport staff asked her if she would like to go to the VIP lounge, but she refused. She loved people, Well, most people!!

She was happy signing her autograph and having her photo taken with her fellow passengers and was genuinely having a good time. Nobody really noticed that the smell that was wafting around the airport was from her. Or if they did, they were too polite to say anything.

After about 25 minutes an announcement came over the speaker - it sounded like somebody was holding their nose as they spoke.

"Will passengers for flight number A13 MAS to Hogan, Australia, please proceed to gate number 63?"

Chapter Seventeen
The Smartalex

Annabell along with hundreds of other passengers made her way to the departure lounge.

Shortly afterwards she was told to board the plane. And what a plane it was! It was huge. She was to travel to Australia on the biggest plane ever built. Annabell, when she saw this aircraft, wondered how something *so big* could possibly fly.

She walked through a tunnel that led to one of the many entrances to the giant aircraft. A beautiful stewardess was standing at the door guiding passengers to their seats.

"Hello Annabell," said the smartly dressed stewardess in an Australian accent. Her voice didn't match her beauty. She spoke with a rather squeaky voice and she spoke very quickly, like she wanted to get the words out of her mouth as fast as possible.

The stewardess was wearing a gold skirt with a silver top and a gold and silver hat which matched the colours of the aircraft.

"You've been allocated a VIP compartment.... compliments of the Airline," the stewardess said proudly. But Annabell didn't want this.

"The *cheapest* seats will be good enough for me," said Annabell. "I don't want to be treated any differently from other passengers."

The poor stewardess didn't know what to do and she got herself in a right old fluster and her face turned bright red.

"But Annabell, you have to... it's my orders, I've been told that I have to look after you, I'll get into trouble. You're a very important person."

Annabell thought about what the stewardess had said and then she replied, "No, you won't get into trouble, why would you get into trouble? and everybody is *important,*" said Annabell and then she hugged the stewardess tightly.

"Don't worry, I'll have a word with your boss, it'll be alright. It's what I want, I'd rather be with ordinary people. I don't like people who think that they're special. What's your name?"

"Madge," came her reply.

"Ok, Madge - now don't worry... now where am I sitting?"

Madge reluctantly showed Annabell to the *cheapest* seats. Which was third class.

When the other passengers saw that she would be sitting with them they gave out a almighty cheer and clapped her.

Annabell didn't like all the fuss that was being made of her, but little did she know that this *fuss* was only the beginning of the *fuss*, because the Australian people knew that she was on board, and that the most famous person on earth was coming to their beautiful country. This was going to be the event of all time for them. To actually have a living *icon* coming to their land was something very special.

The Australians also had this magnificent aircraft that was making its maiden passenger trip as well - there were, of course, as you would expect lots of very famous and wealthy people on board including the President of the United States of America whom Annabell knew quite well.

The presidents are usually transported in their own private aircraft *AIR FORCE ONE* but in today's world the leaders of countries were just figure heads with no powers. The world was being run by computers. Man had no real say in any important decisions regarding weapons.

Every President of America had kept in touch with Annabell, over the years. The Prime Ministers and Presidents or leaders of most countries were on board. Anybody who was anybody wanted to be on this aircraft. It felt like history was being made. Just like it must have felt to the passengers who sailed on the ill-fated liner *The Titanic* in 1912.

Tickets were like gold dust (as they say) and were changing hands at phenomenal prices.

Annabell wondered how her Pa had managed to get her on this special flight at short notice. He hadn't told her that a *special* ticket had been allocated to her, because of who she was. The airline company who owned the plane were delighted to have such a famous person as her on board on this very special flight. Mr Jacobs didn't even have to pay for the ticket, but he hadn't told Annabell that.

The designer of this new aircraft came to see Annabell. His name was Alex Smart - Alex, was a brilliant inventor he was getting on in years now but was still a very clever man. He explained to Annabell about the concept of this aircraft - he'd always had a dream, he told her, of building a gigantic aircraft. He always believed that five thousand people could travel at the same time. The most people carried on an airplane at that time was one thousand five hundred.

Alex set about turning his dream into a reality. The plane was called the *Smartalex,* named after its inventor. Special longer runways had been made all around the world's airports to accommodate this wonderful new plane.

The time was fast approaching for this aircraft to take off. Everybody was now on board and they were told to fasten their seat belts. The giant engines revved up, and the plane manoeuvred down towards the runway. The time now was 11:40am, just five minutes before take-off.

The plane had huge wings with six engines on each wing. The interior of the plane had twenty separate compartments, which were divided into VIP class - first class- second class, and third class. The VIP class seats were situated at the front of the aircraft.

The aircraft was fitted out with numerous bars and restaurants, and there were plenty of play areas for the children and games rooms for the teenagers. Alex Smart's dream was to make a plane like an ocean cruise liner. This plane was built for long haul flights.

The plane was ready to go. Its twelve engines revved up and screamed as the airplane sped down the long runway at an incredible speed, then its nose lifted off the ground and the plane took off. There was a huge cheer inside the plane as it left the ground.

It quickly reached 50.000 feet, this would be the plane's cruising height

The skies were like roads and had strict speed limits. The *Smartalex* was capable of reaching a speed of 3000 mph if all engines were running at the same time, but a maximum speed limit of 2000mph applied in the skies today. Once in its cruising speed, half the engines were turned off.

The plane only needed all its engines to take off and to stop the plane once it had landed. It governed its own speed automatically, everything on board was fully computerised. The plane flew by itself, even taking off, and landing was carried out by computers. The only manual control needed for this plane was to manoeuvre it to and from the runway.

The plane was now ten minutes into its flight. The speaker system came on with a *Ding Dong* sound. "This is your captain speaking," came a voice, "my name is William Smith." Captain Smith spoke with a broad Australian accent. All the crew of this airplane were Australians.

Alex Smart himself was an Australian - but the plane had been built in America, and was a joint enterprise carried out by the Americans and the British who had the technical knowledge to be able to build such an aircraft. All the engines of the plane were made in Great Britain along with some of the computer parts. The Americans mainly built the rest with some help from other European countries.

"Welcome to the *Smartalex*," said the captain. "This magnificent aircraft has been named after its inventor, who I'm proud to say is on board with us today. Would you all please give a show of hands for Alex Smart?" Not many people could see Alex in person because he was in the VIP compartment but they were able to see him on the viewing screens that every passenger had.

With those words the passengers all clapped their hands for Alex. When the clapping had died down, the Captain came in again. "I would also like to welcome somebody that you would all know very well – Annabell, who is on board with us." There was an almighty cheer followed by loud clapping.

"Thank you very much," said the captain. I'm sure Annabell would like to thank you for the incredible acknowledgment that you have shown her, and she certainly deserves it.

We also have with us today some other very important passengers including your President George Grant." The was a small clap of hands for him. "We also have the Prime Minister of Great Britain, Clifford Sparks." There was a sound of somebody clapping inside the aircraft but it didn't last very long.

Ding-Dong. The captain came in again. "I would just like to tell you something about this splendid aircraft. Its fully automatic, and as its name suggests- it's very *smart!-* It's even smarter than *me!!*" The captain laughed, and there was a small ripple of laughter from the passengers. "I'm sorry about that," said the captain, "but it is true. In fact, I'm not really needed on board. I'm more or less a passenger like you. But under aviation law fully trained pilots have to be on board in case of an emergency, which I'm sure will not occur. Our destination, of course, is Hogan airport,

Australia. Unfortunately it's raining there at the moment." This brought a groan from the passengers who were in somewhat of a party mood but then the Captain came in again. "But I've got good news for you. According to the weather reports it will clear up before we arrive. We're now flying at a height of 50.000 feet and going at a speed of 1989 mph - your flight will take approximately five hours and twenty minutes. I'd like to take this opportunity to wish you all a pleasant trip and thank you all for flying with *AMERBRIT AIRWAYS.*"

With those words the Captain signed off.

All the seat belt signs were now turned off. The passengers were free to explore this incredible plane. Lunch was now being served at the many restaurants that were provided.

The children in Annabell's compartment were all crowding around her they kept touching her to see if she was real! And their eyes were fixed on her eyes, because they sparkled like stars.

"Are your eyes real?" One of the children asked her.

"Yeah," replied Annabell, "of course they're real, and I'm a real person." And then she laughed. Annabell found this very amusing, she adored children. She told the small child to *pinch* her skin. Which she did. *"Ouch!"* said Annabell and then she laughed again.

She picked up the small child and gave her a cuddle. "I'm only joking with you, I didn't really hurt," said Annabell smiling. The small child smiled back.

The flight was going very smoothly, everybody was enjoying themselves. The five hours soon went. Time always seems to go faster when you're enjoying yourself.

People used to get very bored on long haul flights, but this plane was designed to entertain people and it had certainly lived up to that.

The plane would soon start its descent to Hogan airport which was now only thirty minutes away.

Passengers were requested to return to their seats. Stewardesses were securing the luggage racks, so that nothing could fall out - children were being strapped into their seats. Everything was being prepared for landing. All the bars and restaurants were now closed and secured.

The giant plane was now on its descent, it was dropping altitude very slowly, it was in glide mode, now all you could hear was a gentle swishing noise. They were now only twenty minutes away from landing. Suddenly and surprisingly warning lights started flashing on the cockpit's instrument panel.

Captain William Smith and Co-pilot Cecil Murgett were stunned. Then a siren started sounding. "***WARNING! -WARNING! -WARNING!***"

"What's wrong Captain?" asked Cecil, anxiously.

"I don't know, Cecil," replied the captain looking very worried. "I don't know what's wrong. **Quick! get out the check list, Cecil,"** shouted the captain.

Cecil got out the check list and went through it with the captain, but they couldn't find any reason why the warning sign had come on.

The captain radioed Hogan airport air-traffic control informing them that flight A13 MAS' warning system had activated and they were unable to find out the reason why.

Hogan airport technical officials asked the captain to switch his control panel to them. Which he did with a flick of a switch. They informed him that they would check out why the planes warning system had come on.

Several minutes later Hogan airport technical staff radioed back telling the captain that there was nothing to worry about. All his instruments were fine and that he was to '*ignore*' the warning signals and let the plane land.

The captain acknowledged the command and felt relieved that all was well. But a few minutes later the second back up warning system activated. **"WARNING! -WARNING !-WARNING!"** It bellowed.

Captain Smith and the Co-pilot and the rest of the cockpit crew now became very concerned.

"What the hell is going on?" shouted the captain. **"HOGAN AIRPORT."** He yelled, **"HOGAN AIRPORT.** Come in please. This is flight A13 MAS. We have a problem. I repeat …We have a problem."

There was an immediate response from Hogan Airport. "What is your problem?" asked air traffic control.

The Captain shouted out. "The secondary warning system has activated and we don't know why - please investigate immediately… This is a emergency. I repeat …this is a emergency."

Two minutes later Hogan Airport responded. "There's nothing wrong A13 MAS… I repeat ….there's nothing wrong…please proceed to land."

Suddenly the whole of the instrument panel lit-up with warning signs - everything electrical on the plane was going berserk but according to Hogan Airport, there was nothing wrong.

Just when the Captain thought that his nerves couldn't get any worse, the radar warning system activated indicating that there was something ahead. But nothing could be seen.

"Hogan airport, this is flight A13 MAS. There's something ahead of us. Please investigate."

Captain Smith was trying to stay calm, but this was a very stressful situation. Nobody knew what was happening, but the *Smartalex* was picking up something that wasn't supposed to be there. But what it was, was as yet unknown.

"A13 MAS," came a voice …"This is Hogan Airport …There's nothing wrong…I repeat there's nothing wrong… There's nothing out there!…please proceed to land."

"But there is something out there!" shouted the captain "I don't know what it is, but this plane has picked it up." Then suddenly the captain was heard to scream!!

***"HELP !- OH-NO!- MAYDAY! -MAYDAY!* What the hell is this…?"**

Seconds later there was a noise that sounded like glass smashing and then there was nothing

Flight A13 MAS had mysteriously disappeared from Hogan Airport's radar screen. Panic set in at the control tower. There were five thousand souls on board, if anything had happened to this aircraft this could be the worst air disaster of all time.

Chapter Eighteen
Levid

Unbeknown to Hogan airport air traffic control. The plane had been hit by a blinding flash of bright light. The energy from this light was so intense that the entire electrical systems of the plane had been *consumed!* All twelve engines had been disabled, all computers were dead. Every battery-operated appliance on this aircraft had been drained of its power. Mobile phones. Music players. Watches. Everything was dead.

There were twelve listed passengers on board who had heart pacemakers fitted. These had stopped working, which left these people in a desperate situation. If their batteries weren't charged soon they would all die.

This magnificent aircraft was now *out of control!* The Captain and Co- pilot whose job it was to fly this aircraft manually in case of an emergency had been *blinded* by the mysterious flash of light energy force that had hit the plane.

The cockpit window screen had a round hole, about the size of a football that had been burned through when the light hit it. The energy force was now inside the aircraft. It went through the aircraft blinding every single person, except for Annabell. The light stopped and engulfed her - it seemed to know that Annabell had powers.

The light was a living force of pure electrical energy. It drained everything electrical in its path, it was also getting power from the sun. If this devil wasn't stopped it would eventually consume all of the sun's energy.

Annabell realised that this was what the parchment had warned her about. This was the Devil Levid *solar and electric it will consume.* The parchment had told her. *She would see it when others won't.*

Annabell screamed at the light. "I know who you are - you're Levid, and I know that you're evil, you've come for me, haven't you? But you won't win. You'll see. I will beat you." Annabell's face was stern as she faced this evil.

The light circled around her, keeping her enclosed in the centre but it didn't touch her.

Annabell was very concerned about the passengers, she didn't know about the twelve passengers whose heart pacemakers had failed but she did have powers to save them as long as she had time to.

She had to defeat Levid first though. She shouted at it again. "Go away or I will destroy you. I can, you know." Annabell thought that she could but she didn't know how.

The light showed no sense of any fear - it just kept going around and around her, like it was waiting for her to do something. It seemed to be wary of her though.

Annabell thought back to the parchment that was in her pocket. The parchment had warned her that she would encounter Levid soon but she hadn't expected it to come this soon. Annabell got the parchment out of her pocket and read it again. She knew that she didn't have much time. She could see everybody around her had been blinded and she could hear the screams from the passengers.

She read the parchment. It said:

This devil is solar and electrical too
You will see it when others won't

You have the seed of Land and Water

One seed will alter and one seed will falter

You must choose but beware of your choice

Choose wrong and Levid will become strong

Choose right you can extinguish it's light

and you will gain its flight

Annabell realised that she had to use the seeds to defeat this Devil but she didn't know which one to use.

"Which one?" she spoke to herself. "If I choose wrong this Devil will become *strong.* I mustn't do that."

Annabell was puzzled. "I don't know what to do, this is awful. I don't know which seed is which. The parchment said one seed will *'alter'* and one seed will *'falter'.* **Which seed shall I use?"** she yelled. "I don't know."

All the time that she was thinking the plane was descending on a course for a crash but she didn't know this. She obviously knew that something was wrong but she didn't know that the plane was going to crash. The plane was at this moment in time still gliding, and she had no idea that the cockpit crew had been blinded and that the plane was out of control.

She looked at the two seeds that were on her necklace they were glowing with all the colours of the rainbow but they looked exactly the same. She didn't know which one was the land seed and which was the water seed.

"Oh, creator," she shrieked, "why do you do this to me?"

She removed the two seeds from her necklace and she placed one in her right hand and the other seed in her left hand. She looked at the right hand seed. "Is it you?" And then she looked at the left hand seed. "Or is it you?

One seed will *'falter'* and one seed will *'alter'*. Alter means to *change.* she muttered to herself. "Right then - change must be the seed that will alter it. But wait! The other seed will *'falter'* it. That means it will weaken it.

"Oh, dear," she yelled "How can I choose a seed when I don't know what seed is what? It's impossible to choose, and if I choose wrong, the devil will become strong - and I would have lost." Annabell was starting to panic.

The energy force seemed to sense that Annabell was in a quandary, it was making a humming noise as it circled around her. The sound was like the sound that you would hear from a power station as electricity was being generated. The humming got louder and louder.

Annabell could sense that the force could feel what she was thinking. If she made a mistake and picked the wrong seed, this Devil force would become everlasting, and would surely destroy the Earth.

This would be the only opportunity anybody would ever have of destroying it. If Annabell failed, this evil force would be free to roam and would cause havoc on the Earth forever, and ever! and ever! and ever! and ever!

The time had come for Annabell to choose a seed. It was to be a fifty- fifty chance of picking the right one. Levid was now humming very loud it was as if it sensed Annabell's dilemma.

She had to choose now. A decision had to be made. She closed her eyes and went to throw the seed that was in her right hand. She didn't pick this hand for any particular reason. She pulled back her arm and went to throw the seed at Levid but suddenly she stopped herself at the very last moment. She'd realised something that was very important. If she used the seeds separately neither of them would work. '*Alter* and *falter*' - wouldn't mean that Levid wouldn't be destroyed - all that it would do was to weaken or change it.

Annabell's mind was racing - she was beginning to work it out - "If I don't know the difference between the two seeds. It's obviously *not possible* for me to choose, so maybe I don't have to choose." She looked at Levid to see if there was any reaction to her thoughts, but there wasn't.

"YEAH!" she yelled, "that's it - that's the answer. Now let me think."

She closed her eyes. "Um, the land seed? Land also means *Earth* in electrical terms, if a fault occurs in electricity it will go to Earth. So if I throw the land seed at Levid it would consume all of the land seed's energy and grow stronger. It's the land seed that will make Levid an everlasting force. It must to be able to use the power from this seed," thought Annabell.

"If I throw the water seed it would definitely weaken it, because electricity doesn't like *water,* everybody knows that. Water could destroy it, yes. But the parchment said that it will *'falter'.* So the water seed won't stop it. It would only weaken it."

Annabell's mind was working overtime on the puzzle.

"I have to use *both* seeds at the same time, I'm sure of it," she muttered to herself. "But if I'm wrong - God help us."

Annabell had worked out that if she threw *both* the seeds at the Devil Levid at the same time - it would have to react to the *water* seed first - it would automatically try to defend itself and would go to land seed. Which would have to become its *Earth*.

Levid knew what Annabell was thinking and its humming noise started to decline and it then started to retreat away from her. This was the sign that she had been looking for. Levid now showed signs of *fear*. She now knew what to do.

Annabell had also worked out that if she threw the seeds at Levid they wouldn't work, because once she let go of them, the seeds would lose their power. Annabell only had the power of the seeds if they were within her person. She would have to physically touch Levid while still holding the seeds. This would be very risky for her - it could even *kill* her! Because she would lose all her power when she did this. The power would all be transferred into Levid. If Annabell was wrong with her thoughts she would certainly die along with all the passengers of flight A13 MAS.

"HEAR!" she screamed, **"see if you like these - you evil, nasty thing."**

She then *touched* Levid with the two seeds at the same time.

There was a loud bang followed by a puff of smoke. Annabell was thrown to the floor by the force of the bang and her hands were badly burnt.

Annabell screamed with the pain that she felt and was very weak now that she didn't have the power from the seeds but Levid was gone!

The two seeds were lying on the floor about ten feet from her.

Levid had done exactly what Annabell had hoped it would do - it knew that a fault had occurred when it was touched by the water seed, and instinctively it ran to the only place that it could go - *Earth*! Which was the land seed. But it entered the land seed as a weakened force. Levid had been *captured* and was now inside the land seed, where it would remain forever. It would now become part of Annabell's powers. She realised now why Levid hadn't attacked her. She was wearing the seeds of life, the power from these seeds was obviously stronger than Levid's power when they were combined.

Annabell although still very weak and hurt gave out a loud shriek of excited emotion. She had defeated the second devil, Levid - she had chosen *correctly.*

She crawled across the floor on her hands and knees in terrible pain and picked up the two seeds. Instantly the seeds glowed with all the colours of the rainbow and she felt a surge of the most incredible energy go through her body. The burns on her hands healed instantly and she felt stronger than ever now.

⸻◄❯►⸻

Chapter Nineteen
Saving The Passengers

Annabell had defeated Levid, but now she had to turn her attention to try and save the five thousand passengers and crew on this *doomed* aircraft.

It was now at twelve thousand feet and heading for oblivion. Hogan airport had absolutely no idea where the plane was or what had happened to it. The airport was in turmoil. There was a huge plane out there somewhere but nobody knew where it was. They knew that it hadn't crashed because there hadn't been any reports of any major incident.

The Australian air force had now been scrambled and were in the skies looking for the *Smartalex*.

Passengers were screaming, yelling and shouting, they didn't know what had happened to them. Most were in deep shock, hundreds had fainted. Children were screaming and sobbing uncontrollably. Thousands of people were yelling the same words.

"I CANT SEE -I'M BLIND-WHAT HAS HAPPENED? - HELP! - HELP!"

There was absolute total panic inside the aircraft. Because of the noise inside the aircraft, nobody knew that the plane's engines had stopped. The plane had speeded up and was now descending rapidly. The only person on this plane that could save these unfortunate people was Annabell but she wasn't sure what was going on herself.

She ran to the cockpit as fast as she could. When she got there, she was shocked to find that the aircraft had *no power* and was out-of-control, and that the pilot and cockpit crew *were all blind.* And they were all in a state of shock.

There was a howling wind coming through the broken cockpit window. The crew's flight documents were being throw around the cockpit like confetti.

Annabell was now aware of the serious situation they were all in. She knew that she had to act quickly but what could she do? She had fantastic powers, but flying wasn't one of them. "If only I could fly," she yelled.

She didn't mean fly the aircraft. She meant fly herself! She knew that there was no hope for this aircraft. It wouldn't be possible to start the engines of this plane now, because there wouldn't be time.

She believed despite the hugeness of this aircraft that she would have the strength to be able to guide it down *physically*, but she needed to have the powers of flight. She couldn't fly, she knew that, she'd had tried and failed.

She knew that she wouldn't die, but there could be very little hope for the passengers and crew of the plane.

The plane was now descending at a rate of one-thousand feet per minute, *luckily* (if that is an appropriate word to use in this situation), the plane was still in its glide mode, otherwise it would have nose-dived to Earth within seconds.

Annabell knew that she had to take control of this desperate situation.

The captain and crew were not in a position to help her. She had less than twelve minutes to decide what she was going to do.

Her first priority was to try and inform Hogan airport of the desperate plight of this plane but all communication between plane and airport was lost. She had to think quickly. She had an idea but she needed a mobile phone. None of the crew had mobiles, because they weren't allowed in the cockpit.

She ran out of the cockpit and went to the first passenger who was an Asian man. She tapped him on his shoulder. "Sir, I'm Annabell. I know that you can't see me, but I need a cell phone or mobile phone as some people call them. Have you got one?"

The man couldn't speak English but Annabell could understand his language and asked him again in his own language.

"Yes...yes," stuttered the man. He was obviously in shock, but was aware of himself.

"I do have one. But what is happening?" asked the man in a distraught voice.

"I'm sorry, but I haven't got time to tell you. Please can I borrow your mobile, sir? It's an *emergency*. **Quickly! - quickly!** I haven't got much time," yelled Annabell.

"Yes, yes of....of... course you can," said the man. He took the mobile from his pocket and gave it to her. The battery was dead. Annabell touched it with one of the seeds, it didn't matter what seed she used - the water and land seeds powers didn't apply in the same principle as it did when fighting Levid. The mobile phone battery instantly re-charged as soon as it was touched by the seed.

Annabell went back inside the cockpit and tried to ask asked the captain what the number was to get in touch with Hogan airport traffic control but the captain and crew were too shocked to be able to answer her. She looked around the cockpit but was unable to find the number so she called the Australian emergency services number which she did know. She managed to get through straight away. The call was answered by what sounded like an elderly woman's voice.

"What service do you require?" asked the voice in an Australian accent.

Annabell screamed down the phone.

"Listen to me -I don't have much time. My name is Annabell. I'm a passenger on flight A13 MAS. Please inform Hogan airport that the plane is *out-of -control* - I repeat, the plane is out-of - control, it's going to crash! - I repeat it's going to crash! I promise that I will do everything in my powers to save it. I have to go," yelled Annabell. "Please confirm that you understand this message."

There was a short pause before the woman operator responded.

"Yes," came her reply. "Yes, yes…. Oh, my God!" The woman was clearly shocked. "Yes, my dear, I will pass on your message immediately. God help you all."

"Thank you!" said Annabell. She ended the call.

The plane was now only nine-thousand feet from the ground and all the time it was speeding up. Annabell needed to communicate with the other passengers. She felt that they had the right to know what was going on.

There was now less than eight minutes before this plane was going to crash.

"Captain!… captain!" yelled Annabell, "I need your help," but the captain didn't respond. He was just sitting there staring with a *vacant* look on his face.

Annabell slapped the Captain across his face, again and again. "I'm, Sorry! - sorry!" she screamed. "Come on captain… snap out of it."

The captain shook his head and slowly came to his senses but he was still blind, and was still very confused.

"What!… what is it?" asked the captain. And then his body shook and he muttered something that was not understandable. It was as if he didn't really know what was happening.

Then his body shook again, and he screamed. He'd remembered the bright light. "**What was that light? It's blinded me. I'm blind! - I'm blind!**" he yelled in panic.

"I can't explain right now captain I haven't got time. We're in a very serious situation. This plane is going to crash sir."

"*Crash?* What do you mean we're going to crash? This plane can't crash. Who are you?" asked the captain, now aware of what he was saying.

"I'm Annabell, captain. Everybody on this plane is blind, except for me. All power has been drained from the plane... we only have a few minutes left before we will crash. I desperately need to inform the passengers. I need to connect to the speaker system, sir. How do I do that?"

"It's not possible," said the captain. "The speaker system is run by batteries. If we've lost all power the batteries will be dead, it can't be done. It will take hours to recharge them. Oh, God we're all going to die," said the captain mournfully.

Annabell shouted at the captain. "**Stop it, captain, get a grip of yourself please. I need your help. Where** are the batteries for the speaker system? Quickly, quickly sir, we haven't got much time."

The captain felt around with his hands and located a catch. "They're here. But what use will they be?" He pulled the catch and exposed the batteries. Annabell touched the batteries with one of the seeds. Instantly they came to life.

"How do you work the speaker system captain?" asked Annabell

The captain told her. She pressed a button and she heard the familiar sound of the *ding-dong.* She pressed it again and again making sure that she had everybody's attention. Ding-dong...ding-dong-ding-dong.

"Please, please can I have your attention?" she yelled, "all of you please listen to me. I'm Annabell and I can see. I know that you've all been blinded. I haven't got time to explain to you as to what has happened but I cannot lie to you. This plane has lost all of its power."

Annabell could hear the screams as panic had now set in. She wondered if she had done the right thing by telling the passengers.

"We're going to crash- We're all going to die," screamed some of the passengers. They were all now aware that their lives were in danger.

Annabell had to get a grip with the situation. She tried to stay as calm within herself as was possible. But of course she felt the pain and anguish that the passengers must be feeling.

"I know…" She paused for a second to try and compose herself. "…I know that you'll all be terribly afraid but I promise you that I will do everything in the powers given to me to save you all, I know that it's difficult but please try to stay calm. We haven't got much time now. Will you all make sure that your seat belts are fastened and please try to assist other passengers - and I'm so sorry to have to say this…" Annabell paused and then she closed her eyes, she was filled with emotion. A single tear drop came out of her left eye and rolled down her cheek and fell to the floor. "Oh, God" she muttered. She could barely get the words out of her mouth…. "Would you all assume the *crash position.*" With those haunting words Annabell turned off the speaker system.

The plane was now only six minutes from crashing.

Annabell guided all the crew out of the cockpit and sat them down with the passengers. While she was doing this a small girl bumped into her leg. The little girl was only about three years old. She was a rather beautiful mixed race child with striking brown eyes and dark thick curly hair. She was wearing a red dress with white spots. The little girl was sobbing. She had her arms stretched out in front of her trying to find her way, like a blind person would do if they never had a stick. The little girl had somehow strayed away from her parents. They obviously wouldn't know where she was, because they wouldn't be able to see her.

Annabell picked up the child and held her affectionately in her arms. "Mummy...mummy - is that you? I can't see," sobbed the child. The child spoke English.

"I'm not your mummy," said Annabell tearfully. "What is your name, little girl?"

"My...my....name...is....is.... Trin...Trinity."

"Hello Trinity, that's a lovely name. I know what your name means - maybe it's a sign? Yeah...." muttered Annabell. "*It's a sign,* I really hope so.. My name is

Annabell ...it sounds like a fairy's name doesn't it? Like *Tinkerbell*."

The little child nodded her head and answered, "Yes... are you a fairy, Annabell?"

"No, no. I'm not a fairy, Trinity - well I don't think that I am, but maybe today I am. Do you know who I am Trinity?"

"Yes... you're the *red lady*. And you do look like a fairy, because I've seen you on the telly."

"That's right, I'm the red lady. And you are right, I suppose that I do look like a fairy sometimes." Annabell was trying to calm the child.

She tapped the captain on his shoulder to draw his attention.

"Captain, I'm putting this child on your lap, I don't have time to find out who she belongs to. Would you please look after her?"

"Yes, of course I will," said the Captain. Annabell placed the child on the captain's lap and buckled her up and then gave her a kiss on her cheek.

"This kind man is going to look after you for a little while, Trinity, is that all right?"

Trinity answered, "Yes."

Annabell was very emotional now. She adored children. These were the *innocents* of this situation, who had hardly started their lives and there were 187 on board this aircraft. Annabell wiped away her tears.

The plane was now only 4000 feet from the ground. There could be no more than four minutes left.

The plane was lacking in oxygen, it was becoming very hard to breathe. Not for Annabell, she didn't need to breathe oxygen, but the passengers were clearly suffering.

"Captain... captain how do I get oxygen to this plane?" shouted Annabell.

The captain told her to release the oxygen masks that were above everybody's head and let them just dangle. This would produce enough oxygen for the passengers to be able to breathe. He told her that she would have to do it manually. There was a lever inside the cockpit that she would have to pull down that would release the oxygen masks.

Annabell ran to the cockpit and found the lever and pulled it. Which released the masks.

The plane was now only 3000 feet from the ground, there was very little time left now. The plane suddenly and *alarmingly* started to nose dive. *this was it!!* There would now be only seconds before the plane crashed.

There was no time left for Annabell to do anything. She felt helpless. There was really nothing that she could do to save these poor unfortunate souls. There was no-point in her remaining inside this doomed aircraft.

Annabell ran to the cockpit with tears streaming from her eyes. She smashed out the window and jumped out.

She found herself drifting in space. She felt like an *Angel.* The pieces of the Holism were glowing, making her white dress which she had changed into look like it was made from a rainbow.

Annabell at this moment in time was very unhappy. This was the saddest day of her life.

"I couldn't save them... I couldn't save them," she was saying over and over again.

"If only I could fly. God please let me fly." With those words the land seed that captured Levid suddenly began to glow brighter.

Annabell was now several hundred feet behind the aircraft and all the time she was moving farther and farther away from it, and all the time, she was herself plummeting to the ground. She knew that any second now there was going to be a huge explosion and a massive loss of life and there was nothing that she could do about it. As she was falling through the sky her thoughts were on the little girl, Trinity.

Annabell was very distraught. She closed her eyes trying to blot out what she thought was the inevitable. As she was tumbling through the air, something strange happened. She felt a surge of energy go through her body. There was something different about this energy.

When she opened her eyes, to her amazement she realised that she was no longer falling downwards. She was in fact, going *forward* and at an incredible speed. She had gained the power of flight. The surge of energy that she had felt was the new power.

Annabell had forgotten what the parchment had told her. It had said that:

If you choose right you'll extinguish its light and gain its flight.

Annabell had defeated Levid and had gained all of its powers. One of which was the power of flight.

The plane was now only thirty seconds from hitting the ground and there was something else that was very disturbing, the plane was on course to hit a densely populated area. Annabell didn't have much time she rapidly caught up with the aircraft and positioned her back underneath the cockpit. She held out her two arms to form the shape of a cross to support the plane. This looked ridiculous. She didn't know if it would be possible for her to support this huge aircraft. She knew that she had super human powers but was she strong enough to be able to do this? The answer was yes, because when the plane was only seconds away from hitting the ground, it suddenly slowed down and then started to climb upwards when it reached a safe height. Annabell levelled the plane out as gently as she could.

She could see Hogan airport in the distance. All emergency services had been activated. All other flights had been diverted away from the airport, so everything was now clear for her to bring the *Smartalex* in to land.

The plane had now been sighted by the airport air traffic control but it wasn't showing up on their radar. They could see Annabell underneath the front of the aircraft. It looked ridiculous to everybody who was witnessing it.

The giant plane slowly made its way towards a runway, it was coming in on a smooth approach to land.

Hogan airport were aware that it was Annabell who was bringing it in but they could hardly believe what their eyes were seeing. It was an incredible sight.

The plane glided down to the runway but there was a problem, it had no wheels! It wouldn't be possible for it to land in a normal way.

Annabell had realised this and brought the plane to a complete stand still, while still in mid-air. She then lowered the plane gently as she could down to the ground but it still hit the ground with a *bit of a bump*! but nothing that would cause any damage to the plane or harm the passengers.

The passengers' ordeal was now over, everybody had been saved.

People at the airport couldn't believe what they had just witnessed. A rather beautiful slim twenty-one year old woman had just landed the biggest aircraft the world had ever seen with her bare hands!!

The huge crowds that had gathered at the airport to welcome this plane and its celebrities, especially Annabell, had been told to leave when the plane went missing. Only the emergency services were at the airport.

Somebody had captured this whole incredible event of Annabell landing the plane on film. The world would now get to see what this remarkable woman had done. She had saved the lives of all the passengers and had prevented a disaster happening on the ground.

Annabell flew up to one of the aircraft doors and pulled it open and she went inside. "Is everybody alright?" She said feeling terribly relieved. "That was a bit rough, wasn't it?" She kind of joked, but it wasn't a joking matter really.

Annabell was just trying to ease the minds of the passengers. They had all suffered a horrendous ordeal.

She was informed by the passengers that some people had pacemakers which had stopped working. So Annabell quickly went around the aircraft and saved all those passengers, everybody was saved.

"You're all safe now," said Annabell. "I'm pleased to tell you that the *Smartalex* has landed." There was a huge roar from the passengers mainly with relief that they were still alive.

"Please everybody remain in your seats and I know that's it's difficult, but please try to stay calm, help will soon be on its way. Does anybody need immediate assistance?"

Nobody said that they did. Suddenly passengers were shouting out that they could now see again. The blindness that Levid had caused was only temporary.

Then one of the passengers started to sing:

"For she's a jolly good fellow

for she's a jolly good fellow..."

and then all the passengers joined in to sing the line ...*"and so say all of us."*

This once doomed plane was now filled with happiness. These people were very lucky to be alive, and they all knew it.

None of them were aware what Annabell had done but they all knew that it was she who had saved them. They had no doubts about that. They knew that it couldn't have been anybody else.

Fleets of ambulances, coaches and fire engines and other vehicles were fast approaching the plane. The whole airport was filled with the sound of sirens. It sounded like an air raid was about to begin.

Walkways were quickly assembled to all the entrances to the plane and passengers were now slowly disembarking, most of them could now see, but some needed the help of the emergency service staff. Miraculously it appeared that nobody was seriously injured.

Passengers and were being taken to the airport reception rooms to be checked over by doctors.

Annabell was helping escort passengers off the plane when she caught sight of the Captain carrying Trinity down the walkway from another door. Annabell was so excited and ran over to greet them. **"Captain!- captain!"** she yelled with great emotional excitement. "Please, please, can I carry Trinity?"

The captain replied in a broad Australian accent. "Of course you can, young lady. My God what did you do? How did you manage to bring this plane down?"

Annabell smiled and said, "It's a story captain that you won't believe, I can hardly believe it myself. I can't believe what I've just done... Oh, my God. How was I able to fly?" Annabell was shaking her head in disbelief at what she had done.

"I'll tell you something young lady," said the captain. "I don't know yet how you did this incredible thing, but you are..." and then the captain paused. He was filling up with emotion himself, tears could clearly be seen rolling down the his cheeks. He coughed to clear his throat and carried on where he had left off "... without any doubt the most unbelievable human being there has ever been on this planet... and that's a fact. May I kiss you, my dear?"

"Of course you can, captain," said Annabell feeling just a little embarrassed.

The captain leant over, and he kissed her on her red cheek. "Thank you - thank you - my dear. I owe you my life. We all do. I'm humbled to be in your presence, you are clearly somebody very, very special." And then he handed Trinity to her.

Her sparkling eyes sparkled even more when she held Trinity in her arms and she cuddled her as if she was holding a teddy bear. Trinity was holding a soft toy bear that had coloured dots on it that somebody had given to her in the plane.

"Hello, my darling, you're safe now," Annabell whispered. "Can you see Trinity?"

"Yes," she said in a soft voice. Her tiny hands were trying to touch Annabell's sparkling blue eyes.

"Are they sweets?" she asked inquisitively.

"No darling they're not sweets they're my eyes, I'm not like other people. I don't know why. Trinity, we must find your mummy and daddy." Annabell gripped Trinity's small hand. "What do you call your teddy bear, Trinity?"

"*Spotty pants!*" replied Trinity with a grin.

"That's a nice name," said Annabell smiling. "It's a funny name, I like that."

Annabell paused for a moment, she wasn't sure if Trinity would be able to understand what she was about to ask her. "Umm – Trinity, do you know what your mummy's name is?" Annabell spoke slowly.

Trinity looked up at Annabell, and answered, "Yes, my mummy's name is Sally and my daddy's name is daddy!"

That confused Annabell. "Um. Trinity, do you know what a surname means? Everybody calls me Annabell but my surname which is my family's name is Jacobs - so I'm called Annabell Jacobs. Do you know what your full name is? We know that you're first name is Trinity. But Trinity... What?"

Annabell wasn't too sure what Trinity was going to say or if she understood the question.

"Jelly," she replied

"Jelly? Are you sure Trinity? That's a wonderful name."

Annabell was pretty sure that Trinity didn't understand what a surname was. We all know what jelly is, and it seemed rather strange for Trinity to say that.

"Yes, my name is Trinity Jelly," she said confidently. "That's my name and my mummy's name is Mummy Jelly, and my daddy's name is Daddy Jelly, and I have a brother called Chevron Jelly, and a sister called Chevaze Jelly..." Trinity then took a deep breath. Annabell thought that she had finished, but no, she then carried on.

"... and another brother called Sean Jelly and another sister called Serena Jelly and another brother called Remi Jelly, and a sister called Melody Jelly, and another brother called Neo Jelly," and then she stopped.

"Wow!" replied Annabell. "You've got a lot of brothers and sisters. I always wanted a brother or sister, especially a sister, but my ma couldn't have any more children. So there was only me, you're so lucky to have all those brothers and sisters, Trinity.

Do you know what jelly is?" Annabell was trying to find out whether or not Trinity knew what she was saying.

"Yes, it's my name and it's what you have with ice cream - it's like a wiggle-waggle on a plate."

"That's right," said Annabell. "So your name is like the wiggle-waggle on the plate?"

"Yes," replied Trinity. "My name is wiggle-waggle," and then she laughed.

Annabell walked over to a policeman who was waiting by an ambulance.

"Officer," she called. "I'm going to the reception with this child. I don't know who her parents are but she says her name is Trinity Jelly - it's a bit strange I know - and I have no way of knowing if that's her real name but if anybody asks about her please tell them that she's with me."

The policeman wrote it down in his notebook and assured Annabell that he would keep a look out for anybody asking the whereabouts of a small child with that name.

A short while later, Trinity was re-united with her mummy and daddy and all her brothers and sisters and Jelly was her surname, but it was spelt Jelley.

All the newspapers around the world had pictures of Annabell carrying Trinity in her arms, and the headlines read:

"INCREDI-BELL SAVES PLANE"

The world had witnessed the most incredible real life rescue it had ever seen. 5000 people had been saved by this young lady. Everybody in the world now knew that Annabell could not possibly be human!! No human being was capable of what she had just done. What or who she really was, was a mystery, but it didn't matter. The people of the Earth were mighty pleased that she was here.

News of Annabell's amazing rescue of the plane had obviously been relayed back to America - Annabell had saved the life of the President of the United States of America, amongst others. She was red hot news. The press not for the first time had gathered at Mr and Mrs Jacobs' farm. All wanted to ask the same question.

"Who is Annabell?

Mr Jacobs always knew that his daughter was going to be somebody *'special'*. But even he didn't realise just how special she would become. She had become a person of the like the world had never seen before.

They had seen *Super* people portrayed in comics and films but they were fictional characters, Annabell was real.

What the angel had told Mr Jacobs had now come true.

"Only time will tell just how special she will become," predicted the angel.

What Annabell had become was a *SUPER WOMAN* and there was more to come…

The press had nicknamed her *SUPERBELL.* From now on she would always be known by that name to the media. But not to her mother and father.

Chapter Twenty
The News Conference

The Prime Minister of Australia, John Brown, bestowed the highest honours of his country to Annabell. Other countries soon followed. Some religions around the world had also taken her to be their divine person - *like a Goddess!*

All the world now knew that Annabell was somebody very special and they were very proud of her. Annabell was of course humbled by the accolades that were being bestowed upon her but she was here in Australia for a reason. She had to find the third piece of the Holism. But the news media wouldn't give her a minute's peace, everybody wanted interviews with her. She tried her best to avoid them but in the end realised that she had to bow down to the requests of the world's press, so she decided to hold a press conference and face the world's media.

A day was set, hundreds of the world's press were invited to a selected venue, it was to be held at Hogan Town Hall.

The day arrived and the hall was buzzing with excitement, at last the journalists would now get their chance to ask the questions the world wanted to know.

Prime Minister John Brown followed by the President of the United States of America and the Prime Minister of Great Britain entered the room along with Annabell.

The moment that they saw Annabell there was a huge roar, followed by loud clapping from the journalists. Cameras were flashing like a firework display.

The four dignitaries sat down at the front of the large room behind a long table - on the table were lots of microphones with the names of the various media companies.

Everybody was eager to ask Annabell questions, but she didn't want a free-for-all. So selected journalists had been chosen before the meeting started to ask the questions that all of the journalists would have asked anyway.

First person selected to talk to Annabell was a reporter from England. She was a reporter representing a newspaper called the *Daily Earth.* The reason why she was chosen was because she was a passenger on the near ill-fated aircraft.

When she stood up, the room went into a ghostly silence. Everybody in the room was waiting for an answer from Annabell to the question that the world wanted to ask. Pamela would be the first person to have the opportunity to ask it.

"Hello Annabell, my name is Pamela Jones from the *Daily Earth,* England."

Pamela was a smartly dressed woman in her early thirties - she had her blond hair tied back in a pony tail and was wearing spectacles. She had hesitation in her voice. She wasn't nervous, this was an emotional hesitation. She cleared her throat and started to speak.

"First of all Annabell, may I say thank you for saving my life, and I know this will apply to all passengers on flight A13 MAS. I think that you are a remarkable woman - unique in fact. You are somebody that the Earth has never witnessed before..." Pamela stopped speaking for a moment thoughts had come into her head at what she had just said and then she carried on "...well maybe there are some other people that are remembered in the same divine way as yourself?" Pamela then stopped. Again the emotion of it all was getting to her, she wiped away a tear and cleared her throat. "Sorry!" she said. "There is a question that I think people all over the world would like to know. But I don't want to ask the question, it's clear to me that you are somebody who has been heavenly sent to us. Thank you, Annabell," and then Pamela sat down in tears. A woman next to her gave her a tissue so that she could wipe her eyes.

Next person to stand up was Charlie Newman, a very experienced journalist, who was working for the *Australian Times* and various television channels.

It was thought in the twenty-first century that newsprint papers would completely become extinct, but this wasn't to be. Newsprint papers made a strong comeback and were now a very popular way for people to get their news.

Charlie Newman was a very distinguished man in his late fifties. He thought that he'd seen it all in his thirty-two years as a journalist, but he'd never seen anything quite like Annabell. "Hello Annabell. Umm, my name is Charlie Newman, representing the *Australian Times* and television news. It's certainly a pleasure to be talking to you. Er...um.." For some reason Charlie was also finding it hard to find the words. He knew what he wanted to ask her, it was what everybody wanted to ask her. "Um…Sorry! Um- er… like Pamela, I would also like to thank you for what you have done, you've saved thousands of people's lives-I can't begin to understand how you did it, but on behalf of the people of Australia we thank you. Like Pamela there are questions that I would like to ask you, but I believe it's not really for us *mortals* to question something that it would be impossible for us to comprehend, there's something clearly involved here that must be *divine.*

"I must be honest with you, Annabell, I really didn't believe in what people call God…" Charlie paused to wipe his brow with a handkerchief that he took out of his top pocket.

I don't think he could believe what he was saying. This man had been an atheist all of his life but here he was faced with something that he was unable to understand. He carried on with what he was about to say "…with your presence with us here on Earth today, Annabell, I feel that I have to change my mind. Thank you!" and then Charlie sat down.

Nobody was still any the wiser as to who or what Annabell the Super woman was.

Next up was Fiona Brewster for the *New York World News.*

So far Annabell hadn't been asked to answer a single question! Fiona like Charlie had vast experience in the media world.

"Hello Annabell or, should I call you *Superbell*?" There was loud clapping in the hall.

"As you know, I've known you for a long time, in fact I was one of the journalists at the hospital the day you were born, we Americans have witnessed some unbelievable things you have done in the past but this time, Annabell, you have even surprised me. I would like to take this opportunity on behalf of all 1375 Americans that were on board that flight - including 76 American children, whose lives you have saved. No words can describe how we, Americans are feeling, we're so proud of you - I've only got one question. *Are you related to God*?" The room went very quiet. Before Annabell could answer the question which was ridiculous, of course.

The next person chosen to speak, stood up. His name was Neil Pepper. Neil was a portly man in his late fifties, he'd been chosen because he was Australia's

Prime Television News reporter, and was very well respected.

Everything had been going very well at the press conference but as usual there's always somebody who doesn't have the same thoughts as other people.

When Neil went to speak something seemed to happen to him. His face went bright red and he started nodding his head up and down and then from side to side. And then he started to glare at Annabell - it was a rather hideous and frightening glare. His eyes glazed over and turned red.

People in the room were looking at Neil and wondering what was wrong with him.

The Prime Minister, John Brown, asked him if there was anything wrong, He knew Neil Pepper very well but Neil didn't answer, he didn't even seem to realise that he had been spoken to. Then the Prime Minister asked him again. "Neil are you alright? Do you need attention?"

Suddenly Neil Pepper let loose. He sort of *growled,* then he yelled at Annabell. It was like he was in pain. **"YOU'RE NOT GOD! - GO ON TELL US - WHO YOU REALLY ARE?"** And then he turned to the people in the hall, most of them, he knew very well, some of them were his closest friends.

He screamed out. **"All of you are like me."** Everybody was baffled as to what he was talking about. They believed now that he was drunk. And then he turned his attention back to Annabell.

"You may fool them, but you don't fool me: GOD? That's a laugh." Then he began to laugh out loud. And then he shouted out "Look at the colour of her skin. Do you think God would have red skin? She's like a tomato!" And then he laughed again, but it was a hideous kind of laugh. "Maybe we should call her *Tomato bell?*" and then he laughed hysterically, but nobody else was laughing, everybody was stunned at what this man was saying.

The people in the room did not like what he was saying and they started *booing* him.

Suddenly the room erupted in uproar. People were screaming at him to shut-up. But he carried on giving Annabell verbal abuse, he was saying the most ridiculous and hurtful things to Annabell but she didn't say anything to him. She just looked at him and wondered what his problem was.

He was trying everything he could to insult her. He was a man clearly out-of-control of himself. It was like he was *possessed.*

Fiona Brewster and Pamela Jones were sitting on either side of him. They were telling him to shut up like the rest of the people but he wouldn't shut up. Suddenly Fiona saw the *red mist* (as they call it). She stood up and swung her handbag at Neil, hitting him on the back of his bald head! The force of the blow knocked his full set of upper false teeth out of his mouth. The false teeth slid across the wooden floor and embedded themselves in a leg of the front table.

Pamela Jones stood up and she started having a go at Neil. Both *(ladies?)* were swinging their handbags with all their might at Neil's head. Suddenly, Charlie Newman who was sitting in front of Neil Pepper threw a right hand punch, hitting Neil's nose with full force. Then other people started to join in the *fight.*

The press conference had turned into a brawl. Nearly everybody in the hall was shouting and yelling uncontrollably. And they were all trying to get their hands on Neil. These unbelievable scenes were being relayed around the world, this would be very embarrassing to the Australian nation.

Annabell was appalled by what she was seeing. She got up from her chair and yelled at the top of her voice. **"Stop that at once. How dare you?** Leave the man alone. He has the right to say what he feels without being attacked, you should all be ashamed of yourselves. Do not touch him again, do you hear me?"

Annabell was very angry. **"Prime Minister!."** she yelled. John Brown was sitting in his seat next to Annabell, he was shocked at what he was witnessing.

The Prime Minister of Great Britain was spellbound, and The President of the United States of America was flabbergasted.

"Prime Minister!" screamed Annabell. "Please put a stop to this immediately, what is wrong with these people?"

The Prime Minister, John Brown called the police.

Fiona Brewster and Pamela Jones were arrested and handcuffed - all the other people who had participated in the *fight* were also arrested and handcuffed and they were all frogmarched out of the hall into a waiting police vehicle and would now face charges of assault.

The police managed to regain law and order. Neil Pepper was lying on the ground. He had cuts to his face and his nose was bleeding and appeared to be broken. His lips were split and bleeding. He also had severe bruising to most of his body.

One of the policemen realised that Neil was in a bad way and asked if there was a doctor in the hall.

Annabell said that she would see to Neil. She got up from her seat and went over to him. She was very distraught. She was shaking her head in disbelief at what she had just witnessed. And she was muttering to herself "What is wrong with these people?"

She kneeled by his side. Neil was barely conscious.

"Do not be afraid," she said in a gentle voice. But Neil Pepper wasn't aware of Annabell. She ran her hand down and across his body. She didn't touch his body, her hand was about one-inch distance from it.

"I'm very sorry for what has happened," she muttered. "But these people don't seem to know what they're doing."

Within a few seconds all of Neil's injuries had healed. This brought a gasp from everybody in the room. They had witnessed yet another miracle from this remarkable woman. Annabell had the power of being able to heal, but she already knew that.

Neil got up to his feet, he was still a very angry man, he glared at Annabell again, and said. "You see, this is what people are really like everybody has wickedness within them, you just have to release it. They wanted to hurt me...and, what did I do wrong? Did my words hurt them that much? And it really wasn't anything to do with them."

Annabell had to agree with what Neil was saying.

"Who are you, sir?" asked Annabell in a gentle voice. "Why do you say such horrible things about me? Is it because of the colour of my skin? You likened me to a tomato, sir. That's not a very nice thing to say."

Neil Pepper raged at Annabell, "No, it's nothing to do with the colour of your skin, you ,silly woman. It's you! Everybody's afraid to ask you the question."

"What question is that, sir?" asked Annabell. She was puzzled.

"Well... who are you? You're not like us! You're obviously not human! that's for sure. Are you an *alien*?"

Annabell was taken back by Neil's statement - "You're not human...are you an alien?"

Annabell had never known what she was.

Neil Pepper was still a man on a mission. Annabell asked him again.

"Who are you, sir? Don't worry who I am. The question is who are you? I know that you're Neil Pepper, but who are you at this moment?"

"Who am I, madam?" he yelled. "You know who I am." All the time Neil was talking his face was contorting.

"I do?" replied Annabell. "But I don't."

"Yes, you do," replied Neil. "I'm *Iveld.* And I've come to warn you."

"Ah?..." muttered Annabell. She was very puzzled

"Who's Iveld? And why have you come to warn me? Warn me about what?" She didn't know the name Iveld.

As soon as Neil said the name Iveld his attitude seemed to change. He was suddenly in a state of unawareness. It was like something had been released from his soul, and his eyes turned back to normal.

"Who's Iveld?" asked Annabell. Neil didn't answer. So she repeated the question.

"Who's Iveld?"

"What...what?" stammered Neil.

"Iveld… Who is Iveld? Please tell me." Annabell was screwing up her face and giving one of those looks that only women can give.

"Come on, please tell me who Iveld is."

Neil shook his head, "Iveld? I don't know. Why would I know… Wait a minute."

He was slowly regaining his senses now. "What's going on here? Why have I got blood on my clothes? And why is everybody looking at me? And why are all these police here? Has something happened?"

Annabell looked at Neil. She was baffled herself as to what was going on with him.

"Have you lost your memory, sir?" asked Annabell, peering deep into his eyes trying to get a clue as to what had happened to him.

"No, I haven't lost my memory," replied Neil. "Why would you say that? I'm just about to ask you some questions, it's my turn. That's what I'm here for. Where's Fiona and Pamela? Where's everybody?"

It was clear that Neil had no idea of what he had said or what had happened to him. It was a total mystery as to why he had changed into another personality. There was no explanation for it at all. Neil seemed to spark off when Fiona asked Annabell if she was God.

Somebody then shouted out "Has anybody lost their teeth?" It was a man named Fred Grumble.

Fred was sixty-seven-year old man who worked at the town hall, had done for the last forty-one years. He was dressed in a smart council uniform with a simulated gold service medal attached to his lapel.

He should have retired two years ago but Fred thought that he was indispensable. The council didn't like to tell him that he wasn't, so they kept him on.

Fred was what is generally described as a *jobsworth*. He was a sort of security guard cum handy man. He had in his hand Neil's false teeth. Neil recognised the teeth as his. **"They're mine,"** Neil shouted out in embarrassment. "What are you doing with my teeth, Fred?"

"Oh, they're yours, are they, Neil?" and he handed them to him. "Watch out they don't bite you!" and then Fred gave out a little snigger of a laugh. It was clear that this man was not used to laughing but the teeth had found his little bit of sense of humour.

Neil wiped the teeth with a bit of tissue paper that he had in his pocket but it stuck to the teeth and made a right old mess. So he wiped them with his tie and cleaned them as best he could but when he put them back into his mouth, they wouldn't go in, he had teeth already in his mouth. "That's strange, I was sure they were mine," said Neil looking very surprised. "They look exactly like mine and I should know - I've had them for twenty years." Neil examined the teeth more closely. "Yes, they are mine!" he said with confidence. "But what would my teeth be doing out of my mouth? Fred, where did you get these teeth from, mate?"

"Oh, I found them over there on the floor. They were trying to eat the table leg," laughed Fred. It was the second time that Fred had laughed which was very unusual.

Neil put his fingers in his mouth to check his teeth and was shocked. His teeth now weren't *false*, they were real!

When Annabell had healed his wounds her powers had created Neil a new set of upper teeth. "What's going on here?" asked Neil. "How can I now have real teeth, when they were false when I put them in my mouth this morning? These teeth are definitely mine. This is madness. It's impossible. You can't grow new teeth at my age."

Annabell laughed. "You know what they say, sir - *don't look a gift horse in the mouth!*" And she burst out laughing. Everybody that was left in the hall burst out laughing, even Fred! This episode with the teeth had created a different atmosphere in the hall, it was now full of fun.

"What does that mean?" asked Neil. "Don't look a gift horse in the mouth?"

The Prime Minister of Great Britain butted in. His name was Anthony Stark-Raven. He was a rather arrogant sort of chap, well-bred aristocracy, and a horsy man.

"Um -I know what it m-eans." He seemed to extend his words as he spoke. "It um - m-eans um, if umm, someone gives you a g-ift - accept it thank-ful-ly, sir."

"What's my teeth got to do with horses?" asked Neil rather abruptly.

"Well, um - well - er - umm..." The British Minister thought for a moment and started fiddling with his tie "...um, well- well umm." He had a rather annoying stutter in his speech

"...Well - you can tell the a-ge of a horse by its te-eth - so -so- um... " and then he mumbled something that nobody was able to understand. "...so - er, um, the saying is- er, um- um sa-ying if a horse is giv-en to you as a g-ift - um, er- don't look in.. its mouth to see how old it is, because that would be classed as um, umm an in-sult, sir."

All the time he was speaking, he was fiddling with that tie, it was like a comfort thing to him, like a baby's dummy!

"Would it?" said Neil rather abruptly "Well I wouldn't want an old clapped out horse for a gift sir," said Neil in his broad Australian accent.

He then threw his false teeth in a waste bin that was close by. "These are no use to me now," he said looking at the British Prime Minister. "Maybe your old horse would like them, sir?" The British Prime Minister didn't respond. But Fred Grumble did, he marched over to the bin, took the teeth out of the bin. "You're not allowed to put teeth in there, sir. It's only for waste paper - it's more than my jobs-worth to allow you to put them in there. Cant you read, sir? *Paper!* That's what it says on the bin, sir. It doesn't say *teeth!* Do you want me to get the sack?" And then he handed them back to Neil with a frown on his face. Neil put the teeth in his pocket and moaned at Fred and gave him such a look of disapproval.

"Don't you look at me like that," said Fred. "I'll have you removed from these premises, sir, with any more of that sort of attitude, I'm only doing my job."

Annabell turned to Neil and asked him if he wanted to *press charges*.

"Charges? What charges?" Neil laughed. "What are you talking about? Why would I want to press charges against Fred? He's only doing his job, the silly old fool."

"That's enough of the 'old fool'," said Fred.

Annabell told him what had happened and then she asked the Prime Minister John Brown the names of the people who had been arrested.

He sent one of the policemen out to find out. A short while later the policeman came back with a list of names. And read them out to Neil.

"Oh, this is madness," said Neil. "For God's sake, let these people go, some of these people are my friends. I couldn't possibly charge them - I don't remember them doing anything to me. Please let them go at once. Of course, there will be no charges. How ridiculous!"

Annabell asked Neil if he remembered what he had said to her.

Neil said that he didn't.

A short while later all the people arrested were released and came back into the hall.

As they walked in they all gave Neil a *daggers* sort of look - Fiona and Pamela were both swinging their handbags like they had unfinished business and Charlie was practising fresh air punching.

They didn't know that Neil was alright now.

The Prime Minister John Brown asked Annabell if she would like to continue with the press conference. He said that under the circumstances maybe it would be in everybody's interest to end the meeting now.

Annabell said that she would like it to carry on. So the meeting continued.

Neil Pepper stood up to speak like nothing had ever happened - everybody held their breath. It was a tense moment in the hall. They all wondered what he was going to say. They didn't want a repeat performance. Neil got up and spoke, he had a slight lisp in his voice now, he hadn't got used to his *new teeth* yet.

They had no need to worry. Neil just said the same as the rest of the journalists.

All the dignitaries at the table then said their piece. It eventually came to the last speaker which, of course, would be Annabell herself.

She stood up and she looked at Fiona Brewster and said, "I don't think that I'm related to God, Fiona - I might be called a lot of things, but a relation of God is not one of them," and then she looked at Neil Pepper. She paused for a moment, "...I don't think that I'm an *alien,* Neil. But you never know. And my name is not *Tomato bell?*" and she laughed.

Neil Pepper looked puzzled. He obviously didn't know what she was talking about, and then she turned to Pamela Jones. "I like your handbag Pamela, but maybe you should use it as a handbag, girl!" This brought a laugh from the room.

And then she turned her attention to Charlie Newman. "Charlie have you ever thought about taking up Boxing, sir? You have a mean right hand!"

The people in the room laughed again. Everybody was now happy in this hall. And then the meeting came to an end.

Annabell had no idea what had caused Neil to go berserk. She didn't know who Iveld was. None of what happened in this hall this day made any sense. But there was a reason for it. Annabell had been taught a lesson, but she wouldn't find out what it was until nearly the end of this story. But it was something very alarming.

⋯⋯◆⋯⋯

Chapter Twenty One
The Search For Kevin

Annabell was invited to stay as a guest at Prime Minister John Brown's country residence.

Annabell told the Prime Minister that she was looking for a person named Kevin Zoolagong. She told him that she needed him in her quest to find the third piece of the Holism. It was absolutely vital that this person was located. She told him.

"Oh, don't worry about that," said the P.M. "That won't be a problem, anything for you my dear. I'll get one of my staff to search the birth registration files, it shouldn't be too difficult," he said confidently. "Zoolagong is not exactly a common name, it sounds aboriginal. We'll soon find him for you. Now you just sit back Annabell and relax while I'll sort this out for you."

The Prime Minister picked up the phone and asked someone on the other end of the line to look up the files to find a person named Kevin Zoolagong.

"There, that's done - shouldn't take long." said the Prime Minister. He sat back down in his chair.

Annabell was excited about meeting Kevin but wondered why he was so important. The parchment had said that *'without him'* she wouldn't be able to find the seed.

One hour passed and there was news about Kevin but it wasn't good. It appeared that no such person was living in Australia with that name and there was even worse news. There was not a single person even with the surname of Zoolagong in Australia.

"But there must be," said Annabell, despairingly

"Annabell there isn't. I can assure you, they tell me that they've triple checked."

Annabell read the parchment again, all the clues seem to point to Australia. Had the owl made a mistake? Maybe it wasn't Australia where Kevin was. She needed help. She was baffled as to what to do next.

Annabell asked the Prime Minister if he knew anybody who could help her solve the puzzle on the parchment. He told her that he knew the very man and to leave it to him.

A few hours later Annabell was introduced to a man named Phillip Manwannie.

Phillip was a very clever man. He had won a competition to find Australia's brainiest person - Phillip had won the competition very easily

He was a man in his early fifties, never been married, he'd always studied, it was like a compulsion to him, he felt that he had to learn more and more. Knowledge he felt was the reason for life.

When he was introduced to Annabell she thought that he was a rather scruffy looking man, his hair was long, grey and unkempt. His clothes were rather old fashioned, he had the appearance of what people would call a *vagrant* or a *hobo* if you're American but Phillip wasn't a vagrant, it was just that he didn't take any pride in his appearance. What he needed was a good woman! But he had no time for other people, his time was for his books. That was his love, his passion, his life.

Phillip was a happy man though and very friendly but a little bit eccentric. He was very well known in Australia and people accepted him the way that he was and they loved him for that.

"Hello, Annabell," were his first words to her, he held out his hand for her to shake. Annabell shook it and replied, "Hello."

"It's a pleasure to meet you Annabell, a mighty pleasure indeed," said Phillip.

"And it's a pleasure to meet you, Phillip," replied Annabell. "But can I have my hand back, please!"

Phillip was still shaking her hand, he couldn't let go of it. It was like he sensed something within Annabell.

"Oh, sorry," he said apologetically and reluctantly let her hand go.

"You know, Annabell …you're even more beautiful in real life if you don't mind me saying so?"

"Thank you Phillip," replied Annabell thinking that she couldn't return the compliment, because Phillip wasn't very good looking and she didn't know him anyway.

"Now then… what can I do for you, Annabell? The Prime Minister tells me that you have a problem that I may be able to sort out for you."

"Yes," said Annabell. "It's this Phillip." Annabell handed Phillip the parchment. "It's a sort of puzzle - the owl said it meant that I had to come to Australia to find a person named Kevin Zoolagong, but it appears that no such person by that name lives here… can you work it out, Phillip?"

Phillip thought for a moment. "An 'owl' told you?" Then he laughed. He was beginning to think that somebody was having a joke on him but he'd heard the stories about Annabell being able to talk to animals.

Although Phillip was the brainiest man in Australia, he looked completely baffled by the parchment. "I'm sorry Annabell, but I can't read the writing on this document, it's all in strange writing. This is a joke, isn't it?"

"No," replied Annabell. "No- it's not a joke, please don't think that. Oh, I'm so sorry! I forgot that nobody is able to read it."

"I thought you wanted me to decipher the writing," said Phillip. "I'm good at languages but I haven't a clue what this language is!"

"Well that's not surprising," replied Annabell with a grin on her face. "Nobody can read it Phillip, it's not any known Earth language. It's not from this world."

"Really?" replied Phillip looking very bewildered. "Well, who wrote it?" laughed Phillip. "Was it an alien, Annabell?"

"I don't know whether or not the creator is an 'alien' - Phillip. But the creator wrote this, sir."

Phillip shook his head. "No- no-no, I don't believe in God, Annabell. God is a fantasy."

Annabell shook her head. "No, sir. God is not a fantasy, and it's not a joke," she tutted. "Oh, how can I convince you that it's all real?"

Annabell had an idea. She called for the PM. "Sir, do you have any animals as pets?"

The Prime Minister said that he had a dog. "Can I see the dog, sir?"

He said that she could, but before he fetched the dog Annabell asked Phillip to think of some questions that he would like the dog to answer.

Phillip was very clever. He laughed. "Yeah, I have some questions.

Prime Minister can I see the dog's registration documents, please?"

The PM went out and brought back the dog and its registration documents. Phillip held the documents in his hand and read it. "Right then... Annabell...can you please ask the dog what time and date it was born and who was its mother and father?" Then Phillip laughed out loud. Annabell spoke to the dog and a few seconds later gave out the correct information that Phillip had asked. Phillip was of course flabbergasted. He knew that what he had asked Annabell she couldn't possibly have known.

"Sorry Annabell," said Phillip, "I should never have doubted you but I really thought that somebody was having a joke with me."

Phillip was clearly shocked and took a step backwards and combed his fingers through his grey hair. "Um, you said." and then he paused. "...Um... you said, that the writing is not *of this world,* Annabell... what world does it come from then?"

"I don't know, sir," she replied shaking her head. "I just know that it's true."

"But how do you know... who told you that?" Phillip was now becoming fascinated, this was learning far beyond his comprehension.

"The computer told me Phillip," replied Annabell.

"What computer?"

"The computer, *NOALL,* that knew virtually everything about the Earth - it had been working non-stop for well, years, and years, and years. The parchment was put into *NOALL,* but it blew itself up trying to find the answer to the questions. But it did find the answer before it - well, died! It said that the parchment was '*not of this world*'. I'm sorry for the computer. But I don't think that it was my fault, and the building where the computer lived burnt down Phillip!! I feel so bad about it but I wasn't to know what was going to happen, and poor Pamela was so shocked. I feel so guilty but I will put it all right when I can."

Phillip didn't really know what Annabell was on about.

"Can you read the writing on the parchment?" he asked her.

"Yes I can," Annabell answered proudly.

"How do you know that God, the creator, wrote the words on the parchment, Annabell?"

"Because, the magpie told me, and the professor told me that it was something *divine.* And the parchment is signed *the creator.* The creator is God, isn't he, Phillip? I have to find the seeds that created all life on Earth. The professor called them a *holism.* They're the seeds that created everything. But I believe that God created the seeds. The seeds exist, Phillip, that's a fact. I have two of them already and so do the devils exist... they're so evil. So the creator must exist: don't you think?"

Phillip had to nod his head in agreement. There were things happening here that was beyond his intellectual knowledge. He now believed that if there was no reasonable explanation for something that had actually happened there must be an unknown force to make it happen. Annabell's ability to be able to communicate with animals was not normal. He knew that she was clearly somebody very special and he felt privileged now that she had asked for his help.

Phillip asked Annabell exactly what it was that she wanted him to help her with.

"I have a puzzle for you, Phillip," she told him

"It has to be worked out - I have to know the answer. I really hope that you can work it out."

"Oh - I love puzzles," replied Phillip rubbing his hands together in anticipation of something that he would be interested in. "Please tell me the puzzle."

"Well it says in the parchment that I have to find a person named Kevin Zoolagong but to find him I *'have to go backwards before I can go forward'*. The owl that worked out the clues said that Kevin was here in Australia but according to the records he's not here. What do you make of that, Phillip?"

"Well that sounds interesting," replied Phillip pouting his thin lips. "But this is not a puzzle, Annabell, it's more of a riddle. Leave it with me for a while and I'll have a think about it." Phillip left the room to try and work out what the parchment was trying to tell Annabell.

Annabell was kind of confident that Phillip would work it out but when she thought back all of her help had come from animals. So she wasn't really that sure now.

Annabell sat down on a sofa and happened to notice a pile of old books that was on a table in the corner of the room, some were on fishing. The Prime Minister was a keen angler, Annabell wasn't the least bit interested in fishing but there was one book amongst them that caught her eye. It was a very old book titled, *The Lost Children of Nala- Seivad* - all its pages were brown with age. Time had not been kind to this book. It was a book that had been written over two hundred years ago. When Annabell picked the book up she sensed a strange feeling go through her.

She felt compelled to read the book. Annabell was able to read a book in a matter of seconds. She just flipped through the pages, just like publishers do when they're not really interested in somebody's story.

The book was about disasters that happened to the Earth and another planet in another solar system called Nala-Seivad sometime in the future.

When Annabell read it she was shocked to find her name mentioned in the book. She was referred to several times in the book by her name, Annabell. She knew that it was her because the author called her the '*red lady*' with the incredible powers.

Although the story was supposed to be fictional, Annabell knew by her instincts that the story was actually going to happen at some time. She couldn't understand this, because if this was true her task to save the Earth must have *failed!*

The devils were trying to destroy the Earth, that was a fact but she was confident of beating them which she had done so far. So why had she failed? She had to find out. The man who wrote that book had to be found. How could he have possibly known what was going to happen in the future, and how did he know about her?

Annabell thought that this man may know something about Kevin.

A couple of hours passed and Phillip came back into the room. Annabell was sitting on the sofa thinking about that book. It was worrying her.

Phillip had a broad grin on his face. "I think that I may have solved the riddle for you Annabell," he said confidently.

"Have you? Oh, that's great," she said with not much conviction. Her mind was on that book.

"What does it mean Phillip?" Annabell asked politely.

"Well it says that you have to go '*backwards*' before you can go '*forward*' to find Kevin. That can only mean one thing. If there's no such person alive now with that name and the owl was right that Kevin did live in Australia the only possible explanation is that the person once lived *back in time* ... To find him, Annabell, I believe that you have to go back in time. You have to look at the old records to see if this person existed in the past which is what the parchment is telling you to do.

If Kevin Zoolagong is registered in the past then that must be the answer and the riddle would have been solved."

Annabell was flabbergasted. "But how can that help, Phillip?" Annabell was touching her teeth with her fingers in thought.

"The parchment says I need to find him but what good is it… if he's *dead*? This is hopeless Phillip. This can't be right."

But she already knew that Phillip was right, the answers were in the past and the author of that book knew what the answers were.

Phillip held Annabell's hand to try and comfort her. "Believe me, Annabell, it's the only explanation. I'm sorry, but that's that answer to the riddle. I'm certain of it."

Annabell thanked Phillip for his help, but didn't really know what to do next.

The Prime Minister came back into the room and saw that Annabell had a frown on her face.

"What's the matter, Annabell?" asked the Prime Minister. "Wasn't Phillip able to work it out for you?"

"Yes he has worked it out for me, Prime Minister but I don't understand it…Phillip says that the person that I'm looking for may have lived in the past but he must be dead."

"Oh, dear," said the PM. "I can see your problem. Shall I check to see if Phillip was right?"

"Yes, you may as well, I suppose," sighed Annabell. She was very glum.

The records of births and deaths were checked again and sure enough Phillip was right. There was a person named Kevin Zoolagong who had lived in the past, but not much was known about him - all the records said was that he was found dead on the 14th of July 1999 and that it was believed that he may have been an illegal immigrant.

"I'm baffled Prime Minister," said Annabell. "What good is a dead man?... Why would I have to find a dead man?" Annabell had that old book on her mind and asked the PM if she could borrow it. He said that she could.

She didn't tell the Prime Minister why she was interested in the book.

Annabell spent the rest of the day thinking about it, but she couldn't come up with any answers as to how a person from over two hundred years ago could know about her.

That night when she went to bed her mind was still racing, trying to work out what it all meant. She was talking to herself. "You have to go backwards before you can go forward. Phillip said I have to go back in time. He was right but I have to really go back myself in time. But how do I do that? It's not possible to go back in time but I've got powers... I wonder if I've got such powers to be able to time travel? ... No, that's impossible... but nothing is impossible for me." Then she remembered that Bambalata had gone back millions of years to find Pete.

Suddenly Annabell realised something. "If he knew about me..." (that's the author of that book she's talking about) ...then he's seen me, I must have gone back in time." Annabell suddenly realised something, today's date was the 13th of July. It would be two hundred years tomorrow when Kevin was found. She wondered if she had done this.

Annabell was very excited. "I wonder how I did this?" she muttered to herself.

Annabell picked up that book. It had been signed so she knew that the author had been in personal contact with it, but it was a long time ago.

She opened the page with the signature on it and put it flat against her head, she hoped that this would act as a contact for her to get in touch with the author of the book - Alan Davies. Me!

She closed her eyes and went into deep concentration. She didn't realise just how powerful she was. At the precise time that she was trying to get in contact with me, I was out fishing in England. I was at that moment getting under a live cattle wire fence so that I could get to the river.

Annabell's power was immense. I felt her power and accidentally touched my head on the live wire fence - an electrical current went through my brain, killing me instantly. At this moment a clone of me was created. Myself and the clone were teleported to Australia in the year 2222 next to a river. The police and ambulances were called and both bodies were taken to hospital, where they were put into the morgue.

Only Annabell would be able to bring me back to life. My clone had never been alive.

Annabell had to find the bodies. She shouted out in frustration. "Creator, you've got to help me, I don't know what to do. Please! Please! help me, I have to I find Alan Davies, but I don't know how to do it. I know he's here in Australia but I don't know where." Annabell could sense what she had done.

Suddenly a bright light flashed in the room, it was like a bolt of lightning but it was just for a split second. Annabell found herself now no longer in her bedroom. She was now in a morgue and she was standing next to two dead bodies that were lying on slabs with white sheets covering them.

She knew that the people were dead because they had tags attached to their toes that were sticking out from the bottom of the sheets. Annabell had no idea if the people were male or female but a hairy arm was dangling out of a sheet indicating that one must be a man, or a very hairy woman! She read the tag attached to his toe - she really didn't want to do this but she knew that she had to.

She read the name on the tag. It was the author of that book - Alan Davies. The very person that she was looking for. She read the file that had his name on it. It read:

Name: Alan Davies

Cause of death : Electrocuted.

Cause of accident: unknown.

Nationality: English

Annabell read the toe tag from the other body and she smiled. She had found Kevin Zoolagong. She removed the sheet from the face of the other body - she could instantly see that it was a clone of me. Annabell now realised what it had all been about. She read his file. It read:

Name: Kevin. Zoolagong: (not real name)

Somebody had noted this was an unknown person and a name had been made up for him. He was found by a person named Kevin, and he was found next to the river Zoolagong so they called him Kevin Zoolagong.

Cause of death: Unknown

Age: Unknown

Country of birth: Unknown.

Annabell realised that no such person as Kevin Zoolagong had *ever* existed. She had created Kevin without realising it. She had incredible powers but they were a bit erratic sometimes. She had no idea that she had the power of telekinesis.

Annabell now knew that she had gone back in time and had found the person that she was looking for but this person would always be a mystery, nobody would ever know anything at all about him.

Annabell had no idea why this person was so important if he had never really existed, but she knew that she had to bring him to life. But first she brought the other dead person back to life. Me! She knew it was very important that I lived. It was only right for her to do this, because she was responsible for my death. But obviously she didn't mean to kill me.

Annabell placed her hands on Kevin's forehead so that all her fingers were in contact with it. Her powers instantly activated his brain and Kevin shuddered but his heart wasn't working yet. So he wasn't alive, Annabell was working on instinct. She had already brought me back to life. I didn't know that I had been dead!

I was watching everything that Annabell was doing. It was fascinating. I later wrote an account of what I had witnessed in the book *The Lost Children of Nala - Seivad.*

She put her hand on Kevin's heart. His body shuddered violently, it was like Kevin had been touched by one of those electrical heart revivers that the hospitals use to stimulate somebody's heart after it had stopped.

Kevin's heart started beating and the ghostly white appearance of his face slowly changed to a reddish brown colour. Kevin was now alive but he couldn't stay where he was and he needed some sort of memory - Kevin was just really a *blank!!*

Annabell created a memory of some sorts for him and she had implanted some part of my thoughts into Kevin's mind - she had to try and find out how or why I wrote that book. Annabell waved her hands over Kevin like she was performing a magic trick and then she touched him with her fingers. This worked because Kevin suddenly disappeared into thin air.

Annabell searched my brain to try and find out why and how I had written that book. She couldn't find the answer. What Annabell didn't know was when she sent me back, I touched my head on that wire fence again trying to get back. This time I was just stunned, this gave a chance for the devil to implant the story into my brain. The devil was trying to unnerve Annabell and he'd succeeded. Because Annabell was baffled! She couldn't see the date the day the book was published because it was so dilapidated. It was published three years after their encounter.

Annabell sent me back. I found myself back to where I had come from, still lying on the river bank with my fishing rod in my hand but with lots of stories in my head. But not the story, The Lost Children of Nala- Seivad.

That would come a few minutes later.

Annabell was now alone. She shouted out, "Creator what do I do now?"

Suddenly there was a bright flash of light. Annabell found herself back in her bedroom at the Prime Minister's house. The time was still 11.58pm. It was like time had stood still.

Annabell wasn't too sure what had just happened. She didn't know if it was real what she had just done. Had she brought Kevin to life? It was all very strange. She went back to bed but her sleep wasn't sleep as we know it. Annabell didn't get physically tired but she got mentally tired. She had to rest her brain.

She was woken the next morning at 9:am by somebody knocking on her bedroom door.

"**ANNABELL -ANNABELL,**" somebody was shouting outside her door. "**WAKE UP -WAKE UP...** there's good news."

Annabell got out of her bed and opened the door. It was the Prime Minister.

"What is it? You seem anxious, sir. Has something happened?"

The Prime Minister was standing there shaking his head. "I really don't know how it could have happened, Annabell, but Kevin Zoolagong has been found. You won't believe this, but I've just been informed that there is in fact a person of that name. He appeared at a police station, not far from here early this morning. He walked into the police station wearing no clothes." Annabell laughed.

"The police recognised that name and informed us this morning. Kevin has spent the night in police custody, because apart from his name he doesn't know anything about himself, and he's not registered in this country as being a national. It's a bit of a mystery, Annabell, I can tell you. I'm so sorry, I didn't mean to mislead you."

"Not to worry, no harm done, I thank you for your help, sir."

Annabell felt very guilty, because she knew that she was responsible for Kevin being alive now but she couldn't really tell anybody, because she knew that they would never understand. She wasn't sure if she understood it herself. But she was happy that she had fulfilled her task of finding Kevin. She knew that she still had a lot to do in Australia, and she didn't know what to expect from the devil seed, Elvid, whom she would have to encounter. She had no idea where the third piece of the holism was.

⚬═❮◆❯═⚬

Chapter Twenty two
Meeting Kevin

Several hours had passed since the revelation that Kevin existed - it was now early afternoon. Annabell was having lunch with the Prime Minister and his wife, Helen when there was a knock on the dining room door.

The Prime Minister was just about to put a forkful of peas into his mouth when a voice outside the door said: "Sorry to disturb you, sir, but there's a person here that you wanted us to bring to you - you said that I was to tell you the minute that he was here ... well he's here. It's Kevin Zoolagong."

The Prime Minister gave out a yell - his peas went all over the table! But he didn't care about that. "Did you hear that, Annabell? They've found your man for you."

Annabell's skin got goose pimples. She was so nervous but also very excited, although she was responsible for his very being, she had no idea what he was really like.

"Is it alright, sir..." said a voice from outside the door. "...if I let him come to the dining room? Or shall I make him wait in the lobby?"

"No, - no send him here straight away," said the Prime Minister scooping up the loose peas that were all across the dining table with a spoon.

A few moments later there was a knock on the door. "He's here, sir," said a voice.

"Please come in," said the Prime Minister excitedly.

Kevin entered the room - Annabell's sparkling eyes lit up like a beacon, when she saw him.

Kevin was a rather handsome man. He had long, black, curly hair, beautiful sparkling blue eyes and he had a small snub nose similar to Annabell's nose. He was fairly tall, about six feet, and he was very muscular. Kevin had a very strange skin colour. It wasn't brown and it wasn't red but it was something in between.

Kevin had gone through a remarkable transformation in his appearance since Annabell had seen him last night.

Annabell couldn't take her eyes off him. It was crystal clear that she fancied him from the very moment that he walked into the room.

Kevin looked at Annabell, and he couldn't take his eyes off her.

"I don't mean to be rude," he said, his accent was that of an Englishman. "But what on earth are you?" He was referring to Annabell. "My, you're a strange one but you're so beautiful." Although Annabell was famous throughout the world Kevin didn't know who she was.

Kevin spoke to the Prime Minister. "Um, sir. I'm sorry but who are you? … and why have I been brought here? And who is this strange but beautiful lady? And I'm sorry, madam, I don't know you either." He was looking at Helen. The Prime Minister's wife.

"Please sit down over there," said the Prime Minister pointing to a blue and gold upholstered chair that was next to Annabell. "All will be explained to you."

Annabell's sparkling blue eyes, sparkled even brighter when Kevin sat down beside her.

"Would you like to have lunch with us Kevin?" asked the Prime Minister.

Kevin said that he would but Kevin had never eaten anything before. He didn't even know what food was!

The Prime Minister stood up from the table. "First things first. I would like to introduce you to this wonderful lady: this is Annabell. Kevin… I'm sure that you must already know her, everybody in the world knows this lady."

Kevin looked puzzled. "Do they? Well I don't, sir."

The Prime Minister was a bit taken back, he didn't expect that. He thought that Kevin was joking though.

"Really? Well, you must know me? I'm your Prime Minister, Kevin."

"Prime Minister?.. Sorry, sir, but I don't know you," replied Kevin looking very puzzled.

"Oh," he replied, "this is all very odd…umm…Where do you come from Kevin? Wasn't you born here in Australia? It's rather strange that you have an English accent."

Kevin thought for a moment. "Um… er…umm - born?" Kevin didn't know what this word meant.

He was getting into trouble here and Annabell knew it. She had to step in and save Kevin from himself his brain memory wasn't up to much yet. Annabell needed to do some more work on him and pretty quickly.

"Prime Minister, Kevin doesn't come from this country he was born in England, I think?" Annabell wasn't sure what she was talking about, she didn't really know how Kevin was here. But she knew that she hadn't put enough knowledge into Kevin's brain.

"Can I have a moment with him in private please? There's something that I need to personally ask Kevin." She looked sheepishly at the Prime Minister.

"Yes, of course you can," said the PM. "Come on, Helen, we need to give Annabell a bit of privacy."

They both got up from the table to leave the dining room. "Please let me know when you want us to return," said the Prime Minister thoughtfully.

"Yes I will, sir," said Annabell, "thank you."

"Oh, dear Kevin, what are we to do with you?" said Annabell peering into Kevin's blue eyes.

"What?" he replied. "What do you mean?"

Annabell held his hand like she was holding a child's hand. "What are you doing?" asked Kevin.

"Nothing!" replied Annabell "I'm just going to put some sense into you. Please come with me." She led him away like a child!

Annabell took Kevin to the Prime Minister's study - there were hundreds of books in there. Annabell touched Kevin's head and made him un-aware of anything.

She then transferred as many books from her brain into his as she could. She flicked through the pages and then touched the centre of his forehead with her finger transferring the contents of the book into his brain instantly. She picked out book after book from the shelves on any subject including the Prime Minister's favourite subject *Fishing.*

Kevin would now have a reasonable intelligence to be able to have a conversation without embarrassing himself. The Prime Minister had several books that she had written, so she implanted them into his mind so that at least he would know who she was. She also put *The Lost Children of Nala-Seivad* into Kevin's mind. In a short space of time Annabell had transferred vast knowledge into his brain. She knew that when she brought him back to awareness he wouldn't be the same person.

She touched his head with her finger, Kevin was now aware again.

"Hello Annabell," he said cheerfully. "What are you doing here with me?"

"I'm having dinner with you, Kevin, don't you remember? We're having dinner with the Prime Minister and his wife Helen."

"Oh yeah, I remember now," he said rubbing his forehead, he had a red mark where Annabell had been constantly touching it. And he had lost his English accent.

"I hope the Prime Minister likes Fishing?" said Kevin

"Well he does," said Annabell, "so you're in luck."

They returned back to the dining room. Annabell pressed a button that was on the wall. This was used to summon one of the Prime Minister's aides. A smartly dressed man came into the room. "Can I help you madam?" he asked politely.

"Yes, you can," said Annabell. "Can you please tell the Prime Minister that we're back at the dining room."

The man left and shortly afterwards the Prime Minister and his wife came back into the room. The dinner was now cold so a fresh menu was ordered.

"Right let's start again," said the Prime Minister. "This lady is Annabell, Kevin."

"Yes I know who she is, sir," said Kevin looking puzzled.

"Oh," said the PM. "I thought that you said that you didn't know who she was."

"I was only joking," said Kevin with a smile

"Do you know who I am, Kevin?"

"Yes sir, you're the Prime Minister of Australia and I understand that you like fishing. I'm a keen angler." (That wasn't really true. Kevin had never been fishing in his life but he had a lot of fishing knowledge implanted in his brain).

The Prime Minister's eyes lit up. "Really, what type of angling do you do Kevin?"

"All types sir. Anything you like. I'm a master angler, you know."

"Really, Kevin? You're that good then, are you? Well, we'll have to have a competition between me and you - I rarely get beat you know. I'm a fair angler myself. Maybe after lunch I'll show you photos of my catches."

"Yeah, but I bet they let you win, sir. You being so important and all that. I wouldn't do that. I wouldn't let you win."

The Prime Minister's face dropped. "No .. no, surely they wouldn't do that. I win fair and square, Kevin." He was a little bit annoyed by Kevin's statement.

"Right then young man," said the Prime Minister. "Me, and you are going to have to have a match."

Annabell was getting fed up with this conversation and tried to divert the chatter back to something she wanted to talk about. But Helen intervened.

Nobody had mentioned the strange marks that were on Kevin's forehead., and that Kevin's accent had mysteriously changed into an Australian accent.

"Kevin what are those marks on your head are they tattoos? They look like finger prints. I know that you, young people, like to decorate your skin but they're rather unusual. And how come you've changed your accent? You have an Australian accent now, whereas before you had a English accent? "

"No ma'am they're not tattoos they're birth marks, I was born with them. And I don't know what you mean by changing accents, I've always talked the same way."

The Prime Minister's wife was a bit embarrassed and wished that she hadn't asked the questions now.

"Oh, I'm really sorry Kevin I didn't mean to offend you," she said looking perplexed.

"Oh, not to worry ma'am," said Kevin. "I rather like them really, and I suppose they do look like finger prints." (Kevin had seen the marks in a mirror and guessed that they were birth marks)

"Well, that's fascinating isn't it? And they are very unusual birth marks," said Helen trying to save face.

Annabell sat there with a smirk on her face, she knew exactly what those marks were. They were her finger prints!

All through the conversations Annabell was holding Kevin's hand affectionately but she finally had to let it go.

"Is your meal alright, Kevin? And happy birthday for yesterday," said Helen.

"It's the best meal that I've ever had, ma'am," said Kevin crunching his teeth on something hard. "And I didn't know it was my birthday ma'am? But thank you anyway."

(It wasn't Kevin's birthday yesterday - Helen had been told that Kevin had arrived at the police station wearing his birthday suit!!)

Kevin was eyeing Annabell up and down.

"Alright Kevin, what is it?" said Annabell sharply. "Why are you looking at me like that?"

"I don't know," said Kevin. "But I get the strangest feeling that we've met before, but I can't for the life of me remember where. Have we met before, Annabell?"

Annabell didn't answer immediately, she was thinking about last night and then she blurted out by mistake.

"Yes, we have met before…" then she stopped, she'd realised what she had just said.

"Where?" said Kevin

"Last night," said Annabell

The Prime Minister butted in. "It couldn't have been last night, Annabell, we didn't know that Kevin existed until this morning."

"Oh!" said Annabell. "It must have been in my dreams then!!" And then she laughed.

They all finished their meals and the Prime Minister stood up and said: "We'll leave you two alone now. I'm sure you've got lots of questions that you would like to ask Kevin and I'm sure Kevin is bursting to know why he's been brought here."

"You can say that again, sir," said Kevin. "And don't forget our fishing match, sir."

"No I won't," said the Prime Minister. "You can rest assured of that, Kevin. Letting me win, umm," he muttered to himself as he left the room with Helen.

The two of them were now alone.

Annabell was very curious to know more about the person that she had created. There was something that she needed to find out. Was Kevin really an accident or was he supposed to be here? He was personally mentioned in the parchment and she knew that she had to find him so it couldn't have been an accident, it was all supposed to happen.

(Me touching my head on that live wire was supposed to happen. This created the connection between myself and Annabell).

"I must ask you something, Kevin. Do you have a hand print where your heart is?"

Kevin looked at her in disbelief. "How would you know that?" he said, shocked.

Annabell answered, "Because I do Kevin." She repeated, "Because I do."

"You're very odd, Annabell, you know that?" and then Kevin repeated, "Very odd."

"Yes I know that I'm 'odd' Kevin, but I am what I am, and you are what you are."

"But what am I, Annabell?" He had feelings that something wasn't right.

"I don't know, Kevin. I don't know who you are, or why you're here, but there is a reason for you. but what it is I don't know, I was hoping that you may know. Do you have anything in your mind Kevin - that you can't understand?" Annabell was trying to find out what Kevin knew about his being.

Kevin shook his head indicating that he didn't know what she was talking about.

He turned to her and said "Wow! look at those eyes, they look like stars... wonderful!...beautiful!... you look like an angel, Annabell ... I think that you're an angel."

Suddenly Kevin shuddered. "What's wrong Kevin?" Annabell was very concerned.

"I've just had these thoughts come into my mind. I've seen my father, I think? He was lying in a very cold place and he had the same marks on his head as mine and he had a hand print like mine on his heart but then he disappeared. Was that real, Annabell?"

"Why are you asking me, Kevin?" But Annabell knew what Kevin was saying was true.

"I don't know - I just feel that you know...you do know... don't you, Annabell? What is that story *The Lost Children of Nala -Seivad* about Annabell?"

Annabell sighed, "I don't know Kevin I was hoping that you would know. It's very worrying to me. The person who wrote it knew about me, but I didn't tell him that story. If I didn't tell him - who did? Because his story is..." Annabell stopped "... I believe his story is going to come true Kevin! And I have to try and stop it from happening."

Annabel had to tell Kevin the truth. "I've been sent to find you, Kevin. The parchment said that I had to. You have been chosen - I need your help."

"Help to do what? I don't know what you're talking about, Annabell, and what's this about a parchment?"

"You've been chosen, Kevin and I don't know why. I receive parchments and your name was on one."

"You're talking in riddles, Annabell - you say that I've been 'chosen' but you don't know why - how can that make any sense?"

I really don't know, Kevin," replied Annabell, nodding her head.

"Chosen?...chosen for what? Who chose me?" asked Kevin intrigued.

"The creator!!" replied Annabell.

Kevin took a deep breath and laughed. "The creator? Who is the creator?"

"I think that it's God, Kevin."

"No- no -no this is silly Annabell. Why do you think that's it's God? What would *Yahweh* want with me? I'm not anybody special."

"What did you say? Kevin, who is Yahweh?"

"I don't know, the word just came into my mind."

"Ah!" muttered Annabell and then she took the parchment from her pocket and showed Kevin - "Look!" she said.

"It says that I have to find a person named Kevin Zoolagong and that if I don't, I won't be able to fulfil my task."

"Show me that," said Kevin, quite sternly. He pulled the parchment from her hand and appeared to read it.

"You can't read that!" said Annabell. "Why are you pretending to read it? I'm the only person on this earth who can read it - it's not of this world Kevin."

"Who said so?" said Kevin rather sarcastically. "And I can read it, Sheila - so there."

Annabell was really taken back by Kevin's revelation that he could read the parchment. But could he really read it? Or was he just pretending. She had to find out.

"Ok, Kevin read it out loud, what does it say?" Annabell pointed to her ear. "Come on, let me hear you read it. And don't call me *Sheila*, my name is Annabell."

"Alright, I'll read it for you. I don't know why you don't believe me."

Kevin was able to read it. Annabell was shocked. Kevin was obviously somebody very special. He was reading something *not of this world*. Maybe Kevin was not of this world either, she thought or maybe Annabell had somehow transferred the language into Kevin's mind. She wasn't sure.

"Kevin do you know who your mother and father are, or were?"

"Um-er-um." Kevin thought for a moment. But no answer came from his mouth.

"You don't know, do you?" she knew that he wouldn't.

Kevin admitted that he didn't know.

"But I must have a mother and father - everybody has," said Kevin, "...everybody does." He looked despondent.

"Can you remember anything about yourself, Kevin?" Annabell was nibbling on her finger nail, in her mind the questions were lining up.

Kevin thought for several moments. "No, I can't Annabell. What's going on?"

"When were you born, Kevin?"

"Um...let's see...um... so I was born in...um... I don't know!! But Helen said it was my birthday yesterday so I was born on yesterday's date."

Kevin was happy with this statement.

"Yes, but what was yesterday's date and what year is this, Kevin?"

Kevin shook his head - "I don't know Annabell. What year is it now?"

"It's 2222."

"Oh!" replied Kevin, "You know, Annabell I don't -I don't - I don't. I don't know anything. I don't seem to have any memory about myself but I know a lot about other things. I know the Prime Minister, Helen, and

I know you. I must have lost my memory somehow. Have I been in an accident?"

"No, Kevin you haven't," said Annabell feeling very sad for him, she didn't know whether to tell him the truth about himself or not - How do you tell somebody that they're not a *real person*? Annabell thought that she shouldn't tell him.

Chapter Twenty Three
The Outback

Now that Annabell had found Kevin she could continue her task of trying to find the third part of the holism. The seed that had created all plant life.

The Prime Minister said that he would give her all the help that she needed.

Transport in the way of a robust land vehicle was provided along with tents, pots and pans, and everything that was needed to survive in the outback. This trip was not going to be easy, the outback can be a very dangerous place.

The following day Annabell and Kevin left the Prime Minister's residence and headed for the bush. Kevin drove the vehicle. The Prime Minister had fast tracked Kevin and Annabell to get their driving licences, because they never had a licence to drive.

Kevin was also allowed to become an Australian National.

Kevin was remarkably a good driver considering that he had never driven before. Annabell had put into his mind a book on advanced driving. She wasn't going to take any chances.

They drove all through the day. Kevin never stopped asking Annabell questions he wanted to know about himself but Annabell didn't tell him anything. Which annoyed him.

They reached the edge of the outback just as it was about to get dark. It was too late to go into the dense bush so they camped for the night.

Kevin had no idea why they were going to the bush. She hadn't told him - she just said that she wanted to go there. They pitched their camp, they had separate tents - it was just as well because Kevin could snore for the world!

In the morning over the camp fire Kevin asked where she was going.

"Into there! Kevin," she replied, pointing to the bush.

"But why do you want to go in there?" asked Kevin.

"I'm looking for something that's very important, I'm looking for a seed, Kevin."

Kevin laughed out loud and then he rolled around the ground in uncontrollable hysterics. This lasted for several minutes. Annabell just stood there thinking what a fool he looked.

"Have you finished?" she asked sarcastically.

"You're looking for a seed in the outback?... Are you mad, Annabell? The outback must have *billions* if not *trillions* of seeds - *a needle in a haystack* comes to mind. Please tell me how you're going to find a single seed?"

"I'm not!! You're going to find it for me Kevin," said Annabell pouting her lips.

Kevin laughed. "Am I? And how, pray tell me, am I going to do that?"

"I don't know, Kevin but I think that you can. The parchment said that I have to find you and if I don't I won't be able to fulfil my task. So you must know where it is."

"Well I don't," said Kevin. "How would I know? Anyway what sort of seed is it? And what does it look like?"

Annabell revealed her necklace that contained the two seeds that she had already and showed Kevin. "The seed that I'm looking for Kevin will look like these. But it won't be glowing - it will just be a drab grey colour."

"Wow! Why do they glow? They don't look like seeds."

"I don't know why they glow but they give me powers, Kevin - I activated them - they only work for me."

Annabell explained to Kevin what the seeds were.

Kevin was slowly beginning to remember parts of Annabell's past that she had implanted into his brain. He had all the knowledge of her adventures but his brain was new and it was sometimes slow to activate the information.

"They look like jewels, Annabell. They're made of metal, aren't they?"

"I don't know what they're made of Kevin, but I know that they're indestructible. My Pa tried to destroy one, and he failed."

"But how can metal be a seed? How would it grow?" Kevin was baffled.

"I don't know, Kevin all I know is that I've got to find it but there are dangers here. There's a devil plant here somewhere that I have to destroy - if I don't, it could mean the end of the Earth - Kevin. So this is a very dangerous thing that I'm asking you to do. I can't ask you whether you want to do it, because you have to, Kevin. I'm sorry about that."

"But the outback is huge, Annabell, how am I supposed to find a small seed? There's no real point in trying, is there? We might as well go home." Annabell frowned at him.

"Kevin, you're not listening. It's a matter of life or death for this planet. We have to find it. If we don't everything will die."

"Oh, dear," he sighed. "God help us because we're going to need some help."

"I'm sure that he will, Kevin. Now come on let's get going we haven't got all day! Oh, I mustn't say that - that's what Polp used to say."

Off they set, there were sort of tracks that led into the bush. The soil was like rust and the truck kicked up a vast dust cloud as it made its way deeper and deeper into the unknown.

Annabell had no idea where she was going she just let Kevin drive where he wanted. The parchment always told her to *follow the signs*. But what were the signs? - she couldn't see any.

They drove for a week and were getting deeper and deeper inside a dangerous place. All the time it was getting harder to drive as the tracks became narrower and bush, denser. It was obvious that not many people ventured this far into the bush.

Kevin was getting more and more agitated and several times an hour he told Annabell that it was a waste of time. But she turned a deaf ear to his moaning. She knew that Kevin was here for a reason and was confident that he would lead her to the seed.

They drove on for three more days until finally the track ran out - it appeared that nobody ever went beyond this point. This was the end of the road, and it was in the middle of nowhere. It felt like the end of the Earth to Annabell.

"Right, this is it," said Kevin. "As far as I'm going. No point in going on, end of the road! - end of the line for me. That's it! - No more!- Finished!"

Annabell didn't take any notice of him. "We're not turning back, Kevin so you might as well shut up, make yourself useful and unload the gear out of the truck, we'll have to walk from here."

"Oh, no!" said Kevin, "women drive me crazy! This is madness beyond anything that I have ever known."

"Well, you don't know much, Kevin, take it from me. Come on, we haven't got all day. Oh, I mustn't say that - get the gear out."

This was a very dangerous place to be if you didn't understand the bush but Kevin although he didn't know it yet was an expert on the bush. Annabell had seen to it that she wasn't taking any chances. She wondered what she would encounter when she met up with the devil Elvid - she knew that wherever the seed was so would be Elvid. That's what the parchment had told her.

They were now two weeks into the trip and were slowly trekking their way through the dense scrubland. Annabell had enormous strength and carried most of the equipment. It didn't really look right for a woman to be carrying this load but Annabell was no ordinary woman, she was physically stronger than Kevin.

All their food was now gone they would have to rely on Kevin's expertise of surviving in the bush, eating bush tucker, meaning grubs! And other not very nice things.

On the sixteenth day they made their camp, they were well into the bush now but they still hadn't seen any signs, but something strange was happening.

Kevin not once had asked where they were going, he seemed to know without realising it. Annabell didn't say anything to him, she just let him get on with it.

They pitched their tents. Annabell put a woman's touch around the camp while Kevin was the hunter gatherer!! Went out searching for their dinner. Annabell wasn't really happy about eating this kind of food. She'd been in this position before when she was younger. With that bird/reptile thing! Bambalata. But she knew that if she didn't eat she would get moody, and there was already signs of this.

Annabell was invincible as long as she was wearing her necklace with the parts of the holism. She didn't complain so much now about the food that she knew that she would have to eat. She knew that this was the way of the bush, and she had to put up with it.

That night when Annabell was resting her brain she was woken by noises outside her tent. It was pitch black outside but she could see. She was amazed at what she saw and couldn't believe her eyes. The trees and plants were moving about like people. It was like a Saturday afternoon shopping trip in town. The whole bush was a mass of activity.

"What on earth is going on here?" she muttered to herself. "I've never seen plants walking before!!"

An old tree about 30ft tall with a crooked trunk came stomping along. "I say - I say, tree, can I have a word with you please?" said Annabell politely.

"Yes, of course you can." replied the tree. "What can I do for you?" In a rather gruff voice. "You'll have to hurry, because I haven't got much time. Now then, I don't want to be rude but what do you want?"

"What are you all doing moving about, tree? It's rather unusual, plants and trees don't usually have a walk about."

"I'm moving home," said the old tree.

"Moving home! Trees don't move home - they stay where their seed is rooted *forever!* What are you talking about 'moving home'? I've never heard of such a stupid thing. This is ridiculous."

"I don't want to rude," said the tree "But are you deaf or something? I told you that I was moving home and that's what I'm doing."

"Umm, you're a bit grumpy, tree, there's no need to be rude. You said that you didn't want to be rude but you are," said Annabell kicking the ground.

"Well, why don't you listen? I've got every right to be rude and grumpy." said the old tree. "You would be grumpy if you were *forced* from your home after having lived there for the last 200 years - I thought that I'd see my days out there but oh, no there's always something to upset you, isn't there?"

"What's wrong tree? Why do you have to leave your home?" Annabell was intrigued.

"Haven't you heard?" moaned the tree.

"Heard what?"

"We're all being forced out by some nasty piece of work, it's an interloper; doesn't belong here but it's taken over our land."

"What's taken over your land?" asks Annabell bemused.

"I don't know what it calls itself but it's the devil's work - it's nasty. *Chokes* everything in its path, it strangles! And if it catches you, you're dead! Exterminated! It grows so fast, it's spreading like wild fire and those are two words that I don't like. We've all been on the move for months now. None of us can settle anywhere; we're running or should I say walking for our lives. Oh, I'm so tired. I shouldn't be doing this at my age, I don't know how much longer

I can keep going. I can only travel at night and I have to get my roots back into the ground before the sun comes up otherwise that would be the end of me. I'm getting so weak. Oh, what a life - maybe I'd be better off dead! It's only a matter of time anyway - we're all doomed! Sorry but I can't stop and talk to you any longer, time is life, you know."

The old tree stomped off moaning and groaning to itself as it stomped.

Kevin was snoring away in his tent and was unaware of what was going on outside.

Annabell went back to bed and fell fast *abrainsleep.* (That's not a word but it applies to Annabell).

In the morning she was woken up by Kevin. "Sleep well?" asked Kevin rubbing the sleep from his eyes.

"No! I didn't," moaned Annabell. "The trees and bushes were moving about last night. They woke me up, there's something very odd going on here in this bush."

Kevin laughed his head off. "Have you been drinking Annabell?"

"I don't drink alcohol, Kevin. I tell you the trees and plants were moving about, and I don't tell lies."

"Well it's all quiet now," said Kevin, still laughing.

Annabell looked outside the tent. When they made camp last night there was a big tree no more that 20ft away from their camp but it wasn't there now. Surely Kevin would notice that?

"Kevin, where's that tree gone that was over there?" Annabell pointed her finger to the spot.

"I don't remember a tree," said Kevin.

"You must do, you had a *pee* behind it!! Oh dear," moaned Annabell "How can you not notice that where once was a tree, there is no longer a tree. Can you not see a big hole where the tree stood, Kevin - have you not noticed that the bush is all different this morning?" Annabell spoke very quickly.

"No!" replied Kevin.

"A tree told me, Kevin, that he was being forced away from his home by some sort of plant. He called it a *'devil plant'* and he said that it strangles and chokes everything in its path and that it grew so fast. This sounds like it could be Elvid. The parchment said that Elvid will be where *'only it can live in its soil'.* It's Elvid, Kevin. I know it is. You've guided me straight to it. You knew where it was all the time, didn't you?"

"But I didn't," insisted Kevin. "I swear, I didn't know, Annabell."

"What did you say? 'Not in a billion or a trillion chance of finding the seed'. Where Elvid is, will also be the seed, Kevin. You've beaten the odds of a trillion to one. How did you do that?"

Kevin shook his head. "I really don't know, Annabell - I'm baffled, maybe it was luck?"

"No, Kevin 'luck' had no part of it. You guided me straight to it. You must have been here before."

But Annabell knew that this couldn't be true, it wasn't possible but some sort of miracle must have happened for Kevin to have guided her here, without him being aware that he was doing it. This certainly was a mystery.

They broke camp. Annabell was eager to be on her way, she knew that she was close to finding the third piece of the holism, and Elvid.

As they moved through the bush it was becoming sparse. This was a very strange sight. Most of the plants had gone. It was like a barren land now. It was obvious that everything had been moving away from something. Some plants hadn't made their roots back in the ground in time and had died, and were shrivelled up, and there were a few old trees that were now fallen and dying. Annabell felt very sad at the sight of them she wondered if they had just given up.

The old bent over tree that she had spoken to during the night had said that the devil plant grew rapidly so she knew that it couldn't be that far from here. They walked all through that day but they didn't see any sign of Elvid.

Annabell didn't know what Elvid looked like. Some bushes and trees were still living, these were the very old and sick ones who couldn't move very fast, so Elvid hadn't been this way yet. It was getting dark again so they decided to make camp for the night.

The darkness soon came and the bushes and trees were on the move again. Kevin witnessed it this time.

Suddenly Annabell could hear the noise of something big approaching she wondered if this was Elvid. Annabell and Kevin huddled together, or should I say? Kevin huddled Annabell.

A few minutes later two huge trees came ambling along. They were interconnected, branch in branch. Annabell thought that maybe they were husband and wife. They were both very wrinkly and withered looking, and looked very old. And they moved very slowly.

"Excuse me sir, sorry for troubling you. I know that you're in a hurry but I need to ask you a question that is very important to me," Annabell spoke sincerely.

"And what might that question be young lady?" said the old tree in a very kind and gentle voice. "I'm sorry but we have to keep on moving – can't stop! I don't know where we're going to go, though."

"That's alright, I understand," said Annabell. Politely.

She walked by the side of the two old trees. "Is this your wife sir?" asked Annabell.

"Yes she is, this is my good lady Mildred, and my name is Cyril. You know I'm 250 years old, the same age as Mildred and who might you be? We don't see many of your kind around here. I know that you're human but I didn't know that humans were able to talk to us trees, it's a first for me. You're a funny looking though, but you're very beautiful. Are you another species of human?"

"No, sir. Well I don't think so. My name is Annabell, and I'm quite famous."

"Oh, yeah. We've heard of you alright. Mildred, this is the famous Annabell. Well, that explains your funny appearance. We've heard that you're *special.* Have you come to help us? There's something very nasty not far behind us - have you heard about it?"

"Yes I have," said Annabell. "And I promise you, sir, that I will do everything within my powers to stop it; whatever it is. I think that it's a devil seed, sir. Sent to destroy your kind and the earth - I need to ask you a question, Cyril."

"Anything for you, Annabell, my dear," said the old tree. His roots were scraping along the ground. Annabell wondered how the trees managed to move, it was a strange sight. The roots seemed to be able to wave about like snakes (like sidewinder snakes).

Annabell showed the old tree the parts of the holism that she already had.

"Have you ever heard of any stories about an object like these? There's a piece like these somewhere very near here I think, and I have to find it."

The old tree looked at it. "What are they? They're very beautiful."

"They're seeds, sir. One created all water life, and one created all land life on the Earth. I'm now seeking the seed that created all plant life, it's what made you, and all the plants on earth at the beginning of time, sir. And it is very near here."

"I'm sorry," said the old tree, "but I haven't seen anything like that. I wish that I could help but I can't. Do you know anything, Mildred?" "Have you ever seen one of those things around here?"

"No, I haven't seen one, Cyril, but there was a story that I heard years and years ago when I was very young - let me think - umm, it was a long time ago, my memory is not so good these days. Now what was it? It was a rather strange story - that's why I never forgot it."

"Well you've forgotten it now," butted in Cyril.

"Oh, be quiet dear, I haven't forgotten - it just takes me longer to recall it. I remember it now. There was a very old tree that used to live here... What was his name ?...I think it was Roger, or Dodger? But his name doesn't matter. He's long gone now. Do you remember him, Cyril? He was a grumpy old tree, just like you !! He used to tell a story to us younger trees. He told you as well about something that his father had told him. The story had been passed down for millions of years," so he said.

Annabell was all ears. "What was the story Mildred?" asked Annabell. She was like a child waiting for her mother to tell her a bedtime fairy tale.

"Well, he said that there was something in the bush that made plants grow, it created new species every year. Hundreds of new plants and trees were born to the earth - the plants created flowers and the flowers became seeds. Birds and other creatures sometimes ate the seeds but when they go to the toilet they released the seeds to another place so life for that plant would start somewhere else, it could be anywhere in the world. Isn't that fantastic? The old tree said that every time a new plant was created it would glow with all the colours of the rainbow for one day only. But one day the new created plant didn't glow and it withered and died and never again was there another plant created."

Annabell was excited by this story. The creator had told her that evolution on Earth had ceased that's why he wanted the seeds back. So this story made sense.

"Do you know where this spot was where the plants were *created*, Mildred?"

"No I don't know where it is but there's a dead spot here somewhere where nothing will grow. Roger or

Dodger, the deceased tree said that it was here that the plants were created. All that I know is that the dead spot is said to be shaped like a *diamond*."

"What are you babbling on about – you, silly old goat?" said Cyril. "Yes I do remember that story. But it's nonsense, Mildred. Don't take any notice of her, Annabell. It's an old *wives tale* as you humans say. I think that she's going senile believing a story like that … it's ridiculous. Come on, Mildred, we have to get a move on. That *thing* is after us. I really hope that you can save us Annabell."

"So do I," said Annabell. "You go carefully now."

With that the two old trees started moving just a little bit quicker. The old man tree, Cyril, seemed to change his branches like he was holding onto to Mildred's shoulder.

Annabell looked at Kevin and screwed her face up. "What do you think of that, Kevin - do you think that there's anything to Mildred's story?"

"If you want my opinion, Annabell, I think she's a twig short of a branch," and then he laughed out loud.

"Oh, you're so funny, Kevin, be serious for a minute, this could be important. Mildred said that the plant glowed like a rainbow. Well, these seeds that I have glow like a rainbow. It must be the holism, Kevin. What else could it be? It's all starting to fit together – 'follow the signs'. These are the signs, Kevin."

They had their supper by the camp fire. Kevin had caught a bird of some kind. It wasn't hard to catch, though, because the bird had a broken wing and was hopping around the ground in a lot of discomfort. Kevin did the poor unfortunate creature a favour by putting it out of its misery. It wasn't wasted. Nothing in the bush ever is. It made an excellent meal, even Annabell didn't complain about her dinner like she usually did. Annabell could complain for the world!! But tonight she was quiet. She had been fed so she wasn't moody.

There weren't many trees or plant life moving about now. The bush was becoming very eerie. It was so quiet, like nothing was living. They finished their meal and went to bed, they had already decided to make an early start the next morning.

As soon as it was light, they were up and ready for the day. Annabell knew that this was likely to be the day when she would have to face the devil seed, Elvid. She hoped that she would be strong enough.

"I must find that diamond shaped land where nothing will grow," she said to Kevin.

"I have to leave you for a while, Kevin. I'm going to use my powers of flight to see if I can locate it. I don't think that we have much time." Kevin was saddened by this comment.

Annabell flew high into the sky and she flew around and around for over an hour and then she came back.

"Well," said Kevin, "did you find it?"

"No," she replied. "But about two miles ahead there's something very strange, there's a huge patch of land that is covered by just one species of plant. It's a beautiful plant, it's not very big - it can't be Elvid, surely? It has beautiful red and blue flowers - it's a gorgeous plant but I don't know what species it is. Come on Kevin, let's go and see what it is."

Annabell was eager to see what this plant was. It certainly was prolific and it was odd that there was nothing else growing in that area but that plant. The riddle said that *only it can live in its soil.*

They left their camp as it was, and just packed their cooking equipment, and a few other essential items, like water. And then they trundled further on into the bush, it was easy to get through now because there wasn't a single living plant in sight and it was very quiet, there weren't even the sounds of any birds or animals.

They walked for a couple of hours, they were getting very close to where Annabell had seen that plant. Suddenly Annabell moaned of something, it was her usual moan.

"I'm needing food, Kevin. We haven't had anything to eat today."

"That's because we haven't got anything, Annabell," said Kevin. "We ate all the food last night."

"Well, go and find us something then, you're the man, it's your job," moaned Annabell.

Annabell was very bossy towards Kevin but he didn't seem to mind. He knew that when she started to moan, it was best to say nothing.

"Oh, all right, I'll see what I can find," said Kevin. "But I don't think that there's much food around here."

"Well hurry up," said Annabell grumpily, "I need food."

Kevin was gone for about half an hour. In the meantime Annabell got out the primus stove and the pots and pans in anticipation of Kevin finding something nice to eat.

Kevin returned. "I hope that you've found something really nice to eat, Kevin? It better not be those big white grubs. I don't want to be eating grubs, and I'm not eating anything that hasn't been cooked."

Kevin laughed and put his hand into his pocket and produced some huge *white grubs.*

"Oh, no," tutted Annabell, "not again! Isn't there anything but grubs to eat in this bush?"

"What's the matter with you, Annabell? You're always moaning and groaning," said Kevin.

"I don't moan unless I have to eat, Kevin. That's my one weakness."

"These grubs are really tasty, they're a well-known bush food, you've had them before. I remember your story about Bambalata. That was funny, and you don't have to cook these bugs, everybody likes them, they're full of protein. And anyway, that's all that I could find. Right here we go. Hold out your hand. One for you - one for me - one for you - one for me -one for you- one for me. Oh, there's a spare one."

"You have it, Kevin," said Annabell, "I'm not bothered."

"No, no, no," said Kevin, "we share everything equally."

He then bit the head off of the spare grub, all its bodily juices splattered over Annabell's face and then he handed the rest of the unfortunate creature's lower half of its body to Annabell. "Here, this is your bit."

"UGH!" shrieked Annabell. "That's horrible!"

"No it ain't," said Kevin. "It's delicious!" He was chewing on it, like he was eating a piece of the finest steak.

"UGH!" said Annabell again. She was not having the same experience as him. She *chucked* her half of the poor unfortunate grub as far away from her as possible which was a considerable distance. Instantly a rat came from nowhere and grabbed hold of the headless bug!

"Quick!" said Kevin, excitedly. "There's a bush rat … I'll see if I can catch it, that would make a good meal."

Kevin went running after it like a man possessed but the rat was too quick for him. It dived down a hole and was gone. "Oh, blast! It's got away," moaned Kevin. He was very disappointed.

But Annabell wasn't, she was very relieved. This left Annabell, though, with three whole bugs that were wriggling in her hand.

"I'm sorry Kevin - I've had enough of these bugs, I'm not going to eat them - I'm going to let them go."

"Well, you'll have to get moody then," said Kevin quite sternly. "You have to eat this food, Annabell, it's the way of the bush, if you're hungry you eat what's there."

She took one last look at the grubs that were in her hands, closed her eyes and picked one up and bit into the juicy part of its body, there was no way that she was going to eat its head!!

She started stamping up and down and was yelling at the top of her voice.

Kevin was really laughing at her antics. "Oh, you're such a big baby, Annabell, that wasn't so bad was it?"

"Yes it was!" she yelled and she gulped the grub down. "Ugh!...it's horrible ...it's the way that they wriggle and they stare at you with those beady eyes."

Annabell shook her head. "Like you do when you've eaten something that you really didn't want to. Ugh!" she moaned.

"Come on Annabell, eat up your dinner like a good girl," laughed Kevin.

Annabell reluctantly ate the last two grubs but left their heads - it was like eating prawns.

"Did you enjoy those?" laughed Kevin.

A loud "NO!!" came her reply. "Ugh! I would have rather eaten the rat - I think. Maybe not, and they didn't fill me up - I'm still moody - is there anything else to eat in this bush besides grubs?"

Chapter Twenty Four
Gone Fishing

Kevin thought for a moment. "Yes there is, do you like fish? I should have thought of that before - there's fish here, Annabell."

"What sort of fish are you talking about Kevin - I don't see the sea anywhere around here?"

"Well, you'll have to wait and see, won't you?" said Kevin mysteriously.

Kevin took something out of his pocket. "I'll see if I can catch you something out of that stream that we passed earlier."

"How are you going to do that?" asked Annabell. "Are you going to catch them with your hands? Fish are very slippery creatures you know. I really don't think that you'll be able to catch them with your hands, Kevin, whatever fish they are."

"Yes I know that," said Kevin. "But I'm not going to catch them with my hands, Annabell, I've got fishing line and hooks, all that I need now is a pole, any old piece of branch will do as long as it's about 8ft long and bendy. There's an old tree over there that's fallen, I'll see if I can find a nice branch off it."

Kevin went over to have a look. He came back with a piece of a branch that had all its shrivelled leaves still attached.

"I'll just have to trim off these bits." He had a knife in his hand which made him look very menacing. He trimmed off the branch until it was smooth as a baby's bottom.

"That's it, perfect!" said Kevin, pleased with his work. "I'll just tie the line onto the end of the pole and tie a hook onto the end."

Kevin connected the line to the pole and the hook to the line.

"That's great! That should do the job," Kevin tested the strength of the pole by holding the line and pulling it against the pole. The pole bent nearly in double, this was the indication that it was a pretty perfect pole for fishing.

"We're ready now, come on Annabell, let's go and find that stream."

Annabell for this moment in time had put finding the holism and the devil seed out of her mind. Her moodiness for food had overridden her mission.

They walked back from where they had come. It was about a ten-minute walk back to the stream - the stream was about 10ft wide and pretty shallow but on the bends it was deeper. There would normally be plenty of plant life around the banks of the water but there was virtually nothing.

"This is where I'm going to fish, Annabell," said Kevin getting pretty excited. It was like he was about to have a fishing competition.

"Fish like deep holes. This is where they hide. Fish are pretty crafty and cunning... you have to be quite skilful to be able to catch them, and as you know, I'm a bit of an expert."

Annabell was a little bit puzzled. "What do fish eat, Kevin... hooks?"

"Don't be so stupid, Annabell - why would a fish eat a piece of metal?"

But then Kevin thought for a moment. The fishing knowledge that Annabell had put into his mind started to kick in. "Well yes, they do eat metal sometimes. Well, they don't actually eat metal but they get fooled into believing that the metal is a real fish. They call them lures, and you spin with them but we won't be using them today - I'm going to be using worms. Have you been fishing before, Annabell?"

"No I haven't, but my Pa goes fishing - we have a river on our land that's full of trout. Is that what we're going to catch today, Kevin...trout?"

"No, there's no trout in here, Annabell. As far as I know there's only one species of fish that live in these streams."

"And what might that be, Kevin?"

"Well wait and see - I may not catch one - but if I do - I know they're pretty tasty fish to eat so we may be having a real good bit of tucker for our lunch."

"But you're going to have to be quiet, Annabell... We're near the water's edge now - you have to be stealthy when you go fishing."

Kevin's mind was relating to the books. He really didn't have a clue about fishing. It was all in his mind.

Kevin had dug up some worms for bait before they reached the stream.

The stream was now about 30ft away. "We have to crawl to the water's edge from here, Annabell."

Annabell looked at him like he was loony. "You've got to be joking...I'm certainly not getting on my hands and knees," she blurted out.

"But you have to, Annabell, it's part of fishing; you won't catch anything unless you're really quiet - so if you want to eat tonight, come on, get on your hands and knees, we've got some crawling to do."

Annabell reluctantly got on her hands and knees and crawled behind him.

It had rained during the night, and it was quite muddy. The mud was getting all over her face and her clothes. Annabell was not amused. "Is this really necessary, Kevin?" she moaned.

"Shut up Annabell! Do you want to eat or not?" said Kevin with stern authority.

"You have to be very quiet when you go fishing, Annabell; if the fish see you they'll be off like a shot and I won't catch anything. And I don't want that to happen, I'm hungry as well, you know."

Annabell put her tongue out to Kevin in a gesture of defiance of his orders.

"We're here, now be very quiet, Annabell," whispered Kevin. "Shush!"

He gently baited up the hook with the biggest worm that he had caught and lowered the creature gently into the crystal clear water. The worm wriggled as it felt the cold water and it slowly sank out of sight. The water was about 6ft deep here. Kevin was right, the bends were considerably deeper than the rest of the river. Kevin placed the pole gently on the bank, and let go of it.

"How do you know when you've got a fish, Kevin?" asked Annabell.

"Will you be quiet for a minute?" said Kevin. "Can't you see I'm trying to concentrate."

"Sorry, I asked," said Annabell. "But it's a sensible question, isn't it?"

"Yeah, I suppose it is," said Kevin. "Well, you wait for the fish to pull the top of the pole. If the pole tip moves then something has got hold of the worm and it will try and move off with it - this will bend the top of the pole." Kevin was well pleased with his fishing knowledge and felt very manly.

"That sounds very exciting," whispered Annabell. "When will that be then, Kevin?"

"Well how would I know? I don't even know if there's a fish here," said Kevin abruptly

They both sat there in the mud. Annabell dared not make a sound, there was absolute silence now.

Annabell's thoughts were on her possible fish lunch.

Ten minutes passed and nothing had happened. This was proving too much for Annabell. and she broke the silence.

"Oh, this is really boring Kevin...Why is fishing so boring?.. What's the point of sitting here doing nothing? There's no fish here ... let's try another spot."

"Will you shut up, Annabell? ...Can I please have a day off from your moaning?" moaned Kevin!! "Fishing requires patience, fish don't just jump on your hook, you know...there's a lot of skill involved."

"SKILL?" laughed Annabell "What, sitting on your bum doing nothing! Where's the skill in that?"

"Shush!" moaned Kevin. "Be quiet, will you."

Kevin picked up the pole and brought the worm to the surface and then he lowered the pole letting the worm slowly sink back to the bottom of the river, and now he started *jerking* the worm - just little jerks. He was trying to entice a fish to take the bait.

Five more minutes went by and still no fish. Annabell was quick to say something.

"I told you that there was no fish down there, woman's intuition you know. Why don't you admit it; you've failed, you're not such a good fisherman as you think you are?"

Just a second after Annabell's rant - the pole tip gave a little pull.

"Shut up Annabell, I think I've got a bite," said Kevin excitedly.

"Well, catch it!" screamed Annabell.

"No, I've got to wait for the bite to develop into a stronger pull. You have to give the fish time to get the worm into its mouth."

A few seconds later there was another pull on the tip of the pole but it wasn't enough to catch the fish. Although Kevin nearly *struck*. (That's the term fishermen use when they pull the pole to try and hook the fish). Kevin was on edge now. He took a deep breath, his hands were shaking.

Annabell was also quiet now, her eyes were fixed on the pole tip.

She whispered to Kevin, "What sort of fish is it, Kevin?"

"I don't know. It might not be a fish, it might be a crayfish."

"Well, that would be alright, it's a fish," said Annabell

"A crayfish is not a fish Annabell … it's a crustacean, but we could still eat it."

Then there was another pull - this time it was a strong pull, in fact, it was so strong the pole started being pulled along the bank - whatever had grabbed the worm was *big!*

"KEVIN! - KEVIN! " yelled Annabell, "Pull it quick!"

Kevin got up from the ground and dived on the pole just before it was going to be pulled into the river.

The pole *bent* right over. Kevin screamed, "Annabell WOW! this *is huge!* I don't think that I can hold it !!" The pole was now taking on an alarming bend, Kevin dug his heels into the soil trying to get more grip on his footing. But it didn't help, he was being pulled by the fish down the slippery bank. The fish was leading Kevin - like he was a dog on a lead.

"What is it?" yelled Annabell.

"I don't know," yelled Kevin. "But it's the biggest fish that I've ever hooked."

Well it would be because, this was the first fish that Kevin had ever hooked.

"Don't lose it Kevin," shrieked Annabell.

"I'm trying my hardest," yelled Kevin, who was still running along the bank with the fish towing him along. Suddenly the fish stopped, it had reached shallow water - it was only inches deep in this spot so the fish went back up the stream from where it had come.

"My arms are really aching, Annabell... I don't think that I'll be able to hold onto this fish for much longer. It's too big," moaned Kevin in despair.

"Don't give up now, Kevin," yelled Annabell in encouragement. Annabell was thinking about her fish supper.

"No, I won't give up but I think this fish will break my line or my pole."

The fish ran up the river, straight past where it had been hooked until it reached more shallows - it then turned back round and swam back down the river. Kevin was exhausted now and could hardly get his breath but luckily for Kevin the fish was also tiring - its runs weren't so fast now. The fish and Kevin had reached the end of their tether. The fish now was no longer moving but was sulking on the bottom.

Kevin pulled as hard as he dare to try and get the fish to come to the surface. The pole and its line were at its maximum limit. This was now going to be the fight to the finish. "It's me or him," shouted Kevin in desperation.

Kevin kept the strain on the fish, slowly it began to rise to the surface. Annabell was getting very excited.

"Kevin it's coming, you've nearly beaten it," she yelled.

Kevin was perspiring profusely due to the mighty fight this fish had put up. Suddenly the fish appeared on the surface, there was an almighty swirl as the fish revealed itself.

Annabell screamed. "It's a snake Kevin!! Get rid it of it quickly - I hate snakes!"

Annabell cowered backwards and fell over onto her bum! Annabell was now covered head to foot with mud, her skin no longer looked red, she was now brown looking!

"It's not a snake," shouted Kevin. "It's an eel, and it's huge! It must be over 5lbs. WOW!! This will make a lovely meal for us. These are good fish to eat…. Oh, what a treat! This is what I was hoping to catch."

But just as Kevin said that, the fish pulled again and it took Kevin by surprise, he went sliding down the slippery bank and fell *head first* into the cold water. Luckily for him, it wasn't that deep, it only came up to his waist! The pole was on the surface of the water, but was being pulled downstream by the fish.

Kevin half swam and half walked and managed with some difficulty to grab hold of the pole. Annabell was in fits of hysterics!

"Oh, no you don't," said Kevin "You're not getting away from me now, oh no, not now." Kevin pulled the eel back to him, it was getting very tired now and not fighting so much.

"Annabell!" screamed Kevin. "Come on, give me a hand. I need to get out of this water. I won't be able to land this fish unless I get out."

"Well I couldn't care less," screamed Annabell. "Look at the mess I'm in now Kevin… and it's all your fault. This fishing is rubbish, all that you get is filthy dirty."

Annabell who had massive strength, reluctantly grabbed hold of Kevin's hand, but her strength meant nothing on the slippery bank. She slid down and went feet first into the river to join Kevin, and the eel.

"Oh, Kevin look what you've made me do - I'm soaking wet now. Let the snake go and get me out of here. I've had enough of this."

"You're stronger than me," Kevin informed Annabell. "You'll have to get me out, and I'll tell you something, I'm not letting go of this fish. Oh, no, no way."

Annabell grabbed Kevin's hand as she flew out of the water. "Hold on tightly," she yelled.

She pulled Kevin out of the water but he still had hold of the pole.

Annabell, Kevin and the eel were now dangling in mid-air with water dripping off all three of them.

Annabell gently lowered down the fish onto the bank but she was not so gentle with Kevin, he landed with a bump! and then she flew away.

"Come back here, Annabell," shouted Kevin. "Where are you going? Come and have a look at this beauty."

Annabell reluctantly came back but she didn't think that the eel was a *"beauty"* - she thought that it was rather ugly. She'd seen an eel before of course, but that was a Conger eel, and it was a lot bigger than Kevin's eel, his eel did look like a snake.

The eel was lying on the bank exhausted, its mouth was opening and closing rapidly.

Kevin, with shaking hands, got the hook out of the eel's mouth.

The eel was free now, it seemed to know, and it made a dash to try and get back to the water. It wriggled along the bank, just like a snake.

Kevin ran after it and made a dive. He managed to catch it, just inches away from the water edge but the fish was very slippery. Kevin kind of scooped the fish with his hands away from the water, so that it was now facing inland. He grabbed hold of it again but it slipped out of his hands and was now heading in the direction of Annabell.

Annabell screamed, "Get that snake away from me, Kevin."

Kevin tried to grab it but every time he had hold of it - it slipped out of his hands, like a bar of soap. The eel was being *tossed* in the air like it was being *juggled!* After about ten attempts, the Eel finally gave in and remained still. Kevin now had it in his hands securely and was holding it like a baby!

"It's alright, Annabell. I've got it now. You're safe!" he told her convincingly.

"Are you sure?" said Annabell. "That's a horrible thing."

"No it's not, it's a beauty," said Kevin proudly. "It's the most beautiful thing that I've ever seen… well apart from you that's it." And then Kevin gave the fish a kiss.

Annabell was a bit taken back by Kevin's statement, he had said that she was *beautiful,* but then he kissed the fish he had never kissed her!

"Your catch is not beautiful Kevin, it's just a slimy snake and why have you kissed that thing? Do you want to marry it or something?"

Suddenly the eel spoke. "I'm not a 'slimy snake' I'm an eel, if you don't mind, and please tell this person to put me down," said the eel angrily. "I don't fancy him at all, and please tell him to refrain from kissing me again."

Annabell looked at the eel and laughed.

"Tell this person to put me back into the water at once or I'll bite him! -I have teeth you know." The eel was obviously not happy.

Kevin could sense that Annabell was concentrating on the eel but he didn't know that the eel was talking to her.

"Kevin, the eel said that he doesn't *'fancy you,'*" and she laughed out loud! "And he said that you are to put him back immediately."

"Well, he can't go back," said Kevin. "I caught it fair and square, it belongs to me."

"Why have you pulled me out of the water?" moaned the eel. "That's my home, I've been living there for over ten years, nobody even knew that I was there - what do you want?"

"We want to eat you," said Annabell rather brutally. "Well, not me ...him!!" pointing to Kevin. "He wants to eat you but I wouldn't want to eat you. I wouldn't eat a snake. I'm sorry to be the one to tell you eel, but you're to be his lunch."

"Eat me?" said the eel shaking in fear. "He ain't going to eat me ...tell him if he tries to hurt me, I'll bite his finger off... tell him to clear off."

"But you ate his worm," said Annabell. "The worm was your dinner and now you're Kevin's dinner - that's fair. Isn't it?"

"Well, when you put it like that, I suppose it is but who eats you?"

Annabell thought for a moment.

"Well, um, Lions. Tigers... er...Crocodiles. And I'm sure that there are lots other things. But they can't eat me, they can eat Kevin."

"Oh, how I wish that there was a Crocodile around here right now to eat him," said the eel.

"I don't want to be his dinner, is there anything that I can do to save my life?"

Kevin was standing there in amazement at Annabell having a conversation with a fish, obviously he didn't know what the fish was saying to her but he had a rough idea.

Annabell thought about the eel's pleas.

"Eel. There is one thing that I would like to ask you. Do you happen to know the whereabouts of a place that is shaped like a diamond where nothing will grow?"

The eel thought for a while. "Um...yes...yeah.. I think that I do know of such a place. As you know I've been in this river for over ten years every now and again especially when the river floods I go on a swim about. There is a place about one mile from here that is really scary. It's a lake and it is shaped a bit like a diamond - nothing will grow in it, the water in the lake is very black and dead. Maybe that's the place that you're asking about? But I wouldn't go there if I were you, it's very frightening place, whatever goes in there may never come back."

"That's interesting," said Annabell. "But how do I find this lake, eel?"

"You have to follow the river until you come to two dead trees that have crossed themselves to form the letter X - there's a tributary here. You can't see it... but it's there. The tributary flows into the diamond shaped lake. But I must warn you there's something really horrible at the lake."

"What?" Annabell was all ears, this was sounding like what she was looking for.

"It's some nasty plant and it's heading this way, all the other trees and plants have moved away from it."

"Yeah I know," said Annabell. "What is this plant, eel?"

"I don't know, it just started growing, but it grows so fast, it smothers everything, it's completely surrounded the lake so that nothing will grow only itself."

"How do you know this, eel? How would I know that you're not just making this up to try and save your life?"

"No, I'm not making it up; honest, I'm not - I've seen the lake."

"You've seen it? Well, how did you see it and get back? You said that whatever goes there never comes back. But if you've been there - how did you come back?"

"I have been there, and I have seen something, and it was very frightening…I'm lucky to be alive," said the eel shivering with fear.

"Tell me eel, this plant that keeps the lake hidden, does it have flowers?"

"Yes," said the eel. "It does, it has blue and red flowers, but the flowers are not so sweet."

Annabell's eyes lit up, this is what she was waiting to hear. *Follow the signs?* The parchment said the Elvid's flowers *were not so sweet,* the eel had just said the same thing. She now knew for definite that the eel was telling the truth.

"Please tell me what happened when you went to the lake, eel. It's very important."

"Well..." said the eel. And then it shuddered in a manner like it didn't really want to tell its story. "....the river was high, so I decided to have a swim about, I made my way downstream. I always knew about the two crossed trees, and I've never liked the look of them. I had no idea that there was a tributary behind them. I always swim on the opposite bank to avoid them, those two old trees frightened me. You never know what might be lurking behind them. Anyway on this day the current was so strong that it swept me towards the trees. Suddenly I felt myself being sucked. The two trees must hide the flow to the tributary but on this day they weren't able to hold the volume of extra water so the river started to flow towards the trees at a rapid rate. I was pulled under the trees, and down the tributary. I wasn't able to fight the current and was dragged right down it.

"Eventually the current stopped and I found myself in pitch black darkness, as dark as I've ever known - it took me a while to adjust to the darkness but when I finally did, I found myself in a lake that had been completely covered over by a plant - it was a bit like being inside a tent..." (Annabell didn't ask the eel how it knew about tents) "....I thought that maybe this was not so bad a place after all, there could be some good food here. Well that's what I thought but no matter how long and hard I searched there was no food here at all. I swam around hugging the bank for safety, after a while I realised that it was a strange shape like a diamond. I was in the lake for a whole week. I couldn't find a way out. "On the first day something very strange happened. I could see a rat that was scurrying around on the bank, it was a really big rat, it may have been washed down like me in the floods...well I was watching it from underneath the water when all of a sudden the rat dropped down dead!! Just like that, and for no reason that I could see. I thought that I'd take a closer look to see if I could find out what had happened to it.

"So I rose to the surface very cautiously and there it was, the rat - stone dead! lying on the lake shore. Suddenly I was aware of something hitting the water very close to me. There was a noise like it was raining. I could hear swooshing noises. I soon realised that it wasn't rain but spikes!! And they were being fired at me!! But there was nobody there firing them!! I tell you, I was so I frightened. I quickly went back to the bottom of the lake my old heart was thumping I can tell you."

"So what do you think was happening eel?" asked Annabell with great interest.

"I'm not sure," said the eel. "But it must have something to do with that nasty plant, it couldn't have been anything else."

"Why did you say, that the plant's flowers are not so sweet?" Annabell was very eager to know the answer to this question.

"Well," said the eel, "strangely something shot out of the flowers with a horrible head and it only appeared when the rat appeared. I swear that it wasn't part of the plant before that. The plant just had blue and red flowers but when that thing appeared the rat died."

Annabell was shocked. "What do you mean? Do you think that there was something hiding in the flowers that killed the rat, eel?"

"Yes I do," replied the eel. "It couldn't have been anything else. Well I say that but there was something else there at the lake, but it was in the water."

"What... what was it, eel?" spluttered Annabell.

"I don't really know but whatever it was - it was huge! I really didn't see it that well."

"But how do you know that there was something in the water if you didn't really see it?" asked Annabell.

"Because..." the eel paused and gulped in a large breath of air.

"Oh, I'm sorry eel..," said Annabell. "My apologies, you're in need of some water, you're a fish. All fish need water."

"No, no, it's alright," said the eel. "I can go without water for a long time. I'm alright to carry on now... well, as I was saying, believe it or not, the plant picked up the dead rat somehow, maybe with its roots? and threw or should I say, hurled it into the water."

"Really?" said Annabell.

"Yes, really. The rat was floating on the surface for only a few seconds when suddenly I got the shock of my life. A huge creature swirled on the surface and ate the rat in one gulp."

"What was it, eel?" screamed Annabell.

"I don't know," said the eel taking in another gulp of air.

"But whatever it was, flashed like gold lightning, and looked like a dinosaur."

"No, eel there's definitely no dinosaurs around here, I can assure you of that - it wasn't a dinosaur. Maybe a bolt of lightning hit the water?"

"No, it wasn't that," said the eel. "It was definitely a gold dinosaur."

Annabell was puzzled by the eel's story of the giant creature that flashed like gold lightning and that it looked like a dinosaur, and that a plant seemingly was feeding it. This sounded too incredible to be true but Annabell did believe the eel.

Her thoughts were on the parchment, it said that *Elvid guarded a croc of gold.* The eel had mentioned gold so Annabell thought that this must be a sign.

"How did you get out of the lake, eel?"

"Well, the river finally went back to its normal level, the current down the tributary eased off. I slowly made my way up it - it was very difficult but I'm used to being able to handle most currents. I can also crawl parts of the way on land but I didn't dare go on the land for fear of that plant. I eventually reached the two crossed trees and managed to escape. I would never go anywhere near that place again. If you're thinking of going there, well don't. You can let him go, though," meaning Kevin.

"Eel, when did all this happen?"

"Um, er- um, about three or four weeks ago. We had a lot of rain at the time, that's why the ground is so muddy," said the eel.

Annabell turned to Kevin, she had heard enough and believed the eel. "Let the eel go."

"No I won't," said Kevin defiantly. "It's the biggest one that I've ever caught, and I'm hungry and it will make a lovely meal."

"Put it back Kevin, this minute, do you hear me? The eel has been very helpful. Let it go." Annabell was very insistent.

Kevin moaned and groaned, but he didn't dare argue with her, she was already grumpy and he didn't want to make her any worse. So he reluctantly went to the water's edge and slid the eel back into the water but before he let it go he had a message for the eel.

"I'll get you again one day." He promised the eel. "You're days are numbered eel - do you hear me?"

The eel swished its tail as it entered the water splashing Kevin's face with the spray and it quickly swam back to its home and was gone - probably forever!

"What a waste!" moaned Kevin. "If you're more grumpy, Annabell - well… it's just too bad - it's all your fault. Anyway what did the eel say? I hope that it was worth it."

Chapter Twenty Five
Elvid

"Yes it was worth it, Kevin. The eel told me that there was a lake about a mile downstream from here, he said it's shaped like a diamond. The eel said that the lake is hidden by two crossed trees that form the letter X. This is where I believe the devil seed Elvid's main roots are, Kevin.

The eel told me that he believes that the plant killed a rat and fed something that was in the lake. This is so interesting. I must follow the stream and find those two crossed trees."

"Why don't you just fly there, Annabell? It would save a lot of trouble," said Kevin intelligently.

"Yes it would, Kevin," said Annabell. "But I can't do that."

"Why?" said Kevin. "It seems like a good idea to me."

"Because, the plant who I think is Elvid is growing fast - I flew over the area less than two hours ago and I couldn't see any diamond lake. I couldn't even see the river. The plant has covered everything, Kevin, all the plants in the bush have moved away from it now so it can't be far from here. The way to the two crossed trees would be impossible to find. The only way is to get into the water and go downstream, I'm sure of it, Kevin, and that's what I'm going to do."

"Right then, let's go," said Kevin putting his rucksack on his back.

"Oh no, I'm sorry but you can't go, it's too dangerous, I've told you what the eel said. You've done your job and guided me here. So that's it. Thank you very much - I'll meet you later - so bye, Kevin."

"Oh, no you don't, " said Kevin angrily. "I'm going with you, I'm not going to let you go on your own. Something might happen to you. I'm a man and you're a woman. Men are supposed to look after women!"

"Well-well-well, aren't we the manly man?" said Annabell with a grin on her face. "Well, I'm one woman that doesn't need looking after Kevin, nothing can harm me but it can harm you - you'll be in my way. I'll be the one looking after you, I don't want you to go. The answer is a definite no, Kevin."

Kevin frowned at Annabell and very reluctantly let her go on her own.

She went into the water and waved Kevin goodbye but he didn't wave back.

She made her way downstream. She didn't swim, she just lay on her back and let the current take her. When it got shallow she paddled.

It wasn't long before she encountered that plant. It was moving across the ground at quite a speed. It was like it was water, sort of flowing. It flowed over the stream creating a tunnel effect. Suddenly the plant started covering Annabell, it twisted its root around her legs. She pulled at it, and broke free from it, the pieces of the plant that she had broken off started re-growing with such speed that they attacked her again. This was a nasty plant. Annabell now realised why all the plants had moved away from it.

She didn't know what to do so she flew out of the stream at a tremendous speed straight through the plant creating a hole in it but the hole covered back over in seconds.

She knew that Kevin could be in serious trouble from this very destructive plant and that the plant wasn't that far from him now. She knew that if it caught up with Kevin he would have very little chance of survival if he broke off a bit of the plant. Annabell flew back as fast as she could to where she had left Kevin, but he wasn't there.

"Oh where are you Kevin?" she moaned.

She flew around but Kevin was nowhere to be seen. Annabell feared for Kevin's life. She flew to where she had come from following the stream back. On the way she encountered Kevin who was in the stream. He had defied her and had been following her.

"Kevin," she screamed, "you've got to get out of here - you're in terrible danger. Why don't you listen for once in your life - I told you not to come – you, stupid man."

Annabell was very angry with Kevin, She knew that he didn't realise the danger that he was in. The plant was rapidly approaching him. It was only about twenty feet away. Annabell got hold of his hand ready to fly him out of harm's way but suddenly she stopped.

Kevin shouted, "GO! GO!GO! quickly Annabell, what are you waiting for? Get me out of here."

"Shut up, Kevin," said Annabell, "something has happened to the plant, it's not moving anymore. This is very strange," whispered Annabell. She dare hardly breathe.

"I wonder why the plant has stopped growing?"

"I've got no idea," whispered Kevin. "Maybe it's frightened of me?"

"Don't be so stupid, Kevin. This plant wouldn't fear anything," said Annabell. "I don't like the look of this. Don't move! Stay right where you are."

Annabell waded up to where the plant had stopped growing and broke off a piece of the plant to see what would happen when she did this before it grew roots rapidly but not this time, there was no movement from it at all.

"This is weird," said Annabell "Why would it suddenly stop growing? And do you notice something, Kevin? It doesn't have any flowers. There must be a reason but I don't know what it is." Annabell was worried about this plant, she knew how deadly it was, the eel had warned her. So she wondered what the plant was playing at.

Annabell looked around to see if she could find an answer - it was all very, very quiet here, you could hear a pin drop! But suddenly the silence was broken by Kevin.

"**ANNABELL!**" he yelled at the top of his voice.

"What Kevin? What do you want?" Annabell was very moody, because she hadn't eaten anything today.

"We'd better find some shelter it's going to rain. Look at those clouds!"

Annabell looked up at the sky, it was black as thunder in the distance. There was definitely a storm on the way. The sun was now blocked out by the storm clouds.

"That's it !" shrieked Annabell. "The plant needs sun, Kevin. It obviously stops growing when the sun doesn't shine. Oh, this is good news," said Annabell, relieved.

"So I can come with you now, Annabell?" pleaded Kevin.

"I don't know. If the sun shines the plant will start growing again but I suppose it's safer for you to stay with me, I can't trust you. So you might as well follow me but don't wander off!"

They made their way down the stream. They could hear a violent storm above them but the plant was acting as sort of shelter.

About ten minutes passed it was fairly dark in the tunnelled river. Annabell could see alright but Kevin couldn't - so he went into his rucksack that was on his back and got out a torch. Which he attached to his head like a miner.

They waded and sometimes swam and sometimes paddled for a further ten minutes until they eventually came to the two crossed trees that the eel had described. The plant had covered the trees, it had just gone over the top of them, it was like being inside a massive tent.

You couldn't see the tributary that the eel said was there behind the two trees - the plant was very dense. On the banks it would be impossible to hack through it and even if you did when the sun shone again the broken pieces of plants would grow with even more ferocity.

Annabell didn't know what to do about Kevin. She needed to get past the two trees and get into the tributary but she didn't want Kevin going with her.

The two trees seemed to act as a barrier between the plant, she told Kevin to get between the two trees underneath where they had crossed and stay there. She told him that under no circumstance was he to move from this spot or to break off any of the plant.

Under protest, Kevin said that he would stay where he was.

Annabell climbed over the two trees but she couldn't see a way in. The plant had covered up everything.

So she climbed back to the other side where Kevin was and dived under the water between the trees. It was very deep here, about fifteen feet but there was a hole, it wasn't very big - just big enough for her to get through.

She swam through it. This is where the eel must have gone through, she thought.

She managed to push her way through and sure enough it led into a river. It was pitch black darkness and very eerie in there. She swam for a while, but for no apparent reason the river became very fast, she didn't need to swim, she was being carried along like she was being drawn or pulled. About a quarter of a mile down the river she came to a sharp bend, dead trees were blocking her path now, her body thumped against the trunks of the fallen trees. She was suddenly swept underneath them and found herself tangled up in the branches of the trees, they acted as a sort of *net!*

She somehow managed to manoeuvre her way through this and was now in open water again but not for long. Several dead trees that had fallen across the river completely blocked her path. Annabell knew that the eel had managed to get through this, so she dived under the water and on the right hand side of the first tree, there was a small gap that she went through but her way was now blocked by the another tree. She found a gap, this time it was to the left of the tree.

This pattern continued all the way down the river sometimes it was left and sometimes it was right - it was as if the trees had been placed there on purpose to stop something getting in or possibly out.

Annabell was now clear of the obstacles but was being swept down the river and all the time the current was getting faster and faster. Suddenly she found herself falling down a waterfall and she plunged feet first into a lake. Annabell looked around. The eel was right, it was very dark in here and the water in the lake was very murky.

Annabell swam around the lake, she could swim very quickly. The eel was right, the lake was a sort of diamond shape but she felt that it resembled the shape of the holism more than a diamond. It was a fairly large lake. Bigger than Annabell had imagined. This was a very strange place to be, it was like being in a domed tent but the roof of this structure had been made by the plant. The only sound that Annabell could hear was the sound of running water that was being swept over the waterfall.

She wondered how the eel managed to get up the waterfall but remembered that this place had been flooded when the eel was here. The water in the lake must have been still very high and had covered the waterfall. This was probably why it didn't mention anything about the waterfall, thought Annabell.

Annabell swam to the shore line, there was a gap of about thirty foot between the lake and the plant. It had formed a kind of circle around the lake.

The gap between the plant and the lake was all sand it was like being at the seaside. There was nothing growing in this space apart from one small bush. Annabell wasn't sure what this bush was.

She started walking around the dome looking for any signs as to where the third piece of the holism might be. The parchment always told her to follow the signs but she couldn't see any sign as to where the holism was.

She'd been in the dome for about half an hour, just exploring - suddenly a chink of light shone through the plant roof and was shining onto the small bush.

The storm had passed and the sun was shining now. She hoped that Kevin had stayed where he was. She really liked him although she knew that he thought that he was God's gift to women!! Maybe he was, thought Annabell.

It got lighter and lighter, the plant was letting the light come in the dome. It was like a sunny day in there now and was quite pleasant. Flowers started appearing. The whole of the domed roof was soon covered in beautiful red and blue flowers. This place now appeared to be like the garden of Eden. Instead of the *hell hole* that the eel had described

Annabell was puzzled though. Why hadn't the eel mentioned this? She thought that maybe this didn't happen when the eel was here but the eel saw flowers and said they could kill! But these flowers seemed harmless enough or was this some sort of trap? Annabell didn't know.

Her eyes were drawn to a plant that only moments ago was a fairly small bush but it had now grown to substantial size, a mysterious stem appeared from the centre of the bush. The stem was ten feet tall, and attached at the top of it was a thick growth of green foliage. The stem and the foliage suddenly produced beautiful blue and red scented flowers. Annabell thought that this was one of the loveliest plants that she had ever seen.

The dome filled with a sweet-smelling scent that the flowers were producing.

She had always believed that Elvid was a weed. A devil weed, and a very nasty plant, but this plant seemed to be something else - it was so beautiful. Annabell thought that she would really like to have a cutting of this plant to take home with her to plant in her garden. The beauty and the smell of the plant were drawing her towards it, like a magnet! She walked over to it. The parchment had told her that its flowers are not so sweet, had she forgotten? Or had this plant fooled her?

The plant's foliage suddenly changed: its once beautiful flowers disappeared and the foliage at the top of the stem changed into a hideous devil head. The devil head had four spikes, the flowers had gone but had left their stamens. The evil looking head had slanted eyes that looked like butterfly wings, the pupils of the eyes were red. It had a diamond shaped nose and a mouth that didn't open. The plant then produced two leaf arms that enabled it to pick things up, its head and stem had turned red and was now covered in hairs. Annabell now realised that this was the real Elvid - she had been deceived into thinking that its flowers were so sweet and had walked straight into a trap!!

Elvid started firing its stamens, which were like arrows, and they were coming at her from every stamen that it possessed on its evil face and stem. The spikes were hitting her at point blank range! But they just bounced off her. They couldn't harm Annabell but she knew that these spikes would kill a normal living animal. Suddenly the plant stopped firing, it had fired all the stamens. The plant then reduced back in size to what it had originally been. Which looked for all the world like a harmless plant.

"Wow!" shrieked Annabell "You're a nasty piece of work, aren't you?"

A few moments later she felt a tap on her shoulder, she turned around. It was Kevin!!

He had sneaked down the river unnoticed.

"OH, KEVIN," she yelled, "GET OUT OF HERE! - YOU'RE IN TERRIBLE DANGER!"

"Why?" But that was Kevin's last word!!!

It was too late! Elvid had seen him coming and had reformed back to its evil self. Thirty spikes hit Kevin. Killing him instantly! Kevin fell to the ground with a sickening thud and was lying on the sand, stone dead! The spikes were sticking out from his body. Kevin looked like a pin cushion!

"Oh, Kevin," shrieked Annabell, "why did you follow me? I told you not to."

Annabell started to get hysterical and started shouting at Elvid.

Elvid started to move forward towards Kevin. It had a long main root that enabled it to move. The two leaf arms grabbed hold of Kevin and went to throw his body into the lake. Annabell started kicking and punching Elvid. "Get away from him!" she shrieked. But it didn't take any notice of her. And she didn't know how to stop it.

Annabell pulled the branch arms off Kevin's limp body and picked him up and flew to the other side of the lake. This would give her a bit of time to decide how she was going to defeat this devil. Elvid had attached to it a single main root that was at least one foot thick. The root resembled a giant snake. This, thought Annabell, was its main life line. Elvid was able to stretch this. To defeat Elvid this main root had to be detached somehow.

Annabell realised this and went over to it and tried to break it in half, but even with her tremendous strength she couldn't do it, because Elvid was able to alter its root molecular structure to anything that it wanted. When Annabell pulled it, it became like elastic and wouldn't break. Kevin had a knife attached to his belt, so she got that and tried to cut it but it was like cutting metal! It had changed its structure again. The knife didn't leave the slightest mark. When Elvid felt threatened it just changed itself to suit the threat. It feared nothing.

The parchment had given her clues of how to defeat it. But she would have to work them out for herself. There was no other way and she had very little time.

Annabell was at her wit's end. She loved Kevin more than anybody that she had ever met. This was the man for her, she had given him life - surely it can't end here, she thought to herself.

Her emotions got the better of her and she screamed out, "Kevin, I love you!" But she knew that her declaration was a futile statement, because Kevin was dead!

Elvid was making its way around the lake. Nothing could stop this plant.

Annabell took out the parchment from her pocket and read it. It read:

beware of the devil seed Elvid

only it can live in its soil

its flowers are not so sweet

look at soil - look at water

it's something that you can alter

take Elvid's route - but it's not the way

It's written down for you to see

Elvid guards the crock of gold

Annabell was shouting at the clues on the parchment.

"What does it all mean? Beware of the devil seed Elvid - yes I know that," she screamed. "Only it can live in its soil. I know that - its flowers are not so sweet: oh, I know that," she yelled. "Look at soil - look at water - I don't know what that means, - it's something you can alter."

Annabell was trying to work out the clues but she was finding it very difficult. She realised that the main clues were in the words soil and water, something you can alter. Annabell read the last line out loud.

"It's written down for you to see. I know that it's written down for me to see, that's obvious." She wondered why the parchment had even bothered to say that it's written down for you to see. She looked at the parchment again. The words were in her mind. "It's written down for you to see."

Suddenly she realised what the parchment was trying to tell her. The clue of how to defeat the devil was the word 'down'. She followed the first letter of every line down - it revealed the letters 'b-o-i-l i-t'.

Annabell screamed she now knew how to defeat Elvid. To defeat Elvid she would need boiling water!!

"That's it, boiling water would kill any plant if you put it on it. But how do I get boiling water?" Annabell was thinking all the time. "I can get water out of the lake but I need a container."

Annabell noticed that Kevin still had his rucksack on his back and she could see billycans strapped to it so she knew that she had a container to be able to boil the water. But she didn't know how she would be able to make a fire to boil the water.

She opened up the rucksack and inside was the very item that she needed - it was a primus stove.

Annabell yelled, "Yes!" she now realised why Kevin was so vital in her quest to find the holism and to defeat the devil seed Elvid. Everything that was happening was supposed to happen. Catching the eel was supposed to happen. Kevin being there with her, was supposed to happen. Even Kevin being dead was supposed to happen. It was part of parts of everything: like it had all been planned previously.

Elvid was close to Annabell now so she picked up Kevin and flew him back to the other side of the lake. This would give her several vital minutes.

She placed the stove on the sand, and ran to the lake with a billycan and filled it with the lake's water but she needed to light the stove. She went through the rucksack but there was nothing in it to light the stove.

"There must be a light here somewhere," she screamed. "Oh, no- I need a light. Kevin where did you put the lighter?" Obviously he couldn't answer.

She went through Kevin's pockets and luckily found a lighter but it was wet and wouldn't spark so she blew on it, to dry it out but she had wasted several seconds trying to get the lighter to spark. Eventually it did spark and the lighter had a flame.

She lit the stove and placed the billycan on top of it but it would take quite a while before the water would be at boiling point and all the time Elvid was getting closer and closer. Elvid wanted Kevin's dead body. The eel had said that it had fed on something that was in the lake.

Annabell wondered what on earth it could be. She wasn't going to let Kevin be food for whatever it was though. She screamed at the primus stove, "Hurry up, and boil, please." Elvid was now only about ten feet away from her. She went to pick up Kevin and fly him back to the other side of the lake but she stopped.

Elvid for some reason went back within itself and then a few seconds later started to grow big again, it had made a mistake by doing this. Annabell didn't know why it had done this but she was pleased that it had, because this would give time for the water to boil, she didn't care about the spikes that were about to be fired at her.

Elvid let loose its weapon and once again hundreds of spikes were aimed at her but they didn't harm her. Elvid, once it had fired all the stamens had to go back to its original self to regenerate which would only take a few minutes, but these were vital minutes. Annabell looked at the water that was in the billycan, she could see bubbles forming, it was nearly ready.

Elvid grew back to its nasty self. It seemed to sense what she was going to do. It fired its spikes again in another attempt to defeat Annabell but its weapons were hopeless against her - once again it went back to its original self but this would be for the last time she hoped. The water was now at boiling point. Annabell picked the billycan off the primus stove and calmly walked over to Elvid.

"Here!" she yelled. "See if you like this." She threw the boiling water at the plant and hit it full on its ugly face. Elvid reeled backwards in shock, its face distorted like it was in terrible pain and its grotesque face drooped, and dropped off and then Elvid shrivelled up to nothing.

The Australian bush and the world was now free from this evil plant. Annabell had fulfilled her task and had defeated another devil.

Annabell went over to Kevin's body. She wasn't unhappy now she knew what she had to do. She started pulling the spikes out of Kevin's body.

"Why didn't you listen to me?" she muttered to herself. "Look at the state that you're in now? You look like a pin cushion!!!" Obviously Kevin couldn't hear her, because he was of course, dead!

Annabell had created life for Kevin once before. She knew that she could do it again. She placed her hands upon his head in the exact position as she had done before. Kevin's body shuddered. She then ripped open his shirt to reveal his chest. There were hundreds of tiny holes in it. She placed her hand over the exact position that she had done before. But nothing happened. Annabell burst into tears. "I can't bring you back, Kevin. Why can't I bring you back to life?" Annabell lay across his dead body crying her eyes out.

Just when she thought that things couldn't get any worse she heard a noise behind her. She turned round to see Elvid had re-grown!!! She hadn't killed it!

"Oh, no!" she screamed, "God help me!" Why did you not die? Why didn't the boiling water kill you? I'm sure that's what the parchment said I was to do."

Annabell read the parchment again. But she couldn't see the clue of how to defeat it. She thought that she had done what it had told her to do.

She felt that it was definitely boiling water that she had to use but she didn't have time to think. Elvid was growing back at a phenomenal rate.

Elvid was no longer interested in Kevin - it wanted her! She was a serious threat to its very existence.

Annabell picked up the billycan, primus stove and the lighter and flew back to the other side of the lake. This time she left Kevin. She lit the primus stove again and put the billycan on top of it and waited.

When she looked around Elvid wasn't there, it had disappeared but she could see its root sliding into the lake. Elvid had changed its tactics and had gone into the water. Annabell now wondered if it was Elvid that the eel had seen in the lake. Was Elvid the monster?

A few moments passed, Elvid reappeared on Annabell's side of the lake. It approached her, it had grown. It appeared to be even bigger this time and had more and bigger stamens on its evil face than it had before. The plant had definitely changed its tactics. The stamens were double the size.

"Oh, God!" moaned Annabell, "This thing is horrible." She looked at the billycan but it wasn't boiling yet. Elvid fired its nasty spikes again at her - it didn't seem to understand that they couldn't harm her. It then reduced back into itself.

Annabell had a few minutes to think. She read the parchment again. There was one thing that she didn't really understand. It said, "Take Elvid's route - but it's not the way."

She knew that route meant the way to go, like follow something. But the parchment said that 'it's not the way'. She thought that if it's not the way, then it can't be referring to the true meaning of the word 'route'. Then it clicked!!!! The parchment was telling her *root* - it's Elvid's root that is its weakness. She now realised that she had to put the boiling water on its root."

Elvid was back to its evil self again, and was getting bigger, and bigger in size. It now stood thirty foot tall, and looked very menacing.

It started to follow Annabell around, it was trying to catch her but she was dodging out of its way. It was like a child's game of *tag* - but this game of tag was a little bit different - it was to the death!!

Annabell led Elvid as far away from the primus stove as she could and played its game. After about five minutes she ran back to the primus stove. The water was now boiling. She picked the billycan off the stove and hid it behind her back. Annabell didn't want Elvid to see it. She didn't know whether or not it would remember what she had done to it before.

Annabell allowed Elvid to catch up with her, she was beckoning it to come, like teasing it. She was motioning it to come to her with her hands.

When it was close to her she let it fire all of its spikes at her. She knew that when it had fired these, it would have to go back to within itself to re-generate - this would be her chance to attack it. Which she did.

She calmly poured the boiling water over its main root. This root had spread havoc in the Australian bush and would have eventually spread throughout the world. Choking everything to death!

The root didn't change its molecular structure this time, because it wasn't afraid of water. In fact, it needed it. But before the plant realised that it was boiling water, it was *too late.* The plant root smouldered like it was being *cooked*! and then it softened up - Annabell quickly got hold of the root and snapped it in half.

Elvid exploded into thousands of pieces!! This really was the final end of this evil devil plant. The rest of the plant that smothers everything disintegrated into dust with the demise of its leader.

Annabell went back to Kevin's body and slumped herself by the side of it. "I'm going to save you Kevin," she whispered into his ear. "I know that I have the powers but I don't know why they're not working." She placed her hand on top of her hand print on his heart. But nothing happened. "Come on Kevin - come alive - it's time to wake up," she said in a soft voice. But Kevin didn't wake up! "Why don't you come alive? Come on, Kevin please come alive."

Annabell was screaming, "Why-?-Why-?- Why? Why won't it work ? It worked before!" She tried for over half an hour to bring Kevin alive. She was going through the same routine as she had done before. But nothing worked. Kevin was really dead this time. Her powers didn't appear strong enough to work.

Annabell slumped over his dead body crying her eyes out - she eventually got up to her feet. But was in a raging mood. She went over to the remains of Elvid and started shouting, "You killed Kevin, I hate you!" and she started kicking the pieces of its remains around the ground and she was stamping on them. After about ten minutes of getting out her anger she eventually came to reality - she knew that she still had to find the third piece of the holism. It was around here somewhere, but she didn't know where. The parchment had told her that wherever Elvid was, so too, would be the holism.

She thought that it must be somewhere in the diamond shaped lake. So she dived into the murky water to search for it.

She swam around and around probing, but she couldn't find it. She eventually came to the conclusion that maybe it wasn't in the lake after all. She swam to the surface and started to make her way to the shore line. When suddenly without any warning at all something grabbed hold of her, and it was huge!!!

Chapter Twenty Six
The Monster In The Lake

Annabell had been grabbed by the waist by some sort of monster. It had razor sharp teeth and was spinning her around and around in the water. The water was erupting with violent fury with this awesome creature's power. It had a big pointed head, and sometimes it crashed onto the surface of the water sending up plumes of spray. The monster was clearly trying to eat her. This was the beast that the eel must have caught a glimpse of, thought Annabell. The creature was a golden crocodile, and it was ferocious and very angry.

It kept swimming around the lake and every now and again it would leap out of the water, big waves were breaking on the shore line as the creature spun Annabell around and around on top and then under the water. It was trying to crush and drown her but it wasn't succeeding.

The crocodile was twenty feet long and was becoming more and more angry. Its mouth was contorting to strange shapes, as it tried to chew Annabell. Annabell had enough of the crocodile and finally spoke up,

"Have you finished?" she yelled but not angrily. "Let me go at once, you stupid beast, you can't eat me!" The crocodile was shocked that his dinner could talk and he let her go, but not for long. He circled around her several times eyeing her up and down, and then he came at her with his huge jaws wide open showing his big razor sharp teeth, and attacked her again.

This time he grabbed her by her head! He closed his strong jaws in an attempt to bite off her head, but no matter how hard he bit on it, he couldn't bite it off. In frustration, he lifted his head rapidly up throwing her up into the air. Annabell did a complete somersault and landed head first back in the crocodile's open mouth. Eventually after some considerable time the crocodile realised that trying to eat Annabell was a hopeless task and it let her go. Annabell found this amusing.

The crocodile growled with anger and said in a rather gruff voice. "I've eaten…" but before the crocodile finished what it was going to say it coughed. "…Um… I've eaten some horrible things in my time but..." and then the crocodile coughed again, "...but you're by far the toughest piece of..." and it coughed again. "...meat that I've ever come across."

And then the crocodile jumped clean out of the water in temper, and growled. It then swam to the shoreline and staggered up it.

All the time it was shaking its huge head and moaning, "I'm so hungry! I'm so hungry!" and then it roared out loud. The crocodile's hunger got the better of it and it slid craftily back into the water and emerged underneath Annabell knocking her over. "You must..." and the crocodile coughed again, "...be food! everything is food," it growled.

Annabell knew what it was like to be hungry but she'd had enough of this angry crocodile. Annabell was herself in a raging mood, because Kevin was dead, and she couldn't bring him back to life, and she was hungry.

"You haven't listened to a single word that I've said, have you? What part of you *can't eat me!* Do you not understand crocodile?" she yelled.

The golden crocodile lowered its head in disappointment that Annabell wasn't going to be its dinner. "But everything…" and then it coughed again "…is food."

"Well I'm not!" said Annabell. "And if you think that I'm so tough why don't you stop trying to eat me? You'll only break your teeth and then you won't be able to eat anything, unless it's mashed up like baby's food, will you? Who are you anyway? And what are you doing in this horrible place? The eel warned me that there was something in this lake but I didn't expect you." But Annabell then thought about what the parchment had said.

It guards a croc of gold She realised that this is what the parchment meant.

Elvid was guarding the golden crocodile. But she didn't know why.

The crocodile had at last quietened down and was now reduced to *begging!*

"You haven't…" it coughed … "… you haven't got any food have you?" "I'm starving um, can I have a bit of your arm? Just to keep me going please, I haven't eaten…" and then it coughed again ,"…for ages."

"NO!" yelled Annabell. "How many times do I have to tell you? You can't eat me, it's not possible."

The crocodile had a really gruff voice and was obviously finding it hard to speak at times and its coughing was really annoying - it was like humans get when they've got a tickle in their throat.

"What are you doing in this God forsaken place, crocodile? And please speak slowly, because I can hardly understand a word that you are saying. I'm an American you know and find your gruff Australian accent hard to understand. Would you please speak English?"

"I am…cough …speaking English!" said the crocodile quite grumpily.

"Well, it doesn't sound like it to me, and what's wrong with your throat? Have you got a cold or something? Do crocodiles get colds?"

"No, I haven't got a cold, I've had this sore throat ever since I've been here. I'm a prisoner."

"Why are you a prisoner?" Annabell was interested to know the answer to this question. She knew that it was Elvid who was keeping the crocodile a prisoner.

They both made their way to the shore line and got out of the water.

"It's evil you know!"

"What's evil, crocodile?" asked Annabell adjusting her wet trousers.

"That plant!"

"Well it's gone now, I exterminated it. I knew that it was evil. I came looking for it. Now then. Why did it make you a prisoner?"

"Because it said that I had something, ...cough... but I don't know what it is, never have," said the crocodile shaking its head from side to side.

"I've been here... cough ... for years," moaned the crocodile.

"And there's never been enough food. I only get what comes floating in from that river and it's always dead! I haven't eaten... cough... fresh meat for years. The last meal that I've eaten was a dead mouse! And that was three days ago. How am I... cough...supposed to survive on a mouse? And it was a small one! When I saw you, I was really happy, because I thought that I was going to have a lovely fresh meal. But oh, no, that's my luck! I had to have you! You're tough as an old boot!

I haven't eaten a human before...cough...and was really looking forward to eating you.." Then the crocodile licked its lips at the thought of what could have been.

"What's your name, crocodile?" asked Annabell who was now feeling quite sorry for the poor creature.

"Herbert, missy …cough…what's yours?"

"My name is Annabell."

Herbert caught sight of Kevin lying dead on the ground. "Ah!" said Herbert. "There's another one of you and it's meat! it's dead! It's not fresh but it's better than nothing. I can eat that…cough… can't I?"

"Oh, no you can't," bellowed Annabell. "That's my friend you ain't eating him!"

"But he's dead!" moaned Herbert.. "He's no good now, why…cough…can't he be my dinner? I won't last much longer if I don't get something to eat."

Annabell looked at Herbert right in his big eyes and yelled.

"NO!-NO!-NO! you can't eat Kevin." With those words, she kicked Herbert, you can keep your beady eyes off him, because I can assure you if you so much as touch a hair on his body you'll end up like that horrible plant. Do you understand?"

"Alright! - alright! I've got...cough... the message, there's no need for that behaviour. I can't see what your problem is. He's dead, ain't he? He's good for nothing, so what's so wrong with him being my dinner? Go on missy...cough ...spare a thought for a starving crocodile, please let me have him for my dinner."

"NO!" yelled Annabell in a very high-pitched voice.

"Ah!" said Herbert, "you've got a bit of a temper!... cough...haven't you?

What are you doing here anyway? Nobody ever comes here; nobody knew that this place existed... cough...it's supposed to be a secret place well that's what that plant told me."

"Well, the eel knew," said Annabell quite rudely. "He came here and saw you."

"Well, he's lucky, because if I would have seen him that would have been the end of him."

"Herbert!"

"Yes, missy."

"There is another reason why I've been sent here. I'm looking for something that's very special, it's a divine object. I was told that it was here, somewhere."

"What is it, missy? And what does divine mean?"

Annabell showed Herbert the parts of the holism that she already had. "It's one of these. Herbert, have you seen one? It's very important. I must find it."

"No, No…cough… I haven't seen one of those, and I've been here for years."

"Oh, for God's sake, Herbert, let me take a look at your throat, let's see what's making you cough. Open your mouth, and don't try to bite me otherwise, I'll pull all your teeth out! I can do that, you know." Herbert didn't say anything.

He opened up his huge jaws showing off his teeth. And exposing the back of his throat.

Annabell put her head into Herbert's mouth and looked at the back of his throat. She couldn't see anything wrong with it at all, it wasn't sore, she was baffled as to why Herbert was coughing all the time. So she put her hand at the back of his throat and started to feel around with her fingers, she put her hand deeper and deeper down his throat. Suddenly she came upon something that was embedded in it. She could feel it with her fingers. She pulled it out like she was extracting a tooth.

Annabell screamed with excitement when she saw what it was that had been in Herbert's throat. It was the third piece of holism!! "I've got it! - I've got it!," she screamed with excitement.

Suddenly the holism lit up with all the colours of the rainbow and Annabell felt a tremendous surge of energy go through her body.

"What have you got?" asked Herbert.

Herbert realised that he didn't cough anymore. And he was talking clearly now.

"Ah, that's better, was there something in my throat?"

Annabell showed Herbert the piece of the holism.

"This is what I've been looking for Herbert, this was in your throat all the time, that's what made you cough."

Annabell was so pleased that she kissed the crocodile. "Oh, you're a darling. Thank you. Herbert."

Chapter Twenty Seven
Kevin Is Resurrected

Annabell was so happy at finding the holism but her happiness didn't last for long.

She caught sight of Kevin lying dead on the ground but she felt stronger now and sort of, by instinct, she knew that she could now bring Kevin back to life with her added powers.

She placed the third piece of the holism on her necklace and went over to Kevin's body. The necklace was glowing even brighter with all the colours of the rainbow.

Annabell muttered, "You're not going to be dead, Kevin; I won't let you: GOD!" she spoke calmly, "I don't want Kevin dead, I love him. I want him back. Please give him back to me." It was like she was asking for divine intervention.

Annabell placed her hands on Kevin's heart to form a cross. Instantly his heart started to beat, colour started to return to his body. His blood was now flowing through his body and then he started to breathe.

Annabell then placed her hands onto her fingerprints on Kevin's brain. Instantly Kevin started to shake and shudder from head to foot. Kevin's eye lids were moving rapidly indicating that his brain had re-activated.

Annabell was shouting at Kevin, "Wake - up, come on - time to wake-up."

She bent over and gave him a huge kiss on his lips. "Wake-up, Kevin."

Suddenly there came a moaning noise from Kevin and he opened his eyes and saw a bright light. He didn't know that it was Annabell who was kneeling over him.

She looked like an angel - her eyes were glowing brightly.

"Where am I?" he muttered, "Am I in heaven? Where's Annabell?" Kevin was very confused.

"I'm here Kevin, and no you're not in heaven - you've been asleep for a little while; that's all."

"Ugh! I feel like death warmed up, Annabell." Then Kevin sort of laughed.

But Annabell didn't laugh, she knew that what Kevin had just said had been true.

"Why didn't you listen to me, Kevin? I told you to stay where you were. Why did you follow me? I told you not to." Annabell was quite angry but was very happy to have Kevin back.

"I'm sorry Annabell," said Kevin apologetically. "But I couldn't let you go on your own. I was worried, I don't want anything to happen to you - I love you."

"I know you do," said Annabell. "But you're a stupid person, Kevin, you could have got hurt. You've got a *dong* for a brain!!"

"What's a dong, Annabell?"

Annabell just laughed and told him that it's a coin of some country that's not worth very much.

"Very funny," said Kevin, who was still lying on the ground. He hadn't yet realised that his hands had changed colour and were like Annabell's. They were now red! Kevin's body colour was slowly changing. He was becoming like Annabell.

"You should have done what I told you to do, Kevin. You've caused me great worry."

Before Kevin could answer. Annabell gave him a kiss, as she kissed him she squeezed his red hand very tightly but Kevin didn't feel a thing. Annabell now realised that Kevin had gained some sort of powers, because he didn't feel pain.

"Thank you for being so considerate," said Annabell. "It was good of you to be worried about me but you had no need you know. Nothing can harm me!" Annabell paused for a few seconds and then blurted out, "or you now!"

Kevin looked at Annabell. "What do you mean nothing can harm me? I'm not like you."

Annabell laughed but didn't tell Kevin that he was metamorphosing into something similar to her.

"What's been happening here?" Kevin was looking around the area.

"Where are all the plants gone? It's like a desert here now, Annabell! What's been going on here? Have you found the piece of the holism?"

"Yes I have Kevin," said Annabell, looking very pleased with herself.

"Oh, that's great! where was it Annabell?"

Just at that moment, Herbert came creeping up behind Annabell. Kevin jumped to his feet

"Look out behind you! Run Annabell," shouted Kevin.

"There's a golden crocodile and it's huge," Herbert opened up his great big mouth and pretended to bite Annabell.

"Get away from her, you beast," screamed Kevin.

Annabell laughed out loud - she loved the joke that Herbert was playing on Kevin.

"Oh, you're so manful," laughed Annabell. "But don't worry, it's only Herbert having a bit of fun, he won't harm me - he can't anyway. He's already found that out, haven't you, Herbert?"

Herbert swished its giant tail in acknowledgement and said, "Yes."

Kevin appeared to be shocked. "What's wrong, Kevin?" asked Annabell but she had an idea what it was.

"Uh!" Kevin couldn't get the words out of his mouth."Uh! Uh! I heard the crocodile say, 'yes'. How come I can understand what it is saying, Annabell, what has happened to me?" And then Kevin noticed his red hands. He didn't know that his whole body was now red, and that his hair had turned to a gold colour. Exactly like Annabell's. And that his eyes were blue and they were sparkling.

Kevin was very confused, he hadn't quite recovered from being dead.

Herbert butted in. "I thought that you said that your friend was dead?" Herbert was a bit disappointed, he still thought that he had chance of eating Kevin but he knew that it was hopeless now that Kevin was alive.

"He doesn't look very dead to me!" Herbert moaned. "Is that why you wouldn't let me eat him, because he wasn't really dead?"

"Shush Herbert! Be quiet!" said Annabell holding her hands over her ears. She knew that she was in trouble now.

"What did you say crocodile? Annabell! What's been going on here?" Kevin looked stern and was giving Annabell eye to eye contact and clearly wanted answers. But Annabell laughed, she could see his appearance had totally changed and he didn't know. Annabell fell to the ground laughing.

"What's wrong with you - why are you laughing at me? What have you done to me Annabell?"

Herbert stepped in - he wasn't able to mind his own business. "You were dead mate! I wanted you for my dinner but missy here wouldn't let me eat you."

"Why don't you shut up, Herbert?" yelled Annabell who was very annoyed with him.

"I'm only telling the truth: what's wrong with that? And there's another thing. You've turned red! You look like a beetroot mate!" and then the crocodile laughed. Both Annabell and the crocodile were in hysterics. Even though Annabell was red herself she could see the funny side of Herbert's comments.

"Anyway," said Herbert, "you wouldn't have been much good to eat, you're all bones, there's not much meat on you, and I don't like red meat: well I do, but...." Herbert didn't finish what he was going to say. He was laughing so much then they both laughed out loud again. Old Herbert had quite a sense of humour, he made Annabell laugh, but poor Kevin wasn't laughing.

"I'm not all bones," boasted Kevin. And he flexed his biceps to show the crocodile his muscles.

"Umm, not too bad, I suppose - maybe I've underestimated you?" said Herbert.

He opened up his big mouth and pretended to take a bite out of Kevin.

"Herbert!" shouted Annabell. "Behave yourself please. Otherwise, I won't change you back to as you once was."

"I'm only kidding missy," said Herbert with a smirk on his face.

"We've got to get out of here," Annabell told Kevin.

"But what about me?" sighed Herbert.

"You're free to go wherever you want to now," Annabell told him.

"Why don't you find yourself a lady crocodile and have some babies?"

"But I'm gold," said Herbert soulfully. "Nobody would want me."

"What does colour matter, Herbert? You are what you are," said Annabell

"Yes I know that but I was once black, and I want to be black again - you said that you would turn me back to what I once was."

Annabell understood this, she'd been different to others all her life.

"Ok, ok Herbert, you've made your point." She then touched Herbert with all the pieces of the holism, which instantly turned him back to how he once was.

"There you go, Herbert - you're black now," said Annabell proudly.

Herbert went to the water's edge to make sure. He saw his reflection in the water of the now crystal clear diamond lake. "Oh, just take a look at me, would you? - I'm so handsome! Do you think that I'm handsome, missy?"

"Yes, Herbert - you're the most handsome crocodile in the whole world. Now then, what are we to do with you? This is not a bad place, Herbert, would you like to stay here?"

Herbert lowered his head and started thinking about it. "Well, I would but there's no food here for me to eat, and I'll be so lonely."

"Yes, you're right, Herbert, now let me see how can I help you. First we need some fish in this lake for you to eat and then we need to find you a mate, right: I need to go off for a while. Can you keep an eye on Kevin for me, Herbert? You've got to stay here, Kevin, I don't want you following me - you've caused me enough trouble. Herbert!"

"Yes missy."

"Keep guard on him, make sure he doesn't follow me. He can be your prisoner if you like. If he moves, bite him!!"

"What!" said Kevin shocked. "You're telling the crocodile to bite me?"

"Yes, that's right, Kevin." Annabell knew that Kevin couldn't be hurt anymore, and she knew that the crocodile wouldn't bite him, but Kevin didn't know that.

"Right," said Herbert with a great deal of authority. He then placed his huge tail over Kevin. "You're not going anywhere, mate," said Herbert to Kevin.

Annabell flew off and was gone for over an hour.

She came back carrying two large containers - The first one contained many thousands of fish eggs with all different species of fish that were native to Australia. The second one contained nine crocodiles. five females and four males. She released the crocodiles and introduced them to Herbert.

"Herbert, these crocodiles have come from a place where they were not happy, and all wanted to come here with you. Herbert's eyes immediately lit up when he saw one of the female crocs and her eyes lit up when she saw him - she seemed to like Herbert.

All the crocodiles agreed that Herbert was to be the leader of diamond lake.

Annabell then poured all the fish eggs into the lake and touched it with the seed that had created all water life. Instantly the fish eggs hatched out into small fish - she then touched the water again and the fish grew twenty times their size, instantly. They were now big enough to be food for the crocodiles - Annabell didn't really like doing this but it was part of nature. It's the way the Earth functions.

She then removed the trees that had been blocking the tributary and placed them down the far side of the lake to create a barrier - this would be a safe haven for any fish that entered it and a breeding area for them in future. She told the crocodiles that under no circumstance must any of them ever enter this place. They all agreed.

Nature would look after itself in the future. The lake was now teeming with fish.

All the plants and animals that had been forced to abandon this place when the devil plant was here, would soon return making diamond lake a paradise.

Herbert and his newfound friends were very happy with their new home.

Annabell wished Herbert all the best for the future and hoped that he would be happy here at *Herbert's lake.*

"What! It's named after me?" said Herbert excitedly.

"Yes, of course it is, Herbert - this is your lake, has been for a long time. It's only right that it should be named after you. This will be a crocodile sanctuary forever. When I get back to civilization I will inform the Prime Minister of my wishes. You will be protected, Herbert. Now come over here."

Herbert came swaggering over to Annabell and she gave him a cuddle, and kissed his head. "Bye, Herbert. I promise that I'll see you again one day and please don't eat any humans, don't forget they'll be looking after you." Herbert gave his word that he wouldn't.

Chapter Twenty Eight
Kevin Gains Powers

Annabell and Kevin made their way back to their camp site on foot. Annabell could have flown back with Kevin but she needed to talk to him. As they walked, Annabell told Kevin that he possessed some sort of powers like her.

"What do you mean? What sort of powers?" asked Kevin looking very puzzled.

"I don't know - I just know that you have powers. The crocodile was right, you look like me, in fact you're the spitting image," said Annabell with a grin on her face.

"Uh!" said Kevin. "How can I be the image of you? You're a woman and I'm a man."

"Well that's debatable," laughed Annabell.

"Why would I have powers, Annabell?"

"I really don't know, Kevin. But I know that you have. Give me your hand and I'll show you something."

Annabell held Kevin's hand and picked up quite a large stone from the ground and told Kevin to hold out his hand while she hit it with the stone.

"Are you mad, Annabell?" said Kevin not quite believing what Annabell had just said.

"No, I'm not mad - now then - let's see, if as you say, you're a man – let's see how brave you are."

Kevin reluctantly held out his hand for Annabell to bash, but he closed his eye's first, and waited for the expected pain. He didn't believe that Annabell was really going to do it. But he was wrong.

Annabell hit his hand with the stone as hard as she dared. Like she was hitting a conker. She knew that it wouldn't hurt him.

"Come on then!" said Kevin. "Hit it! Go on break my hand if that's what you want to do."

But Annabell had already hit it!!!

"I've done it already," said Annabell. You can open your eyes now."

"No, you haven't," said Kevin. "You're just kidding me."

"No, I'm not - I've hit your hand, and you didn't feel it - see I told you that you had powers. Annabell gave Kevin the stone. "See if you can crush it, Kevin."

"Don't be silly, Annabell you know that I can't do that - how could I crush a stone?"

"Go on, have a try; crush it - you can do it, I know you can."

Kevin held the stone in his hand and squeezed it. Annabell was right. The stone turned to dust! And the dust ran through his fingers like sand. Kevin stepped backwards in shock. "Annabell, how did I do that?"

"I've no idea. I'm as baffled as you, Kevin," said Annabell, nodding her head from side to side in acknowledgement that she really didn't know.

"Wow!" said Kevin "This is brilliant!" He was like a little boy who had been given a new toy.

Kevin opened up his shirt, he knew that Annabell had done something to him.

"What's this Annabell?" he yelled.

Kevin could see two imprints of a hand in the shape of a cross where his heart is- not was Where there should only be one.

"Did I die, Annabell? Herbert was telling the truth, wasn't he?" Kevin got hold of Annabell's hand and placed them on his chest, they matched perfectly with her hands.

"These are your hand prints, Annabell - what did you do to me?"

Annabell looked at Kevin with a sort of innocence but she knew that she had to tell Kevin the truth.

"I touched you Kevin with all the powers that the holism has given to me. And yes, you were dead as they call it but you weren't dead for long so no real harm was done, but you can never be the same person again. I'm sorry about that." Annabell didn't really know if she was sorry or not.

"But I didn't know who I was before," moaned Kevin.

"Come on now," said Annabell holding Kevin's hand like she was holding a baby's hand. "Let's go, let's not think about it. We'll fly back from here."

"Oh, no-no- no, I'm not flying with you," said Kevin with stern authority. "You may drop me!"

"What if I do?" said Annabell. "Nothing can harm you. And in any case, I've got no intention of carrying you - you can fly by yourself."

"I can't fly," said Kevin. "I'm not a bird!"

"I think that you can, " said Annabell confidently, and you don't have to be a bird to be able to fly, Kevin. I'm not a *bird*, and I can fly - Go on; give it a go."

"Well, what do I do? You have to tell me, you're the expert."

Annabell told Kevin to flap his arms as if they were a pair of wings.

Kevin stood there and flapped his arms but no matter how fast he flapped them he wasn't able to fly.

"See, I told you I can't fly," said Kevin moaning and groaning at Annabell. "I don't know why you thought that I could fly? No human can fly, except for you, of course."

"You can fly Kevin but how do you expect to fly when you're not making a bird noise? You have to squawk." Annabell turned her head when she said that so that Kevin couldn't see her laugh.

"What sort of squawk?" asked Kevin, "I don't hear you squawking when you fly."

"Well I don't have to now," said Annabell. "I'm an expert as you say." She was trying hard to hold back from laughing.

Kevin started flapping his arms again and gave out an almighty yell - yelling the word *squawk*. But nothing happened. He didn't move the slightest bit off the ground.

Annabell turned around so she was facing backwards to Kevin, it was becoming impossible for her to keep her composure.

"It doesn't work - I told you that I couldn't fly. You're not laughing at me are you Annabell? **ANNABELL!**" yelled Kevin. "Turn around and face me. I can hear you laughing."

Annabell turned around and faced Kevin and wiped away a laughter tear from her left eye.

"I'm not laughing," replied Annabell wiping away another laughter tear from her right eye. She was crossing her fingers - so she considered that the lie - didn't count.

"I don't think that you were squawking loud enough, Kevin. You only yelled out one squawk - and you have to do at least five." Annabell was now sniggering and had to bite her bottom lip to try and stop her from losing complete control of herself.

Kevin scratched his head in bewilderment. "You're having me on, Annabell. I know you are." But Kevin did as he was told and tried again, his arms were flapping faster than ever and he squawked five times very loudly.

This finally became too much for Annabell and she burst out laughing. she'd fooled him or so she thought, because all of a sudden Kevin shot up into the air like a rocket! He really could fly.

"HELP!-HELP!" screamed Kevin. "Annabell, how do I go down?" Kevin was now about forty feet in the air and was spinning out of control.

"Well, you can stop flapping your arms," laughed Annabell. "That's not doing you any good at all." She was laughing so much that she had a laughter ache in the side of her body.

"You have to hold your breath, Kevin - that's how you come back down to the ground."

"You're kidding me again," yelled Kevin. "You're such a naughty person Annabell."

"No, I'm not kidding you this time, I admit that I was just having a bit of fun with you but I'm telling the truth now. You control your flight by the way that you breathe - when you take a deep breath, you take off - a short breath is how you control your speed, the quicker you breathe in and out, the faster you go and if you want to go higher you take in deeper breaths."

"That's all very interesting, Annabell, but how do I get down from here?" said Kevin, twisting around, and around in the air.

"You hold your breath, Kevin and you'll come down - but just before you land you have to take in a short breath and you should land comfortably. It's a bit like flying a plane. Go on, hold your breath."

Kevin held his breath and came back to the ground quite quickly, in fact, too quickly. He landed with an almighty bump, he'd forgotten to take that short breath that Annabell had told him about but he was now safely on the ground.

"Thank goodness that I'm back on the ground," said Kevin shaking his head. "Phew! That was quite frightening, you were right though - that's how I landed, I held my breath."

"See, I told you so," said Annabell, cockily.

Kevin was pleased that he could fly but it had been a horrendous experience for him.

"How did I fly, Annabell ? I know that it wasn't by flapping my arms and squawking."

Annabell thought for a moment. "You must have said the magic words, Kevin."

"What magic words would they be, Annabell?" asked Kevin expecting another joke from her.

"Well you must have said, 'please let me fly' and then jumped up in the air. Thats how I fly. Did you say, and do that?"

"Well, yes I did; I think," said Kevin, somewhat surprised that Annabell would know what he had muttered under his breath.

"Well, there you go then, that's how you did it - now come on - that's enough of the fun and games. We have to get back to our camp. Now remember what I've told you, and say the magic words, follow me."

Annabell flew up into the air, followed by Kevin.

They managed to get back to the camp but Kevin's flying was a bit erratic.

They broke camp, and went back to the vehicle and started their long trip back. It would take them about two weeks but they didn't mind, they had a lot to talk about.

Annabell loved Kevin and Kevin was realising that he loved Annabell. It was all meant to be.

"I'm coming back here," said Kevin with a determined look on his face. "There's something that I have to do."

"What's that?" asked Annabell but she already had an idea what it was.

"I need to catch that eel, Annabell."

"Oh, no you're not," insisted Annabell. "That eel was very helpful to us - it deserves its freedom, without the eel we would never have found Diamond lake."

"Um," said Kevin thinking about things, "suppose you're right. But I will come back here, I'd like to see Herbert again even though he tried to eat me."

"Yeah, so would I," said Annabell. "Poor old Herbert, he's had a terrible life. That evil plant made his life a misery, it knew that the holism was inside Herbert, that's why it kept him a prisoner. I wonder how Herbert got the holism caught in his throat? I didn't ask him that."

"Maybe he ate an eel?" laughed Kevin. "And the eel had it in its body. Could be, couldn't it?"

"Yeah, could be," said Annabell. "But we'll never know."

Kevin was a little puzzled by something. "I wonder why the evil weed didn't spread past diamond lake until now - what sparked it off?" Annabell already knew the answer to this question.

"It was me, Kevin. It was my presence in Australia. Elvid knew that I was here - it's the same with all the devils - they want to take me on to try and get my powers.

"The Delvi came to life the moment that I entered the water. Levid was the same, it knew that I was in that aircraft. They all know that if they defeat me - it will be the end of the Earth. I've got three of them but there's two more out there somewhere and I must defeat them. I know that they're going to get stronger but I'm stronger now and I've got you."

Kevin was so pleased that Annabell had made this remark.

"Annabell!"

"Yes Kevin, what now?"

"I'm puzzled by something."

"What's that?"

"Why do the parchments that you get, give you the clues of how to defeat the devils? Why don't they just tell you directly how to defeat them? It would save a lot of trouble, and I don't understand why the parchments don't tell you exactly where the parts of the holism are either? It doesn't make any sense."

"That's a very good question, Kevin - but I don't have any answers, I really don't know. But there must be a reason - I wish that they did tell me, because I find it hard to work out the clues."

Annabell and Kevin finally reached the city and headed straight for the Prime Minister's house but when the PM saw Kevin he was shocked to see that Kevin's appearance had completely changed.

"What on earth has happened to you, Kevin. Why have you turned red?" were the PM's first words. "You look like Annabell now."

"I don't know, sir," replied Kevin "But I know that I was de..." But before Kevin could say the word *dead,* Annabell butted in. "Shush Kevin, nobody must know that."

Kevin changed his words. "I don't know what happened to me, I think that Annabell does - but she won't tell me."

"No, I don't know what's happened to you, Kevin, I don't know why you turned red," said Annabell rather abruptly, and innocently. "Nobody must know, Kevin."

"Nobody must know what, Annabell?" asked the Prime Minister.

"Oh, nothing sir, it's just something between myself and Kevin, it has to remain a secret."

Kevin looked at her with glaring sparkling eyes. Kevin didn't have a clue as to what Annabell was talking about, but Annabell wasn't giving anything away.

The Prime Minister wanted to get to the bottom of what had happened to Kevin, and he wanted to know about their adventure.

"Annabell, my beautiful red lady, I want to know your story, I won't let you leave Australia until you've told me why Kevin has turned red," he joked.

"Ok, you win sir," said Annabell rather reluctantly, "I will tell you some parts of the story but there's something that I want you to do for me first." Annabell told the Prime Minister all about the evil plant, and Herbert.

He promised Annabell that he would put a fifty-mile circle around Herbert's Lake for protection for him and the other crocodiles.

"Wonderful," said Annabell. "Thank you very much, sir. Can we have a big sign put up saying that this is Herbert Land?"

"Yes, yes of course we can," said the Prime Minister excitedly. "Just leave it all to me; I'll sort it out. I'm going to see this crocodile for myself, it sounds very interesting. Now come on you two, let's go and have a cup of tea. I want to hear this story, Annabell," said the Prime Minister excitedly, "I'm sure that there's more to this story than you're telling me."

Annabell told the story to the Prime Minister but she didn't tell him the part about Kevin being dead!! She knew that he wouldn't be able to understand this. So there was no point in telling him. She didn't know herself anyway why Kevin had turned red and had gained powers like her. She didn't tell the Prime Minister that Kevin had powers - it would be an advantage, she thought, for the future if nobody knew this at this moment in time.

Two days later Annabell left Australia. She was accompanied to the airport by the Prime Minister, his wife Helen, and of course, Kevin.

Kevin was very sad that Annabell was leaving him and going back home to America but she had to go, her work was done here.

There would be more adventures to come, but she didn't know when. Annabell said her goodbye's and promised Kevin that she would keep in touch. She kissed him and felt an incredible inner feeling within her very soul. Kevin also felt this. "Wow!!" they both screamed, but they didn't say anymore, they didn't need to.

The Earth now had two very special people.

Chapter Twenty Nine
Annabell Goes Home

Annabell boarded the plane and flew back to America. She could have wished to be back in her bed but decided not to this time.

When she arrived at the airport, she was of course greeted by the world's press, they all wanted to know what had happened out in Australia and, they were particularly interested to know who the strange red person, Kevin, was but Annabell didn't want to say anything at this time; she just wanted to get home.

Annabell was pleased to return home to America and be reunited with her Ma and Pa at their farm - she had missed them and her animal friends as well. Of course she was sad to be leaving Kevin but she knew that she would be reunited with him soon.

Annabell told her Ma and Pa all about her adventures in Australia - they already knew about the plane and how she had saved all the passengers.

But they had no idea that their precious daughter could fly. When she had left America she didn't have this power because they knew that she had tried and failed. But nothing really surprised them anymore, Annabell seemed to be gaining new powers by the day.

They were so proud of her but always in their minds were the thoughts they didn't know who their daughter really is. The angel had told Mr Jacobs that she would be 'special' and she surely was, but who was she? And Kevin was now a bit of a mystery.

It wasn't long before the world press were knocking on Mr Jacobs' door. There was a fantastic story for them here, and of course they wanted to know it.

Annabell was very reluctant to speak to them - she didn't like all the fuss that was being made of her. She felt that she was just doing what she was meant to be doing, like it was her destiny.

Mr and Mrs Jacobs of course wanted to know about Kevin.

Annabell was sitting on the couch in the lounge of the farmhouse. Mrs Jacobs couldn't control her thoughts any longer, she was at bursting point.

"Who is Kevin, Annabell?" she asked. "And why is he red?"

Annabell's red face lit up even brighter, like she was blushing. The mention of Kevin's name made her tingle.

"Oh, I love him Ma." Annabell blurted out with a great deal of passion.

Mrs Jacobs gave out a little chuckle followed by a sort of gasp.

"Love him, Annabell?"

"Yeah, Ma. I love him, I know what love is now."

Mrs Jacobs was clearly shocked, she never thought that her daughter would find love, because she was so different from other people. She knew that it would be almost impossible for her to find love from a normal human.

"I'm so pleased for you, daughter, of course I am, but are you sure?" Mrs Jacobs obviously had reservations about this.

Annabell looked at her Ma - her eyes were sparkling very brightly.

"Yes Ma, I am," replied Annabell. "I'm certain Ma. Kevin was made for me!"

Mrs Jacobs looked at Annabell and was a bit taken back by this remark.

"Made for you, Annabell? That's a strange thing to say - nobody is made for somebody else, dear. You can't *make* somebody," said Mrs Jacobs with a look of puzzlement on her face.

Annabell looked away from her mother, she seemed to be a little bit ashamed what she had just told her.

"Yes I know that, Ma, but there is a reason why I say this but I can't tell you - you wouldn't be able to understand, nobody would," Annabell spoke with her head held down now.

Mrs Jacobs was baffled by what her daughter had said but she didn't pursue the matter. She was clearly shocked at what Annabell had said and paused for a moment to compose her thoughts.

"Well," Mrs Jacobs coughed and cleared her throat. "When can we meet this young lad, Annabell? This is very exciting, I would love to meet him - I have seen him on the television. He looks quite nice."

Mrs Jacobs turned round to her husband who was reading the news reports about his daughter on his electronic reader thing.

"BILL!" she called.

"Yes my dear," came his reply from his armchair.

"You want to meet Kevin, don't you?"

"Yes, yes of course I do," but he wasn't really listening to what Mrs Jacobs was saying or appeared not to be. He was so proud to be reading about the exploits of his daughter that he seemed oblivious to what was going on.

"Well, Annabell, when can we meet Kevin?" asked Mrs Jacobs.

"I don't know Ma, he lives in Australia. It's a long way. I don't know if Kevin will come over here just yet."

"Well, phone him up and ask him," said Mrs Jacobs very excitedly. He can stay with us at the farm - there's plenty of spare rooms, here. Go on, phone him up, Annabell."

"I don't need to phone him, Ma," replied Annabell mysteriously.

"Don't need to phone him? How would you get in touch with him if you don't phone him, oh yes, of course you can text him or use the computer I suppose, I forgot about that."

Annabell shook her head.

"No, I don't need to that either Ma. I don't need anything electrical, I just have to think about him and he will know that I want to talk to him. We're telepathic, Ma. He doesn't know that yet but he soon will," laughed Annabell.

Annabell was being a little bit mischievous like a naughty little girl who was telling somebody a secret.

Mrs Jacobs looked at Annabell - she knew that her daughter was capable of anything, but her being telepathic was a bit of a surprise.

"Well, tell him to come over here, Annabell, I want to see who my daughter is going out with - BILL!" shouted Mr Jacobs. She shouted at him, because she could see that he that he wasn't really listening.

"Annabell is going to talk to Kevin and invite him over here to stay with us. Annabell says that she loves him. Isn't that fantastic?"

Bill Jacobs looked up, he was finally paying attention.

"Ah: loves him? Is that right, Annabell?"

Annabell appeared to be a little bit embarrassed by her father's question.

"Yes it is right, Pa, - I love him, just like you love Ma."

"Oh…" he replied "Oh, ok…umm, right then." It was obvious that Mr Jacobs didn't know what to say.

"Well, I'll have to meet this boy and approve of him before I'll allow him to go out with you, daughter," laughed Mr Jacobs.

He was being the typical father trying to protect his daughter from the male species.

Annabell didn't know if he was being serious or not. Mr Jacobs had been reading about Kevin and knew a bit about him from the press report but not much - nobody knew much about Kevin. He was certainly a mystery.

Mrs Jacobs butted in and told her husband not to be so silly.

"This is the twenty third century, husband. I'm sure that Kevin knows how to behave."

Mr Jacobs gave out a groan, and mumbled something that only he could understand.

"It's alright, Ma - Pa can have a talk with him," said Annabell grinning. "I don't mind, Kevin is a lovely person, and he's got wonderful manners. I'm sure that you'll both love him."

"Right then, hand me the phone, Annabell. Let me talk to this Kevin person," said Mr Jacobs with a great deal of authority.

"It's not called a phone anymore, Pa," Annabell informed him. You can't talk to Kevin because I'm going to talk to him using my mind."

"What? Using your mind, Annabell? What you on about, daughter? Using your mind. What does that mean?"

"It means, I'm telepathic, Pa - me and Kevin are telepathic we don't need phones as you call them."

"Telepathic? - Really?"

"Yes, really," replied Annabell. "Now shush Pa - I'm going to get in touch with Kevin."

Mr Jacobs had an expression of not really understanding what his daughter was about to do, he just sat there in his armchair and watched but like Mrs Jacobs he knew that his daughter was capable of anything.

Annabell closed her eyes and went into deep thought. All of a sudden she started to have a conversation with herself - but she was in fact talking to Kevin. The conversation lasted about five minutes and was really odd, then suddenly Annabell stopped talking and told her mother and father that Kevin was coming to America to see them.

"Is Kevin from farming stock, Annabell?" asked Mr Jacobs.

"No Pa, he's not," replied Annabell, she didn't dare tell him that Kevin wasn't a real person or that he was a clone of an Englishman that she had made.

"I'm really looking forward to meeting this boy," said Mr Jacobs.

"He's not a 'boy' Pa. Kevin is the same age as me, and he's a man."

"Well, as far as I'm concerned you're still our baby, Annabell. Now come over here and give your old Pa a cuddle." Mr Jacobs got up from his chair and put his arms around Annabell.

"I've missed you, daughter, it's good to have you home again. How long will you be staying this time?" Annabell gave her father a big cuddle.

"I don't know Pa - I have to wait for the next message."

"Can Kevin read these messages, Annabell?"

Annabell was surprised by her father's question.

"Yes, he can, Pa, but why did you ask that?"

"I don't know but I know that he must be a very special boy - but what do you really know about him, Annabell? You cant fool your old Pa, you know. I've seen things as well."

"Seen things? Really? What things, Pa?"

Annabell didn't understand what her father was talking about.

But Mrs Jacobs did. She told him to shut up. But Mr Jacobs had to say something.

"Oh, I can't tell you, daughter - it was before you were born, you wouldn't understand!!" Mr Jacobs laughed out loud and sat back down in his chair. He felt like he had got a bit back on his mysterious daughter.

Annabell was intrigued by her father's comment.

I could find out what you have 'seen', Pa, if I wanted to. I could read your mind but I would never do that, I don't think that it's right to read people's minds. So what you have seen is *safe,*" said Annabell, peering into her father's eyes to try and unnerve him.

Mr and Mrs Jacobs were very relieved to know that. They didn't want Annabell to know that her father had seen an angel and that he'd seen her before she had been born to the Earth.

Chapter Thirty
The Last Piece Of Parchment

A few days later Kevin arrived in America. Mr and Mrs Jacobs loved him as Annabell had expected. He seemed to be a perfect partner for their daughter.

Several weeks went by. Annabell and Kevin were walking hand in hand in a field on the farm when a black crow, a motley looking bird with holes in its wings, swooped down and landed on Annabell's head. "Hello," said Annabell, "What can I do for you?"

The crow hopped down from her head, and landed on her arm. In the bird's beak was a piece of parchment.

"This is for you," said the bird. It dropped the parchment into Annabell's hand, and flew away.

"Come back here," shouted Annabell. "Where did you get this from, crow?"

But the bird was gone, without so much as a goodbye.

Annabell looked at the parchment and read the words. It read as follows:

The seeds of land - water and plants

you have found - the insect seed is the last

seek out the dragon

Temporal - Hinduism is where you'll find it

see where it flies

beware Videl is here, and it's so loud

it could be turned into a cloud

think of the words 'mo' and 'Wan'

then combine the two and then think of you

follow the signs

The creator

Annabell looked at the parchment and read the words over and over again - it didn't make any sense. *Seek out the dragon.* She knew that no such creature ever existed, it was a mythical monster.

She gave out a snigger, more of a half laugh. "How am I supposed to find a creature that has never existed?" she asked Kevin.

Kevin shook his head, indicating that he didn't know.

Kevin read the parchment but he didn't have a clue either as to what it meant.

"T*emporal - Hinduism.* What's all that about?" Annabell muttered to herself.

She knew that Hinduism was the dominant religion of India, but she hadn't a clue what temporal meant.

She was standing there in the field looking very puzzled. "*mo- wan,* what's that Kevin? And who's *Videl?*"

Kevin shook his head. "I'm sorry Annabell, I don't know what it means."

The parchment said that it was *loud* and that it could be turned into a *cloud.*

Annabell screamed out in frustration as she always did and sat down on the grass trying to work it out, but she realised that it was beyond her - she needed some help, and she knew that Kevin wasn't it.

She walked slowly back to the farmhouse. She hardly said a word to Kevin on the walk back. All her thoughts were on the words of the parchment.

Her Ma was in the kitchen making a meat pie for Mr Jacobs' dinner - this was Mr Jacobs' favourite food

- beef pie, with lots of thick gravy. He had this nearly every day.

Annabell interrupted her Ma, "Sorry to disturb you but what does 'Temporal' mean?"

"I've got absolutely no idea darling, why do you ask?" said Mrs Jacobs rolling out the pastry.

"I've got another piece of parchment, Ma, and it says that I have to seek out a *dragon* and that T*emporal - Hinduism* is where I'll find it. Hinduism is a Indian religion, isn't it, Ma?"

"Yes I think so, darling, but I don't know what 'Temporal' means."

"Look ma," Annabell showed her the parchment.

"I can't read that, daughter, - you know that it's just squiggles to me, you're the only person in the whole world who can read that writing." said Mrs Jacobs.

"Kevin can read it, Ma.... can't you, Kevin?"

"Yes I can," replied Kevin, looking very intelligent.

"Well I never, you must be a special person, Kevin."

"Yes he is, Ma. He's very, very special," said Annabell proudly.

Annabell gave a little smile. If only her Ma knew how special Kevin really was! But she obviously didn't, and Annabell certainly wasn't going to tell her.

Mrs Jacobs turned to Annabell to try to help her.

"I'll see if I can find the electronic dictionary for you, daughter - now where did I see it ? I think that you father had it last, I know he was trying to find out how to spell a word only the other day. I wonder where he put it? I'll go and ask him."

Mrs Jacobs left the room and was gone for about five minutes - when she returned she had the dictionary in her hand. She handed it to Annabell.

Annabell sat on the chair and went through the pages until she came to the T words.

She followed the words down with her red finger - finally coming to the word 'Temporal'. "Ah, here it is, Ma. 'Temporal' it says that it means *near a temple or temple's* but it also means *not permanent or eternal in time.*

So the *dragon* is near a temple - that may not be permanent, somewhere in India."

Annabell was so pleased with herself for working out the clues as to where the last piece of the holism might be; she hadn't realised how ridiculous it all sounded, but Mrs Jacobs had.

"Darling daughter, there are no such things as dragons, and even if there were, there must be thousands of temples in India - how would you know what temple to look for? And it may not be there anymore."

Annabell's head dropped. "Oh you're right, Ma," she said, grinding her red teeth. "It all sounds so stupid I know, but I must go to India - it says that I must *follow the signs.* The signs point to India, I'm sure that there'll be an explanation, there always is. It says here, Ma, that when I find the dragon I must see where it flies. Maybe the dragon will lead me to the last piece of the Holism?"

"But Annabell, dragons don't exist darling," Mrs Jacobs had to reiterate what she had already told Annabell. "How can you find something that doesn't exist?"

Annabell shook her head, "I don't know, Ma. And there's something else that I haven't told you .... Ma, listen to this." Annabell read out the rest of the parchment.

"Combine the words *mo and wan and think of you* and it says *Videl* is here, and it's *loud* but it can be turned into a *cloud.*" Annabell couldn't help but laugh.

"What does that mean, Ma?"

"I don't know," said Mrs Jacobs. "Maybe your father can work it out? Because I haven't got a clue darling… sorry."

Annabell nodded her head "Oh no, Ma - not Pa, he's hopeless at these things, I had to get the owl to work it out the last time. That's who I'm going to ask. The owl will know. Yeah, I'll ask Colin."

Annabell went into the barn where Colin lived, but he wasn't there. She yelled out his name. "Colin! Colin! Where are you?" But there was no answer.

Suddenly a squeaky voice answered, "It's no good calling for the owl, because it's gone and thank goodness for that - that owl was vicious… it tries to eat us you know."

"Who are you?" asked Annabell. She bent down and picked up a mouse, and held it gently in her hand. The mouse wasn't a bit frightened of her.

"I'm Norris," replied the mouse. "I live here, have done for quite some time. Didn't you know that I was here?"

"No," replied Annabell. "Where's Colin the owl gone?"

"It flew away about a week ago - it said that it was starving." The mouse laughed.

"We were too clever for it. It couldn't catch us - so it left, it won't come back, it's getting old, and slow, and its eye-sight was going anyway. It had a pair of spectacles but we got them off him when he fell asleep. It went off to pastures new after easier prey.

"We're all glad that it's gone. It's eaten some of my friends and family you know. He a murderer that owl, somebody should shoot it - put it out of its misery."

"But that's nature mouse; it's normal," said Annabell.

"You're on this earth for a reason, I don't like telling you this mouse, but you were his food and you're food for other creatures too. There's loads of animals that would like you for their dinner, but I'm not one of them, thank goodness."

The mouse twiddled his whiskers in relief.

"What am I going to do now?" said Annabell thoughtfully. "I was hoping that Colin could help me out. I don't suppose you know how to work out riddles - do you mouse?"

"No, I wouldn't know how to work out riddles and by the way, my name is Norris. You're going to need an owl to help you - they're not called 'wise' for nothing, you know."

"Yeah, I know that," said Annabell, that's why I'm looking for the owl. Where am I going to find another owl at short notice?"

"Oh, I know where one is," said Norris smugly. "But..." The mouse didn't finish the sentence. It just started laughing for some reason.

"Why are you laughing, Norris? What's so funny? You do know where an owl is, don't you?"

"Yeah," replied a squeaky voice.

"Where?" said Annabell excitedly.

"It's in your loft in the farmhouse- it's been there for years, I'm surprised that you didn't know that it was there."

"Well I didn't," replied Annabell. "Thank you mouse... umm... I mean, Norris, for your help."

"That's alright - it's a pleasure, and thank you for all the nice grain that you've piled up for us here in the barn - there's hundreds of us living here you know, we need a lot food, it's very good of you to give us all this food."

"No! It's not for you Norris - it's for my horse, Charlie, and all the other animals that live on the farm, but I suppose you can have some."

"Thank you," said the mouse. "And good luck with the owl."

Annabell put the mouse back on the ground and then it scurried away laughing its head off!!

Annabell went back to the farmhouse, but was puzzled as to why the mouse was laughing so much. She couldn't see anything that was funny.

She got a ladder and climbed up into the loft - it was really dark in there, but she had powers to see in the dark.

"OWL!" she yelled, "I know that you're here - the mouse, Norris told me, so there's no point in hiding."

"What do you want?" said the owl in a grumpy voice.

"Don't worry," said Annabell, "you can stay here if you want. I won't chuck you out. I need your help with a puzzle. Colin the owl who lived in the barn helped me last time, but he's gone. Did you know Colin?

"Colin? Um..." the owl hesitated. "Umm... I don't know."

"What's your name, owl?" asked Annabell.

"Er...um..." Once again the owl was very hesitant to answer. Then it blurted out, "Colin."

"So you've got the same name as the other owl who used to live in the barn then?"

"What other owl?"

"Oh, dear," Annabell shook her head. "What have we got here?" She mumbled to herself but she carried on. "Colin, now then: I wonder if you can help me with a puzzle. It's very important."

"What's a puzzle?" asked the owl.

"Oh, er... it's like a riddle. Just shush, and listen Colin, and I'll read it to you."

"Who's Colin?"

"It's you – you, silly old fool, you said that your name was Colin."

"Did I?... Why would I say that?... What is my name: do you know?"

"What!!" Annabell was getting very confused. "What have you been talking about, owl? Oh, forget about your name - it doesn't matter." Annabell was getting a bit irate.

Kevin was standing at the bottom of the ladder in hysterics.

"Stop laughing, Kevin - this is very important," said Annabell, quite sternly.

She read out the words on the parchment to the owl. When she had finished reading it, she asked the owl if he knew what it meant.

"No I don't," replied the owl, "I'm what is generally known as being *thick* as in, not knowing very much, in fact, I don't know anything at all."

"Well, you must know something?" said Annabell. "You must know that you're an owl."

"Er...Owl? Is that what I am? What's an owl? I'm sorry, but I don't have a memory, well I've got some memory, but not much, I can't remember anything over ten seconds!!"

"But how can you talk?" asked Annabell, "if you can't remember anything?"

"I don't know," replied the owl. "It must be instinct, whatever that means,"

Annabell realised now why that mouse Norris had been laughing so much. He must have known that the owl had no memory. She knew that it was hopeless trying to talk to the owl and wished it good day and climbed back down the ladder.

Kevin was now rolling around the ground with a pain in his belly through laughing so much. Annabell was not amused though. "Get up Kevin, this is no laughing matter," she informed him.

She went back into the kitchen, where her Ma was taking out the meat pie from the oven. The smell of the pie was wafting through the house.

"Well," said Mrs Jacobs, "did the owl work it out for you?"

"No Ma… the owl that was in the barn has gone. Did you know that there's an owl in our loft, Ma?"

"I knew that there was something up there," replied Mrs Jacobs, "but I didn't know that it was an owl. I thought that it was mice. Couldn't that owl help you?"

"No ma. The owl in our loft, didn't even know that it was an owl! It doesn't have a memory for God's sake." Annabell was really moody now. Kevin laughed out loud at Annabell's moodiness.

"What am I going to do? I don't know anybody who can work out these riddles. I'll just have to go to India and see if there's anybody there who can help me."

"I'll come with you," said Kevin with great enthusiasm.

"No, no you won't, Kevin, this could be very dangerous - I have to do it myself, you'll only be in my way, you can stay at the farm and help my Pa work the land, or go fishing or something."

"Fishing – that's a good idea, alright then, if you don't want me to come with you I'll go fishing. I know when I'm not wanted," said Kevin with a frown.

Kevin didn't seem to be too disappointed though. The mention of fishing soon changed his mind about going to India with Annabell. He knew that there was some mighty big trout in the river that ran through Mr Jacobs' farm and he quite fancied catching some of them.

Annabell informed Kevin that if he caught any fish he must put them back in the river. Kevin reluctantly agreed.

❦

Chapter Thirty One
Annabell Goes To India

A week later Annabell flew out from Barstone airport to New Delhi, India. Word soon spread to the Indian people that Annabell was on her way to their country. Big crowds had gathered to greet this unbelievable woman at the airport.

The people of India were so proud to be having the most famous person in the world coming to their country. Lots of very important dignitaries were at the airport to greet her, including the Prime Minister and the Queen of India. who's name is Queen Meena. The King who's name is King Nillish wasn't there. He had reigned his country for only one year, but had caused havoc - the people of India, hated him.

Annabell alighted from the aircraft to a fantastic welcome, everybody was waving and cheering her. She waved back, feeling like a Queen herself. The dignitaries were all lined up.

The Prime Minister was at the front. Annabell shook hands with all of them one by one, she eventually came face to face with the Queen of India who was at the back of the line guarded by lots of police. She was a very beautiful woman and she was wearing a magnificent gold and red sari. Annabell's eyes sparkled even more when she saw Meena. Annabell bowed in respect of this very important person and shook her hand delicately.

"It's an honour to meet you, your Highness," said Annabell respectfully.

But when she touched the hand of the Queen, she felt great sadness in the Queen's heart. Annabell was very concerned. "Ma'am forgive me for asking; but what troubles you? Because, as you know, I have powers, and I can feel the sadness within your soul."

The Queen burst into tears. "It's my husband, the King," she replied wiping away the tears with her handkerchief. "He's not himself, Annabell, I wonder if you can help me and our people. India is suffering, because of him. I know about your powers. I wonder if it would be possible to cure him of whatever it was that has made him this way with the powers that you possess, beautiful woman."

Annabell thought for a minute. "Your highness, I don't know if I can cure the King - I don't know what's wrong with him."

The Queen asked Annabell if she would stay at the palace as her guest. Annabell told the Queen that it would be an honour to stay at the palace.

The Queen and Annabell were escorted to a huge black limousine. The car was protected on all sides by military men on motor bikes. Hundreds of other armed soldiers, and police were also present at the airport, security was very tight.

When the Queen got into the car all the people that were once cheering were now booing!!

"Why do they *boo* your highness?" Annabell was shocked at this behaviour.

"It's this car that they boo, I hate this car. The people resent it, and us, I can't blame them. We have all of India's wealth while they suffer." The queen started to cry again.

Annabell didn't understand what was happening here, but she didn't ask any questions to the Queen, she could see that she was really upset.

As they drove towards the palace, along the route were countless signs, saying,

"DOWN WITH THE KING" - "THE KING IS A THIEF" - "THE DEVIL KING" and many more.

The Queen held her hands over her eyes as she passed them, and she was constantly crying.

Annabell now realised that something very bad had been happening here in India.

They eventually arrived at the palace of the King of India.

The palace was protected by a fifteen-foot high wall, armed guards were spaced out every fifty yards. They entered into the palace grounds through two huge iron gates that had been skilfully crafted to look like two elephants standing face to face. The palace was set in thousands of acres of lush land.

There were beautiful flowers in abundance, and fruit trees that were laden down with their fruits, and in the fields. cows and horses were grazing freely on the lush green grass.

Annabell found this very odd, because all she had seen so far in India was dry, arid countryside with the bones of many dead animals scattered everywhere.

The animals that Annabell had seen while she had been here in India, (that were alive) were skeletal but here, inside the palace grounds it was fertile, and all the animals were very healthy. Huge sprays of water could be seen watering the land. Massive crops of every kind of vegetables were being grown here.

They drove down a long road and eventually reached the palace, it shone in the sun, it was a very grand palace, the finest palace that Annabell had ever seen. Everywhere inside the palace grounds there were people working, these were peasant people, and soldiers were out in force making these poor people work. It appeared to Annabell that these people were being treated likes slaves!

Annabell thought, what a contrast this place was to the shanty towns that she had passed on her way to the palace. Several servants were waiting outside the palace to greet the Queen and Annabell.

They carried Annabell's bags into the palace and showed her to her room, it was very luxurious but she couldn't help noticing how sad all the servants looked, they all had a look of utter despair on their faces, it was like fear, like they were all very frightened people - none of the servants said anything to her, they just pointed and bowed their heads. The Queen followed Annabell to her room and asked her if she was comfortable. She said that she was. The Queen told Annabell that she would give her time to rest herself and that dinner would be served at 7:00 pm. She would send a servant to her room at 6:45 pm to escort her to the dining room.

At exactly 6:45pm a servant knocked on Annabell's door. "Madam," came an Indian voice, you have been summoned to the dining room to join his Royal Highness, The King, and Her Royal Highness, The Queen. Please follow me."

Annabell followed the servant to the dining room, where she was greeted by the Queen. "Hello Annabell," said the Queen. "May I call you Annabell?"

"Of course, you can, your highness," replied Annabell looking surprised.

"Well," said the Queen, "you may call me Meena. Have you rested yourself, Annabell?"

"Yes, your highness, thank you," replied Annabell. She didn't tell the queen that she didn't get physically tired but she did get mentally tired.

The Queen paused ..."Annabell: my name is Meena, have you forgotten already?"

"Oh, sorry Meena," replied Annabell, "it's hard to remember, not your name, but I'm in the presence of royalty. I find it hard to call you by your Christian name. It feels discourteous to me."

"Does it?" The Queen was a bit taken back.

"Yes it does, because you're a very important person."

The Queen laughed. "Annabell my dear, you are the most important person in the whole world, I'm nothing compared to you - it's *me*, who should be honoured to be in your presence - which I am. So no more of this nonsense please. Come and sit down."

Annabell sat down to the left of the Queen at a huge oak table. The Queen's two sons, were there too. They were very handsome boys. The younger boy, aged three - whose name was Andish, sat next to his mother, and the older boy aged six- whose name was Mandish, sat next to Andish. Both the boys bowed their heads acknowledging their respect for their guest. Annabell was very pleased at the politeness of the boys and remarked to them how handsome they both were.

"You look just like your mother," she told them. The boys appeared to blush, but didn't say anything.

The big oak table was laid out with solid gold cutlery, and the finest crockery - every fruit imaginable was on the table. The grand table could seat at least forty people, but only four chairs were set out - there was at the far end of the table another chair, more like a throne really. Annabell thought that this must be the King's chair, but he wasn't there.

Chapter Thirty Two
Annabell Meets The King

"Meena, where is the King?" asked Annabell. "Does he not want to see me?"

"The King is not himself," replied Meena, looking very sad. "but he has promised to dine with us today, but prepare yourself for a shock Annabell."

"Meena, why would I be shocked? What is so bad with the King?" Annabell was surprised at what Meena had said.

The Queen didn't answer but the two boys got off their chairs and clung to their mother when she mentioned the king.

One of the servants struck a big gong, that echoed through the palace - this was to announce to the King that dinner was ready. A few minutes later *scratching* noises could be heard coming towards the dining room. The two boys dived under the table!

Something could be heard shouting and screaming, it was an insane sort of scream!!

It was like there was a lunatic out there in the corridor.

"GET ON WITH YOUR WORK YOU LAZY SWINES!" something yelled!!

"JUST LOOK AT THE STATE OF THIS PLACE." Annabell could hear the servant pleading with whatever it was.

"But sire, it was clean, we've cleaned it over and over again, just as you requested."

Then something yelled, "GET AWAY FROM ME YOU HORRIBLE GOOD FOR NOTHING, THING: GET ON WITH YOUR WORK OR I'LL GET RID OF YOU."

You could hear the servant begging for mercy, but whatever it was - was showing no mercy. It continued shouting, "WHERE IS MY DINNER? WHY IS IT LATE? YOU KNOW I HAVE MY DINNER ALWAYS AT SEVEN PM - IT'S NOW TWO MINUTES PAST SEVEN. WHAT IS THE MEANING OF THIS OUTRAGE?"

The servant in a scared sort of voice said "I'm sorry sire, but the clock was two minutes slow, I promise that it will never happen again."

"YOU CAN SAY THAT AGAIN," shouted something. "YOU'RE SACKED!"

And the *thing* could be heard hitting the servant. "OUCH!! screamed the servant obviously in pain, then the thing hit the servant again! And yelled.

"GET OUT OF MY SIGHT. YOU'RE A HORRIBLE MISTAKE FOR A PERSON, NOW GET OUT OF MY PALACE!"

Annabell heard everything, and was shocked at the attitude of whoever this person was, surely she thought this couldn't be the King. The two boys were now clinging to their mother's legs for dear life.

Annabell turned to the Queen. "Meena, who is that nasty person out there?"

The Queen bowed her head in shame, before she could answer. '*It*' entered the room.

Annabell screamed!! "What is this horrible thing? Meena, what is this?"

A grotesque creature had entered the room - you could see that it was once a man, but it wasn't a man anymore. Its face was very pale almost white, and skeletal - its chin was long and pointed, it had open sores on its face that were weeping *red slime*, its eyes were an angry blood red colour that had sunken deep into their sockets. The creature's hair was all gone, bar one single long grey strand that was in the centre of its skull - Its hands and feet were claws. The creature's spine was distorted, and had bent over which made it walk like an ape. - It's body odour was repulsive it smelt like the creature was *rotting* away. Red slime was constantly dribbling from its contorted mouth, its teeth were rotten and crooked, and broken, like pieces of glass.

The Queen turned to Annabell and tried to speak, her body was trembling.

She knew that what she was about to say was something that she really didn't want to. Her mouth opened, her lips quivered.

"May I... intro - du-ce... "The Queen stopped and lowered her head tears filled her eyes.

She tried again. "Um... may ...I, intro..." The Queen paused again, she was unable to get the words out of her mouth. She took a deep breath and started again. "May I, introduce the King - King Nillish- ruler of all India." She spoke quickly this time.

The Queen sobbed. Annabell looked at the Queen and felt great sorrow for her.

The Queen was trying to wipe away the tears as fast as they were falling from her eyes, but she wasn't succeeding. She blew her nose and carried on talking as best she could. She spoke much clearer now it was like a huge weight had been lifted off her.

"Husband, this is the famous and wonderful person, Annabell. She has travelled all the way from America to visit us."

The King who appeared to be drunk, replied. "So what!" and spewed *red slime* out of his mouth as he raged and growled at her.

"What do you want? You're not welcome here," said the King, raging.

"Your Highness," replied Annabell. "I've come to your country in search of a *Dragon.* The creator has sent me here to India to find it."

The King growled and then laughed, "A Dragon you say, well madam, - you won't have to look far - just take a look at yourself, for you are the Dragon! Just look at the state of you, what an ugly creature. What are you?"

All the time the King was talking to Annabell he was spraying her with the *red slime* that he was spitting from his mouth. "ALL WOMEN ARE DRAGONS AND CHILDREN ARE THE CREATIONS OF DRAGONS," the King yelled.

Annabell wiped the slime off her face and stood up and confronted the King.

"Please forgive me your Highness for saying this, but you're not exactly the most handsome person that that I've ever seen - in fact, I do believe that you're the most *ugliest* man in the whole world: that's if you are a man?"

The King growled and grunted in rage, "HOW DARE YOU A WOMAN DRAGON SPEAK TO ME THAT WAY?" And he turned to the Queen. "AND YOU WITCH. Where are my two horrible brats? I haven't seen them for weeks." Red slime went all over the Queen's face, and the dinner table. And then the King *sniffed,* "Ah, I can smell them – they're here somewhere." He carried on sniffing until he realised that they were under the table.

"COME OUT!" he growled. "COME AND SEE YOUR DAD-DY." And then he laughed - with an *insane* sort of laugh. By this time the whole of the dining table, and floor was covered in the red slime that had been coming profusely from his mouth.

The two boys were petrified of their father and wouldn't come out from beneath the table.

"WELL, STAY THERE," shouted the King. "IF YOU WANT TO BE LIKE SCARED RATS - THEN- BE RATS - SEE IF I CARE."

The King then turned his attention back to Annabell.

"YOU BETTER NOT HAVE BEEN TOUCHING MY MONEY." As the king shouted, a big blob of slime hit the wall, and slowly trickled down towards the floor.

The king shouted out for his guards - instantly six armed soldiers came running into the dining room but the floor was now so slippery that they all slid on their bums right across the room and ended up in heap at the far corner. They tried to get to their feet, but every time one stood up, he slid back down bringing all the rest crashing down again.

The King was now getting very angry and started growling like a lion. "SEARCH THAT DRAGON WOMAN," he yelled, "SHE MAY HAVE SOME OF MY MONEY."

By luck one of the soldiers managed to get to his feet, he sort of skated over to Annabell and apologized to her for what he was about to do.

"I have to frisk you ma'am, it's the Kings orders, and I have to follow orders. I'm very, very sorry."

Annabell felt sorry for the soldier and allowed him to frisk her, although she didn't much like the idea.

"She's clean!" The soldier informed the king. But his hands were covered in slime, so she wasn't *clean* in the other meaning of the word.

"WELL, LUCKY FOR HER," the king shrieked, and the red slime sprayed all over the soldier's face and uniform.

The King went over to the door and kicked all the soldiers one by one out of the room and shouted at them telling them that they were a bunch of useless good for nothings, and he went on to tell them that their next week's duties was to clean out the toilets.

He then donged the dinner bell, and shouted, "WHERE'S MY DINNER?" and then, he slipped on the slippery floor, and went flat on his ugly face! Everybody laughed, including his two sons.

"DON'T YOU DARE LAUGH AT ME," the King yelled. He tried to stand up, but fell flat on his bum and his legs went up in the air, and he farted! with the loudest fart imaginable.

Annabell, the Queen, and the two boys went hyper hysterical with laughter.

While the King was lying on the floor Annabell noticed that the king had three two's on top of his bald head and a fourth two was half showing. She obviously knew that the year was 222 2, so this had a meaning. She knew she still had time to save the king from whatever it was that had made him this way.

The King managed to get up from the floor, but he was covered head to toe in his own muck.

"You're the same colour as me now," laughed Annabell, but the king didn't answer or he didn't hear her. His mind was on his belly. He donged the dinner bell again and shouted out with even more fury than before. "WHERE'S MY DINNER? I WANT IT NOW - NOT TOMORROW."

A petrified chef in a white apron and hat came into the room. He too slid across the floor!

He was holding a big plate that was full of piping hot vindaloo, unbelievably, he managed to stay on his feet. He placed the plate, despite shaking hands neatly on the table in front of the king who was now seated at his throne chair.

"This had better be hot!" grunted the king, "you know that I like it very, very hot, plenty of hot curry powder, and hot spicy sauce."

The chef who was still standing next to the King was shaking uncontrollably with fear, and now he was also covered in slime, replied, "Your highness we've used the hottest spices known in the world, you can't get the vindaloo any hotter."

The King yelled back at the chef. "I don't want any excuses, that's what you're paid for you little shrimp."

The chef replied, "But highness you haven't paid me for years - I work for you for nothing."

"Well you're lucky to have a job then, aren't you? And where's my bottle of whisky? You know that I have a cold drink with my dinner. I've got this horrible dragon woman staying here with us and she's doing my head in."

The chef slid back out of the room. As he got to the door the King shouted to him to bring two bottles of whisky.

The chef shortly came back with the king's two bottles, but this time he was wearing a pair of skis, and had two ski sticks that he used to propel himself forwards. He had the bottles of whisky in a bag that was around his shoulder. He put the two bottles of whisky on the table.

The King grabbed one bottle, like there was no tomorrow and drank the whole bottle in one go!

The Queen turned to Annabell and asked her what she would like for her dinner.

"Nothing for me, thank you Meena," replied Annabell now feeling quite sick.

"For some reason I seem to have lost my appetite," Annabell was looking at the king while she said that. She was still trying to wipe off the slime from her face as she spoke.

The king was gobbling up his vindaloo, snorting like a pig.

"Husband, can you not eat your dinner more slowly? And do you have to make that disgusting noise," pleaded the Queen.

The King raged and got up from his seat. "SHUT YOUR MOUTH YOU OLD HAG, DON'T TELL ME HOW TO EAT; HERE YOU CAN HAVE MY DINNER."

He then threw the plate of vindaloo over the Queen's head! The plate remained on top of her head like a crown! While its contents trickled down her face and all over her beautiful gold and red sari.

Annabell was shocked at what the King had just done to his beautiful wife and asked him what makes him so angry.

"I'M NOT ANGRY," he yelled, as he took a swig from his second bottle of whisky.

"Why do you always have to shout? Can you not talk without shouting?" asked Annabell shielding her face, because she knew what was about to follow.

"I'M NOT SHOUTING - I'M TALKING NORMAL - THERE MUST BE SOMETHING WRONG WITH YOUR HEARING, DRAGON WOMAN."

Annabell shook her head to try and get some of the slime off her face. "May I touch your claw...er...I mean hand, your highness?" asked Annabell.

The King yelled, "Why would you want to touch my hand?" Once again Annabell got splattered.

All the time the room was getting more and more covered with the gooey muck.

"Because..." answered Annabell "....I may be able to find out what troubles you."

The King didn't like what Annabell had just said, and grunted.

"There's nothing wrong with me - it's everybody else, everybody is useless. All women are useless, and I hate babies - what good are they? They can't even go to work, all they do is eat and poo. So I can't make any money from them, well I suppose I can make something. I've put up the prices of the food they eat, and their clothing and the filthy nappies. That was the best thing that I ever did, put a tax on babies. If any of those horrible women creatures want to have a baby, I make them pay dearly for it, but it doesn't stop them, they still carry on *breeding* - I'm going to have to ban babies. That's the only answer," and then the King laughed out loud.

While the King was ranting Annabell grabbed hold of his claw hand. The King screamed in pain and his claw started smouldering, like it was about to catch fire.

"LET GO OF MY HAND AT ONCE!" the King yelled. But Annabell wouldn't let go of it. The King screamed, and screamed, to him, Annabell's hand was *red hot*!

Suddenly a puff of *red smoke* came out from the King's mouth!

"What on earth is that?" shouted Annabell.

The King pushed her away, which made Annabell let go of his hand.

The red smoke returned back into the King's mouth.

"Just look what you've done to my hand, it's all burnt," moaned the King.

Annabell shouted at the King. "It's not a hand, it's a claw! What is wrong with you?"

"I'll have you put in prison, you ugly woman," shrieked the King.

The King yelled for his guards. The same six soldiers as before came rushing into the room. Once again they all slid over.

Annabell quickly opened the door that was on the other side of the room, and all the soldiers slid from one side of the room and out of the door to another room. Annabell quickly shut the door and locked it so the soldiers couldn't get back in.

"You're not going to put me in prison," said Annabell. "Anyway it wouldn't be possible to lock me up, because I would be able to escape easily," she bragged. "I've got powers you know."

She was really starting to get angry with the King. "Can't you see that there's something wrong with you?"

"There's nothing wrong with me," the King yelled, as he took another swig from his bottle of whisky, by this time the King was really drunk.

He then grunted and yelled at the Queen. "*YOU!*" pointing to the Queen. "GET THIS DRAGON WITCH WOMAN AWAY FROM ME - WHY HAVE YOU BROUGHT HER HERE? I TOLD YOU NEVER TO BRING ANYBODY INTO MY PALACE. ALL MY MONEY IS HERE - AND IT'S ALL MINE."

The King then poured the rest of the bottle of whisky all over the Queen's head and shouted, "HERE HAVE A DRINK ON ME - IT MAY PUT SOME SENSE INTO YOUR THICK HEAD-BUT I DOUBT IT."

The King then threw the empty bottle at the wall, smashing it. He then staggered across the room, all the time raging like a mad man.

The two little boys were very upset at what their daddy had done to their mummy. Bravely they got up from beneath the table and ran after their daddy shouting at him, telling him not to hurt their mummy ever again.

"We hate you!!" they both shouted at the same time.

The two boys grabbed a leg each of the king. The King dragged them along the floor and was shouting at them, "Get off me you ungrateful brats - I'll put you both in prison if you don't let go of me immediately." But the boys wouldn't let go. So the King side-footed Mandish, who was holding onto his right leg across the marble floor, between two lamp standards that resembled goal posts, and then shouted out *"GOAL!"* And he did the same thing to Andish. *"ANOTHER GOAL!"* yelled the King. "That's 2-0 to me." He then staggered away laughing his head off.

The two little boys got to their feet, but they slipped over. They too, were now covered in the red slime - they crawled on their hands and knees back to their mummy, both were crying.

The Queen who was also crying, cuddled the boys. "Mummy, what is wrong with our daddy?" asked Mandish.

"I don't know, my darling," replied the Queen. "Your daddy is a kind and gentle man, I don't know what has happened to him." The Queen turned to Annabell and said despairingly.

"What am I to do? Please can you help? I can't take much more, Annabell."

The queen and the two boys were now crying uncontrollably. Annabell got hold of all three of them and gave them a big hug.

"Don't worry Meena, I'll sort it out - I promise whatever has made him this way, I will find out, it's clearly not the King."

Annabell asked the Queen if she had any idea what may have caused her husband to go this way. She asked the Queen if she knew what the *red smoke* was that came out of his mouth, when she touched his hand.

The queen told Annabell that she didn't know.

"Meena when did the King change into this horrible person? How long ago did this happen? I must know the exact date, it's very important. Think, Meena."

The Queen thought for a moment and then spoke while wiping away the tears, "It was when he found the *red bottle*."

"Bottle? What red bottle?" Annabell was surprised. "Meena you must tell me about this bottle."

Chapter Thirty Three
The Red Bottle

"One day when my husband was in the wine cellar looking for a nice bottle of wine to go with our meal - usually one of the servants would do this, but for some reason the King wanted to choose the wine that evening himself - I can't remember why Annabell, but there must have been a good reason."

Annabell thought for a moment. "Maybe he was being *lured*, Meena? Believe me, there are powers on this earth that people don't know about. Please carry on, Meena."

"The King picked out a bottle of white wine in a white bottle - when he said the white bottle changed into a different bottle. It became a *blood red* coloured bottle and it looked really old, maybe hundreds of years old. The King said that the bottle's stopper had been sealed in - like somebody had welded it in. It was like somebody never wanted this bottle opened."

Annabell butted in. "Or it was waiting for a certain person to open it, Meena?"

"There was no wine in the bottle, Annabell. My husband said that there was writing on the bottle, like an inscription and that the writing was in a Indian language"

"Did you see this bottle, Meena?" asked Annabell.

"Yes I did, my husband showed me the bottle."

"Look, wife," he said, "See what I have found in our cellar. Wife, I'm certain when I picked up the bottle it was *white*, but then it changed into this *red one*! Isn't that strange?"

"My husband was certain that the bottle changed colour in his hands and he said that he could see writing on it. He handed me the bottle to see if I could read the writing. When I touched the bottle, Annabell, it was *red hot!* I screamed, the bottle burnt my hand, I dropped it to the ground."

"What is it, wife?" asked my husband very concerned.

"The bottle, husband, is red hot, look, it has burnt my hand. I showed my husband my hand, sure enough it was quite badly burnt. Look Annabell, you can you see the scar on my hand?" The Queen showed Annabell the scar.

The King was shocked at what the bottle had done to his wife. "How can this be, wife? It doesn't make sense - it does not burn me. Look!"

"The King picked up the bottle and he was right, it did not burn him, and there was no writing on the bottle, Annabell, I told my husband so.

The King was baffled by this series of events and called for one of his man servants.

He asked the servant to touch the bottle - which he did.

"Does the bottle burn you?" asked the King to the servant.

"No, your highness."

"Do you see writing on the bottle?"

"Yes," replied the servant.

"Can you read what the writing says?" asked the King

"Yes, I can."

"What language is the writing?"

"English, your Highness. Why do you ask such a question? Isn't it obvious?"

"No, no, you're mistaken," said the King. "It's Indian language, Hindi."

"I see the writing in English," said the servant.

The King was shocked, "But how can this be?"

The servant replied that he was born in England. He told the King that English was his first language.

The King was baffled and asked the servant if he would send in a maid. A few minutes later a maid knocked on the door. "Come in," said the King.

"Maid, can you see this writing on this bottle?" The King held out the bottle to show the maid. The maid looked, and looked, and looked, but she couldn't see writing on the bottle.

The King asked the maid to touch the bottle. "Be very careful," he told her.

"Why should I be careful of a bottle?" asked the maid. "A bottle can't harm."

The maid touched the bottle and shrieked, "OUCH! It's red hot your highness."

"Sorry!" replied the King. "I didn't mean to hurt you." And the maid left the room rubbing her fingers.

"Well what do you make of that, wife? This bottle holds some sort of magic. It seems that only *men* are able to see the writing on the bottle and it appears that whoever sees the writing - it will always read the native language of that person. What incredible power this bottle holds!"

"What does the writing say, husband?" asked Meena looking very worried.

The King held the bottle up to the light so that he could read the inscription on it. It read as follows:

If you open this bottle you'll always be

a person that resembles me

you'll have riches far beyond your dreams

but to get the riches - you'll have to be

like I said, a person like me

open the bottle if you want the wealth

but remember - you'll never again be yourself

Videl

The King turned to Meena. "Wife, it says that I can have *riches far beyond my dreams* if I open this bottle - if that is true. At last I will be able to help my people from the suffering that they have had to endure from this terrible drought - I will be able to buy water and food with the riches that are promised."

The King was so happy at the prospect of this and had a look of satisfaction and a kind of relief on his face.

But Meena wasn't so sure, she was not happy at all, at what the message had said.

"Nillish, my dear husband, the words say that if you open the bottle you'll never again be yourself, and who is Videl?"

Nillish thought about this for a moment and said, "It probably means Meena that I wouldn't be *myself* because I will have riches so that I can help my people - which I'm not able to do now - all our wealth is gone - so I would be a changed man, instead of being sad I would be happy again."

The King had convinced himself that is what it must mean.

"But who is Videl, Nillish?" asked Meena again.

"I don't know, Meena," replied the King. "Maybe he's a sorcerer. Yes, Videl the wizard, that's who it is. The bottle clearly holds magic, there's no doubting that."

Meena was very, very concerned. "But Nillish where has this bottle come from? Why hasn't anybody opened this bottle before? And why does it *burn* women? And why can only men see the writing?"

Meena paused for a moment. "Nillish I don't like this- it's some sort of sorcery that is certain, but It may be bad. I don't want you to open the bottle. Husband, you must promise me that you won't. I want you as you are. You're a kind and gentle man, I don't want you to change." Meena pleaded with Nillish not to open the bottle.

The King responded, "I cannot make such a promise Meena, but I will think very carefully before I decide." Then the King left the room and told her not to worry.

The King was never the same man again. When Meena next saw her husband he had two red spots on his forehead and his face was changing into something grotesque and his personality had also changed. Gone was the kind and gentle person, in its place was a ruthless man who hated women and children.

The King had become something very evil. Over the next year the King as promised by the message on the bottle had gained great wealth.

He was now the richest man in the whole of India but his wealth came from his own people. He ruled India without any compassion for his people. Huge taxes were imposed on every one of his subjects. Children were sent out to work at the age of eight.

Everybody had to pay the King 90% of their earnings!! If you didn't go to work, you were put into prison and made to do unwanted labour - like breaking up rocks or sorting out anything useful for the king from the rubbish tips. If you weren't able bodied, and unable to work, you were left to starve to death.

The Indian people were forbidden to help these unfortunate people, but they did help them, but if they were caught helping what the King described as useless people they would receive a flogging and their taxes would go up to 95% of their earnings, or they would be put in prison. The King didn't see any reason why people who didn't work should be on the earth.

Life was very miserable now in India and the country was still in the worst drought conditions it had ever known.

People were dying of disease and starvation - while the king lived in luxury. The two red spots on the King's forehead had now turned into spiky horns: his face was white as a snow and his chin and ears were pointed, and his nose was bulbous. The King had now lost most of his hair, what was left had turned from a black colour to a sickly grey - his once perfect white teeth were now black and like broken pieces of glass.

Many of his subjects had had enough of the King's cruelty and had left the towns and hid in the countryside to avoid paying the huge taxes or face life in the prisons.

Shanty towns sprung up all over India - but the King would send out his ruthless soldiers to knock down these illegal buildings and the soldiers were ordered to arrest these people if they were able to catch them.

The Indian people became very resilient and rebuilt their homes over and over again. Everybody hated the King.

The King's father, King Tallish, had ruled India for over thirty years and was loved by the people – But beacause of ill health he had to hand over the throne to his eldest son, Nillish.

The old King was very unhappy at what his son was doing to the people of India, and tried to stop him, but Nillish was too strong for him. Nillish put his own father, Tallish, and his followers in prison for treason. That's where they were now.

Nothing was now ever good enough for Nillish. He always wanted more, and more. Despite being the wealthiest man in India, it wasn't ever enough.

He had become so evil now that even his wife Meena and his two sons Andish and Mandish hated him. Meena would cry herself off to sleep every night.

Annabell listened to Meena's story with great sadness in her heart.

"Annabell my husband *opened the bottle*. Whatever was in there, has made my husband this way. There was something very evil in that bottle, I tried to warn him, but he wouldn't listen."

Meena then broke down and cried and cried with her hands held over her eyes.

Annabell hugged her. "Don't blame your husband, Meena, he thought he was doing the right thing. His thoughts were kind, but clearly something has gone very wrong here."

Annabell knew who Videl was. The parchment had warned her of this evil seed.

She looked at the parchment and read the clues of how to defeat this evil but she didn't understand what the clues were trying to tell her. It was telling her to think of the words 'mo' and 'wan' and then combine the two and think of you. It didn't make any sense to her at the time but it did now. She knew that she had to find the bottle.

❖

Chapter Thirty Four
Annabell Tries To Save The King

"We must find this red bottle, Meena, do you have any idea where it might be?"

"Yes I know where it is, Annabell," Meena sobbed. "It's in the King's study; it's been there ever since he opened it. Nobody is able to pick it up: it's too hot to touch, not even men can touch it now."

"Come Meena, quickly, we must hurry. Please take me to the King's study." Annabell told the two boys that they must not follow them, but they insisted, they said that they were too frightened to stay on their own in case their daddy came back. Meena agreed, so they followed Annabell and Meena to the King's study. There was no red slime about so they knew that the King hadn't come this way. Meena knocked on the door just to make sure her husband wasn't in there, he wasn't.

They entered the study. The red bottle was still lying on the marble floor where the king had dropped it - it was glowing *red hot* as it had been for months, the smell coming from the bottle was like rotten eggs!! - Nobody was ever able to touch it.

Annabell bent down and picked it up. Meena was shocked. "Doesn't the bottle burn you?" she asked.

"No," replied Annabell "I have powers: it cannot harm me."

Annabell read the inscription on the bottle. "Can you see writing on the bottle?" asked Meena.

"Yes I can," replied Annabell. "This is very worrying, Meena. I know what it is: this is the devil's work - Videl is the devil's servant, Meena. Your husband has given his soul to the devil. Look at the shape of this bottle - it has a crooked neck, and its stopper is missing. Was the bottle this shape before?" asked Annabell

"No, it was just a normal bottle and the stopper was sealed tightly."

"The red smoke that we saw coming from the King's mouth must have come from this bottle. We must find the stopper, Meena: it must be in this room somewhere."

They all started searching the room, but there was no sign of the stopper anywhere.

"It's not here," said Meena. "Why do you need the stopper, Annabell?"

"Because I have to try and get Videl back into the bottle, and seal it in. We have to find the stopper, it's absolutely vital that I find it: I will not be able to stop Videl without it. We must continue our search, I'm certain that it's in this room. It has to be."

They all carried on searching, but it wasn't there. Andish just happened to notice a small hole on an oil painting that was hanging on the wall at the far end of the room, it was very hard to see the hole as it was on a portrait of the King himself. The hole was where his right eye should have been, but his eye had been removed. "That's very strange," said Annabell. "Did you know that there was a hole in that painting, Meena?"

"No, I didn't," she replied looking very surprised. "Andish, did you make that hole in that picture?" asked Meena.

"No mummy," replied Andish.

"Well how did you know it was there ? It's very hard to see."

Andish started to cry, he thought that he was being blamed for the damage caused to the picture.

"Mummy I didn't do it," pleaded Andish.

Annabell pulled the picture off the wall and there was a hole in the wall. She thumped her hand on the wall to break away the plaster where the hole was - embedded deep inside the wall was the stopper.

"Here it is," yelled Annabell excitedly. "It wasn't Andish who damaged the oil painting, Meena, it was the King when he opened the bottle."

"But how did my husband manage to get the stopper out of the bottle Annabell ? It was sealed in so tight, nobody would have been able to get it off without breaking the bottle and the bottle is not broken."

"I don't know, Meena," replied Annabell. She pulled the stopper out of the wall. The stopper was made of glass.

"The crooked neck on the bottle must have something to do with it. The stopper must have exploded out of the bottle with tremendous force to have embedded itself so deeply inside the wall. We must find the King quickly. I have an idea: I think that I may be able to save him, but time is running out. If we don't get to him soon he will surely die today."

They left the study and searched the palace looking for the King. The two boys were always close behind their mother holding on to her sari.

It didn't take long for them to find a trail of red slime. They followed the slime, it led to the King's counting room. This is where he kept some of his money, precious jewellery and gold.

The King was lying unconscious on top of his wealth, his eyes were open and were sunken into their sockets so deep now that you could barely see them. His breathing had become erratic and the two horns were almost fully grown and his face was as white as a ghost. The King was clearly dying, there could now be only minutes for him to live. The devil's servant, Videl had almost completely destroyed the King's soul.

Annabell turned to Meena, who was crying in desperation at the sight of her once handsome and kind husband. Annabell yelled, "Meena you must go quickly and take the boys - you must leave me with your husband - I must act quickly I haven't got much time."

The fourth two was almost complete on the King's head.

Annabell was now alone with the King, she had the bottle and stopper in her hand. She placed the bottle beside the King and grabbed hold of his right hand. The King started shaking violently, red slime was coming profusely out of his mouth, his face was taking on grotesque and contorted shapes.

He shook non-stop for three minutes, smoke was coming from the King's hand (claw) that Annabell was holding. The King started to rotate in a circle. Annabell had to hold on very tightly to his hand. Then the King started to scream, he was in terrible pain, but Annabell wouldn't let go. She couldn't, the King would die if she did.

Five minutes passed, the red slime completely covered Annabell, and the room. The King was now screaming at the top of his voice and then all of a sudden his eyes had turned a deep black colour, like coal, and he was hissing at Annabell like a snake, but she wouldn't let go. Suddenly the King stopped moving, he went limp. Annabell thought that he was dead. A few seconds passed, the red smoke started coming out of the King's mouth, it came out as a long trail.

Six feet came out from his mouth followed by a gruesome grotesque head of the devil servant, - Annabell was now face to face with Videl.

The creator had said that she could defeat Videl, but at this moment in time she wasn't too sure how she was going to do this.

Annabell started to realise what the clues on the parchment meant. The weakness of Videl was women!! The clue said…

Think of the words 'mo' and 'wan' then combine the two and think of you - Mo and *wan* combined together and rearranged make the word *woman*

Annabell was the *you,* (a woman). Mo also means 'moment' and Wan, means 'pale'.

So Videl could be turned *pale* in a specific instant. It was all making sense now to Annabell and the parchment also said that *it could be turned into a cloud.*

The red smoke circled the room looking for a man. but it came face to face with Annabell. It couldn't enter her soul, because she was a woman, there wasn't a man in the room, and it couldn't get out of the room, Annabell had made sure of that.

Videl had no options, it had to go back inside the bottle, or die! Slowly it entered the bottle. When it was completely inside, Annabell quickly put on the stopper. The neck of the bottle immediately straightened up and the bottle turned back to white.

The King's face started to change, his hair started to grow back, the once pointed chin and ears were now normal and his teeth were now straight and white again. The two horns were also gone. The King was now a handsome man again. The devil that was within his soul was gone.

The King was now sleeping peacefully on the floor unaware of what had just happened to him.

Annabell took the bottle out of the palace and went into the grounds. When she was well away from everybody she summoned Videl.

Suddenly the bottle started to grow in size, it grew to three times its normal size and then the neck of the bottle started to bend over. There was an almighty *bang*! as the stopper blew off at a tremendous speed.

The red devil smoke started coming out of the bottle and had to enter the mouth of the person who had summoned it. But this time it had been tricked by the powers of Annabell. She, a woman, had summoned it, and Videl could not enter a woman's soul, but it had no choice it had to enter Annabell's mouth knowing that it would die. Annabell breathed in the devil smoke like she was inhaling a cigarette, but of course she never smoked (nobody did, it was something that people of bygone days did).

When the head of Videl had completely entered her mouth, she exhaled and blew the smoke out as a smoke ring, the smoke was no longer red, but a pale white.

As the smoke ring slowly rose in the air Annabell touched it with the piece of the holism that had created water life. The smoke ring suddenly started to grow at a phenomenal rate until the whole of the Indian sky was blacked out by a gigantic cloud. It went completely dark like night time - suddenly there were lightning flashes followed by thunder and the heavens opened out with torrential rain. This was the first rain that India had seen for over two years and what a welcome sight this was for the people of India! Rivers started to form and flow throughout the country - soon India would become green again.

Annabell looked at the bottle which had now turned back to white - she used the powers of the holism instinctively and touched the bottle with all the parts that she had. The bottle turned into a beautiful diamond pink rose.

Chapter Thirty Five
The King Tells His Story

Annabell went back into the palace to tell Meena the good news about the King.

"The King is saved, Meena, he's back to his normal self now. He sleeps like a baby in the counting room, go to him, he will need your love and support right now."

Meena hugged and kissed Annabell. "How am I ever going to thank you for what you have done for me and India?" Meena wept with great joy.

Annabell didn't say anything, they went arm in arm together to the counting room.

Meena rushed into the room. Her husband was sleeping as Annabell had said, like a baby, and was still lying on his wealth. She bent down onto her knees and whispered softly into the King's ear, "Husband… Nillish. Please wake up." The King slowly opened his eyes.

"Hello, my darling wife," said the King, and then Meena kissed him.

"What am I doing lying on the floor? And what is all this wealth? Did I faint?"

The King was confused. "What is going on here, Meena? What has happened?"

Meena really didn't know where to begin. She had a terrible tale to tell her husband. Over the next hour she told the King of what he had done to his family and the people of India.

"No!" He kept on saying, as Meena told him the dreadful truth.

He couldn't believe what he was hearing. He held his head down in shame.

"Oh my God, what have I done. I didn't mean to do this, Meena."

"I know you didn't, husband," replied Meena. "Nillish, look who's here. Do you recognise this wonderful woman?" pointing to Annabell.

"Of course I do, it's Annabell - what are you doing in our country?" asked the King. "Of course, it's a great honour to have you here."

"Husband, Annabell saved your life and the people of India - you must put right what you have done wrong. Why did you open the bottle, Nillish?"

The King replied, "I'm sorry I never meant to harm anyone, I thought that I was doing the right thing." The King then told his story.

When the King left Meena he took the bottle into his study and read the inscription over and over again, it was very tempting for him, if the inscription was true. The King knew that he would be in a position to help his people. He was a kind and very compassionate man and it grieved him to see the people of India suffering.

He prayed every night for a miracle and he thought that the mysterious magic bottle was the miracle that he had prayed for. He knew that the bottle had unbelievable powers that could only come from something that was beyond the understanding of man. He thought that it was a divine gift from the Gods.

India had suffered the worst drought in living memory. Masses of people had moved out of the rural areas of India and had come into the cities, trying to escape the famine, but there was no escape. India couldn't cope.

Some countries of the world helped as much as they could, but there were other countries who were also suffering the same plight. The price of food and water, and fuel had rocketed to an all-time high price throughout the world. India was a sad, and bankrupt country now.

The King had used up all his wealth trying to help, but it wasn't enough so he borrowed money from other countries. He had borrowed so much that nobody would lend India any more.

The King was a desperate man. He said that he looked again at the bottle and shouted hysterically.

"What have I got to lose? What do I lose if it doesn't work? Of course nothing! But what if it works, I will be able to buy food and water for my people."

The King said that he had convinced himself that there was nothing to lose and everything to gain.

"I will do it," he shouted. "I will get the wealth promised."

The King tried to get the stopper off the bottle, but it wouldn't budge, it was sealed so tightly. Suddenly writing appeared on the bottle - it wasn't the same words as the King had seen on the bottle before.

The King was shocked but also excited. "This really is magic, I must read what it says, maybe it will tell me how to open the bottle."

The king read the words on the bottle. They read as follows:

Videl, Videl will soon come

kiss the bottle and it will be done

great wealth will come your way

if you say, Videl please stay

beware Videl is here, and it's so loud

It could be turned into a cloud

think of the words ' mo' and 'wan'

then combine the two and then think of you

Follow the signs

The creator

(Annabell had seen the same words on the bottle when she summoned Videl)

The King kissed the bottle and read the verse. He said the last three words... *Videl please stay.*

Instantly the bottle started to expand in his hands. It grew, and grew to three times its size and then the neck of the bottle started to bend over - there was an almighty bang as the stopper blew out of the bottle. The bottle then became *red hot.* The king dropped it on the floor. Seconds later red smoke started coming out of the opened bottle. A six-foot trail developed and a grotesque head formed. The head had two horns coming from its forehead and it had pointed chin and ears and its teeth were broken and looked like pieces of glass.

The King realised that he had made a terrible mistake. He had prayed for a miracle and hoped that he was summoning something divine but he had been hoodwinked by the devil!!

When the King prayed, he prayed for wealth but he had made a mistake, he should have prayed for rain, because it was the lack of rain that was bringing India to its knees.

The devil preys on people who ask for wealth especially if they are influential which the King was. It had been waiting for its chance to capture the soul of the King of India, it knew that he was ready to sell his soul to help his people. Kindness is weakness to the devil. The King tried to run from the thick red devil smoke, but all the time it followed him around the room waiting for him to open his mouth. The King held his breath for as long as he could, but it was hopeless, he had to take a breath of air. He gasped for air and he breathed in the red smoke.

Over the coming weeks and months he turned into something very evil - he had turned into the devil!!

Chapter Thirty Six
The King Rights His Wrongs

Nillish broke down when he was told that he had put his father Tallish in prison.

"Oh, please forgive me," he kept on saying over and over again. "I knew not what I was doing - I must put right the wrongs that I have done."

The King suddenly realised that it was raining outside.

"Meena," he cried. "It's raining. Meena... it's raining. India is saved - it's a miracle. God is surely with me today."

Nobody knew that Annabell had created the rain by killing the devil Videl - Videl was now a cloud that was the saviour of India.

The King looked around the room and saw the wealth that he had stolen from his people and it wasn't just one room that was full of India's wealth, there were ten other rooms piled to the brim - millions and millions of India's currency were stacked in the palace.

The King picked up a handful of the money and threw it across the room. "Never again will I pray for wealth, the love of money is the route of all evil, I must give this money back to my people."

Nillish was still in a state of shock at what he had done and was wiping away his tears when Annabell brought into the room his two sons, Andish and Mandish. The boys ran across the room to their father and wept with joy when they saw that he was once again the father that they both loved so dearly. Nillish hugged and kissed them and Meena joined them to create a circle of love. But the joy was short lived when Meena told Nillish that he had to hurry to see his father in prison, because he was near to death.

"OH, GOD!" he yelled. "How could I have done that to my father?" Nillish ran as fast as he could to get to the prison which was located a mile from the palace.

He ran screaming through the dirty streets. The Indian people jeered him as he ran.

Annabell, Meena and the two boys followed.

When he reached the prison he asked the guards to take him to his father.

"Father, father, what have I done to you!" shrieked the King.

The old King was in a cell shackled to the cold wall by his hands and feet and he was barely alive. He was so weak that he couldn't open his eyes to see that it was his son that was talking to him. The King yelled at the guards to release his father at once.

The old King was unable to stand on his feet, his hands and legs were cut and bruised and he was breathing very erratically, like he was taking his last breaths on this earth.

He was clearly near to death. The King was distraught at seeing his father lying on the cold cell floor unable to move. He knew that it was his fault.

He turned round to Annabell in desperation. "Beautiful woman, saviour of India, is there anything that is in your powers that can save my father?"

Annabell knelt on the cold floor and held the old King in her arms and gave him a kiss on his lips. She had given him the *kiss of life.* Immediately King Tallish responded and came back healthier than he had been for a long, long time. He got up from the ground, Nillish hugged him tightly.

"Father I'm so sorry for what I have done. The devil was inside my soul."

King Tallish kissed his son and told him that he knew that it wasn't him.

The King kissed Annabell's hand and thanked her over and over again.

"What powers you possess, beautiful lady. You must be without any doubt a divine person. What else could you be?"

Annabell answered. "I know not what I am your Highness: nobody does."

"Well I do," said King Nillish. "We have many Gods and Goddesses in our beautiful country of India and from today we have another - and I solemnly swear that India will never forget what you have done…from this day forward as ruler of all of India, I, the King, will make you, Annabell, the *Goddess of Everything*."

Annabell looked at the King and said, "I thank you, your Highness for such an honour, but I'm not worthy of this: I'm not a Goddess."

"Oh yes, you are," said the King. And he bowed his head in acknowledgement of his own statement.

"On behalf of all of India, I thank you for what you have done this day."

The King peered into Annabell's beautiful sparkling eyes and said, "Is there anything that I can do for you?"

Annabell nodded. "Yes your highness there is, I have come to India in search of a Dragon - will you help me to find it?"

The King was shocked at what Annabell had just said, "But dragons are mythical, Annabell."

"I know your highness, but the creator has told me that I must find the Dragon and see where it flies. Like you, I do not understand, but here in your land there lives a Dragon."

The King looked embarrassed. "I don't know how I can help you," he replied. "I know of no dragon. How could I, or anybody know of such a creature that doesn't exist?"

Annabell shook her head, "I don't know your Highness."

Annabell stayed at the palace and became great friends with the King and Meena.

The King made a public announcement and an apology to his subjects for his behaviour and promised that he would put right all the wrongs that he had done. Everything taken from his people would be given back. India would change, he told them. Taxes would be minimal.

The King couldn't wait to get rid of his ill-gotten wealth. Over the next few days he went out into the streets personally distributing food and clothing for the needy. He and Meena were now very happy, no longer did they have wealth, but they had something much more important - they had love and happiness.

Two weeks passed. Annabell was out helping along with the King and some of his soldiers delivering food and clothing. They drove up a dirt track towards one of the many remote shanty towns that were way up in the hills. As they approached the town Annabell got a strong *urge* about this town. She yelled out, "It's here! I can feel it."

"What's here?" asked the King.

"This town knows about the Dragon, your Highness."

"But how do you know this?" asked the King.

Annabell paused before she answered, she knew that she didn't know the answer to the question. "I don't know," she replied. "But I know that there is somebody here that I have to talk to."

"But who?" asked the King in astonishment. "How would you know this if you've never been here before? These people are peasants, you're above these type of people, Goddess of Everything - you're different class, these are begging people and they're robbers, and they're a real nuisance. We knock down their disgusting filthy hovels in their illegal towns, but the scum just re-build them, it's a hopeless task. Come, come, Goddess of Everything. You don't want to be associating with these people. Let's just leave the food and clothes and go."

Annabell looked at the King with a frown, she was not happy with what the King had just said. "But I do, sir," she replied in a gentle and soft voice. "People are just people and please don't call me Goddess, I'm not worthy of such an honour, and I will not accept the title if you insist on treating people like this." Annabell shook her head at the King.

"Just because somebody has more money than you, and can afford a better standard of living, doesn't mean that they're better than you. You sir, of all people, should know that now. Have you not learned anything from your experience with the Devil?"

The King bowed his head in shame and was clearly embarrassed.

"Yes, yes, of course you're right, I don't know what came over me to say such things - I just can't get used to it, I've been horrible for so long. I'm trying to change, and I will change."

"I know you will, sir." replied Annabell, "but please try to think of what you're saying before you say it. You're a good, kind man. India needs you."

The King took a deep breath and nodded his head - he knew that what Annabell was saying was from her divine heart. "I promise I will never say such horrible things about people ever again."

Then the King paused. Thoughts came into his head.

"Annabell I cannot go with you into this town, it's too dangerous for me, these people don't know that I have changed, they would surely kill me for what I have done to them. And who could blame them?"

"I understand that," replied Annabell, seeing the fear in the King's eyes. "I want to go in alone anyway."

"No! no!." pleaded the King. "You could be harmed, you must go in with my armed guards they will protect you from these..." The King was just about to say something horrible about the people, but he saw the look that Annabell was giving him, and stopped himself.

"I don't need protecting, sir, I cannot be harmed. I have powers, nothing on this Earth can harm me." Just as Annabell finished her sentence a gun shot was fired from the direction of the town, followed by several more shots. The bullets could be heard whistling over their heads. The people of the town had spotted the King's men and were trying to warn them off from coming into their town. One of the King's body guards grabbed hold of the King and pulled him to the ground and protected him with his own body. All the other guards had already fallen to the ground to protect themselves. Annabell just stood her ground.

"SEE! SEE!" yelled the King. "What did I tell you? These people are nothing but savages, I'm sorry to say that Annabell, but that's what they are. They try to shoot us, normal people would not do this. Please take cover, Annabell, I'll send in my armed guards to deal with these thugs."

Annabell turned to the King. "You will most certainly not send in armed guards, sir, these people are not dangerous - they are frightened people, sir. They do not fire at you, they fire into the air. I must talk with these people."

Annabell walked up a dirt track towards the shanty town. The town could barely be seen from the main road. As she walked she could feel *eyes* watching her from behind the trees and bushes, she knew that people were there but they didn't reveal themselves.

She walked for about a quarter of a mile until finally coming to the town. It was quite a big town, but it was filthy, and all the dwellings had corrugated roofs, and there was rubbish in abundance, she wondered how people could live like this.

The dwellings were really close together, it was like the people of this town were so frightened that they huddled together for protection and the smell of the whole place was repulsive. It was like a rotting smell. Annabell held her nose as she walked further into the town - all around were bits of vehicles and stinking rubbish - suddenly she caught sight of a pack of rats that were rummaging through the stinking food leftovers. Annabell screwed up her face in disgust - this town was without doubt the most disgusting, filthy place that she had ever seen and she still hadn't seen a living person, but she knew that they were watching her.

Suddenly the silence was broken by a scraggy flea-bitten dog that was barking and running towards her. It stopped at her feet and started growling and was showing its large teeth. It was a very angry dog, just like the people of this town, Annabell suspected.

The dog, a German Shepherd, jumped up at Annabell and tried to bite her arm. Annabell screamed at the dog to stop. "Why do you bite me?" she yelled. She knew that the dog could understand her, but it didn't reply it was so shocked that it could understand what she was saying that it ran off yelping like it had been hurt, but Annabell hadn't touched the dog.

The dog's yelping brought the people out of hiding, they thought that Annabell had harmed the dog.

The people came at her from everywhere with sticks, knives and stones in their hands and they meant to harm her. They thought that she was the *Devil* She looked like evil to them because of her appearance.

They surrounded her, and were shouting and screaming. These people were the dirtiest scruffiest people that Annabell had ever seen - they were like hillbilly people in the worst meaning of the word. (Ignorant and unsophisticated) as some people think of them, but these people weren't real country hillbillys. Hillbilly is a friendly name that real hillbilly people give to themselves.

These people were mostly rural people that had been forced out of the countryside to live up the mountains by the King's harsh taxes.

Although Annabell was probably the most famous person in the world - these people lived an isolated life and had no-idea who this strange person was.

They started shouting at her and throwing stones and hitting her with their sticks - some were prodding her with their knives, but the stones bounced off her - the sticks didn't hurt her and the knives didn't harm her at all. Then suddenly a big man appeared from an alleyway. The people separated away from around Annabell.

Annabell came face to face with a portly man. He was over six feet tall and he had a big belly hanging over his worn out leather belt. His shirt was a dirty blue colour and was tattered and the shirt buttons were missing at the bottom allowing his excessive fat around his belly to hang from his belt.

The man had dark rings around his evil looking eyes and he had a scar running all the way down from his left eye to his chin. It was like a knife scar. He hadn't shaved for days, if not weeks, but you could still see that scar, because his facial hair wouldn't grow over it. His hair was matted and long and it stank!! He was wearing no shoes, his feet and face were dirty. This man sure did look menacing, but worst of all he was brandishing a shotgun!! And it was pointed at Annabell.

"What do you want here?" The man yelled with thunder in his voice. "I warned you to stay away were not going to move from here …NEVER! do you hear me …NEVER!" The man was ranting and raving at the top of his voice.

"What's the matter with you? Why are you red? Are you ill? Have you got a disease or something?" All the townspeople quickly moved back further away from Annabell fearing that she was diseased.

"Get away from us," the man shouted. "You'll contaminate us all. We'll all die!"

The man then took two steps backwards and yelled, "Is this how the King plans to kill us by sending in a diseased person? Look at you! What have they done to you? Are you radioactive?"

All the townspeople were now very frightened of Annabell, they thought that she was diseased and so they ran away, leaving the man with the gun all on his own.

A voice from afar shouted, "Shoot her quickly before she spreads the disease, quickly, all our children will die."

"NO! NO! NO!" shrieked Annabell. "You will not die, there's nothing wrong with me. I haven't got a disease, I was born this way." But the man was so frightened now that he panicked and pulled the trigger and fired *both* barrels of his shotgun at Annabell.

BANG! BANG! The sound of the shotgun echoed around the shanty town.

The townspeople came out of hiding expecting to see Annabell lying *dead* on the ground.

The buckshot hit Annabell with full force! But she didn't even flinch.

The man stood there shocked, he was sure that he had hit Annabell. His gun was still smoking. With shaking hands he re-loaded, but this time he worked up the courage to get closer to her, he didn't want to miss her a second time.

He was now at point blank range. BANG! BANG! He fired again, but Annabell didn't move. The man screamed with shock, and turned pale.

"Why are you not dead?" He knew that the pellets must have hit her. He was so shocked that he fell to the ground on his hands and knees and bowed his head.

He could barely get the words out of his mouth. "What…what…what, are you?" He spluttered, he could barely get his breath, through shock and his body was shaking. "You're not human! Or you must be a mutant of some kind. You should be dead, but there's not a mark on you, not even on your clothes…nothing, why did you not die?"

Annabell had a stern look on her face. "Get up, you stupid man." She yelled, "Why did you shoot me? I haven't done anything to you; I've come here to give the people of this town food and clothing; haven't you heard the King has changed now? - he's a good kind man and wants to help his people." Annabell looked the tall fat man straight in his face, he was now standing up, but he wouldn't look at her. "Look at me," she shrieked.

The man slowly raised his head. "I haven't come all this way to be beaten with sticks and shot at, and have stones thrown at me, and knives dug into me."

"I'm sorry; I'm sorry," sobbed the man, he didn't feel so tough now.

"I was afraid - we all were; look at your skin and eyes, you frightened us; why are you red? I've never seen anything like you before - are you a Goddess?"

The fat man was still shaking and crying. He was clearly in shock.

Annabell thought about the question. "I don't think that I'm a Goddess, but your King says I am," replied Annabell. "So the answer to your question is: well, I have to answer 'yes'."

The man was still sobbing and was ashamed at what he had tried to do to Annabell. "Please forgive me," he muttered. "We're simple people here. We thought that you were a threat to us - we don't ask for much, life is a constant struggle. The King won't allow us to live a normal life, we don't really mean to harm people, but they harm us; they beat us and knock down our homes; what are we to do? Surely we have the right to protect ourselves. I'm the leader of this town and try my best, but sometimes the task becomes impossible. I'm really tired of the struggle, we all are. We saw the King's men coming we thought that they come to knock down our homes again, like they always do."

Annabell looked around her surroundings, she could now see small children with rags for clothes and nobody in this town had any shoes - slowly the people were coming out from their homes and gathering in the dusty dirty road. They had witnessed what had happened and now believed that Annabell was some sort of Goddess.

About one hundred and fifty people including many children approached her, when they were close to her they all fell to their knees and prayed.

Annabell couldn't help thinking that maybe the King would be doing these poor unfortunate people a favour by knocking down this dreadful place. This sure was the town from hell, but at the same time she felt great sadness for these people, nobody deserved to live like this, she thought.

Annabell looked at the tall fat man. "What is your name, sir?" she asked politely. She was still holding her nose as she spoke, trying to mask the stench.

"Gunti," came his reply.

"Well, hello Gunti, my name is Annabell. I'm very surprised that you didn't know who I was, but never mind. Now then Gunti, I don't know why but something has drawn me to this town - what do you call this God forsaken place?"

"Rangdo, Miss Annabell," replied Gunti.

"Where does the name come from, Gunti?" Annabell was squeezing her nose as she spoke, but this time it wasn't to mask the smell, it was in thought. This name meant something to her. She knew instantly the reason now why she was drawn to this town. This name was a sign.

"It's just a name that we've called it. I don't think that it means anything," said Gunti. "But I don't really know - maybe it does, but I wouldn't know."

"Well who named this town, Rangdo? Can you remember when you first used the name? It couldn't have been very long ago, most of these towns are fairly recent - is this the first town that you've named Rangdo?"

Gunti thought for a minute and for some reason he bent down to pick up the shotgun that was lying on the ground. This really annoyed Annabell. "What are you doing?" she screamed. "Don't you dare, you don't need that; nasty things, put it down at once." Annabell was very stern with him.

Gunti put the shotgun back on the ground and stood up and faced Annabell.

"Sorry! Sorry!" he said apologetically.

As he stood up, the wind blew in Annabell's direction. Gunti's body odour hit her full blast.

"Phew! Gunti, you stink!!" she said once again holding her nose. "Why don't you wash? Water doesn't cost any money, you know. I understand that you can't afford clothing, that's fair enough, but what's stopping you from washing?"

Gunti stood there, his eyes were locked onto hers just like all the other people in this town - everybody was staring at Annabell like they were all in some sort of trance. Gunti had taken no notice of what Annabell had just said.

Then suddenly without warning he shouted out. "Wow! Just look at you."

Gunti was coming to his senses after the shock that he had had.

"What on Earth are you?" before Annabell could give an answer Gunti noticed that his four blasts from his shot gun had in fact hit Annabell. The buck shot was lying at her feet, hundreds if not thousands of the lead pellets were flattened!! Like they had hit something solid.

"Please tell me how this was possible," asked Gunti. "Are you wearing armour?"

Gunti knew that this was a stupid question because Annabell was wearing just a T-shirt and slacks. He could see that she couldn't be wearing armour under her T-shirt.

"No, I'm not wearing armour, Gunti," replied Annabell. She then laughed, "How can I be wearing armour under this thin shirt, Gunti? Don't be so silly."

"But the lead shot definitely hit you, Miss Annabell. Look it lies at your feet *flattened.* Why did you not get hurt? And why are there no marks on your T-shirt ?" Gunti shook his head in disbelief. He clearly didn't understand what was happening. "How can this be?"

Annabell knew that she had to give Gunti an answer and she thought for a while before she answered, "I don't know why Gunti. All that I can tell you is that I have special powers that have been given to me, I've been sent on a mission to find special objects." Annabell paused again because she knew that what she was about to say next would be hard to be believed by a normal person. "The creator has asked me to find these special objects, Gunti." She waited for the inevitable question.

"Creator?" Gunti nearly choked on his words. "What you mean, the creator? - As in God... the creator?"

Annabell thought for a moment before she answered,. "If God is the creator who has told me to find the parts of the holism, well yes, Gunti. The God for all of us, I suppose. *The One.* The only one that most of us believe in, has told me to follow the signs, and the signs have led me here."

"I knew that you were a Goddess," said Gunti. He threw his hands up into the air and fell to the ground on his knees and was now in awe of Annabell.

"Get up!" shrieked Annabell. "Don't be so silly." Annabell's eyes were sparkling even brighter as the light from the evening sun was slowly dimming.

"Get up, Gunti, I need some answers from you," yelled Annabell. "I don't have time for this silliness."

Gunti slowly rose from the ground but had his head bowed.

"Oh, for goodness' sake look at me face to face, I need some answers - I need to know why this town was named Rangdo," moaned Annabell.

Gunti lifted his head, but to him it was like looking at an angel - she was so beautiful now that he knew that she wasn't *diseased.* He felt ashamed that he had shot at her.

"Oh dear, what have I done? Sorry, I didn't want to shoot you," said Gunti. "I didn't mean to..."

Annabell didn't let him finish. "Oh yes you did-don't lie," replied Annabell. "You wanted to kill me, you know you did."

Gunti nodded his head. "Well, yes, you're right I did. How could I have done such a thing, will I ever be forgiven? My God, what have I done? I've shot an angel, a Goddess. Thank God that I didn't harm you."

"Gunti, please shut up and tell me who named this town Rangdo? This is the third time that I've asked you." Annabell was getting very impatient. She knew that she was so close to finding out why she had been drawn to this town.

"But why is the name so special to you? It's just a name, it doesn't mean anything," said Gunti waving his hands in a circular motion. His fat belly was wobbling like a jelly on a plate as he was trying to express himself.

"Ah, but it does Gunti," replied Annabell. "You see, I'm looking for a Dragon!! Would you know the whereabouts of one, sir ?"

Gunti stood there and laughed out loud, the people of the town didn't know why he was laughing.

"PEOPLE!" yelled Gunti. "This strange beautiful woman, an angel, a Goddess, has come to our town looking for a Dragon. Has anybody seen a Dragon?"

Although they didn't want to laugh all the people couldn't help themselves, they all just burst out laughing. Annabell was a bit annoyed but not angry, she was happy to see the people of this town laughing - they hadn't had much to laugh about over the last few years.

"Please stop laughing at me," she pleaded. "This is no joking matter. A Dragon exists somewhere near here and somebody in this town knows of it. Now then Gunti, who named this town Rangdo?" Gunti was still laughing when he pointed to the person who had named the town.

Chapter Thirty seven
Anja

The person that he was pointing at was the only person that was not laughing. There was a young boy sitting underneath a tree. Annabell made her way over to the boy. He was about eleven years old, but it was difficult to give an accurate age because the boy was very under nourished and extremely dirty.

"Why don't you laugh like the others?" asked Annabell in a gentle voice. As she spoke she pulled a silly face trying to make the small boy laugh. "Everybody knows that Dragons don't exist, that's why they laugh at me, I'm a funny red lady, aren't I?" But the boy didn't say anything, he just sat there staring into space.

"There's no point in talking to him," said Gunti. "You're wasting your time. He can't speak - not for a long time: not one single word."

"But you said that the boy named this town Rangdo? If he can't talk how did he name the town?" said Annabell motioning her hands for an explanation.

"Well, because this was the last word that he ever said, we're not even sure if this is the word that he said because it was muffled, it didn't make any sense really, his mind was jumbled up. It was like he had dyslexia in his speech. We just guessed that he was saying this word, so as a mark of respect for him we named the town with the word that was coming out of his mouth. He's never said another word since."

"So he used to talk then?" asked Annabell.

"Oh yeah," replied Gunti. "He was a chatty lovely boy, life and soul, you couldn't stop him talking, he was so full of fun and then one day, he came back into the town shaking, and he was very pale. He was obviously in some sort of shock, he kept on repeating the word Rangdo, well that's what we thought that he was saying, and then he stopped talking and never said another word."

"But why Rangdo, Gunti?" Annabell knew what the word meant, but she had to find out why the boy said it.

"I don't know why," said Gunti, swatting a fly that was buzzing around his head. "Blinking flies! I hate them!" he moaned. "What possible use is a fly to the world?" And then he tried to swat another one that had landed on his ear, but this fly was too fast for him and he ended up clipping himself around the ear.

Annabell laughed out loud at Gunti's antics and couldn't help feeling that he deserved his clip around the ear.

"What's wrong with the boy, Gunti?"

I don't know Miss Annabell, we think that it's some kind of shock. Something has frightened him, but we don't know what. We took him to the doctors and tried to find out, but they didn't know what was wrong with him."

"How long ago did the boy stop talking, Gunti?" Annabell knew that she was on to something.

"Um... let me think...umm... must be... about ten months ago. He just sits there every single day by that tree, staring; it's like he's looking for something or hiding from something."

Annabell knelt down beside the boy, he was extremely dirty looking. Like all the people in this town his clothes were rags. The boy's face was covered in mud, all you could see were his brown eyes, it was like he was camouflaging himself.

Annabell placed her hands over the boy's eyes. "Do not be afraid," she whispered.

"Listen to what I have to say. Whatever you have seen - wherever you have been - when I remove my hands from your eyes - you will remember."

Annabell removed her hands from the boy's eyes. The boy started to shudder and shake and slowly came out of his shock and looked at Annabell with a strange look but he wasn't frightened of her appearance. It was the look of a person that had seen something unusual before.

Annabell looked the boy straight into his eyes. Her eyes were sparkling and the boy was fascinated by them.

"What did you see, little boy? Did you see the Dragon?" Suddenly the boy's eyes lit up like a beacon he knew this word. Suddenly his mouth began to move, his lips quivered, he was trying to speak his first words for a long time. Suddenly sounds came from his mouth.

"Rang…do - Rang…do." but then his words changed. "Dra…do - Dra….gon…Dra-gon, I saw a Dragon," his speech had got faster.

Annabell was very excited by this. This was definitely the sign that she had been looking for, the boy had the answer to the mystery of the Dragon she was certain of that.

"Where did you see the Dragon, little boy?" asked Annabell very excitedly.

"It was …it was…" and then he blurted out. "Mountain."

"What Mountain?" asked Annabell. "Quickly - quickly please tell me."

Suddenly the boy opened up it was like he wanted to get all his thoughts out of his mind as quickly as possible.

"I saw it on the mountain, it was a *blue* Dragon with big black eyes, it flew around and around me - it was huge and I was frightened I could hear its giant wings flapping and then it disappeared in a puff of smoke."

This was a strange story that the little boy was telling, a blue Dragon that disappeared in puff of smoke. But Annabell knew that it must be true, no matter how stupid the story sounded, something had truamatised this boy and he had given her a sign.

"How big was the Dragon, little boy?" asked Annabell motioning her hands in a outstretched position.

The boy stretched his arms out, but he did it again and again, ten times in all. Annabell guessed that the Dragon was at least fifteen feet long, but she wasn't sure, so she got a stick and drew a big Dragon on the dirt. "Was it this big?" she whispered.

The boy answered, "Yes." Annabell had drawn a Dragon on the dirt that was at least twenty feet long so this creature was a big one.

"Where did you see the Dragon little boy, was it here?" she asked, pointing to the mountain that was behind the town.

"No! no, no many miles away from here," answered the boy.

"What hundreds of miles?" asked Annabell.

As she was speaking to the little boy Annabell craftily looked around to see if anybody from the town could see that the little boy was talking but they hadn't noticed.

The little boy answered, "Yes, a long way from here," and then he started to cry which was a good sign. It meant that the emotions that he had been carrying in his mind were now being released. Annabell put her arms around the boy and cuddled him. She whispered into his ear, "Let it go now little boy, let your fears come out."

The boy began to talk more freely. "I keep thinking that the Dragon will come back for me...I'm watching out for it, but it doesn't come yet. Please don't let it get me."

"Why did you not tell anybody what you had seen?" asked Annabell.

"I couldn't...couldn't talk - I wanted to, but I couldn't get the word Dragon out of my mouth, I don't know why but I could only say the word 'Rang-do' - the word was jumbled in my mind."

Annabell knew why the boy was saying Rangdo. It was what she was told to look for.

The boy was almost back to normal now, all his worries were gone from his mind.

"Why are you red? And why do your eyes sparkle? Are you an angel?" he asked boldly.

"No, I'm not an angel, my name is Annabell."

The little boy laughed, "Your name sounds like a fairy - like *Tinker-bell* Are you a fairy? You look like one."

"No, I'm not a fairy - well I don't think that I am. It's strange that you should say that, a little girl said the same thing as you once. Her name was Trinity. What is your name?"

"Anja… my name is Anja."

Annabell peered deep into Anja's eyes and said, "You're a brave boy, Anja - I'm sorry that you saw the Dragon and that it frightened you but do not be afraid, I'm going to give you a gift and give you back the ten months of your life that you lost. I'm going to put my hands back over your eyes, when I remove them you will have no memory of the Dragon."

Annabell said a few words and removed her hands from the boy's eyes and touched the palm on his left hand with her finger. This left a red dot on Anja's hand that would remain there for the rest of his life. Anja would gain great knowledge with this mark and would become a leading figure in India when he grew up but he would never know that it was Annabell's finger print that had given him this gift.

Anja was also visibly younger in his appearance, but still had the mind of an eleven-year old and he was now back to his normal self. He looked up and caught sight of his mother and father, he yelled out in great excitement "Mummy! - Daddy!" Everybody turned round to face Anja - they were shocked to hear him speak again.

Gunti shouted out. "Miss Annabell, our Goddess. How did you do this miracle? The boy speaks and he looks younger."

"Yes Gunti, that's right. Anja is alright now. I have used the powers invested in me to cure him - it wasn't his fault that he could not talk."

"What was wrong with the boy?" asked Gunti.

"You were right Gunti, the boy was in shock."

"But what had shocked him- what was so bad that could do that to him?"

"He saw a Dragon, Gunti!!! And he's been ever since frightened that the Dragon will return, but he won't remember it now - I've removed it from his mind."

Gunti stood there baffled. "But Dragons don't exist, you and your Dragon, Miss Annabell. No such creature has ever existed, that's a fact - how could the boy have seen a creature that has never existed?"

"I don't know, Gunti," replied Annabell. "But there is a Dragon, your beautiful country India, holds a secret - somewhere here there is a Dragon, and I have to find it. Where did the boy first stop talking? It wasn't in this place I know that."

Gunti thought for a moment. "It was when we were living on the Punjab mountain, we didn't stay there long; it was too cold up there and strange things were happening that couldn't be explained."

Annabell interrupted, "What strange things, Gunti? Explain yourself, please."

"Well, you already know about Anja. There were also these strange bells sounds that could be heard echoing around the mountain especially when there was a full moon. Believe me, we were all very frightened because there was nobody on the mountain with us. We were positive of that, we searched and searched, but couldn't find who was ringing the bells. And there was another strange thing that happened, one of our people said that he saw what he thought was a 'temple' on the mountain, but he said that it was only there for a few seconds and disappeared in front of his eyes. When it disappeared, he said, that a whirlwind got up from nowhere and then just dispersed. He said that this was very strange because it was a very calm day with hardly any wind. He wouldn't go back up there again, but we sent some of the townsmen up to where he said he saw the temple, but they found nothing. We left the mountain shortly after that. We believed that it was haunted by spirits. I wouldn't want to go back there again."

Annabell was fascinated by this story especially 'the temple'. Everything was making sense now. She knew that she was in the right place.

"Gunti, I must ask a favour from you - will you take me to the Punjab mountain?"

"No, no, no, I'm sorry great lady I cannot do that I must stay here and protect my people, soon the King's men will come and knock down our homes; I must remain here with my people, I'm very sorry."

"Gunti, do you want to stay in this place - forever?" asked Annabell.

"Yes, yes of course I do, we all do - it's not much of a place here, but we like it. It will get better if only the King would leave us alone."

"Gunti, if I get permission for you to stay here, would you take me to the Punjab mountain?" Annabell was trying to tempt Gunti.

"Yes, yes, of course I would, but I don't think the King will allow that."

"Well - wait and see." Annabell walked off back towards the King. She turned around and shouted. "Please do not fire anymore shots from that dreadful gun; do you promise?"

Gunti nodded his head.

Annabell walked back down the dirt track and came to the King and his men.

"Where have you been, Annabell? Are you hurt? We heard shots and were very worried about you," said the King.

"There was no need to worry, thank you for being concerned for me, but I cannot be harmed. I must ask a favour from you, sir."

"Whatever it is, Annabell, you can have it, anything for you. Just say what it is, and it's yours."

"Sir, - kind sir, I wish for the people of this town called Rangdo to be allowed to stay here and live their lives in peace and prosper. The creator has touched these people, sir."

King Nillish held Annabell's hand and kissed it. "Your wish will be granted, special lady, as from this day forward this town known as Rangdo, will be known as Royal Rangdo, India's special town. The people of this town will be given help to build a proper town, one fit for a king you might say." The King gave a little grin.

"Thank you sir, just one more thing. The boy known as Anja is a special boy, would you please see that he gets a proper education, because this boy is destined for something special."

The King said that he would.

Annabell thanked the King and made her way back to the town. When she got there all the people cheered and Anja's parents came rushing towards Annabell and kissed her and thanked her for saving their son.

Annabell felt so proud that her powers had truly been a *Godsend,* today.

The whole town was celebrating the saving of Anja - they believed that he had been released from evil spirits. There were no doubts in the minds of these people that Annabell was indeed a Goddess. They had witnessed miracles this day.

Gunti was talking to Anja, trying to get him to say what had been the matter with him, but Anja didn't know what Gunti was talking about.

"Gunti – Gunti," shouted Annabell. "Come here please, I have good news - I've had a word with the King. The good King Nillish has made a promise to me that you can stay here and that your town will be re-built to make a proper town fit for people to live in. The King says it will be 'Fit for a king' and the special boy Anja will be sent to the finest school in India to become a scholar. If this is alright with his parents."

Gunti shook his head in disbelief. "How could this be? And why do you say 'Good King' when I know that he's a very bad person."

"He's not bad anymore Gunti; King Nillish is a kind man - he wants to help his people, it wasn't his fault that he turned bad - it was the Devil that had got into his soul, but he's cured now, Gunti. I cured him just like I cured Anja."

But Gunti wasn't convinced, too much hurt had been inflicted upon his people by the King.

"I know that you're telling the truth Miss Annabell, but I find it hard to believe, because the King was so horrible to us all - I would have to see it for myself to believe it."

"Your wish will be granted, Gunti," said Annabell. "Please follow me."

Annabell led Gunti down the dirt track - she came upon the vehicle that the King was in. She tapped on the window. "Sir, I have somebody here to see you, his name is Gunti. He's the leader of Rangdo town."

The King lowered the window of the vehicle, when Gunti saw the King he fell to the floor in shock. The King told him to get up off the ground, which he did, but his legs were like jelly and he was too frightened to look at the King. In a trembling voice Gunti spluttered out, "I'm sorry... I'm sorry your Highness - we will move as quickly as possible, in fact, right now, but I would be most grateful to you if you could give us a few hours to gather our possessions together and I promise you we will leave all our money for you, your Highness, I promise, we will soon be gone. Please do not put us in prison."

"Gone!" said the King. "Gone - gone where? Have I told you to go?" The King was smiling.

"No, your Highness, but we know that you will; you have in the past. You've always told your soldiers to move us and they take all our money and jewellery and you knock down our homes and put us in prison."

"Yes," said the King in a sad voice. "You're right Gunti, but it will never happen again, I'm a changed man thanks to this wonderful lady. I have promised her that I will let you stay here and live your lives in peace. Your town, Gunti will be re-built to the finest standards and will be known as Royal Rangdo. All the people of this town will be looked after, especially the boy known as Anja."

The King turned to Annabell and smiled. Annabell nodded and thanked the King.

Gunti couldn't believe what the King was saying, but he knew that it was true.

"One thing, Gunti," said the King. "There's to be no guns or any weapons held by anybody ever in this town. Is that understood?"

Gunti gave his promise. Gunti looked at Annabell. He was speechless, he just gave her a big hug and tears ran freely down his cheeks which left lines on his dirty face. At this moment in time Gunti was the happiest man in the whole world.

"Will you now take me to the Punjab mountain, Gunti?"

"Yes," he replied still hugging her. "We're going to need transport though, special lady, it's a long way to the mountain, maybe four days' travel and you will need to prepare yourself for the cold."

"I do not feel the cold, Gunti, I do not need to protect myself, but thank you for caring."

Gunti shook his head. "My, you sure are a strange person, Miss Annabell. Now then, how do we travel to the mountain? We only have very old vehicles here, rust buckets you would call them, I don't think that any of them would be able to make it to the mountain. It's a very long way."

The King interrupted and said that he would provide everything that Annabell needed for her trip to the Punjab Mountains. Annabell had told the King that she believed the Dragon was somewhere up this mountain and that she wanted to go there to find out. It was arranged and Annabell told Gunti that they would start their journey in two days' time.

Chapter Thirty Eight
The Search For The Dragon

Two days passed. The King kept his promise and had provided Annabell with a vehicle and a driver and all the provisions and equipment that they would need for their trip.

Annabell was offered by the King to be put up in the finest hotels en route to the mountains, but she didn't want that. Of course, Gunti did, but Annabell wanted to stay in a tent at night and cook the meals by the camp fire. She wanted to remember her trip to Australia with Kevin whom she missed very much.

The four-day trip to the mountain soon went, but nearly all the time, all that Annabell would talk about was finding the Dragon. Gunti understandably was a bit fed-up with Annabell's conversation and most of the time he didn't bother to listen to her. He pretended to be asleep. He never believed that the Dragon existed, but Annabell did, she was very excited. Every now and again she would look at the old parchment.

The writings said 'Temporal' is where the Dragon could be found - Gunti had said that someone had seen a temple on this mountain, but it disappeared. That was a bit strange she thought, but it was all fitting together and there was one thing that she hadn't told anybody. The reason why she was drawn to the town Rangdo.

This name was no coincidence. The letters of this town's name re-arranged spell the name Dragon!! The parchment always told her to 'follow the signs'. This was clearly a sign.

At about 10:30am on Friday they finally reached the Punjab Mountain.

The mountain was bigger than Annabell had expected, in fact, it was massive - they all were!! Because it wasn't one mountain, it was a range of four mountains! Gunti hadn't told her this.

"Which mountain were you on, Gunti?" asked Annabell but she had a feeling that she knew what he was going to say before he opened his mouth and she wasn't wrong!!

Gunti scratched his head in thought and paused for quite a while and then said, "Good question, the answer to it ...is...? I can't remember - they all look the same to me now."

Annabell was not amused. "Please tell me that you're joking, Gunti."

"I'm not Miss Annabell, our angel - our Goddess."

"That's enough of the angel and Goddess, Gunti, I've had enough of that, please just call me Annabell or if you like Miss Annabell but not 'angel' or 'Goddess'. Is that clear?"

Gunti nodded his head and muttered underneath his breath, "You are an angel and Goddess, but if that's what you want; alright I'll call you Miss Annabell."

"Good," she said, "thank goodness, that's settled then."

They turned off the road and drove down a dirt track for about two miles, finally stopping at a river. The river was too deep for the vehicle to cross, so this was journey's end. "How did you cross this river?" asked Annabell.

"We built a bridge across it, but the King's men must have knocked it down when we left."

There were several tracks that led up to the four mountains. If Gunti didn't know what mountain it was that he stayed on her task was going to be very difficult indeed.

"Come on, Gunti, help me out here, please try to remember where you once lived. Surely it shouldn't be that hard. For God's sake! you lived here, Gunti. You did live here? This was the place wasn't it?" Annabell was getting a little bit ratty.

"Oh yes, this is definitely where we once lived, but that was ten months ago, I really can't remember Miss Annabell, I'm so sorry, but all these mountains look the same to me."

Annabell sighed. "Oh Gunti, why are all men so useless? Kevin, my boyfriend, is the same he's got a pea for a brain. Ok then, there's no point in you staying here: I suppose you've done your job. I'll have to find the Dragon on my own - go on, off you go...go home and look after your family or something." Annabell was shooing him away from her with her hands. She was none too pleased with Gunti. Annabell called over the driver and told him to take himself and Gunti home.

"But how will you get back home?" asked the driver.

"Don't worry about me," said Annabell. "I'll fly home."

"But there's no airport here," said the driver.

"No, you don't understand, I'll fly home: *me,* I can fly."

"Er," said the driver. "What, have you got a plane here?"

"No," said Annabell. The driver looked at Annabell and was bemused, and tried to make some sense of what she was saying, but he couldn't.

Gunti was listening to the conversation between the driver and Annabell and was laughing his head off. He kind of knew what Annabell was trying to tell the driver. Although he didn't know that she could actually fly he knew that Annabell was capable of anything - if she says that she can fly, then she can fly. As in being like a fly!

Gunti turned to the driver to try and help him out. "This beautiful lady my friend, can produce miracles. I've seen some, she's a very special lady; yes, a very special lady indeed, if she says that she can fly, it means that she doesn't need an aircraft, sir. Do you know what I mean?"

"No," said the driver

"This lady can fly sir, like the comic man. The man they called 'Superman' - do you remember the old films? The really old films that they used to put on plastic circles?"

"Oh, yeah," said the driver. "I've seen some of those things in the museum, they sometimes play them on funny machines but the stories are a bit far-fetched, I mean everybody knows that humans can't fly."

"Well, this lady can, sir, I think that she is like the comic man - I believe that she can fly, sir."

"Really!" said the driver. "Can you really fly madam?

"Yes I can," said Annabell. "Would you like a demonstration?"

"Yes I would," said the driver excitedly.

"So would I," said Gunti, also very excitedly.

"Very well then I will show you." With that Annabell told Gunti and the driver to step aside. She then held out her arms towards the sky and shot up into the air like a rocket!!

The two men looked up into the sky in amazement. A flying red woman!! They had never seen that before.

Annabell flew around for several minutes, she was kind of showing off. The two men looked at each other and had an expression, that money couldn't buy. It was a 'Wow!' moment for both of them for the rest of their lives.

Annabell flew back down to the ground and landed gently on her feet.

"How did you do that?" asked the driver. "Have you got a rocket strapped to your back, madam?"

Annabell turned around showing her back to the driver and laughed out loud.

"No sir, I have not got a "rocket" strapped to my back," and then she gave a little giggle.

"But how did you do that? Nobody can fly," said the driver.

"Well I can," said Annabell. "I just hold my breath, and say to myself *fly* and put my hands in the air, and I fly. It's so wonderful, it's like being a bird."

"Well this is as far as we can go, Miss Annabell," said Gunti. He was impatient to get away from these mountains. "I'll just unload all the camping gear for you and all the food that's left and wish you luck in finding your Dragon." Gunti laughed and was just about to unload the gear when Annabell stopped him.

"No," said Annabell. "Don't bother, I won't need anything. The camping gear was for you and the driver."

"But I didn't want to camp, it was your idea," said Gunti. "I would prefer to stay in nice warm hotels. What about food? Where shall I put that? You're going to need food, you'll starve to death up here. There's no food here except for rats and bugs."

"I won't be here for very long Gunti," said Annabell, confidently. "Soon as I find the Dragon I will be going home to America. When I find the Dragon, I won't even have to fly home. I just close my eyes and wish to be home and it will happen."

Gunti didn't say anything. He knew that anything was possible with this woman. He got back into the vehicle and told the driver that he wasn't going to be *camping* on the trip back under any circumstances. Before they drove off, Annabell told Gunti that she would return to India one day to see how his town Rangdo was getting on. He gave a wave and then he was gone.

Annabell was now all alone in the middle of nowhere and there wasn't a living soul to be seen. She flew across the river. There were lots of tracks that led up these mountains. She started walking up a path - she had no idea if this was the right path or even the right mountain, but she had to start somewhere. She was looking for signs of Gunti's old town, but at the moment there wasn't any.

She walked for several miles, all the time the path got steadily steeper, it was very cold as she got higher and higher, but she didn't feel it.

The day wore on and she hadn't come across any signs of the old town or a temple, not even the ruins of one and she hadn't heard any bells, it was very quiet here. It was a soulless place. Suddenly a butterfly landed on her arm.

"Hello butterfly," said Annabell. "My, you sure are beautiful, aren't you? What are you doing up here? It's a bit cold for you here, isn't it?"

"Yes it is," said the butterfly in a soft and gentle voice. "But I was born here, not very long ago. Actually, I'm making my way down to the bottom of the mountain where it's warm, I need to find a mate so that I can have babies. And thank you for calling me beautiful, you're not too bad yourself. You're a lovely colour, aren't you?"

"Thank you," said Annabell feeling rather good about herself.

"You don't mind me resting here for a while, do you? I need to dry my wings. It's a bit damp up here, your arm was an ideal spot because it's nice and warm."

"No," said Annabell. "Rest as long as you want, it's nice talking to you anyway."

"Thank you," said the butterfly, "that's most kind of you."

"Can I ask you a question, butterfly?" said Annabell holding out her arm towards the sun so that the butterfly could get the maximum warmth from it.

"Of course you can," said the butterfly, flapping its wings.

"Have you ever seen a Dragon on these mountains?"

"A Dragon? What's that? Is it a flower? Is that what you talking about? I haven't been here very long so I don't really know all there is to know about the mountain."

"No. It's not a flower, butterfly, it's a big creature with big nostrils, with fire coming out of them and it's got wings and it can fly, like you."

The butterfly thought for a moment. "No, I haven't," it replied. "And… to be honest. I don't think that I would want to. 'Fire' you say, and it's coming from its nose - well I never! I don't think that I'll hang around here any longer. I don't want to be seeing your Dragon. Bye, thanks for the use of your arm." And then the butterfly flew away as fast as it could.

Annabell realised that the butterfly probably wouldn't know about anything that she was talking about. It had only just been born, so would have very little knowledge of anything.

Annabell walked all day, up and up the mountain. It was beginning to get dark, but she didn't stop. In no time at all it was pitch black.

The creatures of the night were emerging from their homes. There were lots of rats up here, big black ones, some of them were a foot long!! And they were scurrying around everywhere searching for food. Annabell wasn't frightened of them, although she had to admit that she didn't really like them.

One came right up to here, and started sniffing at her foot, its ears and whiskers were twitching and its sharp teeth were trying to bite a hole in her boot.

"Go away!" yelled Annabell. "You're horrible! You rats are dirty."

"No we're not," said the rat twitching its nose. "Why are we horrible? And we're not dirty. I wash every day. What are you doing on my land anyway? It's dark up here, how can you see in the dark? I didn't think humans could see in the darkness hours."

"Well I can," said Annabell cockily.

"What's wrong with your eyes?" asked the rat. "Why are they sparkling? That's very strange. They look like stars."

"I don't know why my eyes sparkle I was born like that," said Annabell pushing the rat off her foot with her other foot.

"Don't kick me," said the rat.

"I'm not kicking you, I'm just getting you off my foot."

"Well you get off my land, you don't belong up here, we've got a code of conduct up here, you know; and the conduct code contract says that this is my piece of land during the darkness hours. My piece of land goes right up to that rock and then it's Bill Stort's bit of land. You wouldn't want to be trespassing on his land

I can tell you. He's a big mean rat, that one is, and his family lives there with him, and they're a rough mob.

"He's got four wives and twenty two kids and they're always squabbling. I can't get any peace around here, with all these kids scurrying about. I've asked for a move but the rat council won't let me, they say that I've already been allocated my land, so I can't move unless somebody will transfer with me, but there's not much hope of that, so I try to keep out of the way of Bill Stort and his unruly kids. Now go on, do as you're told please, and push off, otherwise I'll shout for Bill to come and help me get you off my land."

"What are you mumbling on about rat?" said Annabell. "Nobody owns the mountain, it belongs to the people of India, I can go wherever I want to. I'm friends with the King you know, so there, go on, go and get Bill Stort, see if I care, and he shouldn't be having four wives anyway, one is enough for anybody. Why should males be allowed to have loads of wives, when females are only allowed one husband? That doesn't seem fair.

"Us females are equal in this world today If he was human he would be put in prison for bigamy."

"What does 'bigamy' mean?" asked the rat.

"Oh, I can't be bothered to tell you rat, it doesn't apply to creatures like you, anyway. And if you don't like where you're living why don't you go somewhere else? It's a big country, you know."

"Have you any idea how many rats are living here?"

"No," replied Annabell

"Well, let me tell you; there's billions. There's more rats in the world than humans, it's hard to find a decent place to live, the towns are all full-up, that's why I moved to the country. It took me ages to get a place on this mountain, there's a long waiting list you know."

The rat just stood there twitching his whiskers. "I won't get Bill Stort this time, but consider yourself very lucky. Now what are you doing up here on this mountain in the darkness on your own? Aren't you afraid?"

"No, I'm not afraid," said Annabell. "I'm looking for a Dragon."

The rat laughed. "Dragon? What, you mean those fire breathing creatures that fly, that humans..." The rat couldn't stop laughing. "... have created in their minds to frighten their children?"

"Yes, that's the one, rat. Have you seen one?"

"No, I haven't, now push off."

"Oh, dear, it's pointless talking to you, rat," said Annabell and she walked off in a bit of a huff.

She was beginning to think that maybe this wasn't the mountain that Gunti had lived on so she decided to use her power of flight to search for the Dragon or temple elsewhere.

The parchment said that the Dragon would be where the temple was. She could see no signs of either on this mountain so she flew to the next one.

She flew around that one for hours, but could find no signs. So she flew to the third mountain - once again there were no signs of what she was looking for. She was very disappointed and flew back down to the base of the fourth mountain. She wondered now if she had been wrong in working out the clues but Anja had said that he saw a Dragon on these mountains and somebody had seen what they thought was a temple, but where was it? If it wasn't on this last mountain, that would be it, she thought.

The night had passed, it was now morning. Annabell sat by a small river and was pondering as to what to do next. Suddenly thousands of mosquitoes appeared.

When they saw Annabell they thought that they were in for a free meal.

It wasn't long before one of them landed on her hand and tried to suck out some of her blood.

The mosquito thought that it had hit the *blood* jackpot with Annabell because her skin colour was blood red. But it had made a mistake, no matter how hard the mosquito sucked - it couldn't get any blood out of Annabell (it was like trying to get blood out of a stone!! as they say).

"Mosquito," yelled Annabell. "You're getting on my nerves, I'm trying to meditate here. I'm sorry, but you're not having your breakfast from me. Now buzz off please and take your friends with you."

The mosquito didn't say anything, it just flew off in a huff, panting a bit with the effort that it had made trying to get its breakfast. But it wasn't long before another one tried the same thing. Annabell picked up the mosquito between her fingers.

"Please don't hurt me," came a tiny, squeaky voice.

"Why shouldn't I?" said Annabell, "you were trying to steal my blood."

Annabell released the fly without harming it, but it immediately flew back on her arm.

"Oh, I'm starving," said the mosquito. "Can I have just a little bit of your blood - just to keep me going? There's not much food up here you know, only those horrible rats and rabbits - we prefer horses, cows and humans, but there's not many of them up here. In fact, there aren't any at the moment, except you, of course. When we saw you, we all made a dash for you, but you didn't seem right - too good to be true you might say, so Annie went in first to test you out, but she obviously failed, so I've come in as a back-up. Only female mosquitoes eat blood you know, not a lot of people know that. It's alright for those males they feed on plant juices, but us females need blood."

"Why bother to come here if there's no food for you to eat, what's the point?" asked Annabell.

"Ah, there's a good reason why," said the mosquito. "We come to this river to lay our eggs in it. It's a perfect place, because it's quiet here and our babies will be born in peace. We're born here and we die here; we lay our babies and then that's it - it's the end of us, we're all pretty close to the end now, so you may be our last supper."

"How long have you been alive on the mountain, mosquito?" asked Annabell.

"Only a few days, we don't live very long; well, it's a long time for us of course, but in human terms it's obviously very short. Why do you ask?"

Annabell thought for a moment, she knew that it was a long shot, but it was worth asking. "Umm… mosquito… have you ever seen a temple on this mountain?"

She didn't know if the mosquito would know what a temple was. She'd decided after the fiasco with the rat that she wouldn't mention anything about the Dragon.

Surprisingly the mosquito said that it knew about a temple. "I saw the temple today."

Annabell got very excited. "Where? Where? Where?" she shrieked. "If you tell me mosquito - I'll let you and your friends have some of my blood."

"Deal!" said the mosquito. "The temple is…" But before the mosquito could tell her where it was, a strong gust of wind blew the fly off her arm straight into the river.

The mosquito was flapping its wings on the surface of the water trying to regain flight. Annabell put her hand into the water in an attempt to rescue it, but a small fish, no bigger than one and a half inches long, rose to the surface and gobbled the mosquito up. Suddenly the swarm of mosquitoes took fright and they all flew away.

Annabell jumped up and down in annoyance. She'd been so close to finding where the temple was, but maybe the mosquito wasn't telling the truth, maybe it was just after her blood, she thought, but she would never know.

Annabell decided to trek up the mountain rather than fly, she believed that the mosquito was probably telling the truth and she didn't want to miss any signs. But Anja never saw the temple; she wondered why, but if the mosquito was telling the truth and the temple was really here, then the Dragon must be here too, she thought. But why didn't Anja see the temple? It was a bit of a mystery. Annabell was confused.

As she walked along she could at last see clear signs that people had once lived here, parts of buildings were still standing and there was plenty of rubbish lying around, it felt similar to Gunti's town, Rangdo.

They certainly didn't believe in cleanliness, whoever once lived here. Annabell could see why they lived here though, it was because of the stream;

as she walked up the mountain the river had become a stream but it was fresh water.

As she trekked along, Annabell asked every living thing if they had seen a temple, but none of them had. Suddenly a flying ant, a Queen ant, landed on her nose.

"I understand that you're looking for a temple," said the ant. "I know where the temple is."

Annabell yelled. "Where? Where? Where? Ant, you must tell me it's very important."

"We live near it," said the ant. "But I'm moving now, I have to find my own home, it's time for me to go and start my own family, but I must tell you human person, the temple is not always there. It's not there at the moment."

"But where does the temple go, ant?" asked Annabell screwing her eyes up trying to see the ant which was still perched on her nose.

"I don't know," said the ant, "it's a mystery."

"Have you seen a Dragon, Ant ?" Annabell was now throwing caution to the wind, she was unable to control her excitement. She knew that she was close to unravelling the answers to the temple and maybe the Dragon.

"Ah, the Dragon, I was wondering when you were going to ask me that. It's not always there you know, it's like the temple it comes and goes. I'll tell you where it is. It's…"

Just as the ant was about to tell her, a bird swooped down and pecked the ant off Annabell's nose, and gobbled it up!

"Oh, no, not again! Bird, why did you do that?" yelled Annabell.

"Because I'm hungry," said the bird. "And that's what I eat, that was a nice juicy ant that was on your nose, so I ate it. What's wrong with that?"

"Nothing," moaned Annabell. "But I wish that you would have waited a moment, the ant knew something that I wanted to know."

"Sorry!" said the bird. "I didn't know that, but I would still have eaten the ant."

Before Annabell could ask the bird any questions it flew away.

"Will I never find this Dragon?" moaned Annabell. But she now knew that a Dragon definitely existed somewhere near here, so that was good news.

Annabell sat back on the ground and started to meditate again.

The ant said that it had just come from the temple, or where the temple should be, so it must be fairly close by she thought, but she couldn't see it, and she hadn't heard any bells. Gunti said that he always heard bells especially when there was a full moon.

She'd been sitting, meditating for about half an hour, when along came a snail and touched her hand.

"Hello, snail," said Annabell in a friendly voice.

"Who are you?" asked the snail. "You're not going to harm me, are you?"

"No. I wouldn't harm you. My name is Annabell. I don't suppose you happen to know the whereabouts of a temple; do you snail?"

Annabell knew that she was clutching at straws but she thought that it was worth trying.

"I'm blind," said the snail.

"Yes I know," said Annabell. "But I'm desperate. I know that it's around here somewhere.

"Well, you're in luck," said the snail, pressing its antennae on Annabell's hand. "I know where it is."

"Really?" Annabell was surprised. "Where? Where? Where?" shrieked Annabell.

She put both her hands around the snail to make a sort of tent. She wasn't taking any chances this time of something eating it. She looked around her surroundings, when she was sure that everything was safe she lowered her head to the ground and removed one of her hands very slowly, leaving the other hand covering the snail. She then asked the snail in a hysterical sort of screechy voice where the temple was.

"The temple that you seek," said the snail. "It's about a mile from here, just follow the stream and you'll come to it but I must tell you that it's not always there."

"Yes, I know that," said Annabell. "But where does it go?" She was puzzled. The ant, the butterfly, and the mosquito had all said the same thing.

"Snail, how do you know if there's a temple there or not, if you're blind?"

"Because my hearing is my eyes - my antennae are my hearing. I can hear and feel everything. I can hear the bells but sometimes I can't. The bells come from the temple, so if I hear the bells then I know that the temple is there."

Annabell was very confused, she was talking to a creature that was blind and was a mile away from something that he could only assume was there. A mile for a snail is a mighty long way. But the snail mentioned the bells. So she knew that there was definitely something to this story. She had never asked anybody about the bells.

"Snail."

"Yes?" it replied.

"Please tell me how you managed to get a mile away from the temple? That's a long way, you being a snail. You can't travel very fast, can you?"

"No," said the snail, "you're right, but I travelled by way of the stream on a stick - it's what you would call a boat, I suppose? I was enjoying the trip but unfortunately my boat hit something and capsized, and threw me out, I managed to get to the bank, and get out."

"But why are you going downstream snail."

"Well, it's a bit cold up the mountain at the moment - so I wanted to get nearer the bottom where it's warm."

"Oh, alright, that's a good enough reason. I suppose but why go up the mountain in the first place if you have to come back down again?" said Annabell, "and how do you get up there in the first place? Streams can't go up hill."

"I didn't want to go up the mountain but I was taken up there by a bird who thought that I would make a nice meal for it, but lucky for me, the bird dropped me."

"Snail, how do you know that the bells come from the temple?"

"Because I was told, by the spiders; snails and spiders are pretty close friends, you know. The spiders told me that it was a temple that was making the bell noises because I was curious to know. Obviously I can't see the temple, but I wondered where the bell sounds were coming from. When I can't hear the bells, I know the temple is not there."

"But, maybe the bells don't always ring when the temple is there?" said Annabell.

"Ah, but they do, they only ring when the temple is there, the spiders told me that, and I can hear the bells through my antennae."

"Do you only hear the bells when it's full moon?"

The snail laughed. "No, no, no, who told you that?"

"Oh, that Gunti," moaned Annabell, "he's full of rubbish, that man is. Snail," Annabell paused for a moment, "do you know anything about a Dragon?"

"No," said the snail. "Sorry, but… what's a Dragon?"

"Oh, it doesn't matter snail, you've been very helpful - is there anything that I can do for you?"

"Yes there is. Can you find me a nice big stick, or something that floats so that I can travel further down the mountain. I still have a long way to go - I would be most grateful if you could, it would save me a lot of time."

"Of course, I can," said Annabell. She picked up the snail and held it in her hand, she searched and found an ideal stick for the snail and something nice for it to eat. She placed the snail on the stick with the food and gently put it into the water and wished the snail *bon voyage*

Annabell carried on walking around the mountain keeping close to the stream, she was getting very excited now. She walked for what she thought was about a mile, but she couldn't see any signs of a temple. Her excitement and patience soon waned.

"Will I never find this temple?" she yelled and moaned. Her voice echoed around the mountains. *Will I never find this temple - will I never find this temple?* Suddenly something was happening in the distance she noticed a thick mist had suddenly got up, it was like it had heard her voice. The mist was very strange because it was a beautiful sunny day and the mist was confined to just one spot. She made her way towards the mist and walked inside it.

Inside there was something glowing, and it was golden but it didn't have any particular shape. Annabell stood there and wondered what was happening. It was obviously some sort of strange phenomenon. After several minutes the golden glow began to take shape. Suddenly the mist dispersed and Annabell found herself standing at the front entrance of this beautiful Indian golden temple and she could hear from inside it, the sound of ringing bells!

She now knew that she had found one part of what she had been looking for.

Chapter Thirty Nine
Finding The Dragon

On the front door of the temple was a golden knocker in the shape of what she thought was a Dragon's head. Annabell got very excited by this, surely this was a sign, she thought.

She knocked on the door, but there was no answer. She knocked again, but still there was no answer. She pushed the door and to her surprise it opened. The door creaked as it opened up. Annabell shouted through the open door. "Hello...Hello... is there anybody there?" but there was no reply. She removed her muddy boots as respect for this holy place and she walked inside. She was in awe of this beautiful place. The temple appeared to be constructed in solid gold, but she knew that this wasn't possible, because nobody would use gold, it was too soft a material and would be very expensive to be used for construction purposes. Suddenly she could hear a shuffling noise coming towards her and she could hear the sound of a bell.

The bell sound got louder and louder as something approached. She then caught sight of what was approaching her. She couldn't believe what her eyes were seeing. A *normal* person would have screamed and probably fainted at what she was looking at.

She could see a very old man. But this was no ordinary man. He had a long grey beard and long unkempt grey hair. He now stood face to face with Annabell. All the time he was dinging a small bell. Annabell looked at the old man. He was a skeletal man, and she couldn't help noticing that his clothes were very ancient and were just filthy dirty rags. The man's eyes were misty with age. What skin he had left was pale and wrinkly. Annabell thought that this man shouldn't be alive but he was.

"Hello, sir," Annabell spoke very nervously, "er... umm." She paused for a moment. "I hope you don't mind me coming in here uninvited, but I felt that I had to come. My name is..." but before she could finish the old man stopped her.

"I know who you are..." As he spoke dust came out of his mouth! "...We've been expecting you, have been for a long, long time - we left the door open for you." The old man spoke very softly and was reverent towards Annabell. She was shocked by the old man's statement.

"Umm!... expecting me sir? ...What do you mean, expecting me? How did you know that I was coming?"

The old man didn't answer her question. "Please follow me," he said still dinging his bell.

Annabell was led down a narrow corridor; as she walked, she was leaving her foot prints in the thick dust that was on the floor. There was only the foot prints of the old man, when he had approached Annabell, and his foot prints that he was leaving now as he guided her. The old man walked very slowly. It was obvious that nobody had walked down this corridor for a mighty long time. Annabell was wondering what was going on here, but she followed the old man and didn't say anything.

They eventually reached a door. The old man didn't touch the door, it just opened by itself. He beckoned Annabell to come inside, which she did. All the time the old man guided Annabell he was dinging his bell and was now singing prayers and nodding his head.

Annabell wondered why his head didn't fall off!! Because this man was just a walking skeleton, she didn't know how he managed to keep his bones together either.

Inside the room were six other really old men all had skeletal bodies, and old misty eye's and had long grey beards and rags for clothes. The were all dinging bell's and singing, praying and nodding their heads. Suddenly they all stopped dinging their bells, and stopped praying. It went eerie quiet.

"She's here!" said the old man who had led Annabell to the room.

"Isn't she beautiful?" All the old men bowed their heads in acknowledgement of the presence of Annabell. They were obviously holy people and were in some sort of divine awe of her. It was like she was an iconic figure to them already.

Annabell looked at all the men, they all looked so old. These old people had the appearance like they were hundreds of years old!! They were dead people she knew that, but she was inside the temple now.

The parchment had told her this was the place that she had to be. This was all very strange, and pretty scary stuff, thought Annabell. She stood there shaking her head in disbelief at the sight of this incredible happening.

She finally worked up the courage to speak. "Sirs, I must ask you a question - I've been sent on a mission by the creator to find an object..."

"Yes, we know... we've always known," said all the old men at the same time. As they spoke dust came from all of their mouths! These old people hadn't spoken for a long time.

"We've been waiting a long, long, time for you to come, in fact hundreds of years!"

"But...but..." Annabell was struggling to find the words. "But... how did you know that I was coming? I'm only twenty-one years old, how could you have been waiting for me for hundreds of years when I wasn't even born? Why would you do that? And humans can't live for hundreds of years. You must all be dead! Who are you?" Annabell sighed. This was hard for her to comprehend.

There was a long pause all the old men looked at each other. "It's time." said one of them. "Show her."

One of the old men put his hand in his robe pocket and pulled something out, as he pulled it from his pocket a plume of dust came out with it.

"Here, this is how we know." The old man handed Annabell a piece of very old parchment exactly the same as what the creator had been giving her. Annabell looked at the parchment and reeled backwards in surprise.

On the parchment was a picture of her; exactly as she looked now, and it was in colour. She knew that it was her, there wasn't anybody else in the world that had red skin and her sparkling eyes, but this worried Annabell. If what the old men said was true, that they had been waiting hundreds of years for her, and she had no reason to disbelieve them, why were they waiting for her, and how did they have a picture of her when she wasn't born?

There was also writing on the parchment. The same writing that had been on all the parchments. She read the words, they read as follows:

To the guardians of the temple of the
Punjab mountain
you have been chosen to oversee the red lady
that will come in search of thee
she seeks the seed and the dragon too
all of you know what you have to do
when your task is done
you'll all be as one
The creator

Annabell shook her head in disbelief at what she was reading, what does all this mean, she thought to herself. Nothing makes any sense.

She looked at the seven old men. "Sirs how can this be? How can you possibly be hundreds of years old?" She shook her head again and looked at each one of the old men in turn. She faced one of them. "How old are you, sir?"

The old man shocked her with his answer. "I'm; or would be over 2000 years old!! We're all over 2000 years old."

"But why are you not dead, sir? And why are you here now? What is this all about?"

"We've been chosen. We've been waiting for you," said one of the old men.

"But who am I? And why are you waiting for me?"

"That is not for us to say only the creator can tell you who you are," said another one of the old men. "But isn't it obvious who you are?"

"No," replied Annabell. "No, it's not." She was quite stern

"Our time is nearly finished here on Earth but we have a task to fulfil. We have the answer to your question as to who we are. And the reason why we are here with you today. You seek the Dragon divine red lady."

Annabell got very excited, "Yes I do, but how did you know? You do know of the Dragon then? It really does exist?"

"Oh yes," said all the old men together.

"Sirs, I've been told that the Dragon might know the whereabouts of the seed. Please sirs, you must tell me where I can find this dragon. It's very important."

"Yes we know it is, that's why we're here," said one of the old men.

Annabell was getting very excited and impatient. This was the reason why she had come to India, to find the Dragon and these ancient men definitely knew about it. The old man who had led Annabell to the room turned to the six other old men and spoke in a very reverent voice.

"At last, our day has come," he said.

They all formed a circle around Annabell and started walking around her. They were all dinging their bells and nodding their heads and singing prayers. They did this for several minutes. Suddenly the old man who had led Annabell to the room reached out his right hand and placed it on Annabell's right hand.

The other six old men all placed a hand on Annabell.

"Do not be afraid," said one of them. "We will not harm you - you cannot be harmed anyway."

Annabell felt like she was being touched by dead people!! They were very cold.

"It's time for us to go," said the old man who had met Annabell

"The Dragon that you seek, divine one, lives here in this very spot. The Dragon is for whom the bell tolls. We bid you farewell, our task is about to be fulfilled."

All the old men then started to turn to dust. The dust trickled through Annabell's fingers and fell to the ground like an egg timer. Suddenly and very frighteningly for Annabell all the old men's eyes popped out from their eye sockets and dropped onto the ground. Then their heads turned to dust, followed by the rest of their bodies.

Annabell stood there with her mouth wide open in astonishment at this incredible happening. She should have been frightened, but she wasn't, but she did wonder what on earth was going on here.

After a few minutes all that was left of the old men were seven piles of dust and fourteen misty eyes that were spread around the floor, like children's marbles. She knew that she had been right all the time with her feelings regarding these men - they were never alive.

Suddenly the magnificent golden temple started to melt!! It was like it was made of *lead.* But it wasn't lead, it really was made of gold.

The golden temple rapidly melted away and ran like a volcano's lava flow, it flowed into a hole in the mountain. In the space of just a few minutes. The temple and all the old men had gone.

Annabell found herself all alone on the mountain. All that remained was the seven piles of dust that were once the old men and their fourteen misty eyes.

Annabell's muddy boots were lying on the ground where she had left them. So she put them back on and wondered what it had been all about. The old men had told her that the Dragon was here in this very spot, she looked around but she couldn't see any signs of it. There was definitely no Dragon here, and now there wasn't even the temple.

She was getting very despondent. This had all been a waste of time, she thought. She was sitting down on the mountain with her head in her hands not knowing what to do next but out of the corner of her eye she caught sight of one of the little bells that the men had been ringing, the rest of them were scattered all around. She didn't want to leave them here. These were holy relics and belonged to the Indian people. She searched the ground and found all the seven holy bells. And put them into her pocket. The bells weren't very big, they were only about one inch long.

Suddenly Annabell had an idea she thought, maybe you have to *summon* the Dragon like a genie!! Like the magical spirit in stories that has supernatural powers, that will obey the commands of the person who summons it. The old men had told her that the Dragon was for 'whom the bell tolls'.

Annabell took one of the small bells out of her pocket and rang it.

Instantly one of the piles of dust that was once a man rose into the air.

It swirled around in the air like small whirlwind. This was it, she knew that this is what she was supposed to do. She got out the rest of the bells and rang them one after the other. All the piles of dust and the eyes rose in the air to form seven whirlwinds of human dust. And whirlwind of human eyes.

Suddenly the dust and eyes that had once been the old men formed into one mass. A circle of dust was now spinning in the air. Annabell sat there and stared in amazement, she didn't know what was happening.

Slowly the dust started to take some sort of shape. Firstly, a long body appeared, followed by a big black head and then seven of the old men's eyes formed to make a right eye on the black head and then the other seven eyes formed into one and made the left eye. Everything started to happen quickly now. Four wings suddenly appeared and attached themselves two to each side of the body. Annabell was witnessing a metamorphosis. A creature had formed from the remains of the seven old men. The creature was now complete, and was at least fifteen feet long with giant wings.

Anja, the boy from Rangdo, was telling the truth, the poor boy had witnessed this creature, but Annabell couldn't understand why the creature had formed in front of Anja. But maybe, she thought, it was a common occurrence; or maybe this was the sign for her to find this awesome creature. She didn't really know. Anyway it was here in front of her, flapping its wings.

Hovering in front of her was a Dragon but this was not the Dragon that she had been expecting. It did not spit fire from its nostrils. This Dragon wasn't the mythical creature from fairy tales. No, Annabell's Dragon was in fact... A *Dragonfly!!!!* But what a Dragon fly, it was huge!

Annabell stood there and just stared at this mighty creature - this was the mother of all insects that had ever lived on the earth. She was in search of the seed that had created life for all insects, she wasn't expecting to be confronted by the largest insect that anybody would ever see, but she knew that this giant Dragon fly knew where the last seed was.

Annabell had witnessed many incredible things in her search for the parts of the holism, but the sight of the seven old men turning into the Dragon fly - she will never forget.

The huge dragon fly was just hovering in front of her a few feet off the ground. Annabell wasn't sure what she had to do next. The parchment had told her to follow the Dragon and *see where it flies*, but this Dragon wasn't going anywhere. Suddenly the giant insect spoke. As it spoke, smoke was coming out of its mouth but this wasn't real smoke, it was dust, it still looked quite frightening and at this moment it did look like a real Dragon.

"Get on my back," the insect kind of roared, but it wasn't an angry roar it was just a loud voice. "WOW!" shrieked Annabell. "Am I to ride this giant insect?" She was so excited at this moment in time, she was like a child waiting to go on a fair ground ride.

She climbed onto the insect's back and held on tightly. The insect increased its wing speed and flew off just like a helicopter. It flew high into the sky and went to the highest part of the Punjab mountain range.

Annabell had found the Dragon on the fourth mountain but the Dragon fly flew to the first mountain which was the highest. There was a gap at the top of the mountain just big enough for the insect to get through.

The Dragon fly flew through the gap at great speed and entered a tunnel. It flew through the tunnel for about a mile then suddenly the tunnel came to a dead end. It was now solid rock.

The Dragon fly stopped and then started to fall to pieces! It was turning back to dust. Annabell fell through the creature as it disintegrated and landed with a bump on the ground, but she wasn't hurt. Nothing could harm her, in just a few seconds the Dragon fly was no more.

Annabell was now all alone again deep inside a mountain. *See where it flies* - the parchment had told her. The Dragon had taken her here.

"The seed must be here somewhere?" she said out loud, but she couldn't see it - it was pitch black in the tunnel, but Annabell could see. She had the power of sight in darkness. She knelt on the ground and swept her hand over it like a mine detector, but there was nothing but the pile of dust that was once the old men.

Annabell was puzzled. "This must be the place," she muttered to herself. "But where is it?"

The tunnel was at least a mile long if the seed was here it could be anywhere in there, but the giant dragon fly had brought her here to this very spot. She thought that it had to be here somewhere. She ran her hand over the rock face that was in front of her sweeping her hand up and down. Suddenly something lit up, just for a split second. There was something inside the rock. She ran her hand back over the same spot. It lit up with all the colours of the rainbow. This was what she had been looking for. She had found the seed, it was embedded in the rock.

She pulled it out and gave out an almighty cry of joy. The object was now glowing in her hand and she felt an enormous surge of energy go through her body, she had gained more powers.

She now had all the pieces of the holism. Her mission was now complete, or so she thought.

As usual when Annabell finds a seed she wishes to be back at home in her bed. She closed her eyes and made her wish. Seconds later, she woke up in her bed in America thinking everything that had happened had all been a dream, but it hadn't been a dream, because in her hand was the last piece of the holism and in her pocket were the seven small bells that belonged to the old men of the temple.

Chapter Forty
Annabell Gets Married

Annabell now had all the pieces of the holism, but she didn't know what was going to happen next.

One day when she and Kevin were walking hand in hand by the river in one of Mr Jacobs' fields all Kevin's emotions got the better of him. He bent down on one knee and asked Annabell to marry him. She knew that this was *meant* to be, and of course she said yes, she loved Kevin, she had done from the moment that she first saw him. Kevin, she thought was put on the earth for her. He was *made for her* in every sense of the words.

A day was fixed for the wedding. Annabell wanted to get married on her mother's birthday, June 13th.

The months soon went by and the wedding day was now just a few days away.

Annabell was really nervous about the wedding which was surprising considering all the dangerous adventures that she had been through. She really didn't want a big fussy wedding. She just wanted her family and friends to be there, and she didn't want a church wedding. She didn't have any particular faith, she felt that she was of all faiths.

Despite Annabell not wanting a lot of fuss it would be impossible for her to have a small quiet wedding; the people of America, and the world decided that.

The President of the United States of America wanted Annabell to have a state wedding but she point blank refused. She wanted to be an ordinary person, but of course, that wasn't really possible. She was acknowledged throughout the world as somebody who was as special as you could get, she was most certainly not an ordinary person.

She had phenomenal powers now with the four pieces of the holism but she didn't know what to expect next.

June the 13th arrived, it was a beautiful sunny day and was quite warm.

The registrar's office was to be at the White House, the official residence of the President of the United States of America. This was a magnificent old building built between 1792-1800 and was situated in Washington D.C.

For one day only this special building would be a wedding registration office for Annabell and Kevin. Annabell really didn't want this, but she knew that her home town would not be able to cope with her wedding so she reluctantly agreed.

Kevin was already at the White House along with his best man who happened to be none other than the Prime Minister of Australia. Kevin never had any family. It was still a mystery to everybody as to where Kevin actually came from. Nothing could ever be found from his past, no records existed of him, except that it was mysteriously recorded in the population records which seemed to appear from nowhere! No records existed of his mother or father, and Kevin didn't have any memory of his past.

Thousands upon thousands of people had gathered around the White House. The crowds stretched for miles. Nearly every country had somebody representing them, who would be attending the wedding.

Annabell arrived at the White House in a white stretched limousine. She didn't like this car it reminded her of India, when the King was bad but it was only to be for one day.

The roar of the crowd was tremendous as the car drew up. The white limousine glistened in the sunshine. Police were out in great numbers and were trying their best to hold back the crowds but everybody was jostling for position trying to get a glimpse of this iconic woman.

The car was now outside the White House, a red carpet had been laid out as respect for Annabell. Everything was now ready for Annabell to start her wedding.

Mr Jacobs got out of the car first and walked over to the other side to let his precious daughter out. Annabell got out of the car, hand in hand with her father. Her wedding dress was stunning. Annabell had chosen a vintage dress that was designed over two hundred years ago for an English princess.

Every country in the world presented Annabell with a gift, mainly something that was traditional from that country, not all gifts were worth fortunes but some were. Annabell didn't want money, all gifts that were of monetary value would be given to the poor of the world after the wedding, including the dress.

Annabell looked like an angel at this moment in time. She was the perfect woman and she was marrying the perfect man. It was as if Adam and Eve had been placed back on the Earth.

As Annabell got out of the car the crowd surged forward to try and take her picture. In the hustle and bustle Annabell's bouquet of flowers which were *forget-me-nots,* were accidentally knocked out of her hand and trod on and were completely ruined. Annabell was very upset but she didn't complain. The forget-me-nots had a special meaning for her but they were now lying squashed on the ground. Somebody in the crowd picked them up and gave them back to her and said in a soft and gentle voice,. "Please do not be upset on this your wedding day. I know the reason for the flowers. Your heavenly father is with you today."

Annabell felt a strange inner sense of tranquillity in her very soul and felt that she knew this person even though she hadn't looked to see who it was. "Well, thank you," she said. "How kind, what a lovely thing to say."

Suddenly the ruined flowers were back in perfect condition and the colours were vibrant and vivid. A miracle had happened here.

When she looked up to see who it was who had said these words she was shocked to see a figure in a robe, she could not see the person's face or hands or any part of the person's body. It was just a bright light, like the sun, in a robe, that had now changed to the colour blue.

Annabell was shocked, she turned to her father, "Look father, look what has happened to my flowers, there is the person who has picked up my flowers, his face glows and his robe changes colour. How amazing!" Annabell was so excited.

Mr Jacobs looked but could not see such a person that Annabell was describing. "Daughter who are you looking at? Because I have seen no such person."

"Look father, there!" Annabell pointed to where the person was. He was no more than eight feet away. "Sorry to point at you," Annabell said to the person whose robe had now changed to red. "My father does not see you. Father, the person is there! Look!" Annabell almost touched the man in the robe. Mr Jacobs looked in the direction that Annabell was pointing, but he could not see what she was seeing.

Mr Jacobs shook his head indicating to Annabell that he did not see the man. "Father, surely you can see this person, he's standing right in front of you." Mr Jacobs looked in front of him and then looked left, and then right, and then shook his head. "No daughter, I cannot." He was looking very puzzled at Annabell. Annabell shook her head, not understanding why her father could not see what she was seeing.

Mr Jacobs and Annabell stepped onto the red carpet. There was a guard of honour consisting of twenty people, each side of it. They blew a fanfare of trumpets. The crowd yelled in excitement.

Ten small boys aged ten years old, and ten small ten-year old girls walked behind Annabell and traditionally carried her wedding dress trail.

The boys were wearing suits and the girls, long dresses. Their clothes were like patch work quilts. They were made using flags of the world - every nation of the known world was represented in their clothing and they had semi- precious stones sewn into the clothes which made them sparkle.

As Mr Jacobs and Annabell walked up the red carpet they came to a huge door which somebody opened and the traditional wedding hymn of *Here comes the bride* was sung by a choir of singers made up of peoples of the world.

Inside the room were hundreds of very important people - there was royalty, and Presidents and Prime Ministers, and Chiefs of tribes. At this moment in time, there was peace on the Earth.

Mr Jacobs walked up the aisle arm in arm with Annabell. Everybody was cheering and clapping.

Mr Jacobs gave Annabell a kiss on her cheek and wished her all the happiness in the world. "My you're so beautiful, daughter," said Mr Jacobs proudly. Annabell squeezed her father's arm and gave him a kiss back.

"Thank you for being my father," she said sincerely. "You have brought me up well."

Mr Jacobs felt the proudest person in the whole wide world to be walking down the aisle with this unusual, unique woman. The bravest and most beautiful woman the world has ever known.

Kevin was standing at the front of the room with his best man, the Prime Minister of Australia. Kevin was dressed in authentic aborigine clothing and looked very handsome. When he caught sight of Annabell his blue eyes lit up and his smile was that of a man whose dreams had all come true.

Kevin stood next to Annabell with The Prime Minister to his right and Mr Jacobs was to Annabell's left. Kevin held Annabell's hand tightly, as if to never to let it go again.

Annabell looked at Kevin. Her thoughts couldn't help going back to the Australian bush. She was remembering Elvid and the crocodile, Herbert, at Diamond lake.

Elvid had killed the man she was about to marry. Kevin had no idea that he had been dead and that Annabell had brought him back to life with the powers of the Holism but Kevin had been changed, he now looked like Annabell.

Annabell now realised why the divine parchment that she had received as clues mentioned this man, she now knew the reason for Kevin, she believed that she was sent back in time to find her husband, but maybe she thought the reason for Kevin was to catch the Eel. The Eel guided them to Diamond lake but Kevin was already heading in the direction of Diamond lake, it was like he had been there before but she knew that he couldn't have been. The more that she thought about it though, the more unsure she became but it didn't really matter.

The wedding ceremony didn't take very long. Annabell and Kevin were now officially man and wife. As they walked arm in arm towards the exit door all the guests clapped and cheered, the noise was quite loud but Annabell heard somebody say, "I will see you soon." Annabell looked around to see who was talking to her, it was the person in the now yellow robe. Somehow, he had managed to be one of the special invited guests at her wedding but Annabell didn't know who it was. "Pardon me," she said back to the man, or should we say, figure in the blue robe because she couldn't tell whether or not if it was a man, but it had a man's voice; that didn't necessary mean that it was a man. But the figure was now gone, it seemed to have just disappeared.

"Who are you talking to, Annabell?" asked Kevin.

"Oh, nobody," answered Annabell, very sheepishly. "I thought that somebody spoke to me but I must have been mistaken."

"How could you have heard somebody speak to you in this noise, Annabell?" asked Kevin

"Because I have powers Kevin, you know that. My hearing is sensitive."

"I have powers as well and my hearing is quite sensitive but I didn't hear anything." said Kevin nodding his head from side to side suggesting that Annabell was hearing things that weren't really there.

"Did you see that figure standing over there, Kevin, in the blue robe?" Annabell pointed to the spot where the figure last stood.

"No," replied Kevin. "Blue robe, Annabell...? Who would wear a blue robe to a wedding? We're not in a monastery: only monks wear robes, don't they? Did you invite any monks?" Kevin laughed. But Annabell wasn't laughing she was positive that she had seen something and that he had spoken to her.

"Oh, I don't know Kevin. - There might be monks here, who knows? Strange things happen to me; just forget it." But Annabell was puzzled.

She now knew that she was the only person who could see this strange figure in the robe. Kevin was different from other humans she thought that maybe he would be able to see what she was seeing but he couldn't. Annabell thought that it was strange that he could read the parchment when no other person on Earth could read it but he wasn't able to see the figure. She wondered who this strange person was and why he was at her wedding, and how he managed to disappear. It was the same person who had made her flowers regenerate, so whoever it was had incredible powers.

Annabell and Kevin walked through the big doors and were now outside the White House facing a huge crowd, a massive roar went up, the wedding ceremony had been transmitted on huge screens around the White House.

The world press were lined up outside and wanted pictures of the newly- weds for their newspapers. They asked Annabell to kiss Kevin which she did. This sparked great excitement from the crowds, a blizzard of confetti was thrown into the air. The roar and the confetti was an incredible sight. Annabell and Kevin were covered from head to foot with the confetti but they didn't mind, they expected it. It's what people do at weddings.

Annabell did what every bride does at weddings. It's a tradition that goes back hundreds of years. (The throwing of the wedding bouquet).

A selected number of unmarried women who wanted to take part were lined up and Annabell turned her back and threw the flowers over her head.

Tradition has it that whoever catches the bouquet will soon marry herself, (but this was an old wives' tale), nobody ever really believed it.

There was a frantic scramble to catch it; arms were flashing in the air in a scramble to catch this prized object. There was quite a bit of pushing and shoving by the *ladies* but it was caught fair and squarely by a woman named Maureen Driscole; Maureen was thirty-six years old. She was a loving woman with a kind personality but the love of a man had passed her by. Little did she know that the flowers that she had caught were no ordinary bouquet of flowers, these flowers had powers, they would never die and whoever caught the flowers would themselves marry in one year's time. The old wives' tale would now come true for whoever caught this bouquet of flowers.

The flowers were aptly named *forget-me-nots* because nobody would ever forget this bouquet. Maureen would have to throw the flowers on her wedding day, it would be instinctive for her to do this and for everybody who caught the flowers thereafter.

Annabell and Kevin stayed outside the White House for over half an hour. There was thousands of people who wanted to take their photographs.

The scene was quite hectic but orderly. Annabell and Kevin gave a final wave to the crowds before they were ushered back inside the White House by a group of security guards who had been assigned to protect Annabell and Kevin, but they really didn't need protecting. The guards were dressed in smart mauve suits.

Annabell and Kevin were guided by the guards to a large room where over five hundred selected and very important guests were already sitting at their tables.

As they entered the room everybody stood up and clapped and cheered them. Annabell was embarrassed by the attention that she was getting but Kevin loved it. It made him feel important.

They were led to a table that was situated at the front of the room. Sitting at this table were Mr and Mrs Jacobs, The President of the United States of America and his wife, The Prime Minister of Australia and his wife. King Nillish and Queen Meena and surprise guests that Annabell didn't know about, the boy Anja and Gunti, from Rangdo were here at the main table. Annabell smiled at Anja as she walked past him and blew him a kiss with her hand.

Annabell was greeted by her mother and father who both gave her a kiss.

Annabell sat down at the head of the table and the reception began.

The guests would be treated to the best food, cooked by the top chefs of the world, they could drink what they wanted but Champagne seemed to be the order of the day for the people who drank.

Annabell and Kevin didn't drink alcohol. Kevin used to drink beer but since he had metamorphosed into looking something like Annabell he no longer drank alcohol.

Next to Annabell's table was another table where a massive wedding cake stood. The cake was in the shape of a star, and sparkled like it was a real star.

Everybody was wined and dined - the speeches were made, every accolade that could be said for this special person was said. The ceremony of the wedding cake being cut took place, and the wedding dinner was now over.

The guests were escorted out of the White House and into the large grounds, which had been transformed into a huge tented village, stages had been erected, they would be used by the entertainers who would be performing for Annabell and Kevin and all the guests. Most of Annabell's and Kevin's favourite musical artistes were here to perform a concert for them. Annabell's favourite artiste was a man named Bob Dylan - Bob was a singer, song - writer that had lived over 200 years ago. He had become an iconic figure in this era of time for his musical lyrics - just like William Shakespeare was to literature - Bob Dylan was to music. Bob wrote and sang about issues that he thought important in his day but some people believed that some of his lyrics reflected the future. In time these people would be proved right, because the words of some of his songs would have a dramatic bearing on Earth's future. He certainly seemed to be very perceptive for his time. Bob's music lives on and Annabell loved it.

Annabell was to be treated today to a tribute of Bob's songs sung by her favourite singers of her era. First to sing was a man named Nesseye Williams. Nesseye was a folk singer similar to what Bob was. He started strumming the old-fashioned guitar that they used in the 20th and 21st centuries. Nesseye had a very gruff voice but it sounded good, he started singing *Visions of Johanna.*

Annabell was a bit taken back by this song because she knew the meaning of the lyrics.

Bob was singing about a vision of a person that he thought that he had seen. That vision he called 'Johanna' but the 'Anna' that he had seen was in fact, Annabell!!

Annabell had used her powers to go back in time to see this iconic person Bob Dylan. But Bob thought that he had seen some sort of *ghost.* He remembered that her name was Anna something but he wasn't sure of her whole name. So he called her Johanna.

He wrote that he saw sparks and electricity and that these visions of Johanna… conquered his mind.

The *Joh* that Bob had put in front of Annabell's name, had a strong meaning. It means: God is Gracious, Merciful. God has favoured one who wants to improve the lives of others. Which is Annabell of course. How clever of Bob Dylan to know this.

Annabell stood by the stage and listened intently to the words she knew that he was singing about her and she was fascinated by this. Of course she already knew a long time ago about this song but it still stirred her emotions. She thought that she had wiped Bob's mind of all memory of her but obviously something in Bob's subconscious remembered something about her... and maybe other things?

Artiste after artiste was performing for Annabell, this was bliss for her.

Annabell was a kind of simple woman, she liked ordinary things, this music reminded her of the countryside where she was born. She would prefer to be out in the countryside right now if she could but she couldn't today. This was her special day, she was the centre of attraction for the whole world.

The evening was in full swing. Bob's tribute of songs, sung by Nesseye for Annabell had been performed. The music had now changed to more modern music, the younger generation preferred this.

Most people were up dancing and frolicking around, this was a very informal wedding evening. Annabell was up dancing with the President of the United States of America, and Kevin was talking cricket, (which was now the main sport of the world) with the Prime Minister of England and the Australian Prime Minister. England and Australia were once leaders of the world in the sport but China was now world Champions.

The festivities were coming to the end. A spectacular firework display would bring the evening to its conclusion.

Annabell and Kevin's wedding day had now ended. The guests were slowly leaving. Limousine after limousine was picking up these very important people and taking them to where they wanted to go.

Annabell, Kevin and Mr & Mrs Jacobs would be returning to Mr Jacobs' farm. Annabell wanted to be back with her animals on the farm for a few days before leaving for the honeymoon. The President had kept waiting at the airport his private jet to take them home.

The honeymoon destination was going to be Australia. Annabell wanted to go back into the bush to see Herbert the crocodile and she was keen to go back to basic living. They were going camping for three weeks. Kevin was pretty excited to be going home and was looking forward to a bit of fishing. He had aspirations of trying to catch that Eel again but Annabell quickly told him that he could forget about going fishing on their honeymoon, and he would certainly not be catching that Eel again. But Kevin had other ideas, he believed he had unfinished business with that Eel.

They were both looking forward to the peace and quiet of the bush and wanted to have some special free time together. They both knew that there was going to be many more adventures. They were two very special people of the like the Earth had never seen before.

The white limousine pulled up outside the White House. Annabell and Kevin, and Mr and Mrs Jacobs said their goodbyes to everybody and left for the airport.

Chapter Forty One
The Mysterious Figure

The flight would take several hours but the time soon passed and they arrived back at the farm about 5:am in the morning. Mr & and Mrs Jacobs slept for most of the flight but Annabell and Kevin didn't, they talked and talked about their special day.

Annabell was still wearing her magnificent wedding dress. She was reluctant to take it off as she wanted to make the most of it. The dress was very beautiful but she wouldn't be keeping it. It would be sold along with all other wedding gifts and the money given to the poor of the world.

When they arrived home, Annabell went up to her bedroom to change out of the dress. She took off the necklace containing the four pieces of the holism and put it in a drawer. She instantly felt weak as she no longer had any powers without the holism. Before Annabell could change her dress, there was a knock at the door. This took everybody by surprise, because they weren't expecting anybody to call as it was early in the morning and not quite light yet.

Mr Jacobs answered the door but surprisingly there was nobody there, so he shut it.

"Must have been the wind," he muttered to himself.

A few moments later there was another knock at the door; it wasn't the wind, there was definitely somebody there. Kevin answered it this time but once again, there wasn't anybody there. "That's strange," said Kevin, "there's nobody there but I'm sure that I heard a knock."

Kevin went outside to have a look around but he couldn't see anybody, Kevin had powers to be able to see in the dark so he was sure that there was nobody there.

He came back into the house and shut the door and informed Mr & Mrs Jacobs that there was definitely nobody out there. But a few moments later there was another knock on the door. Mr Jacobs answered it again but once again there was nobody there.

Annabell could hear the knocks at the door and shouted down from the top landing.

"Who's at the door, Pa? Is nobody going to answer it?"

"There's nobody there, Annabell," replied Mr Jacobs.

"But I clearly heard somebody knock on three occasions ...there must be somebody there, doors don't knock by themselves, Pa." Just as she said that, there was another knock at the door, this time it was very loud. It was as if the person knocking knew that Annabell would answer it this time.

Kevin went to answer it but Annabell came running down the stairs and stopped him. "I'll answer it," she said firmly. "It must be for me."

Annabell opened the door and was surprised rather than shocked to see who was at the door. It was the figure in the robe that she had seen several times on her wedding day. This mysterious person. If it was a person? - had made her *ruined* bouquet of flowers come back to life. It had been at her wedding and now it was here on her doorstep several thousand miles away from where she had last seen him.

Annabell walked outside. She wondered why the figure had followed her here but she remembered being told that he would see her soon.

But she didn't expect him to turn up on her doorstep a few hours later.

She was also puzzled as to how the figure was able to be here - there was only one flight out to Annabell's part of the world and this figure in the robe was certainly not on the flight.

Annabell didn't feel afraid even though whatever it was had no visible human face. Where a face should have been was just a bright light, as bright as the sun itself. And she could not see what it used for hands of feet.

Annabell felt tingles go through her body. She knew that the figure in the robe was something very special to her but she didn't know what.

"Who are you? And what do you want? I feel that I should know you but I can't see your face. Why haven't you got a face?" Annabell's mind was kind of confused.

Before the figure could answer, Kevin came to the door. He could hear her speaking to somebody but couldn't hear anybody speak back.

Mr Jacobs was standing right behind Kevin. Kevin pulled open the door and was surprised to see that Annabell was standing outside alone.

"Who were you talking to Annabell?" asked Kevin looking very puzzled.

"I was talking to the figure in the robe, Kevin," replied Annabell, calmly.

"But Annabell, there's nobody there in a robe, you're out here talking to yourself." Kevin turned to Mr Jacobs, "Can you see anybody here, Mr Jacobs?"

"Mr Jacobs shook his head. "No, I can't - Annabell you're talking to yourself, daughter. There's nobody out here with you, maybe the day has been too much for you? Now come inside and go to bed and get some sleep."

Annabell shook her head in defiance. "No, Pa, I'm not seeing things and I'm not tired it's just that you can't see what I'm seeing. I'm standing right next to the figure now. Here, it's right here." Annabell touched the figure's robe with her hand. Instantly there was a flash of bright light, like a lightning bolt which lit up the semi darkness for a split second.

Annabell got an electrical shock from the figure and she gave out a yelp, like a dog. Kevin thought that he caught sight of a shape of something. He shouted in surprise and shock. It was like the figure was telling her not to touch it.

"Did you see that, Mr Jacobs?" said Kevin. "Annabell's right, there is something there. I'm sure that I saw something."

But Mr Jacobs had only seen the bright flash of light. He didn't see the shape of the *something* that Kevin thought that he had seen.

Mr Jacobs was very worried about his daughter, and wondered about Kevin now but he knew that strange, unexplainable things could happen; they had been happening all through the life of his precious daughter and they had happened to him.

Annabell was now getting instinctive feelings she knew what she had to do. She turned to her Pa and Kevin and told them to leave her. Her eyes were glowing brighter which was a sign that something was about to happen.

"There's something that I have to do," she said calmly.

"What do you have to do, Annabell?" asked Kevin.

"I don't know yet," Annabell's speech was changing, she spoke very softly and slowly, like a divine sort of softness. The way that religious leaders tend to speak.

"Please leave me now," said Annabell. "It's time." Annabell didn't know what 'it's time' really meant, it was an instinctive feeling.

Kevin wasn't sure what was happening but Mr Jacobs kind of knew.

They both walked away from the door but they didn't shut it, they wanted to see what Annabell was going to do next.

She stood outside in the semi darkness of the early morning, looking like an angel in her wedding dress.

"Who are you?" Annabell whispered to the figure. "Why can't anybody see you?"

A gentle voice came from the robe. It was of no language known on Earth but Annabell could understand it even though at this moment she wasn't wearing the pieces of the Holism, so she shouldn't have had any powers.

"You know who I am," said the voice from within the robe.

"I do?...but I don't...well, I feel that I do - but oh, I'm so confused."

"You must come with me and bring the seeds," said the voice.

"The seeds?" said Annabell.

"Yes," said the voice, "the seeds."

The seeds which were the parts of the holism were in the drawer in Annabell's bedroom. She went back into the farmhouse to get them and ran up the stairs. As she ran, her wedding dress caught on something and she tripped over and hit her right knee.

Annabell screamed, blood was seeping through her dress, it was the first time in years that she had felt such severe pain without the pieces of the holism. Annabell was a normal vulnerable person. Kevin ran to Annabell's assistance, he was so worried about her, he'd never heard her scream in pain before.

Annabell lifted up her dress to her knee to reveal a fairly deep wound that was seeping blood. She ignored Kevin's help and just hobbled the rest of the way up the stairs, moaning and groaning as she hobbled. She went into her bedroom and took out the necklace from the drawer and put it around her neck and fastened the clip.

Instantly the necklace glowed with all the colours of the rainbow. Annabell felt incredibly strong again, the deep cut to her knee healed instantly, she no longer felt any pain. And the blood stain on her dress disappeared.

She ran back down the stairs, very excitedly and passed her Ma and Pa and Kevin as if they weren't there, she seemed oblivious to everything now.

She ran outside the farmhouse, as if there was no tomorrow. Mr & Mrs Jacobs and Kevin followed her outside and stood and watched. Annabell was acting so strangely now.

The figure in the robe glided off. Annabell knew that she had to follow it. Suddenly as Annabell was walking, the ground started to revolve under her feet. It got faster and faster until it was going at a phenomenal speed. Annabell closed her eyes and felt like she was drifting off into another world and another time.

Unbeknown to Annabell she had disappeared from sight right in front of the eyes of Kevin and Mr and Mrs Jacobs. Kevin started yelling "She's gone!…she's gone!" Mr and Mrs Jacobs stood there open-mouthed in amazement, but they weren't shocked.

Suddenly, both their right hands where the angel had touched them started to glow. Mr and Mrs Jacobs were surprised that their hands were glowing, and instinctively they joined their hands together in the form of a friendly handshake. They didn't know why they were doing this but it seemed the right thing to do. Then they both closed their eyes, there was an enlightenment between them, they felt calmness within their souls, they now knew that their daughter was safe wherever she was.

Kevin wasn't calm though, he was hysterical.

"What am I to do?" he kept on repeating himself. "What am I to do?"

Mrs Jacobs tried to pacify him. "She'll be alright Kevin, don't worry," she told him.

"But how do you know this Mrs Jacobs, you don't know where she's gone, how can you be so calm?"

"There'll be an explanation Kevin," said Mrs Jacobs calmly. She knew that her daughter possessed powers way beyond any human being's capabilities; if there was a step past mankind then Annabell was surely it.

Mr and Mrs Jacobs had resigned themselves for this day, they both knew that their daughter was very special. What the angel had told Mr Jacobs all those years ago, had all come true.

Kevin felt better now. He felt reassured by what Mrs Jacobs had said.

"You're right, I've got nothing to worry about…but it's just that I love her so much."

"I know you do, Kevin," said Mrs Jacobs.

"Where do you think she's gone?" Kevin asked, knowing that Mrs Jacobs probably wouldn't know the answer.

"I don't know Kevin." Mrs Jacobs' hand was still glowing but Kevin hadn't noticed it. "I've got a feeling, Kevin," said Mrs Jacobs, "that she's about to find out who she really is. Today is her destiny - the reason why she's amongst us."

Kevin was shocked at what Mrs Jacobs had just said. "But…but - er… she's your daughter, Mrs Jacobs. What do you mean? She'll find out who she really is?"

Mrs Jacobs turned to Kevin, she had quite a serious look on her face.

"I've always known Kevin, from the day that she was born that she wasn't really my child although I gave birth to her, and Mr Jacobs is her father but there was always something strange about Annabell that's clear for everybody to see. No doctors could ever explain her appearance and she has red bones; nobody on this earth has ever been born with red bones, Kevin. And the powers that she gained from the holism, only she had these powers from these mysterious objects. Like you, Kevin, I love her very much, and I'm very proud to be her earth mother."

Kevin was flabbergasted at what Mrs Jacobs was telling him. "What do you mean, Mrs Jacobs: 'her earth mother'?" Do you not think that Annabell is of this earth then?"

Mrs Jacobs thought for a moment and looked at her husband, neither of them had aged a single day since the angel had touched their hand. She smiled at Mr Jacobs and then spoke. "Annabell was born on this earth Kevin, but I do not believe that she is of this earth." Kevin stood there looking at Mr and Mrs Jacobs and was bewildered.

"So...where does she come from then?" He spoke very quickly.

Mrs Jacobs shook her head, her long blond hair swished from side to side. She was reluctant to answer the question. "I don't know Kevin," she repeated herself in a sort of forlorn manner. "I don't know, Kevin, nobody does on this earth, not even Annabell. But I believe she is something divine, heavenly sent to us, you might say."

One single tear rolled down Mrs Jacobs' right cheek which she wiped off with her hand.

"It's best we wait for her return. Maybe we will find out the answers then."

Kevin nodded his head in approval and at this moment, he wondered who he was.

*

Annabell was still spinning around and around when suddenly everything became still. There was a deathly silence. Annabell slowly opened her eyes.

She found herself on a strange dead, dark planet. She knew that she wasn't on earth or hoped that she wasn't because there was no life in this place. There was no oxygen - no sun - no water, and it was extremely cold, with toxic gases.

The figure in the robe was now hovering in front of her. The darkness of the dead planet was lit up where this figure stood.

"Why have you brought me here and where is here?" Annabell was calm, she felt an inner tranquillity and the feeling of love and kindness that was being generated by the figure in the robe but she wondered who it was that she was talking to and had to ask.

"Who are you?"

Suddenly a voice came from the robe. "You know who I am."

Annabell stared at the figure. "Do I?" she said, shaking her head from side to side indicating that she didn't.

"Oh, yes. You know who I am. Don't you remember? I'm the creator. I sent you messages and tasks for you to fulfil."

Annabell found it hard to talk at this moment.

"The creator?" she mumbled. "But…er…isn't the creator, God? That's what earth people believe. Are you God?"

"Yes, that's right," said the voice. "I am God, the creator. I am the creator of the sun. The seeds that you have are the creators of all living life"

Annabell chewed on her little finger on her right hand as she was trying to think of what to say next.

"Why am I here? What do you want from me? Because I don't understand what this is all about."

"Want?" The voice sounded surprised, that Annabell didn't know the answer.

"I wanted you to find the seeds, you knew that, you are the special one. I've waited since life on earth began for you. The day came and you came."

Annabell stood there and listened to the voice she couldn't believe what was happening to her.

"You waited for me?" she blurted out. "Why?… why have you been waiting for me and who is me?" Annabell had so many questions to ask. The old men in India had said the same thing that they had been waiting for her.

"The reason why I've been waiting for you is because: it's time," said the voice, calmly.

"Time for what?" asked Annabell impatiently.

"It's time to create a new world - a living one - a fresh one - earth is complete - mankind was the last piece of the life seeds. There is no more - no more time - earth's time is running out. It's time to begin again - a new beginning - life must go on - and on. There can be no end - it must not end - I will not allow it to end." The voice sounded sad, and desperate.

Annabell had no idea as to what the creator was talking about.

"But why am I so important? Why didn't you get the seeds yourself. If you're God, the creator, surely you can do anything that you want?"

"Yes," said the voice. "Of course I have powers, but I have the power of the sun which is the giver of all life, without it, there can be no life. You have the power of the seeds, you're the activator - there can be no life without you."

Annabell was stunned. "Me?" But how? - Why? Please tell me, how did I have this power?"

There was a long pause. The light within the robe grew brighter.

"Because..." said the voice, "...you are my daughter! I gave you the power."

Annabell stood there stunned and shocked, her mouth wanted to move but she couldn't say anything. She took deep breaths of toxic gases but they couldn't harm her.

She stood there for several minutes, just staring at the glowing robe, until finally she managed to compose herself.

"No! no!...no!... this cannot be, how can I be your daughter? This is silly. You're God, you can't have a human person as your daughter. And in any case I have a mother and father on earth whom I love very much, I don't even know you: nobody does, and I don't think that you're human. I don't wish to be unkind but I don't want you to be my father, and if you are my father as you say - then who is my mother? And do I have any brothers and sisters?"

The light shone even brighter in the robe.

"I cannot answer your questions, daughter, because mankind does not want to know the answers." The voice showed compassion, it knew what Annabell was feeling and understood her anxiety.

"I wanted you to have an earth mother and father. I put the seeds into your earth parents to create you - there was no other way - everything is born from a seed. You must understand that.

"An angel was sent to earth and touched your earth mother and father's hands, and implanted my seed into them, so that they could produce you."

Annabell took another deep breath. She didn't need to but it's what humans do when they're under pressure and don't understand what is happening to them. She knew that there was a question that she had to ask, it was the question that she always feared.

"Am I not human then?" her soft voice quivered as she asked the question.

"No, my daughter, you're not human. You are immortal. You're divine."

This was hard for Annabell to accept, and she wasn't sure if she could accept it.

"But I've had tests," she pleaded. "My blood has been proved to be that of my father. I can't be your daughter - I'm dreaming - please tell me that this is a dream, it's not real…it can't be." Annabell was getting distressed.

The creator calmed her. It knew that she was hurting because she couldn't comprehend what was happening to her.

"What is it that you want from me? What do I have to do? I want to go home. Why have you brought me here? Please tell me. Am I a prophet?"

"No daughter, you're not a prophet. You're a God. Like me."

"We have to work together," said the voice. "We will make a new world, so that all life can begin again. You have the seeds, and I have the sun."

Something was puzzling Annabell and she had to ask the creator the question.

"Why did you not tell me where to find the seeds, and how to defeat the devils? Why did you give me those hard riddles to solve, what was the point of that? Surely it would have been easier just to tell me where the seeds were and how to defeat those evil devils."

"No, my daughter," said the voice, "I couldn't do that, because when life on earth was created, the four seeds of all life, and the sun were infected with the seeds of evil - anti life.

Elvid- Delvi- Videl- Iveld , and Levid were created at the same time. Everything has an opposite. Male -Female. Positive - Negative. Right - Wrong. On- Off.

These are simple examples. The seeds, and the sun had opposites which were evil: they lay in wait, waiting for the day to activate, when earth's evolution was complete. It was time for the devils to activate, but they needed an activator."

"What was the activator?" asked Annabell.

"It was you, daughter."

Annabell was once again shocked by the answer that the creator had given her.

"But...why did you create me knowing that I would activate the evil seeds?"

"I didn't know the devil seeds existed when I created you - it was only when you was born that they showed themselves. The reason why I gave you riddles was because I didn't want the devils to know that you knew how to destroy them. When they found out that you knew, it was too late for them to stop you. The reason why you were created was because you are the only entity who can activate the life seeds but at the same time you were the only entity that could activate the devil seeds. Except for one. The devil knew that one day you would come looking for the life seeds. And the devil knew that you were the only entity who could defeat them, and you nearly did."

"But I have defeated them, so why do you say, nearly did?"

"Think daughter - Elvid - Delvi- Videl -Iveld and Levid."

Annabell's thoughts were going back in time. She remembered Elvid, that nasty plant in Australia that had killed Kevin. Delvi was that horrible slug like creature that was eating all the salt in the oceans.

Levid was that force that she had encountered in the aircraft. Videl was that evil smoke in India.

But she didn't remember Iveld.

"IVELD!" she yelled. "It's Iveld! - Where is Iveld? I did not encounter this devil. What is Iveld? I do remember that man Neil Pepper in Australia mentioning that name but I didn't know what he was talking about, he seemed to go quite mad at the time."

The was a pause from the creator; it was expecting the questions.

"You cannot stop Iveld, daughter, it's too late... it was always too late, you never had a chance. It wasn't possible for you to defeat this devil. You have encountered it, without realising it. Yes, you were right, it was that man that you talk about - he was telling you what was to come."

"But I don't remember seeing it. I would have known. I have powers. I defeated all the others, you could have helped me. What's so special about this devil? Doesn't it have a weakness? All the others did."

"This devil was too strong and very clever - it outsmarted me."

Annabell was confused. "But how can it outsmart you? Aren't you the cleverest entity in the whole universe?"

"Yes daughter, I am but Iveld is my opposite - Earth people call it the Devil. Iveld is the real Devil and it is strong, it cannot be stopped."

"But what has Iveld done that is so bad that it cannot be stopped?"

"It has entered the souls of mankind - mankind will become Iveld. It creates conflict - it thrives on evil."

"What is the cause of conflict?"

"Greed - jealousy - fear and delusion. Iveld is all these things. I stand for the opposites. Mankind has been contaminated with the thoughts of Iveld.

They're waiting to burst out of humans - it's in all of them - it's only a matter of time when they will destroy themselves."

Annabell was listening very intently to what the creator was saying.

"But if I cannot defeat Iveld, what was the point of defeating the other devil seeds if the earth will destroy itself. My mission has been futile."

"No, your mission has not been futile," said the creator. "You have recovered the seeds of life and have defeated four devils who can never return - Iveld will be defeated when mankind dies - it chose its fate - but it will die with mankind, this is what it wanted. Don't worry my daughter, mankind will return to the earth - you'll see to that - but it will take a long time, and much work."

Annabell was very disturbed at what she was hearing and couldn't really understand how Iveld could destroy the earth, and didn't understand why the creator said that she would be responsible for man's return to the earth.

"What power does Iveld possess that will be strong enough to end the earth?" Annabell asked.

"Iveld will turn man against man - religion against religion - it's an ideology that will be the ruination of earth."

"But...but isn't belief.... you?"

"Yes it is, but so too is Iveld; belief - each man believes that his ideology is the correct one. This creates conflict. Of course, there are good people on the earth, but even these good people will try and defend their beliefs against the evil people. It's the fight between good against evil, daughter There is no answer."

"But what is the right belief? Can people not change and all believe the same thing so that there will be no conflict?"

"It's too late for there to be a right one - it's obvious what is right but right and wrong are already on course for a head-on conflict. It's Armageddon, daughter - nobody can stop it."

"But I don't understand," said Annabell looking very despondent. "Isn't religion supposed to be goodness towards others and love thy neighbour, forgiveness, tolerance? Isn't that what religion teaches us? Why would somebody's belief lead to the end of the earth? It doesn't make sense."

"Iveld is anti-religion, anti-God. It's Iveld who will create the conflict between mankind's beliefs - this will cause the end of life on earth before it's time.

"There's 4000 million years left for the Earth's sun to shine but all life on Earth will be gone long before the sunshine.

Mankind was too clever for the Earth, it learnt how to destroy it, and it will do it, because some humans will believe that they should do it. This is why, my daughter, we have to start a new Earth - make a new start, free from the devils, a new home for the life seeds. The time has come."

Chapter Forty two
The New Earth

Suddenly a red crystal with a yellow outer haze appeared from the creator's robe. It moved by itself towards Annabell. She caught it in her hands. Instantly she felt a tremendous surge of energy go through her body. This was stronger than anything she had ever felt before. The crystal in her hands became warm but she felt no pain.

"Wow!" she yelled in excitement, "what is this?"

"It's the final piece of what you have called the '*holism*' daughter, you must join it with the life seeds."

Annabell let go of the crystal, it hovered in front of her. She removed her necklace and took off the pieces of the holism and placed them so that they formed a circle in the centre of the crystal.

The seeds no longer shone so her powers should have ceased but they didn't. She, now, for some reason didn't need the seeds, something had happened to her.

The red crystal instantly lit up, it was like it had been *fertilised.* The seeds started glowing with all the colours of the rainbow.

The creator told Annabell to move away from the holism, which she did.

The holism started to revolve like a child's spinning top. It got faster and faster until it was just a blur then suddenly it shot up into the atmosphere of the dead planet at a phenomenal speed: a few seconds later there was an almighty explosion similar to a nuclear bomb going off.

The red crystal separated from the holism and shot off away from the planet at a speed that no human would be able to comprehend. In a matter of seconds the red crystal hit a dead planet that was hundreds of millions miles away. The dead planet ignited into a new sun which lit up the dead planet that the creator and Annabell were standing on. The darkness of the dead planet had now turned to daylight but the sky was orange. This was because the atmosphere was toxic.

The red crystal came back and was absorbed by the creator.

A few seconds later there was another huge explosion in the orange atmosphere.

The four life seeds flew off in different directions. Wherever they landed, they would start to develop new life on this once dead planet, free from all the devils.

A new Earth had been born, and this earth would forever be a tranquil place. Never again would there be any conflict between humans when they evolve which will be thousands of millions of years from now.

Annabell was shouting **"WOW! WOW! WOW!"** at this unbelievable happening.

She was like a child who had just opened a present of something that she really liked.

"Our task is done daughter, together we have created a new world." The creator's voice sounded pleased.

Annabell couldn't believe it. "Have...I ..." she mumbled. "... helped you to create a new Earth?"

"Yes," came the reply.

"Wow! This is fantastic. Annabell was so excited. "May I now see the face of my heavenly father?" she asked politely.

"No, you may not," came the reply.

"I have no face, daughter, I am who you want me to be, it has always been that way. You have your father on Earth he is the face that you will see, because he is me. Everybody is me.

"I implanted my seed into him to create you, without him, I could not create you. He is your father - I'm your heavenly father, out here in the heavens."

Annabell was confused, excited and sad, all at the same time but had to accept what the creator had told her. She had so many question to ask that she knew mankind wanted the answers to.

She faced her heavenly father and spoke very quickly.

"Why do you not stop suffering on earth, father. Like hunger, disasters and diseases, - and why do we have to endure wars? Is it not possible for you to stop these dreadful things happening?"

The creator replied, "It grieves me daughter to see mankind suffering but I cannot interfere with earth's destiny."

"But did you not alter earth's destiny when you created me?" Annabell felt really proud of herself to ask the creator such a question.

"My!" said the creator, "you are a clever daughter. I may have altered Earth's destiny but not in the way that you think – Earth's destiny had already been decided. Iveld had already decided that- I could not stop it, so your answer is really no. Everything you have done was meant to be."

Annabell had so many questions that she wanted to ask, she couldn't get them out of her mouth fast enough.

"How did life start in the first place if you didn't have the power to activate the life seeds, and I wasn't born so it couldn't have been me, so who activated them? And where did the seeds come from in the first place? And where did you come from? And is there other life in the universe? Where do we go when we die? What came first, the plant or the seed? Is there an end to the universe?"

"Stop!" said the creator. "Some questions can never be answered, because there are no answers."

Annabell stopped her ranting, and understood the answer.

A lot of things had happened to the Earth that were miracles. Every single thing on Earth is a miracle that nobody will ever be able to explain.

"You must go now daughter, our mission has been fulfilled - close your eyes."

"Will I ever see you again?" asked Annabell.

"Oh yes, we still have much to do. Today is just the beginning. Close your eyes daughter."

Annabell closed her eyes and felt herself spinning around, and around. What only seemed like seconds later she found herself being woken up in her bed by her mother.

"Annabell…Annabell, wake up. Here's a cup of tea for you darling."

Annabell opened her eyes. "Hello, mother."

Mrs Jacobs leaned over and kissed Annabell on the cheek and cuddled her.

"What's that for Ma?" asked Annabell

"Oh, it's just that I love you so much, I'm so proud to be your mother. You're a very special daughter."

"Ma," said Annabell. "I've just had the strangest dream. I dreamt that I met the creator. That's God, Ma… and together we made a new Earth and do you know what Ma. The pieces that I found that are on my necklace, were seeds that created all life on earth and I was the activator of the seeds. The creator was the activator of the sun. The creator told me that I was his daughter. Wasn't that a wonderful dream, Ma?"

Mrs Jacobs looked at Annabell, and now knew who she really was, and she knew that it was no dream. Mrs Jacobs burst into tears.

"Please don't cry, Ma," said Annabell holding tightly to her mother's hand.

"Sorry Annabell, it's just that I love you so much, and by the way, we're all God's children, Annabell." Mrs Jacobs wiped away her tears and left the room.

A few moments later there was another knock on Annabell's bedroom door, it was Kevin.

"Where on earth have you been Annabell?" he asked peering into her beautiful sparkling blue eyes.

"What do you mean Kevin? I've been here taking a nap like my Pa told me to."

"No you haven't, Annabell," said Kevin quite sternly. "You disappeared with somebody or should I say something? Where did you go, Annabell?"

"I didn't go anywhere Kevin, I was just dreaming. It was just a dream."

Kevin suddenly noticed some strange marks on Annabell's hands. He got hold of them and turned them so that the palms were showing. Annabell had imprints of the whole holism on both her hands that would remain there forever. This was now the source of Annabell's powers she didn't need the parts of the holism any more.

"Where's your necklace, Annabell?"

"It's in the drawer, Kevin," she replied "I took it off when I came into the bedroom."

Kevin opened the drawer but he couldn't find the necklace.

"There's no necklace in here Annabell, and you're not wearing it." suddenly Kevin noticed a gold chain that was attached to Annabell's wedding dress. "Here it is...but where's the pieces of the holism, Annabell?"

Annabell remembered where they were but thought that it was a dream.

"I don't know where they are but in my dream I used them to make a new Earth...but it was just a dream."

"No, Annabel," said Kevin. "You weren't dreaming darling, look at your hands."

Annabell looked at her hands and saw the imprints of the holism and she screamed. She now knew that it wasn't a dream, it had all been real.

"Where have you been Annabell?" asked Kevin.

Annabell looked lovingly at Kevin and said, "I love you very much but there are some questions that have no answers." And then she laughed out loud.

"Wow!" she yelled, "it was real, Kevin I met the creator...Oh my God - I touched the sun. Kevin, God is my heavenly father. We made a new world."

Kevin looked out of the bedroom window and looked up to the heavens, and wondered where he and Annabell would go from here.

⊷⊶◁▷⊷⊶

Children's books Kirkshaw Forest Stories Books. 1-2-3-4-5

Children's book
The Tablecloth Family Book 1

Young Adult & Adult book
Captain Wirgoil's Challenge